A Normal C

Part 1 (1939-41)

Olga Peters

First Published 2024
Frank Fahy Publishing Services
5 Village Centre
Barna, Galway
Ireland
www.write-on.ie

All characters and events in this publication, other than those clearly in the public domain, are fictitious, and any resemblance to persons living or dead is purely coincidental.

A Normal Couple: Part 1 (1939-41) © 2024 Olga Peters
Email: olgapeterswriter@gmail.com

Cover Image: *DALL-E modified by ©2024 Gerard Fahy from FahyFoto, Galway* info@fahyfoto.com

ISBN: 9798872173557
Imprint: Independently published by Fahy Publishing Services, Barna, Galway.

The Write-on Group wish to thank Galway County Council for helping to fund our various publications and activities.

Comhairle Chontae na Gaillimhe
Galway County Council

The moral right of the author has been asserted. No part of this publication may be reproduced, stored in a retrieval system, or transmitted in any form, or by any means without the prior permission in writing of the Publisher. The views expressed by the author are not necessarily the views of the Publisher.

For Ursula Naumann and Frank Fahy

Preface

The Nazi regime, which came to power in 1933, openly engaged in persecution, repression, and other crimes. The general public was aware of the murders, incarcerations, dispossessions, and injustices inflicted by those in control of the country. However, despite these atrocities, many people continued to live normal and joyful lives. While many, if not most of them, supported the regime, it is important to recognise that a significant portion of the population did not agree with what was happening to their beloved country. They were the silent minority, who were later included among those guilty of having aided Hitler and the Nazis to retain their hold on power until the very end. Only a tiny minority actively resisted, often at great personal sacrifice.

The couple and their families who are the focus of this account lived through extraordinary events while striving to create a normal future for themselves. These events increasingly intruded upon their daily lives, forcing them to adopt positions and make decisions they otherwise would not have chosen.

These individuals represent the millions of people who, willingly or unwillingly, find themselves caught in environments beyond their control. Their lives take unexpected and often tragic, even dangerous turns, leading to both positive and negative changes in their characters.

However, even amidst danger, worry, loss, and oppression, human nature compels individuals to strive for a sense of normalcy. Love, humour, and beauty are sought and clung to for as long as possible, even as the familiar world around them disintegrates into chaos.

In present times, we tend to view the country and era described in this story as a pit of evil and cruelty. However, my research has shown that even in such a time, a normal couple could live a relatively normal life, experiencing many moments of happiness and maintaining hope for the future. Portraying the varied attitudes and compromises which made this seemingly unlikely perspective possible is one of the aims I set myself in writing this book. I believe it reflects the mindset of millions of Germans during these harrowing years. It is left to my readers to judge for themselves whether or not I have succeeded in revealing these shifts in attitude and, by understanding the factors that shaped individuals' characters, to draw their own moral conclusions.

For now, I hope that my readers will relish this detailed account of life in Berlin from 1939 to 1942.

Olga Peters
January 2024

1939

1

16 March: Emma and Leo

The March sun shone mildly through the anonymous windows of the Ministry of Propaganda and State Security, blinding Leo as he and Dr Bischoff stopped at a heavy oak door.

'Well, Dr Gebhardt, now I'll introduce you to the ladies who look after the organisation of our concerts.'

Without knocking, Dr Bischoff opened the door of the office and entered, followed by his companion. The sunlight streaming through the tall south-facing windows fell on a U-shaped arrangement of desks in the centre of the spacious room. Three secretaries looked up from their work and smiled when they saw their boss.

'Ladies, may I introduce Dr Leopold Gebhardt, who joined our foreign department two days ago and is dedicated to spreading our musical genius throughout the world,' and he turned to his companion, a tall man in his mid-thirties with a long, scholarly face. His grey eyes regarded the secretaries with a mixture of interest and benevolence.

Leo smiled as he raised his arm in the German greeting.

'Heil Hitler, pleased to meet you,' he said in a friendly manner, lowering his arm and bowing slightly.

Dr Bischoff politely indicated the eldest of the three, a well-endowed but otherwise unprepossessing lady with short grey hair. 'Fräulein Kolbe, the head of this office, we'd be absolutely lost without her. She's in charge of the contracts and the book-keeping.' Dr Gebhardt and Fräulein Kolbe shook hands.

'Welcome to our department, and I wish you all the best for your work here,' she said politely, with a measured smile that conveyed control and competence.

Bischoff turned to the lady on the left, a heavily made-up young woman with thick blond hair in a plait twisted around her head. 'Fräulein Zimmermann looks after the programmes and the publicity, among other things. She is, so to speak, the link between our department and the public.' A waft of eau de cologne reached him as she glanced at the Party button in his lapel and stretched out her manicured fingers.

'Gebhardt, my pleasure,' said Leo, and took her hand briefly in his.

'So pleased to have you with us,' she replied with a smile.

Then he turned to the third young lady, who, in fact, had caught his eye as soon as he'd entered the office, and Bischoff followed him.

'May I introduce: Dr Gebhardt, Fräulein Marc. Fräulein Marc speaks English very well and has some French too. She's responsible for concert tours to and from abroad, so I imagine you'll be working mainly with her. Fräulein Marc, Dr Gebhardt.'

Leo looked down at the young lady, who was working at a filing cabinet. More than her appearance – her open face, the deeply-set dark blue eyes, the soft black hair drawn loosely away from her forehead to a small twist at the back, her slim figure – , it was the aura of privacy and inner balance she emanated that roused his interest.

'Pleased to meet you,' she said with a friendly smile, and 'The pleasure's mine,' he answered.

But what he really wanted to say was: 'Enchanted'.

'I hadn't expected to meet an expert in English here,' said Leo. 'Dr Bischoff is sending me to a conference on Bruckner in London next week, and I'll be giving a paper there. I'd be grateful if you could go over it with me?'

'Of course! Just call me on the office line whenever it suits you. But I'm not an expert by any means. Please don't expect too much!'

'I'm sure that between us we'll produce a professional text. Are you personally interested in music, or do you play yourself? Anyone who can touch-type can surely play the piano, don't you agree?'

She smiled politely. He could make out little laugh lines at the corners of her eyes.

'I do play the piano,' said Emma, 'I had lessons for many years, but recently I haven't had much time to practise.'

'Well then, I'd be delighted to give you some lessons if ever you thought of taking it up again,' he answered, smiling, and Emma's blue eyes narrowed a little.

'Very kind,' she answered coolly. She turned to close the open drawer of the filing cabinet.

Leo, annoyed with himself, stepped back and turned to Fräulein Kolbe.

'Dr Bischoff has already indicated that the number of engagements that pass through your hands is impressive. I do hope you don't find this kind of work too ... dry?'

'Not at all,' replied Frl. Kolbe firmly. 'It carries a lot of responsibility and that's a challenge that I enjoy facing. I deal with people of all kinds from many different countries, no two contracts are ever quite the same.' And she gave him a confident smile.

Leo, glad of a lead for another comment to Frl. Marc, seized on this theme and looked at Emma again.

'You must experience the same variety in your section, Frl. Marc, handling all those artists from abroad. Those concert tours rarely come off without a hitch somewhere along the line. I'm sure you often work overtime trying to fix things?'

There was a short pause before she replied.

'Overtime? No, I can't say I do.' She regarded him calmly. 'And I don't usually need to solve any problems myself. I just need to find out what the issue is, and which is the proper department for dealing with it. I'm only the go-between.'

'You must be very flexible, then. I'm sure I'll enjoy working together with you. All three of you,' he added, and indicated a bow in their general direction.

'Our ladies are all very experienced,' said Dr Bischoff. 'They are a great help to me in my position, we form a solid team!'

Again Frl. Kolbe answered for the three secretaries.

'The main thing is that we can rely on each other, and that we all enjoy our work. But we're really glad to have you in our department, Dr Gebhardt. Rumour has it that you are personally acquainted with many of the leading international musicians?'

'Yes. For the past six years I was a music critic at a Leipzig paper, and Leipzig, as you know, draws all the top artists, so that I got to know many interesting people – Sir Malcolm Sargent, Toscanini, and people of that calibre. I believe that might turn out to be of some use for my work here,' he added, sending an encouraging glance towards

Frl. Marc. The ladies greeted his modesty with smiles, though he noted that Frl. Marc's did not reach her eyes.

Frl. Kolbe had started collecting papers from her desk and was shuffling them to make a sheaf. Leo caught the hint.

'Well, ladies, we'll be seeing a lot of each other from now on, I imagine. But we mustn't waste your valuable time. And Fräulein Marc, I'll be contacting you in the next day or so, if I may.'

'Of course,' affirmed Emma again.

After a few more polite remarks the two gentlemen said their good-byes and left the room. In the corridor Dr Bischoff turned to his new employee and tapped him lightly on the shoulder.

'Well, Gebhardt, I can see you're the type that doesn't waste a minute. Let me be clear about one thing though: Miss Marc is *my* secretary, and I intend to keep her!' and he smiled complacently.

Leo didn't reply. He was trying to deal with what had happened to him in the secretaries' office. It was a feeling he had never experienced before, at least not since his teenage years. He considered himself a man of the world, but in the past few minutes he had, he thought, lost control of his thoughts and emotions. All he knew was that he was greatly looking forward to working together with Frl. Marc. He'd ring her the next day.

2

17 March: The English Talk

The inter-office telephone rang as Emma was typing a translation of a letter from the UK music publisher Boosey & Hawkes for Dr Bischoff.

'Marc, good morning'.

She could hear a hoarse male voice trying to say something at the other end of the line, then a cough and a loud clearing of a throat. She held the receiver away from her ear and waited until she heard the caller say his name.

'Gebhardt here, Fräulein Marc,' and another harrumph followed. 'My most humble apologies, I suddenly had something in my throat. I'm so sorry.'

'That's all right,' said Emma. 'I hope you're all right now?'

'Yes, yes, thank you. Fräulein Marc, it's that talk in London that I mentioned yesterday. Would you have a moment today to go over it with me?'

'Yes, Dr Gebhardt, of course. I'm just finishing an urgent letter for Dr Bischoff, and then I could be at your office in about ten minutes.'

'Wonderful! Thank you.' And he hung up the phone.

She took a deep breath before placing the letter for Dr Bischoff in the OUT basket. Then she checked her appearance in the little hand mirror she kept in the top drawer of her desk for this purpose.

Dr Gebhardt's obvious interest in her the day before had annoyed her at the time. But sitting in the underground on her way home, she had to admit that he had an air about him that made him stand out from his colleagues in the department. And whether she liked it or not, she would be working closely together with him in the near future. Much better to try to establish their relationship on a professional footing. She would have to try to overcome her antipathy, while at the same time showing him clearly how far he could – or rather, could not – go.

After patting her hair, she stared at herself for a moment longer, then shook her head as she snapped the mirror shut. She picked up her notebook and a freshly sharpened pencil from the drawer of her desk.

Dr Gebhardt's office was on the same floor, further down the long corridor. She knocked on the door.

'Come in please,' she heard him call, and she entered. Dr Gebhardt rose as she did so, and walked around his desk towards her, holding out his hand. This was definitely *not* professional, she thought. You don't shake the secretary's hand when she comes in for dictation. But she extended her hand, and received a firm, dry clasp as a greeting.

'Thank you for coming so quickly,' he said. 'Please, take a seat.' He indicated the chair across the desk from his, and waited for her to be seated before he sat down himself. She noticed him looking at her for a moment, smiling slightly, and she quickly checked that her fitted grey skirt was covering her knees. She placed the notebook on the desk.

'I'm really being plunged in at the deep end,' Dr Gebhardt began. 'The Bruckner Society have been in touch with the Department. Bruckner is completely unknown in England, and there's a music conference in London at the weekend to which a representative of the Department has been invited. It's a golden opportunity for drawing their attention to our great Austrian composer. I've typed out my speech here,' and he drew a sheaf of papers from a manila folder. 'I learnt English at school and I've been to England several times, but I believe you stayed there for some time?'

'Yes,' answered Emma. 'I spent six months there after I left school, six years ago. I was in a college in Cheltenham for two months, and then on the Isle of Wight.' Her mind flew back to the lively crowd of young people who had welcomed her there, and the fun they'd all had, sailing and bathing.

Gebhardt waited for her to continue, but when she remained silent, pencil poised, he stood up and moved over to a table with four wooden armchairs that was standing in one corner of his office.

'Good. Then I suggest we sit over here. I have a carbon copy for you, and perhaps I'll read my text and you can make notes of anything that seems wrong in the grammar or vocabulary.'

'Yes, certainly,' said Emma, and they settled down to work.

Dr Gebhardt had a pleasant speaking voice. Baritone, she guessed. She saw now that he had dark grey eyes with hooded lids. He had a long, aquiline nose, but the lower part of his face was softer than the rest, with a strong chin, and a finely shaped mouth. His dark hair was cut short, but she could see that it was frizzy or even curly, a frivolous contrast to his otherwise intellectual exterior. His hands, she observed, were beautiful, shapely and strong, with long, slightly flattened fingers. She could imagine him playing the piano. There was no doubt that he radiated a presence.

His speech was interesting and easy to understand, but she concentrated on points that she could improve. His pronunciation was decidedly German, and she knew that this could not be corrected in just a few hours. She circled words and phrases on the pages in front of her that didn't sound right. The speech ended after about 45 minutes, and Dr Gebhardt placed his papers on the table.

'Now, what do you think?'

'Well,' she said, 'I'm not an English teacher, of course, but it seems to me that you sometimes use the wrong tense. Here, on page 1, for example, you say: "Bruckner has been born to a poor but religious family." That should be: "he was born." And similarly you say: "he has become a music teacher." Again it should be: "he became a music teacher."'

Dr Gebhardt raised his eyebrows.

'But in German we say: he has been born. It's the Perfect Tense, if I remember correctly. For events in the past.'

Emma swallowed. Could she remember the rules which had been so well explained at the college in Cheltenham?

'In English, the use of tenses is much more complex than in German, and the Perfect Tense is only used for past events that still have an effect on the present. For example: I've had my breakfast. That implies: so I'm not hungry now.'

Dr Gebhardt laughed.

'But,' continued Emma bravely, 'Bruckner is so long dead that the events of his life belong safely in the past, so you would use the Past Tense, not the Perfect. I remember learning that this was one of the most common mistakes made by Germans in English, because in German it's different.'

'I'll make a note of it,' said Gebhardt, and he scribbled on his manuscript. 'What else?'

'Now here, on page 5, you say: "The influence of Bruckner's music lasts up to the present day." That should be: "has lasted up to the present day"'.

Gebhardt's nostrils flared slightly.

'Why that?'

'Well, with "up to the present day" you have a time span from the past to now, and for that you can't just use the normal Present Tense like we do in German. Here you need the Present Perfect. It bridges past and present.'

'You don't think you're being a bit too particular in this, do you?' asked Gebhardt, and Emma was amused to discern that he was piqued by her corrections.

'It definitely sounds more natural in English to say: "His influence has lasted to the present day",' she said calmly.

'All right then.' And again he noted something on his page.

'Another thing I noticed is the sentence structure. For example, here on page two, you said: "Bruckner travelled in 1854 to Vienna for the first time." You should name the place first, and then the time: "he travelled to Vienna in 1854".' To forestall his objections – another eyebrow was being lifted – she added: 'In German sentences, we name the time first, and then the date, and in English it's the other way round. Otherwise it sounds very foreign,' she added firmly, hoping this last sentence would convince him in case her grammar argument failed to do so.

This time he made a note without commenting.

'Here's another point I noticed,' Emma went on. 'It's on the last page. You write: "Never before a composer had devoted himself entirely to the symphonic form." I would say: "Never before had a composer devoted himself etc." But I can't explain why this is so.'

Gebhardt frowned.

'That sounds very strange. Are you sure? It sounds more like a question that way round.'

'Yes, I'm quite sure.'

'Well, I don't know,' Gebhardt said.

Emma was starting to get annoyed.

'Dr Gebhardt, you asked me in here to help you with your text because you believed I had more experience with the English language than you. If you think that you don't really require my help, then I really should get back to my office, where there's a pile of work waiting for me. Your speech is fine as it is and everyone will be able to understand it.'

Dr Gebhardt stared at her. He got up and walked around the little table to stand beside her. She caught a whiff of tobacco from his clothes.

'No, no, Fräulein Marc,' he said, his hand on the back of her chair and leaning over her slightly. 'You are quite right. I must apologise again and beg your pardon. Of course I accept your corrections and suggestions, and I'm extremely grateful for your time.' He stood back. 'And I suspect that there are more such – slips – in my text. It would take too long now for us to go through all of them one by one. Could you rework my text and type a new and much more typically English version? By ... Tuesday? The original and four copies, please.'

Emma had calmed down.

'Yes, of course, with pleasure. Oh, and by the way, you used the English word 'typical' somewhere, but you pronounced it the German way, as if the letter y were a u-Umlaut: ü – tüpical. But in English the y here is like the letter i: tipical.'

'Ah – tüipical,' he tried.

'More of an "I",' said Emma encouragingly.

He tried it again. It still sounded more like the German version of the word, but Emma decided to leave it. She was, in fact, exhausted. She stood up, gathered the manuscript pages together, and waited for him to dismiss her.

'Well then, we'll see each other on Tuesday. And again, thank you so much. I'm in your debt.'

She felt this was overdoing it a bit. After all, it was her job. At the same time she was amused by the obvious struggle he had had against his reluctance to admit a mistake. It seemed he really did want to make a good impression on her.

She, for her part, was quite happy with how composed she had been during the past hour, quite professional, she believed. They could continue working together on this basis.

3

25 March: Dinner at Borchardt's

Emma pulled another frock out of her wardrobe and, holding it in front of her, looked in the mirror. She liked it, but it was not her favourite for an evening date: a black-and white check, with a bloused bodice and padded shoulders, and a sparkle added by a narrow red belt and a kerchief pinned at the throat. Satisfied with her choice, she hung it on the side of her wardrobe and took out her black T-strap heels, a new pair of silk stockings, and her new black and gold embroidered handbag.

She was just beginning to dress when the door flew open and Franzi blew in. She'd been out skating with Moritz, but couldn't spend the evening with him as he was due in his squadron quarters and would be flying back to Spain tomorrow. Her face was glowing and her short brown hair was ruffled from the wind. Seeing her so vibrant and healthy, Emma could perfectly understand Moritz's instant reaction at his first sight of her at a dance he'd attended with a friend. She'd caught his eye as soon as he entered the ballroom, and before he'd even been introduced to her, he announced: 'That's the one I'm going to marry!' They were getting engaged as soon as the Spanish war was over.

'Ma says you've got a date with the new buck in your department! Is that true?!'

Emma smiled. 'He's not a buck, as you'd be the first to agree if you saw him. A very distinguished gentleman! Yes, he rang this morning, he's only free at the weekend and was away in London all week.'

'Where's he taking you?'

'To Borchardt.'

'Wow! Moritz has never taken me there. He says it's the haunt of too many of the political brownies for his liking. He prefers it more relaxed. Still, it's a posh place. You must have made quite an impression on him. Don't actually remember you mentioning him before.' With a mock frown.

'No, well, I hardly know him. I helped him with a speech he had to give in English, and now he wants to thank me.'

'Hm, normally a bottle of Eue de Cologne would have done the job, but Borchardt! There's more to this than mere thanks!'

Emma had been thinking the same.

'What're you going to wear?'

Emma showed her sister what she'd chosen. As she expected, Franzi pulled a face.

'That's rather a stiff get-up if you want to impress him!'

'I don't want to encourage him at all. In fact I didn't want to accept his invitation when he rang me, but I couldn't think of any excuse, and before I knew what I'd said, I'd accepted. I'd much prefer to keep our relationship on a purely professional footing. He's the one who's so keen. Flattering, of course. But at the same time, you know …'

'My darling sleepy big sister. Always so careful. I'd be delighted if Mr Right swept onto the scene and you off your feet. I think that's the only way you can be convinced to accept anyone. Helmi, and Richard, and Reinhard ... none of them were right for you.'

'No, they weren't,' said Emma, 'so that's that. When the right person comes, I'll know.'

Franzi laughed, and then helped her to get ready. Franzi had finished her apprenticeship as a dressmaker in a fashion salon, had excellent taste, and was much more interested in clothes, make-up, hairstyles, and accessories than Emma. She made her put on more lipstick to match the red kerchief, and gave out to her for not doing her nails with varnish. But it was too late for that now.

'And you *must* pluck your eyebrows! They're like two hairy caterpillars!'

Before Emma left she looked in on her mother and father in the drawing room. As she popped her head round the door they both looked up from what they were reading, her mother a Russian novel, her father the *Law Weekly*.

'Enjoy yourself, dear,' said her mother. 'I'm dying to know how you get on. Paul, why have you never taken me out to Borchardt?!'

'Don't be back late,' from her father.

Neither statement was a surprise, and Emma just said: 'Thank you, see you later' and withdrew smiling.

Franzi saw her to the door and blew her a kiss.

'Promise you'll enjoy yourself! And don't be too hard on him!'

Emma didn't know what she thought. On the one hand, she was annoyed at herself, overthrowing her own guidelines so very soon. How would she get through this evening? What if he became too persistent in his attentions? On the other, it was a completely new experience to be dated by someone of Dr Gebhardt's maturity and presence. She would be careful, and in the end perhaps she could learn something which would help her in future situations. Or something like that.

She drew a deep breath and hoped for the best.

At seven p.m. she pushed open the heavy mahogany and glass door of Borchardt's on Französische Strasse and waited just inside the entrance. The high-ceilinged room was half filled with guests, low voices in friendly conversation mingled with the clinking of cutlery as elegant waiters made their way between the tables balancing trays with plates covered in silver domes. It was hard to distinguish an individual face, but already Dr Gebhardt was striding towards her, a warm smile on his face, his hand outstretched. His tall, well-built figure looked very elegant in a single-breasted suit of dark grey wool with a narrow pale stripe. The fitted jacket and wide trousers with high cuffs were the latest fashion.

'How wonderful to see you! Oh, this is really wonderful!' he exclaimed, helping her off with her coat and handing it to a waiter. She kept her little black skullcap on, and he guided her to a table in a far corner. There were niches with pots of mother-in-law's tongues on both walls behind them, and a planter with aspidistras on one of the open sides, so that they were quite secluded.

'Thank you for accepting my invitation at such short notice, Fräulein Marc,' he began, after they had settled and both ordered a drink – she a dry sherry and he a glass of draught 'You have no idea how valuable your help with my speech was.'

'Oh, it was really not so difficult,' said Emma, 'and it was such an interesting text to work on, much better than those contracts I usually have to translate.'

'Well, everyone complimented me on my excellent English. But more than that – you'd never imagine this – but the whole event led to a triumph for our efforts to promote German music abroad. This series of lectures I was at was organised by Sir Adrian Boult, and I managed to arouse his interest in the works of Bruckner. Would you believe it – after hearing my talk he decided to do a Bruckner cycle with the BBC Symphony Orchestra in the coming winter season, all nine symphonies! In the Albert Hall, if possible!'

Emma realised that this was indeed a great success, and she understood his undisguised excitement.

'That is really wonderful!' she said sincerely. 'Congratulations! Dr Bischoff will be so impressed! And especially when you're so new to the department.'

'Yes, I never expected such an honour myself. It just goes to show that proper preparation is everything. I hope I'll have more opportunities to work together with you and profit from your excellent advice.'

Emma smiled politely, unsure how to respond.

The waiter had placed the menus in front of them, and they spent some time studying them and discussing what they would eat. Emma decided on a boeuf bourguignon, and Leo a steak – 'very rare' – , and he also chose a wine for them. He did this very professionally, and Emma, who had been racking her brain as to what they should talk about, chose this as her opening remark.

'You obviously know your wines!'

'My father was a wine merchant in Dresden before he retired, and so inevitably I grew up learning about wines. When I was a pupil I used to travel around with him during my holidays, visiting his customers and the vineyards where he bought the wines. An interesting and very educational experience which, I must admit, has stood me in good stead since then.'

"Since I've come up in the world" was implied but not spoken, Emma surmised.

'I could tell from your accent that you come from Saxony,' said Emma. 'Have you been in Berlin long?'

'No, not at all! As you know I started at the department on the 15th, and until the end of the previous week I was working for the Leipziger Neuesten Nachrichten.' Emma knew this was a conservative national newspaper published in Leipzig, in the state of Saxony.

But Leo wanted to find out about Emma, and before she could ask another polite question, he took over the conversation.

'You, for your part, have a West Prussian accent. How long have you been in Berlin, and where were you living before that?'

'Yes, I grew up near the Baltic Sea, in Elbing, in West Prussia, but in 1933 my father had to ... my father moved to Berlin. I went to England for the six months I told you about, so that I arrived here early in 1934.'

'And do you enjoy living in the big city?'

'Naturally it offers many more openings for social events and activities and also for work than a small provincial town like Elbing. But I loved living there and I still miss it a little, I must say.'

Their starters had been placed before them, and after wishing each other 'a blessing on this meal' they began to eat. Emma praised her salmon mayonnaise, and Leo explained how much he loved soups. His mother had made one every day. There was a break in the conversation, and again Emma wracked her brains. A lot of obvious questions occurred to her, but they were quite personal, and she felt they were unsuitable, as they would only encourage him to delve more into her own personal life. But Leo did not share her inhibitions.

'From your phone number I see that you live in Zehlendorf. Do you have a flat of your own there?'

'Oh no, I live with my parents and my sisters. My middle sister will be moving out soon, though, she's getting married in May.'

'Are you the eldest?'

'Yes.' There was a pause. She thought of asking him whether he had any siblings, then decided not to. He could make the effort to keep the conversation going.

'I'm an only child. I can't imagine what it must be like to have brothers or sisters. I was often quite lonely in my childhood. If I hadn't had my music lessons, and enjoyed them, from early on, I'd have had a very dull childhood.'

Music seemed a safe topic to keep to.

'Did you have your piano lessons at home?'

'I began with the violin. My father plays and he gave me a miniature violin when I was quite small. I started the piano some years later, and I also took up the oboe a few years ago. It seems music was my destiny from an early stage. You mentioned that you don't play anymore?'

'No, I got out of the habit after I came back from England and went to commercial college and then started working.' And because she was proud of it, she couldn't resist adding: 'I'd got as far as Beethoven's "Pathetique" when I had to stop for my time in England.'

'So you're more interested in classical music?'

'I love classical music, especially Brahms. But I must say I also enjoy good popular music.' Emma loved dancing to jazz, but that was out of favour with the powers-that-be at the moment – 'degenerate' – , so she kept this to herself.

'I used to compose popular music for cabarets,' smiled Gebhardt. 'I had a friend who was very good at those silly rhymes, and we had great fun making up frivolous songs.' He hummed: ' "Oh Elisabeth, I dream of you! Those legs of yours – a dream come true". They sold well and helped us to earn our living. But all that's well in the past.'

'Yes, everything seems to have got a lot more serious now,' said Emma, and then wondered if she had gone too far. After all, he was in the Party.

'Well, we do have serious issues to deal with, and those silly nonsense rhymes don't sound at all funny nowadays, when the world is progressing in quite a different direction. But I still believe people need fun and levity as well as serious goals to be really human, don't you? Life would be so dull if we spent all our time in pursuit of earnest, important challenges, especially for young ladies like yourself.'

Emma didn't take the bait. 'Not dull, perhaps, but one-dimensional. I agree, life isn't black and white, there's a lot of grey and beige and so on. We need different experiences to refreshen us and help us to tackle the more serious sides of life – lighter moments, or simple pleasures, such as we encounter every day, often without noticing them.'

'Moments such as this,' he smiled at her, and raised his glass. His grey eyes looked relaxed and happy. She lifted hers by the stem and touched his lightly, producing a high-pitched ping. She was enjoying herself.

'What do you like doing besides working in the office and not playing the piano?' he asked.

Emma laughed. 'I cycle, and in Elbing we often went canoeing. And our parents often used to take us hiking in the mountains in the holidays. Skiing too, of course, though we didn't have mountains or even high hills at home. But we made the most of what we had. In the summers I must say I love sitting on a beach and just watching the sea and feeling the sun ...' She was going to say 'on my skin,' but caught herself in time.

'I spent two years studying in Innsbruck and so skiing and hiking were very much part of my life.' And he launched into a story of how he had been on a two-day hike with college friends in the Alps and had got ill with a very high temperature, and of how his friends had saved him with alternate cures of snow compresses and a distillation of a very high potency bought from a local cowherd. His imitation of the Tyrolean accent had them both laughing.

'I have some photos of myself on that trip I could never show Dr Bischoff. It would greatly lower my standing in his eyes!'

By this time they had finished their main course, and Leo asked if she would like a dessert, which she declined. They decided on a coffee, and the conversation drifted on, back and forth from memories to preferences to dislikes. He no longer seemed the august person she had taken him for; he was a normal being with tastes and opinions and human touches that she was familiar with. His age and his wide musical and professional experience still imbued him with a worldliness that she had never experienced before in any of her closer friends, and she wasn't sure how to deal with it. On the other hand, she noted signs of neediness, due perhaps to his lonely childhood. Nonetheless, the evening was relaxing, not as tense as she had feared, and there had been no indications of how he saw her or felt about her, to her great relief. It was a normal, friendly evening with a new friend. When Leo suggested that perhaps, sometime, she would like to accompany him to one of the concerts for which he always got complimentary tickets, she was quite happy to acquiesce, and found herself looking forward to it.

At twenty past ten he brought her to the station for the underground to Zehlendorf, said goodbye quite formally, and stood on the platform until her train had whooshed into the tunnel. She would be home in under an hour, and was looking forward to reviewing the evening during the journey.

Leo was pleased with himself, and happy, as he walked up the stairs from the station. Emma was quite different from any of the many girlfriends he'd had. There was nothing flirtatious about her at all, she was so self-possessed, almost serious, though that didn't describe it either. She had a lovely, quite infectious laugh, which always came unexpectedly and sent a surprising and delightful tremor through him each time. But she had been very much on her guard, he had noticed. He had been wise to decide beforehand to be very careful, not to be over-enthusiastic in his admiration. His self-control had paid off – now he could look forward to taking her to the Elly Ney concert the coming week. And perhaps he could take her swimming at Lake Wannsee Baths when the weather got warmer in a few weeks. He could hardly wait.

What luck that he had run into his ex-fellow student Meyer in Leipzig that time – it was he who had told him to apply to the Ministry for this post, knew they were looking for someone like him. Now he had this job with all its potential for rising in the hierarchy of the civil service, *and* he had found the woman he wanted to spend the rest of his life with. All in the one week! It was too good to be true. If only his mother had lived long enough to enjoy his happiness! And his father, that obstinate socialist, would come round too. He still believed Leo should have taken up banking, or law. But now that his only child was hob-nobbing with all the great names in the world of music, Toscanini,

Furtwängler, Sir Malcom Sargent, he could not fail to be impressed. Perhaps their relationship would improve as a result.

Yes, indeed, everything had suddenly taken a turn for the best.

He swung open the main door of the Excelsior Hotel, where he was staying, and headed for a quick night-cap in the bar before going up to his room.

4

31 March: The Elly Ney Concert

Again Emma was standing in front of her wardrobe, its door wide open. Was it time for the dark green silk-satin, or had that stage not arrived yet? What else did she have that might do? Elly Ney was a big, big name, the foremost Beethoven interpreter of her time, and the Fifth Piano Concerto was always impressive and emotional. Bruckner's Second Symphony was on too, one of his longest, very august. The concert was taking place in the exquisite little Singakademie Theatre on Unter den Linden. But the conductor was unknown to her, and the orchestra was only the Berlin Concert Orchestra, not the Philharmonic under Furtwängler. No, she'd save the silk-satin for a more prestigious event. She could foresee having to go shopping for extensions to her wardrobe if Leo's invitations should continue to come in as fast as this one, barely six days after she'd been out to dinner with him. He certainly wasn't wasting any time.

She had got home quickly enough, just over an hour. Everyone was in bed when she let herself in.

From the kitchen she got herself a cup of milk and crept up the creaking stairs to her little room. She quickly got into bed, sitting with her knees drawn up, sipping the milk and letting her mind drift over the evening. She was still unclear about how she felt. It was enjoyable and very flattering to be invited to such a posh restaurant, and there was no doubt that Gebhardt was an interesting gentleman and a pleasant companion. But she was unused to being alone in the company of someone so much older than herself. She was annoyed that this should make such a difference. After all, she was twenty-four, not nineteen, she'd been around a bit and had had her share of boyfriends. But they'd been people her own age, they spoke the same language, caught each other's inferences and innuendos, jokes and ribbing. None of them had elicited *respect* from her as a key component of the relationship. She couldn't ever imagine talking to Leo in this way. Still, he had been very funny in that story about the skiing holiday, and they had both laughed heartily at the same things.

Her mind rambled on into the future. What if this turned into something really serious? She was tired of living at home. Her sisters, both younger, would be leaving in the near future, and she would be alone with her parents. She loved her father, but she often had run-ins with her mother, and longed for a place of her own. It really was time to think of getting married, she thought. But that wasn't something you could just plan and then go out and do! The main prerequisite was finding the right partner, and even if you went to a lot of trouble to meet different people, there was never a guarantee that one of them would be Mr Ideal. In the end you might meet him by turning a corner and bumping into him! On the other hand, many couples met through their work, so that her specific and present 'relationship', if it could even be called that, was absolutely normal, even promising. Oh, it was all so complicated, and anyway, nothing might come of it, he'd meet someone more glamorous than she, and that would be the end of it, so it wasn't worth getting herself a headache at this stage, and besides, she was dead-tired. Within two minutes she'd been asleep.

On Tuesday, her office telephone had rung, and it was he. He had two complimentary tickets for the Elly Ney concert on Friday, would she like to come? On the spur of the moment she decided she would. But for the benefit of the other ladies in the office she had to sound very impersonal and business-like.

'Friday? Yes, I think that can be done. What time were you thinking of?'

She could register his surprise at her tone.

'Eh – we could meet at the station in Friedrichstrasse and walk to the Singakademie from there, if that suits you? Say at 7.15?'

'That would be perfect. I'll make a note of it and send you a confirmation.'

She could almost hear him making sounds of exasperation at the other end, so she quickly added, 'Thank you for calling. You'll be hearing from us.' And she hung up, trying not to laugh.

Before she left for lunch, she noted down his office number, so that she could ring him from a call box.

'Dr Gebhardt? This is Emma Marc.'

'Yes, Fräulein Marc?' Very cool.

'Thank you so much for your invitation to the concert, and please accept my apologies for how I spoke to you on the phone earlier. My two colleagues were in the office, and I didn't like them to know I was getting a private call.'

Leo laughed. 'Of course, I understand. I should have thought of that. The worthy ladies would be only too interested in such information. You dealt with that very neatly, I must say!'

'So we'll meet at Friedrichstrasse station at 7.15, is that right?'

'Yes, if that suits you. And I thought we could go for a little meal in the Comic Opera Restaurant afterwards, it's just across the road from the theatre.'

'That would be nice. I'm looking forward to it. Well, I'm sure you're very busy, but we might run into each other in the Department.'

'Yes, indeed. Otherwise, see you on Friday. I'm delighted you can come.'

'Goodbye then, and thank you again,' said Emma, and hung up.

She still had three days till the concert. She pulled out a hanger with a dress or skirt hidden under a full-length cotton sheath, and drew this up to see what it was protecting. It was her shiny brown satin with matching bolero jacket. She'd bought it a few years back with her first salary, thinking it would imbue her with dignity. When Franzi saw it she'd said it made her look like a medieval countess from Transylvania. She'd worn it once or twice after that, in protest, but she hadn't felt well in it and had forgotten all about it. She removed the cotton cover and hung it on the door of the wardrobe. The gored skirt reached to mid-calf, while the sleeveless bodice was cut close to the figure. The short bolero jacket was of the same material, with cream-coloured embroidery. She tried it on. It still fitted perfectly, and her instinct told her that for this event it would be just the right thing – mature, yet elegant and festive. She searched through her modest collection of shoes but found nothing matching. A high-heeled cream coloured shoe, she thought, was called for, and perhaps Franzi would lend her the satin cream clutch with the pearl stitching. She'd drop into Leiser's after work tomorrow; it was the biggest shoe store in Berlin and not too far away from the office by underground. She looked at herself in the mirror of the wardrobe in her little room and was surprised at how it suited her. She wondered how Leo would react.

On Friday she rushed home from work and got herself ready. Franzi was waiting to help her. She had been in a tizzy and glued to the radio since Tuesday, when the war in Spain had ended with the overthrow of the Communists. Moritz's squadron, the Condor Legion, had been supporting the new ruler, General Franco, and now he could be expected home soon. But she tore herself away in order to help her sister.

Franzi had plucked Emma's eyebrows for her the evening before ('Not too much! I'm not a film star!'), and applied transparent nail varnish. There'd been an argument between them about that: Franzi wanted her to use a pale orange varnish, but Emma said under no circumstances could she appear in the office like that the next morning, and on Friday there wouldn't be enough time between coming home and leaving to take the train back into town. Now Franzi arranged her hair for her, parting it on the right and drawing it back softly to a bun at the back of her head, where she secured it with clips and a tortoiseshell comb. Franzi also applied her make-up, a hint of dark eyeshadow to match the dress, an orange tinted lipstick, and pale pink rouge under an ivory-coloured powder. She had found cream satin court shoes with a medium heel in Leiser's. With her little brown skullcap with the small feather brooch, and Franzi's evening bag in her hand, she presented herself in the mirror, and was amazed at how sophisticated she appeared.

'What do you think, Franzi?' she asked, very pleased with what she saw.

'Where's your amber bead necklace?'

She clipped it round her neck; it suited the outfit perfectly. Franzi stepped back to look at her.

'You look fit to be seduced by a prince! Make sure you get home before midnight! Dear Emmi, you look wonderful. I'm sure the Doc will be swept off his feet.'

They went downstairs, where her mother was clearing the remains of the evening meal from the dining room. It was the housemaid's night off. She came into the hall to examine her daughter.

'Well, Emmi, you look very nice indeed. I always said you should wear that brown dress more often. I do envy you going to this concert, I'm sure it will be a wonderful experience. Elly Ney! It's so long since I heard her!' Elisabeth was very musical and an accomplished pianist. 'Ask Dr Gebhardt if he can get me tickets for one of her future concerts, will you?'

Emma caught her breath. She checked the angle of her hat in the hall mirror and said nothing.

Pa came out of his study in his shirtsleeves, and wished her an enjoyable evening. He smiled at her. She was his favourite, though he tried to hide it from the others.

Franzi helped her sister into her best winter coat, which had fur trimming at the collar and the cuffs, handed her her gloves, wafted an air kiss to her cheek, and then gave her a wolf whistle as she walked to the garden gate. Emma moved carefully in her new shoes, rounding the corner to the underground station for the journey into town. Her image of herself in the mirror had boosted her self-confidence and she was really looking forward to the evening.

Olga Peters

Leo arrived at the main entrance to the station in Friedrichstrasse at the last minute. Bischoff had kept him in the office, droning on about some venture in Romania that he wanted him to get involved in. It could easily have waited till Monday; he wouldn't be able to get hold of anyone over the weekend anyway. He was annoyed too that von Borries had instructed him to find and talk to Dr Weil, the music agent, who was expected to be at the concert, about the possibility of getting Dinu Lipatti to Berlin for a concert and recordings at short notice. He hoped Emma wouldn't already be waiting for him; that would be the last straw in what had been a very hectic day at the office, with multiple trunk calls and two calls to Finland, as well as a meeting with an almost bankrupt Italian music publisher during the afternoon. He took a deep breath and tried to calm himself. There was no sign of Emma, and he was considering buying a cheese roll from a stand in front of the station when he saw her rounding the corner. She looked magnificent! Her flowing burgundy coat, her slim legs with pale shoes, her hands and neck nestling in fur, a little brown cap on her head, her deep-set eyes smiling as they caught his look. He rushed to meet her and took both her hands in his.

'I'm so pleased to see you,' he said quickly, and indicated a kiss to the back of her raised right hand. 'You've brought sunshine into what has been such a gloomy day! If Madame Ney's playing is half as beautiful as you look, this will be an unforgettable evening!'

Emma had to laugh out loud.

'Thank you for asking me. I'm sure we'll have a most enjoyable time.'

She allowed him to tuck her hand under his arm and they set off along the back street beside the railway line which would bring them to the theatre.

A Normal Couple

She had to take little hops in between her steps to keep up with his strides, was in danger of damaging her new shoes, and after a minute she said, 'Could we walk a little slower please!' Leo slowed down, and she withdrew her hand to look for a handkerchief in her clutch to dabble her forehead.

'My apologies,' said Leo, 'in fact we have plenty of time.' And indeed, after only ten minutes they were in the foyer, Emma had left her coat in the cloakroom, and Leo was waiting for her with two glasses of sparkling wine. They raised and clinked the glasses, and sipped the wine while looking around at the other concertgoers. Many of the men were in uniform, black SS and mustard Wehrmacht, and a fair proportion of the ladies were in long evening dresses, but Emma was reassured to see that there were others in shorter dresses like hers. Leo, she saw, couldn't take his eyes off her, and she gave him a shy smile.

'You look wonderful,' he said, 'like a princess,' and she coloured, and had to suppress a giggle, for that is exactly what Franzi had said. She felt a wave of happiness.

She was surprised at how many people he already knew, considering he had been in Berlin only such a short time. Strangers kept coming up and shaking his hand and making one or two remarks, to which he replied in a friendly tone, without encouraging any further conversation. After a short while he said, 'If you're ready, I think we could take our seats. Then we won't be disturbed so much.'

She allowed him to hold her elbow as he guided her to their seats near the front of the auditorium. The chamber was resonating with the sounds of people greeting each other, enthusing, discussing, projecting themselves, murmuring private messages, and she decided that tonight she would say whatever she thought, and see what the consequences were.

'You know an amazing number of people here in Berlin, although you've been here less than three weeks,' she ventured.

He tugged at the knot of his tie as he answered, loosening it slightly.

'My work in the past took me to Berlin and the Ministry quite often. Most of the people I met this evening I've known for a number of years. All business acquaintances.'

He fumbled with his programme, a plain sheet of paper with information about the performers, the pieces and that the grand piano was a Bechstein.

'Do you enjoy all these contacts?'

'Well, in my line of business I have to accept them, you know. It's all part of the job.'

'But then you can never go to a concert and just enjoy it as a private person!'

'Once the music starts I can relax. That's what I come for. Unless I have to be there to write a critique, and those days are gone, thank goodness.'

'Was that not satisfying work?'

'Partly. But there was always the pressure of finding something worthwhile, something memorable to say, even if the concert was absolutely normal. I couldn't just give bad reviews all the time. The big concerts in the Gewandhaus in Leipzig were easy, though even there I had to be careful not to step on anybody's toes while expressing judgements which other musicians in the audience would also have noticed. But very often I was at smaller recitals, most of which in fact were excellent. I'll tell you all about that some other time.'

He spoke more quietly: the auditorium had filled, the musicians had assembled on the stage, the buzz of conversation had died down, the lights had dimmed. The first violin tapped his bow on his music stand, there was silence, and the oboe played the clear A, releasing a pleasant instrumental cacophony, the final tuning of the instruments that preceded every concert. After a minute it stopped abruptly, there was a pause, then, from the wings on the left the conductor strode to the rostrum, bowed deeply to the audience, turned to the orchestra and raised his baton. The musicians picked up their instruments, and the concert began.

During the interval, Leo guided Emma to the lobby and organised a glass of water for her – she had refused a glass of wine. He kept half an eye out for Dr Weil, and to his great annoyance caught sight of him almost immediately, so that he had to excuse himself and leave Emma on her own. She drifted around, looking at the other concertgoers, noting their fashions and their sometimes rather exalted mannerisms. She was still under the influence of the mighty tones of the last movement of the Fifth Piano Concerto; it was such overpowering music, and Madam Ney, who was known to consider herself in direct, mystical communication with the spirit of Beethoven, had given her utmost to produce an unforgettable performance. Emma knew she was fondly nicknamed the 'Reich's grandpianomother' – her enormous coif of white hair and her long career, as well as her high standing with the powers-that-be in today's regime, were all reflected in that name.

 She looked around to see where Leo was. He was talking to an elderly, angular gentleman, as tall as he was himself, and it seemed an agreement was being reached, for they were just shaking hands. Leo, glancing in her direction, was clearly indicating that he had other commitments, so that the older gentlemen gripped his elbow lightly and pushed him in her direction, with a pleasant smile at her. She felt a wave of warmth towards Leo, appreciating how his business partner empathised with him and wished him well. She met him halfway and took his hand.

'Let's hide behind one of these thick curtains, and then no one will find you!' she whispered, and he laughed. They walked over to one of the tall windows overlooking Unter den Linden, and Leo was just beginning to tell her how responsive Dr Weil had been to his suggestions and requests when the bell rang three times, and they returned to their seats.

Emma was unable to concentrate on the music for the rest of the evening. She was looking forward to being in the restaurant and sitting at a table together with Leo after the concert. It dawned on her that she was feeling more relaxed in his company, could even risk gentle jokes, and that she was no longer in awe of him.

When the final chords of Bruckner's Second Symphony had faded and enthusiastic applause broke out, Leo was thrilled to see her smiling up at him, her deep-set eyes glowing and her open face beaming. They got their coats, left the theatre as quickly as possible and crossed the wide boulevard of Unter den Linden, holding hands.

5

15 April: KDW

It was a pleasant day in mid-April as Leo emerged from the underground station Zoo near the Kaiser William Memorial Church and looked around. The train had been crowded, and he drew a deep breath. The wide shopping street looked very gay: colourfully striped awnings shaded the windows of the stores, and bright red Swastika flags hung from the tall lampposts. He turned and made his way towards KaDeWe, the huge department store whose name meant Store of the West. It was the biggest, most luxurious and most modern of the many new shopping venues in the centre of Berlin, a faithful replica of the original temples in far-off, much envied New York. Berliners maintained it was the biggest department store in the world.

At the big junction of Kurfürstendamm, Leo waited for the newly installed traffic light suspended in the centre of the crossing to change. From his travels to London and Rome he was well used to the jumble of bicycles, horse-drawn carts, motor cars, taxis, trams, double-decker busses that were pushing and honking and yelling and swerving for precedence from all four directions. The noise level was impressive, and the pungent smell of exhaust fumes hardly less so.

As the light changed he sauntered across. Easter, a week earlier, had been cool, but now ladies were tentatively decked in summery dresses and costumes, with colourful little hats or caps, and some had even retrieved last year's straw wedge sandals from their winter retreat. He wondered what Emma might be looking like right now. He hadn't seen her since their night at the Elly Ney concert; he'd been too busy.

He entered KaDeWe and paused, uncertain where to continue. His mission was to find a birthday present for his dear friend Hilde. He'd known her for many years, for a short while they'd been lovers, but their – or rather her – passion had dwindled and evolved into a close friendship, which both of them felt comfortable with. Her work had taken her to Bremen, four hundred kilometres to the west, so that they rarely saw each other. But they made sure to keep in touch, and had shared several tours, most notably in Italy. Her hobby was photography, and he was hoping to find a book on the latest technical developments, or perhaps a good volume with art photos of southern Italy or Sicily, something like that.

He had located the book department on the lower ground floor and was heading for the escalator when his heart jumped. There, not ten metres away, was Emma and another young woman. He followed them quickly as they were walking away, and when Emma stopped suddenly and took an unexpected step back, he bumped into her. Shocked, she turned, and then beamed as she recognised him.

'I'm so sorry!' said Leo. 'How clumsy of me ....!' while Emma said: 'Oh dear, I wasn't looking where I was going! I hope I didn't hurt you?'

But they quickly agreed that nothing had happened.

Emma turned to her companion.

'Franzi, this is Dr Gebhardt, from the Ministry. This is my sister Fräulein Franziska Marc, Dr Gebhardt.'

Leo looked into a friendly, snub-nosed, pretty face. Franzi's brown hair was cut quite short in the latest fashion, her blue eyes were not as deeply set or as dark as Emma's, and her figure was more womanly. She held out her hand, and Leo guided it towards his lips and indicated a kiss as he bowed slightly.

'So pleased to meet you, Doctor,' said Franzi, without any trace of shyness. 'My sister has indeed mentioned your name once or twice.'

Emma had to suppress a giggle.

Leo was startled, then he caught the ball, and played the game.

'I hope the picture she has conveyed has not been painted only in shades of black and grey,' he said seriously.

Franzi burst out laughing.

'Oh no, not at all. The tones she used were more beige and pale blue.'

Now it was Leo's turn to laugh.

'Well, ladies, are you enjoying your shopping? If you have half an hour to spare, I'd like to invite you to a cup of coffee. I believe there's a famous café up on the top floor that I haven't investigated yet. Would that suit you?'

Both young women smiled their answer and they proceeded to the lift. Up on the sixth floor a huge gallery awaited them, with layered rows of windows sloping up to the roof on the far side, and a blue and white tiled floor stretching off into the distance. Dozens of small round tables and modern steel-framed rattan chairs were occupied by what seemed like hundreds of people; Emma found the noise level unpleasantly high. Long counters with glass shelves on either side of the room displayed the most tempting and colourful delicacies in the way of cakes, tarts, gateaux, patisseries, strudels, confectionary, petits fours, pralines – an innumerable array of cakes. How could one possibly choose?

Leo immediately found a free table and held their chairs for them while they settled, before seating himself. A waitress appeared almost at once. They ordered coffees, and Franzi wandered off to see what she would like to eat.

'Can I order anything for either of you?' she asked.

'A piece of sponge cake for me, please,' said Leo.

Emma wondered who on earth was going to eat all these cakes as long as they were fresh. She wanted none herself. She was too surprised at the unexpected encounter.

When they had arranged themselves, conversation rippled around the pleasant weather until the coffee and cakes had been placed on the little table.

Leo asked Emma how she'd been since they'd last met.

'Well, thank you,' she replied politely. 'I haven't seen you at the office. Were you away?'

'Yes and no,' he answered. 'I was at my desk and on the phone most of the time, but I also had some days of training with my regiment last week. And over Easter I went to visit my father in Dresden. I hadn't seen him since I moved to Berlin.'

A Normal Couple

'Does he live on his own?' asked Franzi, who knew Emma would never have the courage to ask this.

'Yes, he does. My mother died last year.'

Silence.

'I'm sorry,' said both girls at once.

'She had an accident in the house, which went unrecognised.'

Leo was still affected by the death of his mother.

'And is your father managing? Is he still working?' asked Emma.

'Yes, he's quite independent. I may have told you he was a wine merchant. He used to have a delicatessen and wine shop in Dresden, but he gave it up two years ago. That is, he still keeps consignments of quality wine in his cellar and supplies a small number of his old customers.'

'And you have no brothers or sisters?' Franzi wanted to know.

'No, I'm an only child.'

It was strange for Leo to be so frank about his private life with two ladies he hardly knew, and yet he felt perfectly at ease. Franzi was so open that it was easy to reveal himself to her. But now, he decided, it was his turn.

'You have a third sister, isn't that right?'

'Yes,' said Emma. 'Franzi is the youngest, and Lise is in between. She's getting married next month, and we were just organising her wedding present.'

'Oh, how pleasant! What did you decide on?'

'We're giving her six sets of towels and having them embroidered with her and her fiancé's initials. The quality here is very good.'

'Yes,' added Franzi. 'Huge beach-towels, bath-towels, handtowels, guest-towels, and loads of face cloths. All in deep pink. Paps is supplying the large cupboard they'll be needing to store them in.'

'I'm sure your sister will appreciate them. And have you bought your wedding outfits yet? Little frilly hats and gloves to match?'

For a split second, Emma's eyes narrowed.

'Franzi is a trained dressmaker, she's made our dresses already.'

'That's very practical! Are you working in a salon now?' This to Franzi.

'No,' said Franzi. 'I decided to switch horses and I'm doing a physiotherapy course at the Charité Hospital. I'll be finished in September – unless war breaks out before then.'

'Oh, small chance of that,' said Leo easily, spearing his last bit of cake with his cake-fork. 'Our Führer isn't interested in war. The country will profit much more from peace, and he'll make sure to maintain that. Don't you worry.'

They were all silent for a moment.

'Well,' said Franzi, 'I must love you and leave you. I have some more items to buy, and don't forget the shop closes at 1 o'clock. That's in an hour, folks!'

Leo rose to his feet and moved her chair back for her. This time she grasped his hand and shook it warmly.

'It was very pleasant to meet you, Dr Gebhardt, and I hope it won't be long before we see you again. Thank you for the coffee and cake. It was heavenly! Bye, Em, see you later.'

And with a wave she was gone.

Leo sat down again.

'I hope you don't have to rush off too?'

'No, I've got everything I wanted. But what about yourself?'

'No, I'm fine.' Leo had decided he could buy the book for Hilde on Monday; he'd slip out of the office for an hour.

Emma peered into her empty cup, then set it down.

'You mentioned you were training with your regiment, Dr Gebhardt. What organisation are you in?'

'I volunteered for the SS two years ago. It's not a fighting unit, so it's not real training. I think they just want to check that we're keeping fit. I was in a troop in Leipzig and was assigned to a new one here in Berlin recently. So it was getting to know new people and seeing how things are done here.'

'It could become more ... dangerous ... if war did break out.'

'Oh, I don't think there'd be much chance of me being called up. I'm a bit older than the type of soldier they want, and anyway, if there is a war, it'll be over long before they'd be needing my age group. So I'm not at all concerned.'

'Let's hope so,' said Emma fervently.

'Your sister is a very pleasant young lady, I must say,' said Leo. 'Is she musical too?

Emma smiled, and fiddled with her cup again.

'No, she's interested in sports. She has a large circle of friends, all good pals, young men and women from her hockey club and such like. They go boating and cycling and ice-skating together, there's a whole group of them. Sometimes she brings them all back to the house. It gets very lively, as you may well imagine, but my parents love it. I'm extremely fond of her.'

'I do look forward to seeing her again. And to meeting your other sister,' he added politely. 'By the way, there's a film on which I thought you might want to go to with me, if you like? It's American, "Room Service", with the Marx Brothers. Do you know them?'

Of course she knew them!

'Oh, I'd love that, thank you! I do love them. When I was in England six years ago I saw their film "Duck Soup". It was so terribly funny. Do you know it?'

Leo shook his head.

'It's set in a little state called Freedonia which gets attacked by a bullying neighbour and a powerful leader. He's played by Groucho. He was just *so* funny! Can you imagine him as a prime minister, with his big moustache? All he was interested in was getting his hands on this rich, fat woman. In fact it was quite political, I think. In the end the two countries go to war, but the war turns into something like slapstick.'

Leo couldn't imagine this film ever being shown in Germany.

'And then there was "A Night at the Opera",' continued Emma, her cheeks flushed and her eyes shining. She clearly thought this might be more in his line.

'Yes, I saw that,' said Leo.

'Do you remember that scene in the teeny cabin ...' Emma began to laugh '... where the three men have stowed away in the main character's monstrous suitcases ...' she laughed even more '... and all these people start coming in ...' she was gasping for breath, and Leo began to laugh too, without knowing the scene – in fact, he hadn't seen the film at all – , 'the manicurist and the waitress ... fifteen people ... all on top of each other...'.

By now she was laughing so much that tears were pouring down her face and she couldn't speak any more. Leo was enthralled, laughing himself, and at the same time fighting to keep himself under firm control. He would just love to have picked her up and squeezed her and kissed her and carried her off. She was pure delight. His Emma.

6

17–19 June: At the Baltic and in Italy

The white gauze curtains at the open window were waving gently in the afternoon breeze. Gulls were calling lazily outside, and the waves of the Baltic Sea were breaking on the nearby shore. In the distance, Emma could hear children calling to each other on the beach. She wasn't sure if she was on the verge of being bored or just undecided about what she wanted to do. She lay on the bed where she'd been resting, and took a deep breath of the salty air. It was refreshing, and she swung her legs out onto the floor and stretched her arms a few times. Perhaps Marie was awake already, and they could walk down to the café on the pier and have a cup of coffee and some cake. But first she would check the letterbox. There had been nothing from Leo in the morning delivery.

She pulled on her white summer skirt and the loose green silk blouse with the crystal buttons, and fastened a white belt around her waist. A glance in the mirror, a flick of the brush and her hair was settled. She was delighted that she had had it cut in a short bob before the onset of summer. It was so much easier to manage, and much cooler. And when she covered it with the black pixie cap Leo had bought her, she felt really smart – they were all the rage in France, and hardly anyone in Germany was wearing them so far, especially here in this remote bathing resort.

She slipped on her white sandals and ran downstairs. And indeed, there on the little hall table was a letter in the already familiar handwriting. Her heart skipped a beat. She listened to hear if Marie was around, but there was no sign of her, and so she raced back up to her room, opened the door to the balcony and curled up in the wicker chair.

The letter was dated 15.6., Grand Hotel de Ville, Milan, special delivery. That was the day before yesterday, the Thursday. He'd just arrived after a long, exhausting train journey. The heat was killing, he wrote. They had already seen so many wonderful sights and objects, and his one regret was that his darling, beloved Em was not there at his side to share these magical impressions with him. But he was looking forward to the day when he would revisit these places with his sweet little wife, and how he would enjoy her astonishment and delight! Even with 1000 kilometres between them he loved her more than ever before, and sent her thousands of kisses.

She read the letter again. The handwriting was practically only a flowing line, written in a hurry. As the chief delegate of the German Music Department, he would have little time to call his own. He promised to give her a detailed account of all he had experienced when they were reunited.

She held the letter to her face, trying to absorb his typical scent from it. She held it to her forehead for a moment and closed her eyes, then continued reading.

A Normal Couple

Emma knew he was the perfect man for this work. In the three months that they'd known each other, she'd quickly become aware of how qualified he was. His knowledge of music and performances was immense. As a student, even while still at school, he'd worked in theatres and opera houses, training the choirs, arranging and conducting concerts, playing in the orchestra, accompanying singers on the piano. For eight years he'd been one of the music critics at a national newspaper based in Leipzig, and in this capacity he had attended hundreds of concerts and met many of the leading conductors and soloists of the time. He was a staunch member of the Party, but at the same time he was very diplomatic, an important quality when dealing with upstart superiors who enjoyed hearing themselves speak without having a clue of what they were talking about. She was sure he was revelling in the attention lavished on him during this tour of Italy, and she was pleased for him, for she knew he worked hard and long hours in the office.

There was a knock on her door and Marie's blond curls and cheeky eyes appeared.

'There you are! I was looking for you downstairs. I'm dying for a cup of coffee. Come on, let's go!'

Marie was her best friend. They'd been at school together in Elbing, and at the ballroom dancing course held for all the young people from the better families, where Marie had met her later husband Richard. Now they'd been married for three years. Richard was a submarine officer, and stationed in Kiel on the Baltic Sea at present. There was a chance that he would be in command of a U-boat of his own soon. Marie was immensely proud of him, and was looking forward to being the wife of a submarine commander.

Emma and Marie hadn't seen each other for two years, and Emma wanted to know all about Marie's married life in Kiel, a busy port serving both the military and industry. But Marie was more interested in hearing Emma's news.

'Come on, Emmi, I know something is up. What letter was that you were reading when I came into your room? You've dropped so many hints already! Open up and tell your Aunty Marie all!'

Emma laughed.

'Yes, all right. His name is Leopold – Leo. He's ten years older than I am, but he's very charming and attentive ... Oh Marie, I'm really in love at long last. At least, I think so!'

And she told Marie how they had met, how annoyed she'd been at first by his undisguised admiration, how he'd called her some days later, asking for her help in setting up a speech in English since he'd been delegated to attend a music festival in London. So she'd been together with him in his office several times.

'We were both very nervous, but honestly, Marie, you know how they say the air is electric when people are attracted to each other, and that's how it was. We got the speech together somehow and off he went to London for five days.'

Then she described Leo's triumph with Sir Adrian Boult, and how he'd invited her to dinner and to the Elly Ney concert, and how she'd gradually been getting more relaxed in his company.

'That sounds very promising,' said matronly Marie. 'But I hope he isn't just an egghead and that you sit listening to *Bruckner* all the time! Heaven forbid!'

Emma laughed again.

'Not at all. No, we've even been to the pictures together. That's the pleasant thing about him. He's really very normal. At first I was quite in awe of him, but now my legs go weak whenever I catch a glimpse of him anywhere. Honestly, I've never felt like that about anyone before! We don't want anyone in the office to know yet, so we have to be careful. Since the weather got warmer we've been going swimming at the beach at Wannsee, and we've rented a canoe a couple of times. He loves being in the countryside, and then he doesn't talk much, and we just drift along on the river and enjoy the peace and quiet and being in each other's company.'

'H'm. Now, my dear, if he's ten years older than you, he's in his mid-thirties, and at that age most men have covered a lot of ground on the female front. Has he told you anything about his past relationships?'

Emma poured herself a second cup of coffee from the little coffee pot. Marie shoved a big forkful of strawberry cake and cream into her mouth.

'Not really. And frankly, I don't want to know. I don't know him *that* well yet. But *he's* determined that we're going to get married as soon as possible. He talks about it as if it's all settled, though he hasn't officially asked me yet. It's a bit too fast for me. On the other hand, I can't imagine being with anyone else. Every time the telephone rings at home, or the postman stops at our box, I think it must be from him and am disappointed if it isn't. I just want to be with him all the time. I love the feel of him, and his smell, and his voice. He's always thinking of little things to make me happy, little gifts, or excursions, or lovely letters. My common sense ...'

'Of which you have an abundance, thank goodness!' interrupted Marie.

Emma laughed. '... tells me I should know more about him before I commit myself. Is he really honest? Is he reliable? Would he trust me and believe in me? Could I trust him?'

'I think you find out that kind of thing very quickly,' countered Marie. 'I didn't have any such reservations when I agreed to marry Richard. Of course, I may just have been lucky, as he's turned out to be a dream husband! I can rely on him totally, and he trusts me too, even with business things to do with the family. But to come to something much more important: what's your Leo like as a lover?' asked Marie without batting an eyelid.

Emma stared at her, then giggled.

'All we do is kiss and hug. Well, he tries to do a bit more, but so far I've been able to fend him off, even though I find him *very* attractive and love having his arms round me. He's terribly passionate.'

'So what exactly do you love about him?'

This was a question Emma had asked herself a couple of times, and now she thought for a moment before answering.

'He's very charming, and very caring and considerate. He's a good listener, and we're finding more and more to talk about. I feel safe and ... sheltered ... in his company. As if I'd known him all my life. I love his voice, and how he moves, and how serious he can be. And he takes me seriously. Well – up to a point. He has this thing about me being his "sweet little wife" and so on. I think it's because he's so tall. But that's a way of thinking I should be able to get him out of. I want to be his equal, and not his dependant. But as I say, he's friendly, and kind, quite different as a private person than in his public life. We laugh a lot when we're together. It's all quite different than with my other boyfriends. He's very good-looking in a distinguished sort of way. Though my mother is a bit in awe of him.'

'Oh! Your parents have met him?'

'Yes. They were annoyed at first when he started writing me letters. Because of Helmi. I think they regarded him as an interloper.'

'Are you still hanging around with Helmi?' Marie was surprised. 'He's such a stick-in-the-mud. How long have you been together?'

'About two years. It's almost more of a friendship at this stage, to be honest. I don't see him making any great efforts, and I've never been seriously in love with him. But my parents must have been thinking we were practically engaged.'

'Have you talked to him yet?'

'No, he was away on manoeuvres. I'll have to tell him soon. In any case, I told my parents that I thought the relationship with Leo was much deeper, and once they realised it was getting serious they wanted to meet him. He picked me up at the house one evening, and Papa invited him in for a drink. We sat out on the terrace. Mama was there too. It was very pleasant. He wasn't a bit nervous.'

'And what did your parents say afterwards?'

'Well, Papa said he was a very pleasant gentleman, it was just a pity that he was so committed to the ideals of the Party, but in these times we had to live with that. And who knows if it mightn't be useful to have someone from that particular corner in the family. Mama was very taken with him and was pleased that he wasn't so old.' Both Emma and Marie knew that Emma's father was fourteen years older than her mother.

'So it really looks as if he's the man, Emmi. Congratulations, my dear. If you're happy, then I'm more than happy for you. And I'm dying to meet him.' She waved to the waitress for the bill. 'It looks as if I'll be having to visit my dressmaker soon to decide on a suitable outfit. I assume I'll be the matron of honour! Have you any idea when the biggest social event of the year is going to take place?'

Emma smiled and shook her head.

'No. As I said, I need more time and want to get to know him better, maybe meet his father. His mother isn't alive any more. It's all very new for me. And the political situation is still so uncertain. Papa thinks so too. Anyway, *he*'s still reeling from what he spent on Lise's wedding in May. He really did them proud, the dining-room suite he bought them had a walnut veneer, beautiful, and top drawer. I can't put him to that expense again so soon.'

'That shouldn't be the deciding factor. From what you've told me, I don't think a plain pine veneer would put Leo off marrying you as soon as possible. But you really need to be certain, that's true. Once the date is set you won't have much room to negotiate.'

Emma had stood up and arranged her skirt, and now she leaned over her friend and placed a kiss on her cheek.

'Thank you, Marie dear. Thank you for being such a good friend and giving me confidence. Let's go back to the hotel now and sit on the terrace with a lemonade before dinner. I must write to my parents too. And I want to hear all about Richard's prospects from you. What an exciting development! I can understand why you're so proud of him. Tell me more.'

Not unnoticed by several pairs of admiring eyes, slim, dark-haired Emma and curvy, fresh-faced Marie wove their way between the little white tables and left the café.

A Normal Couple

Milan and Verona on Thursday and Friday, Rome on Saturday, Naples on Sunday, and now Palermo: Leo didn't know how he could stand the pace. The receptions went on until 2am – last night it had been 4am, Lohengrin hadn't finished till 1.30 – and then up at the crack for the next flight or drive or train. He'd just had time to write Em a short letter before today's whirlwind began.

He folded it and was sliding it into his pocket when there was a knock on his door. He called out and Dr Eckart, their legal adviser, slipped into the room. He was several years younger than Leo, a lively, likeable young man of middle height and a look of keen intelligence.

'My god, Gebhardt, it's only 8 in the morning and it's 30 degrees outside – in the shade! How are we going to survive?!'

'What's planned for today?' asked Leo, searching through a folder till he found the schedule. 'Oh, they're taking us on a tour of some of the sights. Have you been to Sicily before, Eckart?'

'No, it's my first time. But I know there's no end of fascinating and beautiful antiquities to be seen. I'd really enjoy it if it weren't for this murderous heat.'

'Haven't you got a summer suit?'

'Yes, that's the first thing I did in Milan, I got myself a natty white outfit like all the men here were wearing, and one of those elegant straw hats. These people really know how to live, don't they?! The food!'

'The food is out of this world. All those courses! One more delicious than the next. That saltimbocca last night was a dream. But if we go on at this rate I won't be able to show myself in my togs at Wannsee baths this season!'

Eckart smiled agreement. 'And the wines! Though they're very heavy compared to our German vintages. That dessert wine yesterday, it was really extraordinary.' And he actually produced a little notebook from his pocket and, leafing through it, read: 'Passito di Pantelleria. I must find a bottle of that to bring home to my wife. Amazing.'

Leo was amused and impressed by the young man's enthusiasm. He too had something for his little wife-to-be: the perfect place for them to spend their honeymoon. It was a small, extremely pleasant luxury hotel on a slope above Lake Garda, run by an English chap who charged only 6M for bed and breakfast. The party had been taken there on Friday night. They'd been served a heavenly meal on the terrace overlooking the lake, with the mysterious silhouette of the grotesquely shaped Trentino mountains opposite, and a glorious full moon reflected in the blue-black water. His longing for Em had been so strong that he'd had to turn aside from the other guests to gain control of himself. He could just see the two of them there, he could almost hear and see Emma's quiet yet rapturous comments on the beauty laid out before them. It wasn't a highly frequented hotel, hardly anyone stayed there, even though past guests had included Himmler and other personalities, as the owner proudly told him.

'We'd better go down and see can we find some breakfast,' Leo said to Eckart. 'I need a bit more than those little cakes and all that fruit. Perhaps the kitchen can supply some smoked ham and some of that delicious soft bread.'

They found a table in a shady corner of the cavernous, flag-stoned dining-room – it was cooler inside than out – and managed to order a passable meal. Eckart was practicing his Italian by trying to read the local paper 'La Sicilia'. Leo tried to relax for a few minutes, and his mind drifted back to the opera last night, which had been impressive. But it was clear that Wagner came over better in a German domain. The Tosca they'd attended in the ancient Arena in Verona on Thursday, though – that was a different matter: only Italy and the Italians could produce such a spectacular and yet artistically perfect show. Although he'd seen a dozen Toscas to date, this had taken his breath away. Outstanding singers and choir, perfectly balanced orchestra, just the right level of drama and pathos, and of course the unique setting under a full moon. The German party and their Italian hosts had occupied the central Government Box, which provided a perfect view of the oval-shaped amphitheatre, tiers upon tiers of soft grey stone and the golden scenery on the stage below. After a short speech welcoming the illustrious representatives of the Reich, an overwhelming roar had risen from the audience of 20,000. As the leader of the visiting delegation, he had been standing right in front, conspicuous in his white evening jacket (from a sale in Peek and Kloppenburg for only M62,50). It was as if they were applauding him personally. He'd laughed at himself, but deep inside he'd been thrilled to be here, and he accepted this accolade as his and his country's due. He'd written to Em about it in a joking tone, but between the lines his pride was obvious.

'Signori!' Two waiters appeared with the coffee, toasted bread, jam, smoked ham, cheese, and sweet buns. They asked for some butter, which the surprised waiters hurried to procure.

'By the way, Gebhardt,' said Eckart, 'have you heard that our tour is being extended by one day? We're not returning till Thursday, won't be back in

Berlin till Friday evening. Travelling by train all the way, I believe. 26 hours, they said.' He spread some jam on his cheese. 'I haven't heard why – perhaps they want to fit in a meeting about the subsidies for the festival next year.'

'Why don't I know about this?' snapped Leo. 'Who decided it? Was it Brockhaus?' That was the finance man. How dared he take this decision without consulting his superior! The man was an idiot!

But before he went off to throw more light on the matter and to give Brockhaus a thorough dressing down, he pulled out the letter he'd written to Em and opened the envelope carefully to tell her about the change in plans.

'Can you come to my hotel on Friday evening? I'll meet you at the underground. I'll write to you from Rome, addressed to the office. All my love and 1000 kisses from your Leo.'

7

22–23 June: Emma and Leo go swimming

On Friday evening, Emma was hovering around the telephone in the hall. The train was due at 7.48pm, so by the time Leo was back in the Excelsior Hotel, the huge business hotel where he was lodging – he hadn't yet had time to find a flat – it would be too late for her to be going all the way into town to meet him. She knew he would be dead tired, and much as she was longing to see him, she knew it was more sensible to postpone the reunion till the next day. She had written to him by express to that effect, and she could sense his disappointment over the ether, but his plan made no sense. Her parents wouldn't approve, either.

At two minutes past eight the bell shrilled.

'Leo? Hallo my darling! How are you? Are you in your hotel?'

'Em, my love, oh how wonderful to hear your sweet voice. I've missed you so much, you have no idea what it's been like to be separated so long, a whole week, even longer, because you went to Zempin three days before I left. I'm just dying to see you.'

Leo had been surprised when she said she'd be travelling to the Baltic resort to meet her friend Marie just three days before he was due to travel to Italy. He'd wanted her to change her plans so she could see him off at the station, but she had refused.

'Where are you now, Leo?'

'I'm in a callbox in the Excelsior. The train was dead on time and I took the tunnel to the hotel from the station. I looked into the café, because I was so very sure you'd be sitting there waiting for me! Oh Em, I have so much to tell you, we saw so many wonderful things and had such a good time, though it was exhausting too. The day before yesterday, in the afternoon …'

Emma interrupted. 'Leo, you must be very tired and dying for a hot bath and a bed. Let's meet tomorrow afternoon. Are you free?'

'Yes, I made sure to have no appointments. Should we go to Wannsee? The weather is so good.'

'That would be ideal. Can you meet me at the S-Bahn station at Wannsee at three? I'll bring a picnic and then we'll have all the time in the world to talk. I've missed you too, dearest.'

'How was your week with Marie?'

'I'll tell you all about it tomorrow. I told her about you, and she approves!'

'Well, that's another hurdle overcome!' and they both laughed.

'Oh darling,' they both said simultaneously, and laughed again.

'See you tomorrow,' said Emma firmly. 'Now off to bed with you and sleep well.'

'Good night, my little love. Only another few hours.'

And Emma hung up, smiling.

A Normal Couple

The following evening, Emma ran up the steps from the station tunnel at Wannsee to the street level. And there was Leo, buying some cigarettes at the kiosk. He saw her immediately, waited for his change and then threw his arms around her. And she pulled his head down and gave him a long, intensive kiss. How could she have doubted that she loved him? Just being in his arms like this was heavenly, his smell, his strength, his tenderness, she sensed it all and felt sheltered and greatly loved. A love that she reciprocated. It felt so right. This was how her life was meant to be.

She pushed him away from her to look at him.

'You're not very brown! I thought you wrote that it was 42 degrees in the shade!'

'Well of course! With temperatures like that you make sure to be in the sun as little as possible. It's like being in Africa! But you're as brown as a berry! You look wonderful! Oh I could gobble you up!' And he gave her another bear hug.

'Not a good idea,' laughed Emma. Leo took the bag she'd been carrying and they walked across the road to the bus for the short ride to the baths. An hour later they were settled in one of the big, roofed, wicker bath chairs, sheltered from the wind and the sun (and other people's eyes). They'd had a quick swim to cool off, and Emma started to unpack the cheese and ham rolls, fried rissoles and a bottle of wine that she'd put together for their picnic.

'Are your parents well?' asked Leo, 'And have you heard from your sisters? And have you talked to Helmi?'

'All well, thank you,' answered Em. 'Nothing new to report. You've only been away a week! But yes, I talked to Helmi, the day before yesterday actually. I was dreading it, for him it came out of the blue. He was quite downcast at first, and then, as usual, he got terribly angry. But I managed to keep calm, and we parted with a handshake and a little kiss. I felt awful afterwards, but that's how life goes, isn't it? I hope it won't be long before he finds someone else.'

Leo gave her a little hug.

'What's the news from the office?' he wanted to know.

'The usual chaos, but you'll find that out for yourself on Monday. Tell me how you got on with your colleagues. People often reveal strange new sides of themselves when you're travelling with them.'

'The biggest surprise was Eckart. He really outgrew himself down there. He enjoyed every minute of it, and was very flexible and easy to get on with, a very pleasant fellow. We must have him round for dinner some night when we're married.'

'And Brockhaus?'

'A pain in the ass, that man, full of his own importance, and that awful squawky voice. It wasn't a good idea to send him on a delegation like this, he didn't leave a good impression. Not the right type to represent our government. And he finalised decisions that he had no right to do. It put us in a real fix the last day. But I dealt with him. In future he'll think twice about taking steps he's not entitled to. But let's leave that! Italy is so beautiful, and Sicily is wonderful, only we should go there in the spring when the weather is cooler and everything is in flower. Those Byzantine mosaics in the castle church in Palermo are breath-taking, huge angels in blue and pink and gold mosaics, so old and so beautiful in a strange stiff sort of way. Unworldly. You'd love them.'

'You've put on a bit of a tum,' Emma teased.

'There was no avoiding that. You won't believe this but dinner on the ferry to Naples consisted of eight courses. Eight! And this was only a ferry! But I promise you, I'll do lots of exercising and dieting and by the time we marry I'll be as slim as ... as ... Rudolph Valentino!'

Emma laughed out loud. Leo's familiarity with the cinema had obviously ended with the silent movies, despite their outing with the Marx brothers.

Leo didn't join in her laughter. He watched her, then reached out and pulled her close to him, kissing her softly, and she responded with an intensity which surprised her. His hand moved to her breast. They were well hidden in the big seat, and most people were busy with their children or packing up to leave.

'When can we get married?' whispered Leo. 'I don't know how much longer I can wait.'

Emma allowed herself to enjoy the sensation of skin on skin, warmth on warmth, love struggling to express itself, but then pushed herself gently away and sat up.

'Leo, my love, I love you so much. But we really haven't known each other so very long. I know very little about your family or background or ... or your preferences, or habits, and you've done so many things and met so many people.' She stopped. This wasn't what she wanted to say. Of course she didn't need to know everything about him in order to marry him. She tried again. Leo was staring down at the sand and started drawing figures in it with a fork.

'I think there might be sides to your character that I haven't seen yet, and I don't think it's a good idea to marry – I mean to promise someone you'll live with them for ever, if you aren't very sure that you'll get along with them in any situation. That's the idea of an engagement, isn't it? To give the two people time to find out who the other person is.'

Leo was instantly downcast. 'I'm a very simple person,' he said morosely. 'There's nothing complicated about me. I'm easy to get on with. Anyone in the places where I've worked will tell you so. I know I work hard. I think I'm interested in quite a lot of things besides music. I don't know what there could be about me that you need to discover.'

Although she had known him for only a little over three months, Emma suspected that Leo had a more complex personality than he might realise himself. On the other hand, she hadn't remotely found anything that might turn her against him, or make it morally or aesthetically impossible for her to accept him as a husband. He was very careful with money – sometimes too careful, for her taste. She knew, though, that life had been a struggle after his father had stopped supporting him when he dropped out from studying law and instead took up music at Leipzig Conservatory. He'd done odd jobs like copying music, and acting as a stand-in for the choral conductor at rehearsals. Now he was on a very good salary, and she hoped that he would become more relaxed about money in the course of time. She herself had always had as much money as she needed, which wasn't much. The three sisters had been brought up to be thrifty, but if money was needed for an important extra, it was always provided by her generous father.

'I know everything about you that I want to know, Em,' said Leo. 'You're the most beautiful woman I've met, and you're well balanced, and interested in loads of subjects and can talk about them. You're a bit of a dreamer too, aren't you? I've seen you sitting by yourself and just staring in front of you, absorbed in something that only you can see. And you have a wonderful laugh. It's totally infectious, and I love you so much that it sometimes hurts.'

'Leo, let's plan the future. We'll need a place to live. That's the first thing you'll have to settle. It needn't be a house, nothing big that's going to take a lot of housekeeping or be expensive to run. When we marry, my father will supply the dining room, sitting room and bedroom furniture, like he did for Lise and Benno, and will be doing for Franzi and Moritz. I think that's the first step before we set a date for the wedding. I mean, what would the wedding guests think when they ask us: "Where will you be living?" and we answer: "In the Excelsior Hotel, seventh floor, Room 739"!'

They both smiled.

'You're right,' answered Leo. 'My clever little Em. Leave it to me. I'll look into it tomorrow. I'll ask around in the ministry.'

'Only no one must know about us!'

'No, I'll be very discreet. Everyone knows I can't go on living in a hotel much longer, so it's quite natural that I'd be looking for a flat, and a decent one at that, since I'll be expected to entertain visiting musicians. It shouldn't be too difficult to find something, maybe in Charlottenburg or Wilmersdorf.' These were two upper-class areas of the inner city. 'A lot of Jews are emigrating so that fine flats are becoming available.'

'It seems unfair to take advantage of their unfortunate position,' said Emma.

'Yes, but what can you do? You can't help them, and if we don't take one of those flats, someone else will.'

'I'd prefer if we found a flat that had come on the market in the normal way, because its owner or tenant was moving to somewhere else in Germany or had bought a house or whatever.'

'Well, we'll take it as it comes. At any rate, the pressure on the housing market is not as great as it used to be.'

They decided to go for another swim, and then lay on their towels and sunbathed for a while. Leo fell asleep, and Emma, who knew that he'd be tired after his journey, got out the book she'd brought along and read for a while.

Later, they packed their things and walked hand in hand to the bus. It was not quite eight o'clock, and Leo asked Emma if she'd like to take the underground into town with him and get something to eat in a restaurant on Potsdamer Platz. This wasn't far from his hotel, and she hesitated. It might be difficult to extricate herself later.

'I think it would be better if we got something to eat around here,' she answered. 'We'll get off in Zehlendorf and go to the Balkan Grill there, if you like. Then I can get home more quickly, and so can you.'

'I hate it when you say things like that,' said Leo. 'About us separating at the end of the day. I'm going to get a flat as quickly as possible, and then we're getting down to brass tacks. No more excuses or shilly-shallying.'

'Shilly-shallying you call it,' called Emma in mock indignation. 'I'm trying to plan our lives in a realistic manner, and you call that shilly-shallying! Who did you pick up that expression from anyway? Wasn't there a pretty secretary from the foreign office in your party in Italy? Did you look after her? That's what I would call shilly-shallying.' And she continued to tease him until his mood improved.

They spent the rest of the evening telling each other about their recent trips. Later, Leo brought Emma home, to her father's house, and after a lengthy farewell ceremony on the street outside her gate, they parted, and he walked back to the underground station round the corner.

8

26 June–7 July: Leo finds a flat

Leo was kept very busy the following week. He was responsible for organising musical exchanges between Germany and East European countries, dealing with concert agencies at home and abroad, directing the minutiae of contracts, travel permits into and out of the country, fees, subsidies, replacements for last minute cancellations. Eckart had advanced to being his assistant, and together they formed a competent team. The head of the Department of Music in the administration, their boss, Dr Bischoff, was more of a hindrance than a support most of the time.

'Gebhardt! Thank God you're back at last!' he called from the end of the corridor on Monday morning. Leo wondered if Bischoff thought he'd been AWOL. 'Did everything run smoothly? Were you able to make those contacts with Milan?'

'You can expect my report on your desk in the course of the morning, Dr Bischoff. But I can tell you already: it was a great success, with some small blemishes. However, we achieved our main objectives. Toscanini has agreed to a tour in the

Reich, and Gigli is looking forward to an invitation from Munich.'

'Gigli? Isn't he too expensive? There was that story about him disputing his pay at the Met …. But now, this corridor really isn't the place to be discussing this, Gebhardt!' A frown formed over his long thin nose. Leo recalled that Bischoff, not he, had started the conversation, but he only smiled politely, and held the door of Bischoff's office open for his boss. He took the initiative.

'I can't stay long, Dr Bischoff, I have reports to write for the finance department and several contracts to assess. Is there anything in particular you'd like to know about in relation to our tour?'

'Not really. Was Mussolini in Verona?'

'No, Commendatore di Vasco took his place. But the hospitality of the Italians was overwhelming everywhere we stayed. A really wonderful tour. It spoke of great harmony and good-will between our two cultures. We are clearly of one mind on the importance of music as an expression of our national and political identity.'

'Good, good!' Bischoff tapped his long fingernails nervously on his enormous oak desk. 'Well, don't let me keep you. I have a lot to do, can't spend all morning chatting.' And before Leo had left the room he had picked up the receiver of his phone and asked his secretary to put him through to the Minister.

Leo was still smiling to himself as he entered his own office and got down to work. But first, he rang a rental agent and made an appointment for his lunch-hour. Finding a flat was his highest priority at the moment, whatever Bischoff might think.

Only ten days later, he had his apartment. The agent had shown him two in the same house, 9 Bayerische Strasse in Charlottenburg, a four-storey apartment house lavishly decorated with plasterwork ornamentation on the outside. It was built in the boom years after the German victory in the Franco-Prussian War of 1871, when the enormous French reparations to Germany produced a burst of millionaires. A spacious hallway tiled in bottle-green art nouveau contained not only a wide staircase but also a shaky little wrought-iron lift. It rattled him and the agent two storeys up to a large honey-coloured two-winged door, which opened onto rooms that met all his expectations: high ceilings and bright walls with stucco work, tall windows, central heating. Interconnected dining and sitting room. A study. Several smaller rooms and even a tiny second bathroom. And a balcony, big enough for two chairs and several tubs for plants. At a very reasonable price. Two floors further up the lift brought them to the second apartment, which lay under the attic and had lower ceilings and smaller windows. It was being renovated, and the agent told him the family that had been living there had suddenly disappeared.

It was not a difficult choice.

He rang Emma, and on the following day they saw the apartment together. To his surprise, the owner of the flat was waiting for them, a slight gentleman of about fifty with a careful smile and dark hair sleeked back with scented pomade. He introduced himself: 'Liepmann. Pleased to meet you. Take your time looking around. I'll leave you alone, but if you have any questions, I'll be glad to help.'

Emma was thrilled by what she saw. Apart from the six months in England, she had never lived anywhere other than at home. This would be *her* apartment, her and Leo's. Her own home. It was huge. The house was located on the corner of the

A Normal Couple

block, and the rooms lay on both fronts. The two reception rooms with sliding doors between them created a huge area along one side, while a smaller room and a spacious bedroom lay round the corner. Down the long corridor were the kitchen, the bathroom, two smaller rooms (nursery?), and two tiny maids' rooms with a small extra toilet. It surpassed her expectations on all fronts.

'It's very big. How much is the rent?' whispered Emma. 'Will we be able to afford it?'

'It's only 125M a month,' Leo answered. His net salary was 510M. 'There's something I... . I wanted you to see the place first. We wouldn't need all this space, and Herr Liepmann would like the use of the two tiny rooms, so that he has a place to stay whenever he's in Berlin. I said I didn't object. I mean, there's the separate WC that he can use. And because of that he's lowered the rent so that it's less than it would normally be for such a big place, even without the maids' rooms.'

Emma was nonplussed. This was unexpected. She wasn't sure that she wanted to share her home with a stranger, even if he only appeared every now and again. Would it feel like their own place at all?

They drifted back to the main room, which faced east and south, with a window on each of the outer walls as well as a large French window to the balcony. Herr Liepmann was waiting for them, a cigarette in his hand, sending smoke-rings towards the ceiling. He smiled again when he saw them.

'Well, my dear, what do you think?' he asked Emma.

'It's very nice,' she answered. 'But I was wondering. Can you tell me who lived here before?' And she flushed slightly. Leo frowned.

'Yes, I can. I lived here myself. I bought the flat about nine years ago and lived here with my wife, but since things have got rough for my type here in the city, we've decided to move to a quieter environment. We live out in Klobbicke now. That's out in the country. My mother isn't Aryan. I thought you should know that,' this directed to Leo, with a quick glance at the party button in Leo's lapel.

'Oh, that's of no importance,' Leo said. 'I hope you enjoy living in your new home. Your decision has turned to our advantage, hasn't it? Do you like it, Em?'

'Yes, I do,' said Emma, quietly. 'But I have another question, if you don't mind. My fiancé just mentioned that you would like to keep two of the small rooms. Do you know how often you might be using them?' Again she flushed as she spoke.

'You are quite right to ask, dear lady. I cannot say definitely how often it would be, but not more than once a month or maybe even less. It depends on my business moves. I would just be in the room at night and away again in the morning. We needn't even see each other.'

Emma couldn't quite imagine it would be that easy.

'I might need a little time to get used to this, Herr Liepmann. I hope you understand. How long would you keep the place for us before we sign the lease?'

'I've signed already, all that's settled,' said Leo quickly.

Emma caught her breath. She was speechless. She'd assumed that they would choose the flat together, a joint decision, especially with this unexpected special arrangement. How could he take such an important step, one which affected her as much as himself, without consulting her? In fact, she would be spending more time in their home than he – she would have to resign from her job when she was married, and become a housewife. She stared at him, wide-eyed.

Her voice shook as she turned back to their landlord.

'Well, since it's all arranged, Herr Liepmann, I'm sure we'll manage about the rooms and your visits. And I look forward to getting to know you better. Perhaps you and your wife would like to come and visit us when we're settled in?'

Herr Liepmann bowed his head. 'That's very kind of you. I'm sure my wife would love to see how you arrange everything here. And of course if you've any questions or problems, don't hesitate to call me. The estate agent will fix all the details and give you the keys in the next few days. I'll leave you here now, though, to look around a bit more. Just pull the door closed after you.'

He gave them his card with his new address and a phone number where they could leave a message, they shook hands in the old-fashioned way, and Herr Liepmann quietly left the flat.

'Well,' said Emma. 'It's a lovely flat. But Leo, honestly! I thought we'd be deciding on this together! And I really think you should have told me about the deal with the two rooms before you signed the lease. It'll be strange having him drifting in here every now and again, even if he only uses the little bathroom. You really should have asked me first.'

Leo looked discomfited.

'It's such a good price for this huge place, a real bargain. Normally I could never have afforded anything like it. It's such a wonderful opportunity. I couldn't let it go. And Herr Liepmann made such a good impression on me, I'm sure we'll get on fine, though I'll have to be a bit careful.'

'Why?'

'SS people aren't allowed to associate with Jews. It's one of those silly rules. But no one need know, and if there are problems we'll deal with them when they come.'

'I hope you're right. He seems a really nice gentleman,' said Emma, trying to calm her heartbeat. 'It's such a shame.'

'I know. Wasted potential. I remember we had three top class journalists at my paper in Leipzig. Then it turned out they were Jewish, and they had to go – excluded from the Reich Department of Culture, and so they weren't eligible for employment. You can't imagine the trouble we had finding replacements that in any way measured up to them.'

'What happened to them?'

'I'm not sure. They probably emigrated, like so many others. Look, let's not get into politics now. Just look at these rooms! I can't imagine that anyone else at my level in the department has anything to compare! And we can go ahead with all the arrangements for the wedding. I'll put in an application for our engagement and the wedding as soon as possible.'

Emma managed a smile. 'Don't forget to have a word with Papa first. Look, why don't we go to that little pub on the corner down below, and then we can make our plans over a cup of coffee or a beer.' And she picked up her handbag, adjusted her cap, and they left their new home together.

The pub, 'Bavarian Corner', was only half full and they found a table near the window. Emma ordered a coffee, and Leo a beer and a frankfurter. As usual, he was a little hungry.

'When should we ...' they both started together, and laughed. Emma lifted her hands and made conducting movements, and they continued in unison: '... have the wedding?!' And they laughed again. Leo looked around quickly, then leant over and gave her a quick kiss.

'We need to get the flat furnished, we have to find a maid, I'm due to go to Italy again at the beginning of August. And then there's all the paperwork. That'll take ages.'

'What's involved?' asked Emma. 'I've no idea. It didn't seem too complicated when Lise and Benno got married in May.'

'Well, it's all this stuff the SS want to know. I believe they investigate both our characters and who our parents are. Whether our marriage meets the criteria they've set up for their members. Our ancestry. It's all very much exaggerated, I must say. But they want to keep it an elite organisation and they have their rules. I'll get all the documents when I put in the application for our engagement and the wedding.'

'How long do we need, then?'

'I'd say about two months. Oh, it seems such a long time!' He took out his little pocket calendar.

'Today is 7 July. What about 7 September? Or rather – I'll apply for a week's leave starting on Friday the 8th. We could have the wedding on the Sunday, so that everyone would be able to come, and then we can go away for a few days till the end of the following week. What do you think?'

'That sounds perfect, Leo. I'll ask Mama to invite you for dinner, and then you can talk to Papa. Would you have time on Sunday?'

Leo said he would. They decided to consult his father about where to have the wedding, and then they discussed which friends they would ask. It would not be a big wedding. The times were too unsettled.

Emma was delighted about the flat on her way home, but the shock she'd felt when Leo announced he'd already signed the lease still lay like a warning in her stomach. She would have to watch out.

9

9 July: The Proposal

To his surprise, Leo discovered he was nervous as he travelled out to Zehlendorf on the underground two days later. He took out his large fresh handkerchief and dabbed his brow. It was very hot, and he'd spent a long time deciding what to wear. He wanted to make a good impression, but in this heat a suit was out of the question. In the end he chose grey linen pants and a pale blue linen jacket pleated at the back over a short sleeved white shirt, with a navy tie. He'd taken off the jacket in the underground and only slipped into it as he turned the corner of the street where the Marcs lived.

Emma's mother, Elisabeth, opened the door to let him in. She looked attractive in a soft green cotton dress and much younger than her almost 50 years, and she beamed at him with a knowing smile. Indeed, he sensed that she would like to have taken him in her arms and given him a kiss on the cheek. Paul came out of the living room when he heard that Leo had arrived. His eyes smiled kindly behind his steel-rimmed glasses as he looked up at his guest, and he held Leo's outstretched hand in both of his for a moment. By now, Leo felt quite at ease.

Emma joined them from the kitchen, her face glowing. Disregarding her parents, she stood on tiptoe to plant a kiss on his cheek. Her richly flowered cotton print veiled the nervousness that she, too, felt.

'Let's sit out in the garden for a moment,' said Elisabeth, and they went through the dining room and the conservatory to the patio in the shade of the huge walnut tree. Emma followed with a tray holding four shallow champagne saucers and Papa brought the bucket with the bottle, which he opened with a festive POP. He filled the glasses. In his cream summer suit and Panama hat he reminded Emma of a plantation owner from *Gone with the Wind*, which she had just read.

'I don't think we need to stand on ceremony, my dear Dr Gebhardt,' he began. 'Emma has told me the reason for your visit, and I can assure you that my wife and I are more than happy to entrust our beloved Emma to your hands. We have never seen her so happy, and in these difficult and uncertain days, it is reassuring to know that there is someone who will take good care of her. We welcome you to our family as our son-in-law. Dear Leo, I am your Papa!'

'And I'm Mama,' added Elisabeth, with a giggle, her apple cheeks pink.

They clinked glasses: 'Leo – Mama – Emma – Papa ...' and sipped, and then Paul said: 'To the happy couple. May they enjoy a long, carefree and healthy life together.' And he lifted his glass a few centimetres, as did the others, before taking another sip. Then they all sat down. Emma was moved by her father's words – long, carefree, healthy – what did the future hold for them? She

A Normal Couple

sent a little prayer heavenwards, begging for fulfilment of these simple requests.

After they had eaten – Elisabeth had made a wonderfully tender and succulent pot roast with mashed potatoes and a green salad – they returned to the garden for coffee, and the talk moved on to the formalities laid down by the new administration for couples wanting to marry. It turned out that Paul was an expert on this.

'After all, I'm a judge in the divorce courts, so I deal with the ins and outs of these laws every day.'

'The divorce courts!' said Leo. 'That must give you great insight into human nature.'

'Well, to one aspect of it, yes. My work in Elbing was more diversified and allowed me greater scope for observations on the peculiarities of human motivations. Still, being here in Berlin is preferable by far,' replied Paul, adding more sugar to his coffee.

Emma had never told Leo about her father's background, and she decided that this was the time to introduce him to it.

'Papa was public state prosecutor in Elbing until 1933,' she began carefully, but Paul, who had had the same thought as Emma, interrupted. Like Herr Liepmann two days earlier, he glanced at the party button in Leo's lapel before he spoke.

'You are aware, I'm sure, that none of us are in the party. As a lawyer, I am in any case required to be impartial, and I lay great stress on this, even if my superiors have been trying to influence me otherwise.'

Leo raised his eyebrows slightly but said nothing.

'Well, you're safe in the divorce courts. Tell Leo about the end of your career in Elbing, my dear,' said his wife.

Emma checked that there was coffee in everyone's cup and topped up her mother's.

'Yes, well, as you know, Leo, the early thirties were very turbulent and unruly times. I'm sure you remember the atrocious street battles between the Communists and the supporters of Herr Hitler. It was an unsettling, insecure time for the average citizen. My main task as state prosecutor was to bring to court perpetrators of illegal unrest and rowdyism, regardless of whether they came from the left or the right. As you may imagine, this resulted in my being unpopular in both factions.'

Emma glanced at Leo, who was observing Paul under his heavy eyelids.

'When Herr Hitler came to power in January of 1933, I knew I might be in for trouble. And sure enough, on 1 April, as I was going to my chambers in the Law Courts, a very large young man in the honourable uniform of the NSDAP stopped me and demanded my name. I told him, and he informed me that "my type" was no longer required in this department and to get out. He showed me a paper signed and stamped by the Head of the Department of Justice, my superior, who was a staunch party member. Just that. This was clearly not an April Fool's joke, and I knew what it implied. Arguing would be fruitless. On the way home I passed by the train station and got myself a ticket to Berlin for later that afternoon. At home Elisabeth packed a bag for me and I left the same day. She can relate what ensued.'

He lifted his cup to his mouth and drank. There was silence for a moment. A blackbird began whistling in the tree above them, and they could hear children in a garden nearby calling their mother. Leo sipped at his coffee cup.

Elisabeth took up the story.

'Of course we were in a terrible tizzy, we didn't know what might happen or who to turn to. But we didn't have long to wait. Two evenings later – it was just getting dark – there was a ring at the front door and I opened it. Outside stood a figure, a woman, I couldn't identify her – she was all muffled up, with thick shawls wrapped around her head, and I couldn't see her face. She spoke to me in a kind of hoarse whisper, asking for Paul. I said he wasn't there at the moment. Then she said he should clear out as soon as possible, immediately, he was in danger. And she turned and hurried away. We never found out who this lady was, but we assumed it must have been the kind-hearted wife of one of the party functionaries who knew about the planned arrest of my husband and wanted to warn him. She might even have been someone we'd met socially! And sure enough, two policemen appeared the next day, rather embarrassed, since of course they knew our kind papa well, because of the nature of his work. Anyway, we told them he'd gone to Berlin, and they left, quite obviously relieved, and after that we weren't bothered any more.'

She paused, and Emma continued. 'I'd just done my Abitur and left home for England shortly afterwards. But Mama and my sisters stayed on in Elbing for the moment. Franzi noticed how many of the girls in her school year started avoiding her, and two of her teachers started making pointed remarks. The trainer in her hockey club started criticising her and some of the girls stopped talking to her. So she gave it up. And Mama said several of their formerly "good friends" stopped coming to the house and looked the other way if they met her in town. We were definitely on the wrong side of the fence socially.'

Leo looked down at the cup in his hand. It was not the first time he had interacted socially with friendly people whose political stance was so different from his own. Usually an unequivocal sentence or two pointing out the huge advantages of the present system, and the possible dire effects of a diverging point of view had sufficed to silence them. But these people were his future wife and parents-in-law!

'Well, you know,' he began, but Elisabeth wasn't finished.

'Paul stayed on in Berlin. Nobody here was interested in his past. Attitudes were much more relaxed. It was more anonymous. We all followed him six months later. But then he risked everything at the Congress of Lawyers in Leipzig later that year... .'

Paul tried to interrupt his wife. 'We don't need to go through that.'

'We do,' she said sharply, 'it shows exactly where you stand! What did he do only contradict Hans Frank, who at that time was no less than Hitler's personal lawyer. This was at the Congress of Lawyers in Leipzig in September of 1933. *Thousands* of people from the legal profession were present. Frank put it forward that German lawyers should see the law only as a means to an end; it should be used to guarantee a nation the "heroic strength" – those were his words – required in the struggle to survive. And what does my brave Paul do when he hears Frank say this? He stands up and answers loud and clear: "Our actions will continue to be based not on the wishes of the Party, but on our ancient laws." Right in front of all those people!'

Despite his misgivings about Paul's viewpoint, Leo was impressed. What a courageous stand by his future father-in-law, a slight, round-shouldered man, smaller than his own wife! At the same time, he knew it was futile. Leo understood Frank's argument; the pressure of the times demanded a strong stand. His future father-in-law was fighting a losing battle. More seriously, he was risking his own and his family's safety and well-being in the process. He knew that people had been sent to one of the new concentration camps for less. In a similar situation he himself would have reacted differently. More ... diplomatically. If at all.

'Well,' said Paul, 'I was perhaps a little foolhardy there, but it had to be said. Fortunately, there were no repercussions. In Berlin I was appointed Director of the Divorce Courts, where I settled into separating quarrelling husbands and wives rather than Nazis and Communists.' He finished with a smile, 'And I've been living happily ever since.'

He rose. 'Time for a little liqueur!' And he went indoors.

Elisabeth began to clear the coffee cups. Leo considered saying something, then decided against it. Then thought again.

'These are complicated times. Unfortunate things happen, but many good things have come to pass too. When we think of what conditions in Germany were like ten years ago...!'

Paul was descending the veranda steps with some bottles and tiny schnaps glasses.

'Let's stop talking politics for now,' he said, swinging the bottles on high. 'How can I make you happy, Leo, a cognac? A schnaps? An apricot liqueur?'

The drinks were poured and once more there was silence. The children had gone indoors, and the blackbird could be heard rooting among the compost leaves in the lower corner of the garden. 'Have you thought of what kind of furniture you'd like for your flat?' Elisabeth asked. 'By the way, you know I have a lot of linen here that I got as a dowry and have never used, wonderful tablecloths and bed linen. I don't think you'll need to buy any of that. Lise didn't want any of it.'

Leo spoke. 'My father has promised me the Dresden china service he and my mother were given when they married. The one with the blue onion pattern. It's for 12 settings. Do you think you'd like that, Emma?'

'Of course!' answered Emma. 'It's so beautiful. How wonderful, and how kind of him. A generous gift! When are you taking me to meet him?'

Next weekend was decided on, and the conversation drifted to the invitations.

'We wouldn't want a big wedding, would we, Leo?' asked Emma.

'It's up to you, dearest. I haven't got many people I'd want to ask. My father, of course, an uncle, a strange person ... and I have some cousins in Frankfurt, but ... not for a wedding, no. I'd like to ask my friend Hilde, though. I'm sure the two of you could become good friends.'

'Yes, of course, I'd love to meet her. I'd like to ask Marie. In fact I've promised her.'

'When was this?' Leo asked in mock astonishment. 'We've only just got engaged!'

Emma laughed and blushed.

'And of course Aunt Charlotte.' That was Elisabeth's younger sister, who was unmarried. She was a quiet and unassuming lady, who worked as a secretary in an insurance company. All the family loved her.

'What about Aunt Dorothea von Franken?' asked Paul.

'Yes, of course,' answered Emma quickly. 'Both of them.'

Aunt Dorothea was one of Paul's sisters and Emma's godmother. She had married well, as they say, a banker, but they had no children, and she had designated Emma as her heiress.

'When the day comes,' she proclaimed every now and again, 'all this will be yours!', indicating with a limp wave of her hand her mansion with its opulent furniture, the grounds, and presumably whatever was deposited in the safe. In Emma's opinion she made far too much of her status as her husband's wife, and the 'von' in her name. Franzi put it more bluntly: 'She's a downright snob!'

But while Emma found her company trying, she was polite and kind to her for her father's sake.

'What about Uncle Fritz?' she asked her father.

'If you ask him, you'll have to ask all the others too. And their families.' *All the others* were all of Paul's siblings – four more brothers and another sister besides Fritz and Dorothea.

'Anna and Willi live very far away, I don't think they'd come. But you'd have to ask Otto, you know,' said her mother, with a pout.

Emma made a face. Otto was her father's youngest brother. He was an ardent Nazi, and lived under the impression that his views were shared by all the other members of his extended family. Paul tended to avoid him as much as possible.

'Well, if most of the others come, he won't be able to dominate the party too much,' said Emma.

Elisabeth mentioned some old family friends that she would like to ask, and Emma quickly agreed. They were people she had grown up with and called 'aunt' and 'uncle'.

'That makes about thirty people, I think,' said Elisabeth, 'almost all on our side of the family. That'll make up for the small numbers on your side, Leo!'

'I hope you don't mind,' said Emma, with a small frown.

'Not at all!' said Leo. 'It'll be a great opportunity to meet all of them, I'd like it very much!'

When Leo announced he was leaving, Emma said she would accompany him to the station. As he took his leave, Paul and he shook hands very firmly, and this time Elisabeth reached up and kissed him on the cheek.

'How lucky I am to be getting all these wonderful sons without having had the bother of bringing them up,' she whispered, and then gave him a warm smile. 'I recommend it.'

Leo laughed. 'I'll make sure to remember that!'

He took Emma's hand and they disappeared down the garden path. Once outside the gate, he asked Emma to take a walk with him instead of going straight to the station, and she said that she was just going to suggest the same. So they turned right and then right again, strolled along the sandy footpath, crossed the main road, and went down to the lake.

'First of all,' said Leo, 'I must apologise, my love. I think I was a little nervous this afternoon, and forgot something terribly important. Why did nobody draw my attention to it?' He put his hand into his jacket pocket and drew out a small, cube-shaped box. He opened it. Inside was a gold ring, with a little cut diamond held in an open ray of supports set in a pattern of minute chased dots. It was very understated, yet an exquisite design, and it suited her taste perfectly. Leo removed it from the box and took her left hand in his. He tried to slip the ring onto her finger, but she stopped him with a smile.

'Wrong hand,' she said. 'Have you had a fiancée in England that I don't know about? *They* wear it on the left, love, but *we* wear it on the right.'

'Of course! I wasn't paying attention.' And he gently pushed the ring onto the proper finger, where it settled and nestled as if it had lived there for years. Then he scooped her in his arms and kissed her intensely.

'Now we're properly engaged,' he whispered.

For a while they stood in silence, wrapped in each other's arms, gazing at the water. Mallards were busily foraging and chattering among the rushes near the shore. The air was heavy with the honey scent of the lime trees lining the lake.

'I wanted to say something about why I joined the party,' said Leo. 'I know your family is neutral, but I'm not. What's happening nowadays is very important to me. I believe in it.'

Emma hooked her arm in his, and they turned and strolled along the path.

'I joined in May of 1933, shortly after our Führer was made Chancellor. I had been an admirer of his for many years before that, all during my student days in Innsbruck. He had a clear vision, he had concrete plans, and he could persuade people. I was and still am convinced that he and his movement are what is needed to save Germany, to get us out of the pit we were in since the end of the war. I don't know how much you noticed or can remember of those years, the twenties, you were very young. They were terrible times, absolutely catastrophic. The mass unemployment, not just for workers but in all classes – the streets and parks full of grey, hollow-eyed figures with posters round their necks begging for work, trying to get through the day before returning empty-handed to their hungry families. It was awful. The terrible housing situation, the poverty – large families living in one room, a tenement house with fifty inhabitants sharing one toilet. First the great inflation, then the stock exchange crash and its consequences. The immense reparation payments imposed at the Treaty of Versailles in 1918, that Germany had to and still has to transfer to the victorious countries. Draining us! All because of the betrayal of our mother country by that international conspiracy of Jewish communists – the war was lost because of them. Scum!'

He angrily waved off a persistent mosquito.

'The democratic experiment of the twenties was a total failure. Ten parties – ten! – formed the coalition government of 1920, it was impossible to rule. Constant squabbling, a consensus on policies was out of the question. Or the power to implement anything useful. Then gradually the Führer emerged as a politician who could inspire confidence, and the belief grew that this hopeless situation could be changed, that there was a future for our country. He was able to motivate people and allow hope to develop. He showed strength and purpose!'

He paused to draw breath.

'And I wanted to support this new start, to contribute to the emergence of a new Germany. My own future was at stake!'

Some late cyclists were approaching them on the narrow path, and they stepped aside to let them pass.

'And look how Germany has prospered since he came to power. The mass unemployment has gone, people have enough to eat, the state is sending families to holiday resorts at the seaside or in the mountains. New homes are being built. Everyone is looking to the future with hope and confidence.'

He drew his enamel cigarette case from his pocket and lit a cigarette. Emma waited for him to continue.

'And of course new laws were necessary to bring all this about. Radical laws. Of *course* there are people who have suffered during this time,' he continued. 'It's a kind of revolution, like in France. It's impossible to be fair to everyone. The idea that Germany must be inhabited only by pure-bred Aryans, and that we don't want to intermingle with other races, like the Jews ... well, I don't see the necessity of that, I must admit, when I think of friends I used to have. But there were just too *many* Jews in all the leading professions – lawyers, doctors, academics, businessmen – all the leading positions were occupied by Jews. They passed the positions on to each other and we, the original German nation, were excluded. And not even just in the leading professions. You know, even in Bingen, the wine-town on the River Mosel – when I went there with my father to buy wine, all the winegrowers were German, tending and harvesting the vines on those steep slopes all summer in the heat of the sun; but all the dealers, who merely bought the grapes and hired people to press them and make the wine, all of them, were Jewish. That can't be right. It's unacceptable.'

His voice had got harder. Emma watched him for a moment as he expelled cigarette smoke through his nose. Then she spoke.

'But they were German too! Their families have lived here for ages! And then the brutality and cruelty with which these people are being chased out of the country, you can't possibly accept that either!'

'Well, that's the downside. There seem to be elements in the leading organisations that are operating on their own. I doubt even the Führer knows about this. We can only hope that these actions will stop soon, and the resettlement of unGerman elements will proceed in an orderly manner. Wouldn't it be wonderful if everybody could live in peace and harmony with each other!

The world is so beautiful – wait till you see Italy, my Em. We must go there for our honeymoon. That little hotel near Verona I wrote to you about!'

Emma didn't want to continue the gloomy discussion either, and so they continued their walk arm in arm, Leo telling her about Italy, and Emma listening to him, imagining the wonderful places he was describing.

But at the back of her mind she felt an uneasiness. Despite her belief in the equality of husband and wife, politics was definitely a male domain; she had never been interested in it, and knew too little about what had happened in the last few years to be able to answer him properly. She felt his way of looking at things was too superficial; she was sure it was all more complicated. But she had no idea how to counter him. And in her heart of hearts she knew that nothing she said would make any difference at all.

10

28 August–1 September: Anticipating the War

'Are there any more rubber rings?' asked Elisabeth, pushing a loose twist of hair away from her eyes with the back of her hand.

Franzi shoved an open box of the large flat rings across the kitchen table. She was carefully stuffing plums into preserving jars, then adding a few centimetres of a sugar solution, before sealing them with a rubber ring, the glass lid, and a clip to hold it down. Elisabeth was doing the same with pears.

'How much longer for the beans?'

Franzi checked the timer. 'Another ten minutes. We can do another batch of plums, or maybe the beetroot from the garden. Thank goodness we bought all these extra jars at that sale.'

'Those smaller ones will come in useful,' said Elisabeth. 'I've ordered a kilo of calves' liver from Frau Meier. We'll be able to make loads of liver pâté.'

'If she keeps it for you! Everyone will be looking for that kind of thing now. Did I tell you that

Christel has promised Pa several bucketfuls of pale grapes? They got a huge crop this year. He'll be able to make some wine. Or at least we can bottle the juice.'

'It'd be even better if she gave Paul a cutting of her vine so he could start his own, but of course that wouldn't occur to her. He's been talking about it for so long. They obviously don't want us to have it.'

Franzi ignored the last remark.

Bottling, preserving and jam-making were normal summer and autumn activities in the Marc household, but they had special relevance this year. The rumours of an impending war had reached a climax. Hitler had openly declared his intention of attacking Poland if it refused to return the German territories it had been allocated after the Great War in 1918. Elisabeth remembered all too well the hungry years during that war, when turnips had been the only food available for large sections of the population for several years. This time, if there was a war, it wouldn't last so long, she thought. That the present regime had been pursuing a pro-war policy for the past few years should be clear by now to anyone who used the eyes, ears and brains God had given them. So at the very least the country should be well prepared. But there was no knowing what might happen, and hoarding supplies of food and fuel was only common sense. The garden provided rich harvests of fruit and vegetables, and once sterilised and vacuum sealed in the jars, they would keep for years.

These thoughts were wandering through her head when the timer rang. The two women turned to the stove, where a huge cauldron was emitting soft wafts of steam. Franzi turned off the gas, and together they lifted it down. Elisabeth removed the lid and the long thermometer that was sticking out through a hole in its centre and examined the jars of beans – French, runner, and yellow wax beans – that were stacked in the water bath inside.

They emptied the cauldron and filled it with the next lot of preserves, hauled it onto the stove and added cold water before relighting the gas. Franzi checked the time and temperature from the guide printed on the thermometer.

'Forty minutes at seventy-five degrees,' she said. 'I'll have to leave you now, Ma, and get back to my books.'

'Oh, all right, I suppose I can manage!' retorted Elisabeth. 'It's a pity you didn't start revising earlier, so that you could help me properly now. I'll call you when these are ready.'

The finals of Franzi's physiotherapy course were taking place on Friday, 1 September. That was only three days away.

'That's not fair, Ma! You know I've been working hard on the side, and I've been studying all the time too. There are only so many hours to a day!'

Her mother pursed her lips, and Franzi flounced out of the kitchen.

Elisabeth prepared another batch, this time of sliced beetroot, and then she began to tidy the kitchen. She used to have a live-in girl from the country helping her, but since unemployment had dropped so radically, and openings for young women had appeared in shops, restaurants, hairdressing salons and hotels, it had become more and more difficult to find suitable household help. Of course her daughters had stepped in, but Lise was now living in a small town to the north of Berlin, where her husband had been appointed to a surgery. Emmi would be marrying on 10 September, and then she too would be unavailable. Franzi and that attractive Moritz had finally announced their engagement and would probably marry early in the new year. What a huge change in their lively household, and all within one year. She shook her head – it was hard to get used to the idea that she and Paul would be on their own. Maybe she'd look around for a girl to help her again.

She had twenty minutes before the plums were done, and she decided to sit down at the piano to try to relax. Without removing her apron she went into the sitting room to her Bechstein baby grand, her pride and joy. But lying on the lid was a large envelope which was awaiting her attention: it held the ration cards which had been issued two days earlier. Ration cards! For meat, fats, butter, milk, cheese, jams and sugar. It was incredible. She thought all that had ended twenty-one years ago, in 1918. Surely one such experience was enough for any one lifetime! But here it was again. And what was to follow?

She heard Paul coming up the cellar steps and went out to meet him. In his arms he held rolls of black material, the blinds for the last two bedroom windows. All other windows had already been equipped since the blackout order was issued in July. He'd been hoping one of his prospective sons-in-law would help him to install them, but they had all been far too busy and he'd had to manage on his own as best he could. Do-it-yourself was not his strong point.

'What are we to do about these?' demanded Elisabeth, waving the envelope.

'What is it?' asked Paul, closing the cellar door with his shoulder and coming into the sitting room with the blinds.

'The ration coupons! I can't make head or tail of them.'

A Normal Couple

Tired, Paul placed the blinds on a chair and took the envelope, then sat down heavily in the sofa. He pulled out the pages of cards and the accompanying instructions and scanned them.

'It begins on Friday,' he said. 'Poor Emmi, what an unlucky start to her married life to have to cope with this. Will the catering for her wedding be affected?'

'How should I know? It's that father of Leo's who's doing it all, he insisted the wedding should be in Dresden. The whole thing is ridiculous! He's there on his own, he could easily come to Berlin for a few days, but no, all of us have to make our way down there, find accommodation, buy our meals, bring all our finery in suitcases ... How selfish can you get! No wonder Leo is always so tight-lipped about him.'

'You must get Leo to write to him and clear up that point. Perhaps we can bring food from here. In fact, once the rationing is in place, we'll have to produce our ration coupons before we can even expect a piece of wedding cake! It's so unfortunate! Poor Em!'

'Do you really think there'll be another war, Paul? I just can't imagine it. We all lived through those five long years and know how horrifying and cruel it is. Surely no one wants to go through all that again!'

'I think it's our leadership,' said Paul quietly with a sigh. 'From my experience back in Elbing with those street gangs, I've always been sceptical of the Nazis, but when Herr Hitler overcame the mass unemployment so quickly, I started to come round in his favour. And then, when he succeeded in bringing the Rhineland back to Germany – though he did contravene the Treaty of Versailles – I thought it was a good move.' He pushed his steel-rimmed glasses back up his nose and continued.

'But the annexation of the Sudetenland areas of Czechoslovakia, and then the annexation of Austria – to say nothing of his treatment of minorities, the disgraceful laws being passed against the Jews, the political assassinations in recent years – all this is not the way things should be run. It is not the rule of law. I fear he plans to occupy Poland, and if he does so, then its allies England and France will have to move to its defence. And that, my dear Lissy, means war. So to answer your question, yes, I think there will be a war.'

'But why?! It's all nonsense! I don't think the public want a war. Things have been going so well for most people, they're satisfied and optimistic! What good would a war be to anyone? Who needs Poland?'

'That's the point. In contrast to most people, I've read *Mein Kampf,* and in it Herr Hitler states quite clearly that he believes the German nation needs more land and that it should expand eastwards. And that's what he's implementing now. Step by step he's achieving all the things he set out to do. Everyone should read that book, then they wouldn't be so surprised at what's happening. It's just so hard to read.'

'I thought it was very simply written – what can you expect from a former housepainter, and an Austrian at that!' said Elisabeth, reaching out to pick a dead dahlia from the vase on the little table.

'Yes, simply and badly, that's what makes it hard to read,' said Paul with a sad little smile.

'His mother obviously brought him up badly,' began Elisabeth, but then the timer in the kitchen shrilled, and she hurried out, shouting for Franzi to come and help her with the heavy cauldron.

Two hours later, Emmi arrived back from the office.

'Hallo,' she called, 'anyone home?'

Elisabeth emerged from the dining room.

'Hallo Em! You must be tired. Dinner is nearly ready. I've made a potato soup with sausages.'

'Oh, lovely! How was your day, Ma?' asked Emmi, pulling off her hat and coat and changing into her lighter house shoes.

'Very busy. I've been preserving all day and I'm tired too, so it's just a simple meal. Give me a hand with the dishes, will you? And call Franzi please, she's upstairs at her books.'

At dinner, Paul asked Emmi what things were like in the Ministry.

'Have these war worries had any effect on your work?'

'No, I can't say they have. There's a big scandal because Leo's colleague Klaus approved a series of concerts with the Black Sea Cossack Choir and the Willi Glahe jazz orchestra to tour Prague and the Czeck Protectorate – Romanians and Germans in Czechoslovakia. The idea behind it is to show the cultural bond between our nations. Some bigwig in Prague got wind of it and is shocked because he considers it all too trivial. He said the Cossack Choir was "culturally degenerate" – can you believe it? And he spelt "jazz" with a double "s". How narrow-minded can you get?'

'Those Russian choirs are wonderful!' said Elisabeth. 'Such deep, musical voices! It's folk art, what's abnormal about it? And a jazz group is a perfect contrast. What do they expect? Do they think people want to hear nothing but Richard Wagner and Beethoven all day long?'

'Leo put on his inscrutable mask and dealt with it,' Emmi continued. 'He sent a bland telegram saying that unfortunately nothing could be changed at such short notice, and that they were planning a tour with the German State Opera company next spring. We all had a good laugh about it.'

Franzi asked, 'Any chance of Leo getting his hands on some good jazz records again? Willi Glahe is great to dance to.'

Confiscated jazz records sometimes landed in the Ministry and were 'disposed' of by some of the people working there.

'I'll ask him, but for goodness's sake don't pass them on to anyone else. If anyone asks where you got them from, say one of your uncles gave them to you.'

'Don't worry, sis, I wasn't born yesterday! I was just thinking of the party we're planning at Susi's place after the exams on Friday. I need something to look forward to. I still haven't got over the shock of them cancelling all hockey championships until further notice!'

Franzi's hockey club was practising for a regional championship title, but the previous day the government had issued a proclamation whereby championships in all sporting events were postponed indefinitely.

'It might be only a temporary measure,' said Emmi. Paul and Elisabeth caught each other's eye. 'Anyway, just make sure you're fit for the exam on Friday, and I'll see if Leo can dig up anything to brighten your evening. Will Moritz be there?'

'No, I told you, his leave has been cancelled, even for the weekends.'

'Well, girls,' said Paul, 'thank you for the meal. Franzi, you'll want to be resuming your studies. Emmi, perhaps you could assist me in fixing up these blinds in your and Franzi's rooms? It's much easier with two pairs of hands.'

A Normal Couple

Emmi was glad of a chance to be alone with her father for a while. She helped to clear the table, and then followed him upstairs with the box of tools.

After they had fixed the first blind, her father working very slowly but methodically, they moved into the next room and set up the ladder. Paul took a drill and a tape measure and climbed up.

'Pa,' Emmi began, 'what do you think of all this? Is it as dangerous as it sounds? Or is it all a lot of hot air?'

'I'm afraid it is serious – very serious,' answered her father. 'I was talking to your mother about it. We have to expect the worst.'

Emmi was silent for a minute.

'What will it mean for all of us?'

'Well, it won't affect Mama and me, we're too old. I'll be retiring in a bit over two years. Our sons-in-law are more exposed. Benno, as a doctor, will be all right. It's highly unlikely that he'll be called up for active service. In the worst case he might be assigned to a First Aid station near the front. But it's more likely that he'll be posted to a clinic somewhere in the hinterland, where he'll be safe. In Leo's case, his age is in his favour. His year won't be called up for a few years, and even then he'll be used for some sort of liaison work or a desk job of some kind. And with luck the war would be over by then. Franzi's Moritz is the most endangered. As a pilot, and then in Fighter Squadron Richthofen, he can expect to be in the thick of it.'

'But surely Poland doesn't have an air force worth talking about?'

'No, they haven't. But France and England will join in defence of Poland. Since the time when England knuckled under to Herr Hitler's annexation of the Sudetenland with only a murmur – you remember, not quite a year ago, how Mr Chamberlain was here with his appeasement policy – , they've clearly known which way the wind is blowing. So they've had time to prepare for war, and we must expect the British have been building up a considerable air force. That's where the danger lies for Moritz. Reach me the screws and the screwdriver, will you?'

'But how will it end, Pa?' she enquired anxiously.

'Who knows, my love? At least we're safe from an attack by Russia.'

'How do you know?'

'Russia and Germany signed a non-aggression pact yesterday. It wasn't heralded in the papers, but I have a friend at the courts whose son knows about these things. I never expected Herr Hitler and Stalin to be able to reach an agreement, but it seems they have.'

'So if Poland falls to Germany, then Germany will be attacked in the west, by France and England?'

'Yes, that's the likely scenario. It's far away from us here in Berlin, in the east, and fortunately we have no relatives in the west of the country to worry about. Germany has reaffirmed that it will respect the neutrality of Belgium, the Netherlands and Switzerland, so that leaves only a narrow corridor from Germany to France across the River Rhine to Alsace. But who knows whether the air force will respect that neutrality if they want to fly attacks on Paris?'

'Oh Pa, it's all too horrible. I can't believe that such terrible things will happen. I mean – it seems so remote from our world, from our reality. It sounds like a nightmare!'

Paul climbed down from the ladder. He lowered and raised and lowered the blind to check that it was working properly.

'Well, nothing might happen for quite some time. Let's forget about it now and go down and open a bottle of wine. Leo's father sent us some fine bottles which I haven't tried yet. Don't worry, my love. There's nothing we can do, except to prepare ourselves as best we can for hard times. I wish your married life were starting in happier circumstances.' He stared absent-mindedly at the screwdriver in his hand as if wondering what it was for. 'Strange – Mama and I married shortly before the Great War. And yet we produced you three girls during and just after it, and we've done all right since then. You had a good childhood, didn't you?'

'The best,' said Emmi sincerely. 'And I hope the same will be the case for any children Leo and I will have.'

Her father put his arm around her shoulders and then drew her into an embrace and planted a kiss on her cheek.

'My sweet Em, our dear Lord will take care of you and Leo, as He has always looked after Mama and me. Trust in Him and all will be well. Even without a church wedding.'

Emmi and Leo had decided to have a civil wedding only, and she knew her parents were piqued.

'I know, Pa. Please try to understand. Neither of us feel that way now. But I'm still a member of our congregation, and you and Ma both know that deep inside I still believe in all the things you taught me when I was growing up. I haven't changed.'

'You know your mother would love to have seen you in a white wedding dress.'

Emma coloured. Leo tended towards the new Nazi religion of 'Believers in God', which had replaced all religious symbols with its own Germanic tokens.

Paul sighed as he gathered up his tools and the ladder.

'Well, I suppose it's not as important as it used to be. The climate is changing, and we have to bend whichever way the wind blows. We're no longer in complete control of our own lives and destinies, I fear.'

They slowly went downstairs to the pure, joyful sounds of a Bach Prelude coming from the drawing room. It stopped abruptly, then started again, then stopped again.

'Drat!' said Elisabeth. 'These pieces are so difficult! I must practise more often!'

Franzi was up early on the day of her finals. She had slept well, but was woken at 5.30 by the racket from the sparrows in the virginia creeper at the side of the house. They reminded her of a crazy orchestra tuning up. She swung out of bed and did a few exercises at the open window. The sky was a cloudless blue, and already the air was warm, promising a hot day, not ideal when sweating over exam papers. But it raised her spirits and gave her confidence. She washed and dressed, and tore downstairs to the kitchen, where she made herself a pot of tea and a cream cheese sandwich. Then she moved into the sitting-room and turned on the radio. Five minutes later she was rousing everyone in the house.

'MA, PA, EMMI! COME AND LISTEN!! IT'S STARTED! THEY'VE INVADED POLAND! OH GOD!'

It was Friday, 1 September. The war had begun.

11

1–5 September: Before the Wedding

During the day, Elisabeth was on her own and had the radio running non-stop. Both Emmi and Paul had been able to listen to the Führer's speech in their respective offices. He had delivered a long harangue in which he outlined the reasons for the attack on Poland, his attempts to reach a peaceful solution, the hand he had reached out to the Polish premier again and again, the concessions he had announced – all to no avail. Repeated attacks by Polish soldiers on German facilities near the border, he said, had stretched his patience to breaking point, until he had been left with no alternative but to return fire. He was now the First Soldier of the nation, had donned the honourable uniform of the previous war and would not take it off until victory was his and Germany's.

Whether in Bischoff's office in the Ministry, where Leo stood near Emma while listening, or in the Chief Judge's chambers in the law courts, – not a sound could be heard until the speech was ended. Or rather: not a word was heard, though there were some sharp intakes of breath, a few quickly subdued hisses of repulsion, several amazed but minute shakes of the head from individual listeners.

When it was over, there was silence in both offices, until some officials, in both cases in uniform, straightened up, clicked their booted heels together, gave the German salute, and called: 'Sieg Heil!' and 'Heil to the Führer'. The others fell in with these actions more or less convincingly, after which the groups quickly dispersed. It seemed that in both houses there were elements that did not wholly concur with the Führer's interpretation of events, but no one was prepared to state his mind openly. The time for standing by one's beliefs in public, if they contradicted the official line, had long gone. Now more so than ever.

The atmosphere in the Marc household was subdued in the following days. Leo dropped by on Saturday and Sunday. He still believed the war would not last long, and was more concerned about whether they would be able to get enough to eat. As expected, England and France had declared war on Germany two days after the invasion of Poland, and the Brits had flown air raids against two coastal towns. Moritz phoned on Sunday: he flew a Messerschmidt fighter, and his squadron, Fighter Squadron 2 'Richthofen', was securing the air space over the invading troops. Franzi was reassured – it didn't sound very dangerous. Shopping had become complicated: the ration coupons took getting used to. All private motoring was banned. Theatres and cinemas were closed in the evenings. The population were forbidden to listen to foreign radio stations. But these were isolated incidents during the day, and on the whole life began to revert to normal. The weather remained fine and encouraged excursions to Wannsee and the public baths, people continued with their work, and Franzi and her mother resumed their preserving activities with renewed motivation.

Emma started concentrating on her wedding again. It was now only a few days off. They would be a smaller party than originally planned – several guests had regretfully cancelled because of the uncertain situation. By car and train, they would be making their way to Dresden on Saturday, where her future father-in-law was giving a party in his flat in the evening. The ceremony would take place next morning, to be followed by a dinner in a restaurant nearby. In the afternoon they'd planned a walk to the cemetery where Leo's dear mother was buried, and coffee and wedding cake in a nearby café would round off the day. Franzi and Moritz as well as Benno and Lise would be returning home that evening, since the men had to work the following day. The Marcs, Aunt Dorothea and her husband, Aunt Charlotte and Marie would be returning by train on Monday. The remaining guests and family had made their own plans. The newly-weds would spend the wedding night together in the hotel, and then travel down to the Black Forest for a few days. The trip to the exquisite family-run hotel near Verona that Leo had envisaged was still a dream – it was too far away for the few days they had available for their honeymoon. They would go there some other time, perhaps on their first anniversary.

On Tuesday afternoon she was able to get home earlier than usual. It was her last week in the office: married women were not employed, and her contract ended on Friday. Dr Bischoff had been furious when she'd handed in her notice, and had tried to make her change her mind about getting married. Leo told her Bischoff had even tried to forbid him to communicate with her in the office.

But he had given them a wonderful wedding present, a huge pottery art deco punch bowl and matching ladle, so it seemed he had forgiven them.

Emma came home waving a fat manila envelope in her hand.

'There's been a sudden break in communications, so Bischoff said we could leave early. He's not usually so generous with our time. And look what I have here.'

'What is it?' asked Elisabeth, busy at the stove. There was a delicious smell in the kitchen. She was making Königsberger Klopse, juicy meat balls poached in a rich stock, which was then thickened with roux and enriched with fresh and sour cream, dry white wine, lemon juice and capers, and given a silky sheen with two egg yolks. It was a favourite with all the family, though now she'd had to replace the cream with powdered milk.

'Leo gave me this today,' Emmi said. 'It's our licence. And they've sent back all the documentation we had to submit with our application to get engaged and married. All that stuff the SS wanted to know about me to make sure I was worthy of marrying one of them! It's been processed and returned to us. We won't need it again. Perhaps it can be filed with the family documents, Pa?'

Leaning against the open kitchen door, she removed the papers from the envelope and started leafing through them. She gave a laugh.

'Look, Franzi, here's the questionnaire that Dr Trute and Uncle Bernhard filled in. You'd never believe the kinds of things they were asked! "Is the future bride reliable or unreliable?" Well, that's pretty harmless. Wait – here. "Is she companionable, or domineering?" Uncle Bernhard just answers "Companionable", but Dr Trute writes: "I am of the firm opinion that she will be an absolutely outstanding companion in her marriage."'

They all laughed.

'And this one: "Is she a good housekeeper, or frivolous and vain?" And Dr Trute: "She is very domesticated and much too serious to be frivolous or overly interested in her exterior." And here – this is how he sums up my character: "She is serious and introspective and in no way inclined to be superficial or to do things by halves." Well, isn't it wonderful to know there's at least one person who recognises and appreciates my true qualities!'

Dr Trute was a colleague of her father's, though only a few years older than Emmi. He'd become a good friend, but the girls considered him a bit of a stuffed shirt. The other guarantor, Bernhard Wagner, had been a family friend for many years.

'Let me see!' said Franzi, still laughing. As she read the other questions, her smile faded.

'This is really so primitive. How dare they ask such stupid things about you! I don't think I'd allow anyone to subject me to such an examination! It's humiliating!'

'Uncle Bernhard clearly thought so too. He just wrote "Yes" or "No" or one word in his answers. But at any rate, we have our licence to marry now, that's the main thing. We're all set for Sunday. High time,' she added quietly for Franzi's benefit, 'I can't keep Leo off much longer.'

'What made him join the SS?' Franzi wanted to know. 'They're not exactly a group of do-gooders!' The law enforcement activities of the SS received laudatory reports in the papers, but eye-witness accounts fed the grapevine which allowed perceptive minds to form their own opinion of what these dealings really involved.

'Well, he wanted to take an active part in the reconstruction of Germany, or its new start, as he

105

says. A friend suggested he join, and he liked the idea. It *is* a very prestigious organisation. They don't just take anyone, or at least they usedn't to. At first they only had a few thousand members. It means getting to know a lot of influential people, and learning to accept authority and leadership. He told me something very revealing. He said when he was growing up it was taken for granted that every young man would do military service. It was part of growing up, it would turn boys into men, and as an only child he spent his early years looking forward to the time when he would belong to a group of like-minded young men. But he was too young for the Great War, then the Treaty of Versailles stopped Germany having an army of its own, and now he's too old for this one, so he never got the military training he'd expected as a youngster. He feels strongly that he missed out on something in his education. I think he's trying to catch up. And anyway, he likes the black uniform.'

'Yes, he does look very smart in it,' Franzi conceded thoughtfully.

They went through the other papers, the CVs Emmi and Leo had submitted, the family trees for the Marcs and the Gebhardts, going back to the year 1800 and beyond to guarantee their Aryan descent, the page with precise queries about their parents and grandparents: 'Job or profession? Diseases? Age at death? Cause of death?'

'That's to make sure there are no inherited diseases. The purity of our Aryan blood must be maintained on all fronts, and our government is ensuring that this is guaranteed! Hurrah!'

Emma replied with a wan smile.

Later they were sitting out on the veranda enjoying the peaceful late-summer evening, talking quietly about their fiancés, when the harsh ring of the

A Normal Couple

telephone erupted. Franzi raced into the hall, hoping it was Moritz, and picked up the receiver.

'Berlin 1746, Franziska Marc speaking, hallo?'

....

'Good evening, Herr Gebhardt.'

....

'No, but Emma is here. Hold on one moment please.'

....

'EMMI! Come quick! It's long distance! Leo's father!'

Emmi was at her side immediately.

'Hallo, father. Is everything all right?'

A long pause while Leo's father was talking.

'But for how long?!'

....

'But that's terrible! Everything's arranged! All our arrangements.... And yours ....'

....

'And the hotels?'

....

'All right, I'll tell him, he'll write to you straight away.'

....

'Thank you, I'm so sorry too. Thank you for... we'll see what we can do. We'll be in touch.'

....

'Goodbye.'

Franzi was standing beside her. Her face was taut and pale.

'What's wrong?' she whispered.

'The registry office in Dresden is closed – indefinitely. The wedding registrars have all been drafted. They've cancelled everything. Our wedding – it's off.'

And she burst into tears.

12

8–10 September: Visiting Leo's Father, Part 1

Leo's father Ferdinand carefully pulled one of the large Dresden china platters and several plates out of the sideboard and brought them into the kitchen. From the cold larder he fetched the packets of meats and sausage, the cheeses and vegetables he'd bought for the supper he would be preparing for his son and prospective daughter-in-law. He cleared the kitchen table and set to work, fanning out the thinly sliced smoked schinken and salami and decorating them with radishes and parsley. It was woman's work, but he had often done it when displaying his products in his wine and delicatessen shop in the centre of Dresden before he retired. He'd used the entire month's ration coupons for these things, but he hoped Leo would remember to compensate by leaving him some of his.

This visit excited him greatly. He hadn't seen Leo for two months, and the occasion was a special one. The wedding was supposed to have taken place in two days' time. But now – this mess! And all because of that gangster Hitler and his Nazi gang. He couldn't understand why so many people supported the regime. It was so *openly* criminal! Hitler had removed his political rivals for power by force. By having them murdered, everyone knew that. Even more shocking than the murders themselves was the fact that the general public was *not* shocked by these actions. The apathy with which the butchering of Hitler's would-be rival, Röhm, and his cronies (criminals themselves!) back in '34 was received gave the so-called Führer the backing to continue along this path. No one protested; it was the 'go ahead' for Hitler. The socialists and communists were dealt with next, imprisoned and tortured and worse. He himself – a socialist and a democrat all his life – had had to be careful.

Then it was the turn of the Jews. It began as a slowly burgeoning trail of oppression which was hardly noticed by the non-Jewish population. They were forbidden to follow certain professions, they could shop only in certain stores, at certain times. They lost their citizenship and civil rights, they had to leave their houses. Their children couldn't belong to 'German' clubs, attend 'German' schools, weren't allowed to sit for finals, to study. And so on. Till the culmination on 11 November in the previous year, the Kristallnacht, the night of broken glass, when bricks were heaved through the windows of Jewish owned shops and the synagogues were set on fire, men, women, children driven from their homes, beaten, murdered, their furniture thrown onto the streets – it had all happened in broad daylight! He himself had seen the chaos when he'd gone into town the following day. And the public went along with it! It was incredible!

He recalled the nice family that had been living in the flat above his when he and his wife moved in here in 1932. Brauer was their name, parents and two polite young teenage children. His wife had become good friends with Frau Brauer. Herr Brauer had a millinery shop in town. When the trouble began, Frau Brauer confided to Hedwig one day that her husband was of Jewish descent, and that she had found out that a grandmother of hers had also been Jewish. They were completely assimilated, and her husband had fought for Germany in the Great War, and been wounded, and received a medal.

But it made no difference. As their movements and those of their children were restricted more and more, they decided to emigrate. Herr Brauer was able to sell his shop, though for a fraction of its real value. They moved to Holland. For a while, Frau Brauer wrote to Frau Gebhardt, but then even this became too dangerous – for both the Brauers and the Gebhardts – so they broke off the connection. He hoped they had been able to settle there. But why had this happened? What had the Brauers done to the German people that put them in the category of undesirables, of elements that were harming the German state? Hah! He had asked Leo this question more than once, and never received a satisfactory answer. Because there was none! At least Leo hadn't said: 'They deserved it.' That was the line taken by the real Nazis!

Nonetheless, his son Leo had joined hands with these people, had joined the 'Party' in 1933: organised concerts in their name, wrote for their paper when required, gave talks at their cultural events. How could he be so stupid? Leo was not one to throw bricks through windows – or to burn books, as had happened to thousands of works by dozens of authors not approved of by the Nazis in

'33, shortly after they came to power. When had Leo taken the path away from the freedom promised by democracy to follow this ridiculous totalitarian madman? How could he support, or even merely accept, the crimes that were being committed in the name of the party he had joined? True, he was ambitious, and he had taken the side of the victors, which was working out to his advantage. But to openly condone what they were doing! And now this completely illegal invasion of their neighbouring state! How could that boy be so blind?!

Muttering to himself while rolling balls of butter between a pair of wooden butter pats, he grew more and more angry. He set the table in the good room, banging the cutlery onto the white cloth (but treating his beautiful wine glasses with care). Back in the kitchen, he placed the finished platters in the pantry, then went down into the cellar to get the white wine. The red wine was already acclimatising in the conservatory, where it was a little cooler than in the dining room.

Half an hour before he thought Leo and Emma would be arriving, he placed all the food on the table. He knew they would be hungry. He wondered if Emma shared all of Leo's political opinions. He hoped not – it would be too much to deal with. As it was, he'd have to keep a tight hold on himself not to snipe at Leo all the time.

Emma had been to Dresden several times in the past years, but she never got tired of seeing the skyline of the baroque city. It well deserved its by-name 'Florence of the North': the towers, spires and cupolas of its palace, cathedral, churches, museums, academic institutes, opera house were ranged along the gentle curve of the River Elbe like a backdrop on a stage. As their train slowly crossed the river, she could see the wonderful panorama in dark silhouette against the white evening sky. It was breath-taking. Its grandeur had been founded by Elector August the Strong of Saxony in the early 18th century. He became King of Poland, kept his warfare to a minimum, and instead built up a collection of Baroque artworks and architecture that had guaranteed the city a foremost place among the cultural capitals of Europe to the present day.

She and Leo had decided to visit his father on what would have been the wedding weekend as originally planned. She would stay at a small hotel not far from the flat. On arrival at the main station they made their way by tram out to the suburb where Herr Gebhardt lived. When they rang the bell, the door opened almost immediately – he had obviously been waiting for them.

'Welcome, welcome,' he said, holding the door wide open and ushering them in. His flat consisted of the ground floor of a garden house, built into the extensive back garden of a much larger house to the front. It was surrounded by lavish flower beds, and the only sound was that of the birds sending forth their last messages of bonding and possession before settling down for the night.

Leo embraced his father, who held him close for a few seconds, before turning to greet Emma.

'My dear child,' he said, 'I'm so happy to see you, but how unfortunate that things have turned out like this. Of course it's not surprising with this government, but I wish it hadn't happened to you. Come into the dining room, I have a meal ready.'

She saw that he had indeed prepared a lavish cold spread, and several bottles of his excellent wines were standing on the sideboard, a red already uncorked, and a white in a cooler. They settled at the table while he poured a pale white

A Normal Couple

into clear goblets with long golden stems. Emma was hungry, and this being so, she knew that Leo must be starving. They concentrated on the food for the first ten minutes, and Emma had time to appraise her future father-in-law, whom she had met only once before.

She knew that Leo did not always see eye to eye with his father, but she wanted to form her own opinion. Herr Gebhardt was in his early seventies, almost as tall as Leo, but he was quite portly, though he held himself very straight. His bald head did not detract from a kindly, intelligent face with even features, in which she could detect Leo's heavy cheeks and his sensuous mouth. Leo's distinctive sunken eyes and eagle nose, she realised, stemmed from his mother, whose portrait was hanging on the wall. She wished she could have got to know her too.

It was inevitable that the conversation would turn to the war. But Emma feared that this would lead to a disagreement between father and son, and so she brought up the topic of the postponed wedding instead.

'Have you been able to cancel the dinner and all your other arrangements, father?' she asked. 'I hope you haven't been left out of pocket because of this.'

'Yes, dear, fortunately I was able to do so, and I hope it won't be long before we can enjoy everything the way it was planned. Have you tried for a new date?'

Leo gave Emma a warning look.

'Yes, father, we have, but I'm afraid you'll be disappointed. We got nowhere with the office here in Dresden, but we were able to get a date in Berlin-Zehlendorf, where my parents live. It's for 10 November. Two months later. That was the earliest they could come up with. They're short of staff too, and of course lots of young couples are wanting to get married now before all the young men are called up.'

'It means having the dinner and everything else in Berlin,' said Leo.

'I realise that!' said his father, unnecessarily sharply, thought Emma. 'And I understand completely. The main thing is that you marry as soon as possible. Of course the dinner there will be my invitation, just as it was planned for here. What is your status with regards to military service, Leo?'

'I'd say it'll be a while before they get round to my year, so I'm safe for the moment. I'm just continuing on at the Ministry as usual.'

'And I've withdrawn my resignation,' added Emma. 'Our boss, Dr Bischoff, was thrilled! It's nice to be appreciated, even though he can be quite cutting at times. But anyway, I've handed in my notice now for 1 November. That'll give me time to prepare for the 10th.'

Herr Gebhardt asked how her parents were, and what her sisters were doing, and Emma related some amusing incidents from her childhood, which would give Herr Gebhardt a wider picture of her family life. At half past nine, she indicated that she was tired, and Leo said he'd walk her to the hotel, which was just five minutes away. They arranged to meet after breakfast the next morning, and to visit the cemetery before lunch. The weather forecast had been fine.

Leo was quiet on the short walk, and after she had checked in, he kissed her sadly in front of her room before saying good night. He looked very despondent as he left her, and she realised he needed comforting. But she was extremely tired, and besides, she wasn't in the best of spirits herself, so she let him go.

She fell asleep as soon as she had drawn the eiderdown up to her chin and buried her face in the pillow.

Next morning, Leo and his father collected her, as the hotel was on the way to the cemetery.

She noticed that the atmosphere between them was chilly, but she glossed over it by commenting on the weather. The forecast had once again been wrong, it was cool and drizzling. Emma was glad she'd brought her warm green suit with the long button-through jacket, which had squirrel fur on the collar and on the patch pockets. This was the latest fashion, though in fact she'd had the suit for a few years, and the fur was the result of a hunting expedition of her father's.

The cemetery was huge, and beautifully laid out, with avenues of mature trees, and hedges of yew between the individual sections. Leo's mother was resting in the grave of her parents, together with a sister who had died young. It was looking a little derelict, and Leo stooped and pulled some weeds before standing at the end with folded hands. His father had removed his hat, and Leo did likewise. They were all silent for some moments.

'Well,' said Herr Gebhardt, 'it's such a shame. My wife would love to have met you, my dear. She would really have taken to you. She'd probably tell you that this fellow doesn't deserve you at all, what with the company he keeps.'

Emma ignored the last remark and smiled. 'I can't imagine that,' she countered. 'I'm very proud of Leo, and I'm sure his mother would be equally proud of him if she could see him now, with the turn that his career has taken.' Although she was beginning to feel comfortable with her father-in-law, she didn't dare suggest that he too should be proud of his son.

'She wasn't in favour of him joining that pack of ruffians. I wasn't either.'

Leo intervened immediately.

'Now, father, we don't want to get into all that again. Not now, please.'

Herr Gebhardt took off his spectacles and polished them on the end of his scarf.

'I suggest we have lunch at Luisenhof, on the other side of the river, what do you think?' he said to Leo.

'That's an excellent idea. I'm sure Emma doesn't know it yet.'

Emma didn't. They took the rear exit from the graveyard and walked back towards town beside the river. On this side the placid Elbe was lined with water meadows; on the opposite bank a leafy escarpment rose steeply, dotted with what looked like medium-sized palaces, complete with turrets, pinnacles, huge conservatories and terraced gardens, the mansions of rich industrialists, lower nobility, and political personalities.

A stroll of half an hour took them to one of Dresden's icons, the Blue Miracle, a cantilevered truss bridge reminiscent of a horizontal Eifel Tower, painted blue. They crossed the bridge and arrived at the station of the funicular railway, which transported them halfway up the steep rise, from where a short walk brought them to the famous Luisenhof restaurant. The weather had cleared, and the view was stupendous. Emma was very impressed.

'Yes,' said Leo. 'This has earned the restaurant the by-name of "the balcony of Dresden".'

'It's easy to see why,' said Emma. 'It's been a lovely walk. Thank you for showing me all these sights. Dresden is unique!'

Not many tables were occupied yet, as it was early, and they were given seats near one of the

A Normal Couple

panorama windows; there was a low hum of conversation. Emma tried to pick out landmarks, and Leo and his father were able to identify some of the famous buildings for her. Leo located the Semper Opera House, and began to relate anecdotes, funny experiences he'd had with some of the eccentric artists who had appeared there.

It was a relaxed and pleasant meal. Leo had a wild pork roast with red cabbage and dumplings, Emma breast of chicken with poached vegetables and Father a schnitzel with parsley potatoes.

Towards the end of the meal, they were distracted by a group of boisterous young men in the mustard-coloured uniform of the NSDAP at a nearby table.

'Your friends!' said Herr Gebhardt to Leo, and called the waiter.

'Could you tell those young men to be quieter, my good man. They're disturbing our meal.'

'It's all right,' said Leo quickly. 'I'll deal with it.'

He rose and walked over to the other table. There he gave the German salute, and a few of the group responded. Emma could see that they had noticed his party button, which as usual was attached to his lapel. Leo said something to them, and one of them answered in a normal tone. Leo made another comment, and they nodded and gave short replies, then continued talking quietly among themselves as Leo returned to his chair.

'What did you say?' whispered Emma.

'I just told them to respect the uniform they were wearing and behave properly. And I asked them what they were celebrating. They were nice young lads, from good families. They probably live in the houses around here.'

'You would never have behaved like that at their age! Disgraceful young rowdies!' said his father.

'Well, there were a couple of incidents I was party to while I was a student that I'm ashamed of now, though they seemed terribly funny at the time. These young lads have all been called up. They're off to Poland in the next few days. That's what they're "celebrating".'

'If it weren't for the damn Nazis there'd be no issue with Poland! Frederick the so-called Great robbed Silesia from Austria in the Seven Years War in the 1750s, and with its large Slav population it was given to Poland in the Treaty of Versailles in 1919. That was perfectly in order and Hitler has no business marching in there now.'

'Please Father,' said Leo, in a sharp tone, 'keep your voice down. Emma, would you like some dessert? They make a wonderful apfelstrudel here.'

'No thank you,' said Emma. 'I couldn't eat another thing. It was delicious.' She began to fuss, gathering her things together, in the hope that Herr Gebhardt wouldn't continue his monologue.

Leo called the waiter for the bill. Herr Gebhardt dabbed his mouth with his cloth napkin and avoided everyone's eye.

'I'll pay for the wine,' he said.

Emma could see this didn't please Leo. Clearly he'd hoped his father would foot the whole bill. When it arrived, Leo and his father fumbled with notes and coins, until the waiter said: 'I can change a 20 Mark bill,' picked one up from the money on the table and deftly produced the change. Then Herr Gebhardt paid for the wine. Both men contributed the required number of coupons from their ration cards. Emma had risen and pretended to be concentrating on the view. It seemed neither of the Gebhardts was keen on spending money. She gave a little sigh.

They returned home by funicular and tram. As they entered the garden, Emma saw it wasn't as well tended as it had seemed in the gloaming last night. It was clear that Leo's mother had cared for it. Grass was growing between the clumps of perennials in the beds, and the roses hadn't been pruned for at least a year.

'Let's have some coffee, and then you might want to take a rest, father?' said Leo. 'Is there anything you'd like me to do for you while I'm here?'

'I have no blackout on the window of the guestroom at the back. It's so well hidden that the block warden hasn't detected it yet, but he could come poking his Nazi snout into my back garden at any time. It's ridiculous! As if the light from that room could be made out 100 metres away.' Herr Gebhardt had 25-watt bulbs in all the rooms except the sitting room. 'I don't have a blind, just a roll of black paper. Perhaps you could stick the paper straight onto the panes.'

'I'll take a look,' said Leo.

Emma helped to prepare the coffee, and they sat down in the main room. Herr Gebhardt asked Leo if he found a moment to produce any music himself nowadays, and he reminisced about the time when Leo was little, and he himself used to play the piano while his young son had stood leaning against him, singing in a clear treble. 'Those were lovely days,' he said. Leo described the country holidays he used to have on the smallholding of his great-uncle Blasius, an accomplished violinist, as he thought then, whose house was a gathering point for all the local musicians. One by one they would appear in the door of the kitchen, in their long boots and three-cornered hats, with their instruments: cello, viola, trumpet, clarinet, horn, flute, enough to form a small orchestra. They would practise in his great-uncle's house, and were often called upon to play at weddings and festivities in neighbouring villages and small towns. He himself had witnessed this as a child, and it had influenced him greatly.

Herr Gebhardt said he would, indeed, like to lie down for a while, and he retired to his bedroom. Emma and Leo tackled the window of the spare room. It was small, and sticking on the paper took no time at all. Then Leo wanted to tidy the flower beds, and Emma said she'd help. They found some shoes of his mother's that fitted her – they were much too large for her – and an apron, Leo got tools from the shed, and for an hour they uprooted weeds, deadheaded flowers, and cut back branches and twigs. She could feel that Leo was depressed and didn't feel like talking, so she worked in silence too. Now and again, though, Leo would comment on a particular flower or shrub that his mother had particularly loved, a yellow-flowering azalea, or a thick stand of autumn anemones, which were just starting to bud. 'The pure white ones, with the bright green seed head surrounded by the yellow stamens. She always said they reminded her of young virgins!'

When they re-entered the house, Herr Gebhardt was up. He had found photo albums and spread them out on a side table, together with a bottle of sweet plum schnaps and small glasses. Emma's nerves were near breaking point, and she decided to accept a glass of the fragrant schnaps to help her to relax. She wasn't at all sure that looking at photos of the happy or not-so-happy past, photos that would include his mother, was what Leo wanted right now. She had passed away only eighteen months earlier. There were charming studio photos of him as an infant on a rocking horse, dressed as a corsair complete with plumed helmet and legs outstretched, or in his first school uniform and cap, looking quizzically at the photographer. His mother progressed from an end-of-the-century lady in ground-length skirts to a mature matron in modern dresses which reached only to mid-calf. There were pictures of them motoring with Leo – he had owned a Brennabor while he was working in Leipzig – his mother in a voluminous coaching coat and a white, tight-fitting motoring hat with long side flaps, a strange contrast to her serious, intelligent face with its striking eyes and strong nose.

Supper was a repeat of the previous evening, and she was glad when Leo suggested he walk her back to her hotel.

'I can't stand it much longer,' said Leo, as soon as they were out of hearing range. The streetlights were not on, and he fiddled about with the dimmed torch he had bought, adjusting its blackout lens until he had a low beam of light which showed them the way for the next few metres. 'It's impossible to talk to him about any topic of importance. He's a radical democrat, he hates Hitler and what he stands for, he just won't see what's happening around him, the progress, the enthusiasm. The changes we're all benefiting from. He lives in the past, and it was a bad past, with mass unemployment, insecurity, no future for millions of people. You remember, we talked about it. And I'm surprised he hasn't had one of his outbursts yet. He's got himself under control because you're here, I suppose.'

'Just as well,' said Emma. 'It's only another day, Leo. What's planned for tomorrow?'

'The wedding!' said Leo, and laughed morosely. 'No, I don't know. Perhaps you and I should take off for a few hours. We could go to the Green Vault, or one of the other museums. Or there might be an afternoon concert in the Frauenkirche, where I was baptised, by the way!'

'You told me that before!' said Emma, laughing at him. 'But those are good ideas. He might even want to come with us to a concert. If there was one in the Church of the Holy Cross, I'd like that. Their choir is so famous and I've never heard them.'

'I should be more tolerant of him, I suppose. He's probably lonely. But it's his own fault. He fights with everyone sooner or later, and so he has few friends. The ones he has now are staying in touch purely for my mother's sake, I'm sure.'

'We could get a steamer to go upriver to Pillnitz Palace, if the weather is suitable,' suggested Emma. 'I've been there, but it doesn't matter. It's such a lovely trip and would give us things to talk about that are safe.'

'Right,' said Leo. 'We'll find a suitable programme. But now it's time for us to say goodnight to each other. Dear sweet Em, you've been so brave here, and a great help, I must say.' And he folded her in his arms and bent his head to kiss her.

'You're the best thing that has ever happened to me,' he murmured, as he kissed the top of her head.

They were occupied with each other for twenty minutes. When she finally reached her own room, she collapsed into bed and again fell asleep right away.

13

10 September: Visiting Leo's Father, Part 2

When Leo arrived to pick her up the next morning, he was in a foul mood.

'He's been at me all during breakfast. He's been listening to some foreign station. He can get into such trouble if he's caught! The German army is closing in on Warsaw. I don't know what he wants me to do about it. If the Führer thinks it's necessary, there must be a valid reason for it. Of course I wish it wasn't happening. But he's using it as a pretext for criticising me for all the things I did in the past that he didn't approve of.'

'Let's go over and decide what we're doing today, and distract him from this train of thought. It might be best if you and I went off alone for a while. Cheer up, Leo dear, only another few hours.'

When they arrived at the flat, Herr Gebhardt was sitting in an armchair, reading the paper.

'Good morning, my dear. I hope you slept well and weren't troubled by what's happening in the world around us.'

Emma chipped in immediately.

'Oh, I slept like a log, after that lovely day yesterday. The weather is so fine today, we thought we could all take the steamer to Pillnitz. What do you think, father?'

Herr Gebhardt stared at her for a moment. Leo was busy in the spare room.

'What do you think of all this? This war in Poland? What does your father think? From what I've heard, he's a very sensible man.'

'I know little about it,' answered Emma, 'but we've only just had a terrible war, and we'll be paying for it for a very long time, so it doesn't seem such a good idea to start another one now. I mean, war is always bad, isn't it?'

She was not going to bring her father's opinions into the conversation.

She continued, 'But father, really, let's not waste time discussing this sad situation. Who knows how long we'll be able to do simple things like taking a steamer upriver for a few hours? This was supposed to be our wedding day, and both Leo and I would like to spend it in as pleasant a way as possible.'

Herr Gebhardt pulled himself up heavily from his chair and came over to her. He patted her cheek.

'My Hedwig would really have loved you,' was all he said, and he went out to get his coat.

But when they reached the embarkation stage for the pleasure boats, they experienced a disappointment. Everything had been cancelled. The war. All three were annoyed with themselves for not having thought of it.

'We could go into the Green Vault instead,' suggested Leo. 'That should be open.'

Emma concurred, but Herr Gebhardt said: 'That's not for me. I've seen it so often, and anyway, I think it's all overrated. All those appallingly expensive jewels, sparkling and gaudy, they're not even in good taste! What a waste of good public money! August could have done so much more for his country than to accumulate these baubles.'

'He *has* done something for the city,' said Leo sharply. 'These baubles, as you call them, are a huge tourist attraction, and as you know yourself, that's a major economic factor in the city budget. And anyway, you can't judge past actions by today's standards of morality and ....'

His father interrupted him loudly.

'Don't talk to me about morality! I'm surprised you still know the word. True morality is timeless and was as valid in August's day as it is in Herr Hitler's. Though when I see what that twirp is up to, perhaps I do favour August's way of life. At least his jewellers and their families lived well, which is more than I can say for hundreds of thousands of Jews and Poles right now!'

'Father, how can you dare to talk like this in front of Emma?! You're endangering all of us! Keep your voice down!' said Leo in an icy tone.

'Yes, keep my voice down. Great times these, when a man can't speak his mind in public because he might be arrested and stuck in a concentration camp. Is that what we've come to?! Living like mice while those people lord it over us!'

But Leo had turned and was walking away, and Emma ran after him. She caught his arm.

'Leo, Leo, stop. We must get this under control! Wait!'

He strode on, and she trotted beside him. Then she stopped and looked back at his father. He was standing by himself, leaning on his walking stick with both hands, his head bowed. Despite his mass, he looked old and frail.

'I'm going back to your father,' she called after Leo, and returned to the lonely figure.

'Now father,' she began, before he had a chance to say anything. 'We'll try to sort this out. Leo can't do anything about the present situation, and even less about what Elector August did two hundred years ago. We're here for only another few hours – let's try and spend them in harmony.' She took one of his hands in both of hers.

'Yes, my dear, you're right. I'm sorry. It's just ... He's wasting his talents supporting those criminals. I'm just afraid he'll have to pay for it some day. All right, I'll stop. Can you get that young scoundrel of yours to join us again?'

Leo had stopped to light a cigarette. He drew on it a couple of times, then walked back to them.

Again Emma took the lead. 'Let's get a cup of coffee somewhere. I think we can all do with some refreshment. Then I'd like to see the Procession of Princes, and maybe take a peek in the Church of Our Lady, to see the font where Leo was christened. Have they put up a plaque to him yet?'

Herr Gebhardt gave a little smile to support her attempt to lighten the atmosphere, but Leo remained grim. Fifteen minutes later they were sipping their coffees in the nearby café-restaurant, The Italian Village, and Ferdinand explained the origin of the café's unusual name.

'When August the Strong was offered the crown of Poland, he had to convert to Catholicism. His successor built this church that we can see over there,' – pointing at the cathedral on the other side of the square – 'the Catholic Church of the Royal Court, for which he imported Italian master builders and artisans who were housed in a little village specially built for them. It was located here on this site where the café is now.'

Afterwards they walked around the historical city centre, stopping to have a light lunch at an inn in the street where Herr Gebhardt's shop used to be. Then they decided to return home to have a rest. It had been quite warm and humid, and they were all three tired, and not just physically.

Emma woke from her nap to the sound of loud voices coming from the good room. She tidied her hair, plucked up her courage, and joined Leo and his father. It turned out that Herr Gebhardt had been listening to a Polish station. He had learnt Polish as a child from the mixed German and Polish population in the region where he grew up. Now he was obviously beside himself.

'Father, I'm sure it will be over in ...' Leo was trying to say.

'Don't be an idiot! Do you think when they've taken Warsaw they'll just settle in their armchairs and enjoy the beer? They'll devastate the town; they'll murder anyone and everyone that shows the slightest sign of opposition! It will be catastrophic! Why can't you see that? Where is all this going to end? Hitler won't stop at Poland, mark my words! This will end in a disaster for all of us!'

'Please, father, I hope you're wrong, but there's nothing we can do about it ....'

'Oh yes there is! We can stop supporting the organisations that are behind all this! We can stop voting for Hitler and his cronies. We can leave his Nazi party and speak our minds in public places about why we're doing this.'

'There's no way we can do that, and you know....'

'And why not? Are you one of them? Do you want this to happen? Do you want your wife and your children to grow up in a dictatorship? Where an individual is worth nothing and the state everything? Where we're marionettes of corrupt and dangerous politicians? I wouldn't even want to call them that! We had honourable politicians in the past. These people are scum. Scum!'

And he lifted a book that was lying on the table and banged it down again violently.

Leo turned to Emma. He was pale.

'We're leaving,' he said. 'There's no point in staying here any longer.' He turned to his father.

'Father, Emma and I are going to leave now. This has been the most disastrous weekend in my life. I'm sorry we have to part like this, but I don't want to subject Emma to this kind of talk any longer, and it's not what we had hoped for when we came to see you.'

Emma was highly embarrassed and speechless. Herr Gebhardt glared at them both.

'You do what you like! You young people! You think you know everything!' And he turned and left the room. She heard his bedroom door slam.

'I'm going to pack my things,' said Leo, and also left the room.

Emma collapsed in a chair, shaking. When Leo re-joined her some minutes later, she had calmed down sufficiently to give him a little smile of encouragement.

'I'll just say good-bye to him,' said Emma. She knocked on the bedroom door, and when there was no reply, she opened it carefully. Herr Gebhardt was sitting in an armchair near the window, his head in his hands. She walked over to him.

'We have to go, father,' she said. 'I'm so sorry you're so upset. We'll write to you from Berlin. Please look after yourself. Is there anything I can bring you before we leave?'

He turned to her. 'No, my dear. I think it's best if you both go now. I'm so disappointed in Leo. He's not a bad person, I know that. I just can't understand why he ....'

'I know,' Emma interrupted him. 'But he is what he is. I'm sure you and he will come together again soon, and that we can meet in happier circumstances.'

'I doubt it,' he said grimly, but he stood up and gave her a peck on the cheek. 'Look after him. You've no idea how reassuring it is for me to know you're at his side.'

'Good-bye, then, father.' And she left the room, closing the door behind her softly.

'Don't you want to say good-bye to him too?' she asked Leo. 'You can't leave him like this.'

Leo went into his father's room, and came out after a minute. They put on their coats, Leo took his bags, and they departed for Emma's hotel to check her out.

The sun had set by the time they arrived at the flat in Charlottenburg. They were both starving, so they dropped the bags upstairs and went into the pub on the corner of their apartment block. Leo ordered a bowl of potato soup with two frankfurters and an extra third, and bread on the side, and Emma chose a cheese omelette with parsley potatoes and green vegetables. They both took a dessert too, Emma a piece of chocolate cake with a hot cherry sauce, and Leo a large piece of cheesecake, though there was no cream.

'That feels better,' said Leo, pushing his chair back. 'Poor father. He makes life difficult for himself and all those around him. He gave my poor mother a terrible time. She often cried about him when we were alone.'

'Did they have political differences too?'

'Oh no. But she had ideas of her own about how to do things and about what was right and wrong, and he never granted her any freedom of thought. He has a despotic streak. Everything had to be done the way he wanted, and if his napkin wasn't lying in the proper place he used to get a tantrum. Stupid details that no one would be concerned about. He kept her very short of money too, so that she had to beg for every penny when she went shopping, and to account for every penny she spent. He was a tyrant.'

'It must have been very hard for her when he refused to support you after you decided to take up music instead of law.'

'Yes, it was. She used to send me things whenever she could, shirts she'd sewn or socks she'd knitted. Without telling him. When they both came to Innsbruck for my PhD conferral and she visited me in my digs, she began to cry when she saw how small my bed was. My father was, in fact, proud of me by then, and he even paid for the celebration dinner. We got on better after that. But we still had our moments.'

They both ordered new drinks, he a beer and she a glass of white wine, and chatted about the weekend and what it would be like back in the office, now that they were *not* married. Emma had to laugh when she imagined the faces of her co-workers.

There was silence for a moment, and then Leo said: 'Em, my darling, I want to ask you something. Today was to have been our wedding day. In the normal course of things, we'd be on our own now, or a little later, and tonight we'd be spending our first night together. In my mind, we're married already. We know that we're going to get married officially as soon as possible, and it's not our fault that we aren't already. In spirit we've been married for a long time, don't you feel that too? Stay with me tonight in the flat, and let us celebrate our wedding as if everything had worked out the way we'd planned. – Please don't be upset. Please say yes.'

Emma coloured. She fiddled with the cake fork on the table. She didn't dare tell him that the same thought had occurred to her a little earlier, when he was talking about his mother.

'My parents don't know I'm here already,' she said thoughtfully. 'No one need know.'

'That means yes?'

'It looks like it,' she said bravely, and gave him a lovely smile which made his heart jump. He was smiling himself now, and called the waiter to pay the bill and leave his coupons. He left a big tip on the table.

Together they walked out into the street. The air was cool. It was dark; the only light was that of a candle in the window of the inn they'd just left. At the end of the long straight street they could see a crescent moon greeting them between the thinning leaves of the trees. A late blackbird in the nearby park was issuing its first pearly tones.

'This is just too romantic,' said Emma with a giggle. Hand in hand they slipped round the corner and into the building which was to be their home for the coming years.

14

Early October: Emma is worried

'Emmi, is anything bothering you? You've been much more serious than usual. I'm getting worried about you.'

Franzi had been observing her sister closely since the cancelled wedding, looking for signs of depression. At first everything seemed normal, or at least what might be considered normal in the circumstances, but there had been a change in the past few days that had not escaped her notice. Emma spoke even less than usual, she looked tired, and any time she didn't spend with Leo she hid herself in her bedroom.

Emma gave her a startled look.

'Come up into my room, Fra,' she said quietly. Her parents were in the sitting room round the corner, reading and talking.

'What is it?' asked Fra, when she was settled in Em's little basket armchair. Emma sat on the edge of the bed.

'Didn't you do a basic medical course when you were doing your physiotherapy training?' Emma wanted to know.

'Yes, we did. Why, what's wrong?' Her face expressed concern.

'Do you know how long a period can be delayed, if everything is normal?'

'Emma! You haven't ...!'

Emma coloured deeply.

'When was your last period? When was this one due?'

'At the end of August. It should have started around 28 September.'

'That's a week ago. Today is the 5th. Will you tell me what happened?' Franzi asked carefully.

Emma had already told her family some of the events of the fateful weekend in Dresden. Now she confessed to her sister that she and Leo had returned a day early, and that they had spent the night together in the flat. And that she been there together with him more than once since then.

'Well,' said Franzi, taking a deep breath, 'it's quite possible then that you're pregnant, my love. Oh dear, Em, what a conundrum! You must have been so worried. Why didn't you tell me earlier!'

Emma stared at her feet, turning them from side to side. Franzi moved onto the bed beside her sister and threw her arms around her.

'But you know,' continued Franzi, 'it's not the end of the world. You'll be getting married in six weeks or so, and you won't be showing by then, so nobody need know. Then you'll just say you got pregnant right away. Of course Ma might begin to wonder at how fast you're growing, but she won't say anything. Don't worry, dear Em, it just means you and Leo won't have much time to really get used to living together. Once a child is there you'll have your hands full.'

Emma smiled. 'It sounds as if you've had loads of children already. The voice of experience.'

'The women I treat tell me all about it.' She looked at her strong hands and pulled her fingers through her short, thick hair. 'All with ruined backs from carrying heavy children around.' Franzi had got a job in the physiotherapy department of the Charité Hospital where she had done her training.

'Really – it's wonderful news! I'm *pleased* for you, and you'll be pleased too, once you get used to the idea. I don't suppose you've told Leo anything yet.'

'No, of course not.'

'But Em, you know – how could this happen? Did neither of you use any kind of contraception? A cap? Or a sheath?'

'A what?'

'A sheath, a rubber. Protection. Em, don't tell me you don't know what a rubber is! The man pulls it over his thing, it's like a rubber balloon, so there's no direct ... exchange ... with the woman. So she can't get pregnant.'

'No, I don't think so.'

'And I suppose you don't know what a Dutch cap is either?' asked Franzi more severely. 'I could have got you one.'

Emma shook her head.

'It really was very naïve of both of you. Did Leo not ask you if you had any protection? He must have known what could happen!'

Emma said nothing.

'It was very irresponsible of him! Well, it's too late now, anyway. No point in closing the barn door after the horse has bolted.'

Emma gave a weak smile. 'What an expression!'

'Now tell me, Em, did you at least enjoy your ... experience?'

'Yes and no, to be honest. I didn't know what to expect, how could I? In fact, if you hadn't told me something about how children are produced I would have been so scared. You know that we've hugged and kissed and ... once Leo put his hand inside my blouse and felt my breast. I didn't feel anything, but he seemed to like it a lot, so I let him go on. What I really like is lying in his arms and having him caress me. That feels nice. But the other business – it's really strange.'

'Was it very painful?'

'No, not very. It's better now than it was at first. Oh Franzi, it's all so strange! Why have we not learnt about all this? I mean, is it normal to enter into a completely new experience like this without any preparation? The only advice Ma gave me, just before our first wedding date, was: "Make sure he doesn't come every night." At the time I didn't even know what she meant!'

'I know. It reminds me of when I got my first period. I had blood in my pants at school, hadn't a clue what was happening. We had Fräulein Schiller that day, and I asked her if I could go home, I wasn't feeling well. She asked me what exactly was wrong, and I told her I was bleeding – down there. "Is this the first time?" she asked me, and when I said yes, she asked if my mother had prepared me. I didn't know what she meant, and she gave a loud "Pshaw!" Then she rummaged in her big handbag and produced a sanitary towel. I didn't know what it was, but she told me what to do with it, and then to go home. "And give my regards to your mother and tell her to do her duty by you!" She was very kind. She told me not to worry, that it was normal, it happened to all women, my mother would tell me.'

'And did she?' Emma was smiling, recalling an almost identical experience – and its aftermath.

'Of course not! She just told me to write down the date, and that this would happen every twenty-eight days, and where the sanitary towels were kept, and the rubber bands for clipping them into. But not a word about why.'

'And the pains!' said Emma. 'I had to beg her for something when they got so bad. "It's our punishment for being women," was all she said. Can you imagine! Fra, where would we be now if you hadn't done that physio course?!'

'Really, Ma is hopeless. If I think about it too long I could get quite angry at her. I hope you'll get to enjoy being close to Leo ...'

Emma interrupted: 'Have you and Moritz ...?'

Fra went slightly pink, which she rarely did. 'Well, now you mention it, I think there were one or two incidents of the type you mean. But he associates with very, very experienced men of the world, and he knows about all the precautions and where to get them.'

'And do you like it?'

'Yes, I must say I do. You know, Em, people are different. Lise, for example. She told me that she and Benno have a fantastic ... married ... life. She really goes for it. She says sometimes she can't get enough. She told me it's the most intense feeling she's ever experienced and she couldn't live without it any more. My goodness! I could hardly stop her running on about it! She's mad! But bully for her. It's a big part of being married. Men seem to go for it much more than women, so if you can have fun, like the men do, all the better.'

'My goodness, Franzi! To think you're five years younger than I am, and you know all this!'

'Oh, Lise said she could never talk to you like this. She thinks you're ... shy.'

Lise had actually said 'inhibited', but Franzi thought it a cruel word, and the last thing she wanted to do was to hurt her older sister. She gave her a hug.

A Normal Couple

'You know, Em, it might be a good idea if you took your normal supply of sanitary towels from the store, in case Ma notices they haven't been used and launches into one of her probing interrogations.'

'Yes, I've done that already. I hate going behind her back, but I couldn't face her reaction if she knew. And if she was ranting on about it, Pa would find out too, and that would break my heart.'

'Maybe, and maybe not. In the last resort, he's a pragmatist. But – better let sleeping dogs lie. Just hold onto the towels until you need them again. – My angel, I must fly. There's a refresher course in the institute this evening that I have to attend. Is Leo around at the moment? You'll have to tell him soon. I wonder what he'll say!'

Emma had had the same thought. 'No, he's in the Rhineland, at some conference. He'll be back at the weekend.'

'Thank you for making me an aunt! And Ma and Pa will be delighted to be grandparents. Don't worry. Take care of yourself. Eat well, don't overdo things, and if you feel tired, lie down and get some rest. I'll try to get some more information from my contacts.'

Emma laughed and gave her sister a kiss, and they parted. How lucky she was to have Fra!

15

10 November: The Wedding

The 10 November was grey and drizzly, not the type of weather she would have ordered for her wedding day, thought Emma, as she drew aside the heavy bedroom curtains to let in the daylight. It made little difference. At this stage she didn't much care. The only thing that mattered was that she and Leo should be married today, that no further stumbling blocks be laid in their way – the assassination attempt on Hitler in the Hofbräuhaus only three days previously had caused her to panic. Nothing else must occur to prevent her becoming a legally wedded wife and the mother of a legitimate child.

Franzi poked her head round the door and then knocked.

'I thought I heard you moving,' she whispered. 'Can I help you to get ready? How do you feel?'

'Fine, so far. I bought some oranges yesterday, so I'll be all right if and when I get the yearn. I don't think I need your help, Franzi dear. Perhaps later, with my make-up ...'

'I'll start the breakfast,' said Franzi, and disappeared.

Emma washed and slipped into her new underwear, pale green silk with a matching slip, and then the dark green heavy silk dress she'd bought in August. It was not quite warm enough for November, but it would do. It had a blouse top with a narrow mandarin collar and was buttoned through, ending just below the knee. Her cut bead amber necklace would look very pretty against the green background; the pale orange buckles on her green leather pumps added the perfect matching touch. Leo would be wearing a dark suit with a pale grey waistcoat.

She pulled up and secured her silk stockings and then turned around in front of her full-length mirror to make sure the seams were straight. She stood sideways and examined her waist and stomach, but they were the same as usual. And her breasts? Weren't they more prominent than normal? That would be nice! Give her a better figure, she was really much too flat up there. People would think she had used pads for a special effect for the occasion. She patted her hair, which was fuller today – she'd been to a hairdresser the day before, and Franzi would set it for her later.

Downstairs, the family were already at breakfast. Her parents looked up when she came in. Lise and Benno had motored down yesterday; Moritz would be arriving in his car at 10.00, and the two cars would bring the whole party to the registry office in Zehlendorf town hall, where Leo and his father, Aunt Charlotte and the von Frankens would be waiting. The ceremony was to take place at 11.00.

Lise and Franzi were in high spirits at breakfast, and Emma began to emerge from the strange mood, close to apathy, that she had woken up with. She drank some coffee, and then peeled one of the oranges she'd made sure to have on hand. She hoped her mother hadn't noticed that she was eating them all the time. To play down the orange, she also cut open a roll and buttered it lightly, but felt her stomach retching at the fat, so she pushed it aside.

After breakfast, Franzi and Lise went upstairs with Emma and worked on her hair and makeup. Her heart lifted when she looked at herself in the mirror: a touch of eyeshadow had made her eyes large and dark; lipstick with a shade of orange, and a hint of rouge, gave her face a fresh appearance. Her fingernails had been manicured by Lise and were the same colour. She looked a question at her younger sisters, and they both blew her kisses.

'Don't worry!' said Lise in her husky voice. 'He'll take you!'

The doorbell rang, and Franzi raced downstairs to let Moritz in. Lise and Emma went down to greet him, and as usual whenever she saw him, Emma blushed slightly. He was so handsome, very tall, with athletic shoulders, black hair and straight eyebrows over blue-grey eyes – he could have been a film star! He was in full dress uniform, the Luftwaffe insignia on his right breast and the rarely awarded Cross of Spain in Gold in his top buttonhole. He gave her a warm smile, and instead of taking her hand in his, he raised it towards his lips, with a slight bow indicating a kiss.

'You look wonderful,' he said. 'Fra, you're lucky I saw you first, or you might have been left standing in the queue for a beau.' And he gave his fiancée a peck on the cheek.

Everyone bundled into coats, wraps, hats and gloves, Elisabeth stealing the show with her huge Siberian fox collar, which fell over her shoulders and reached almost to her waist. Pa was in a

A Normal Couple

morning suit with a wing collar and a neck cloth, looking very distinguished in a 1920s manner.

Emma, Franzi and Elisabeth climbed into Moritz's car, a Brennabor, which had a roomy interior, while Lise and Pa squeezed into Benno's little Adler.

Leo and his father were standing outside Zehlendorf Town Hall when they arrived, chatting to Aunt Charlotte and the von Frankens. Of her father's many other siblings, only Uncle Hans and his family, and Uncle Otto, who was unmarried, had come. Everyone else, even her friend Marie, had sent their heartfelt regrets – they didn't want to risk a longer journey right now. Franzi was annoyed to see that Uncle Otto was wearing his mustard-coloured Nazi uniform, while all the other men, except for Moritz, were in formal dress. Under their furs and soft wraps, she could make out the fine materials and glistening colours of the ladies' ornate robes. Apart from the mustard, they were a noble gathering.

Emma had eyes only for Leo, and went straight to him before greeting his father. She still felt it was all unreal, as if it wasn't she who was getting married here. The gloomy morning echoed her mood – it seemed reluctant to produce proper daylight. Leo, by contrast, looked so happy, tall, slightly pale, his eyes glowing – a striking gentleman, and even his father's stern face was wearing a smile as he, too, raised her hand to his lips in greeting.

Moritz had been rooting in the boot of his car and now produced a picnic basket with a bottle of Veuve Clicquot and glasses wrapped in snow-white linen napkins.

'A toast to the bride and groom! They need reinforcement for what's coming at them!' he

141

called. He poured a little champagne into the glasses, which Franzi and Lise handed round.

'To Leo and Emma!' Emma was glad of a sip of alcohol. She felt it making its way through her arms and chest, and felt livelier and more aware as a result.

Uncle Otto cleared his throat and clinked his signet ring on his glass. Reluctantly, the others fell silent.

'Dear bridal couple, dear family and friends, I am proud to be here today in the honoured uniform of my Führer to witness the wedding of my beloved niece Emma! May I congratulate her on her choice of a partner, one who will bring prestige and progress to our family and our race. Leo, my dear nephew, welcome to our family. We, who ...'

'Hear hear!' interrupted Paul loudly. 'To Emma and Leo!' And the rest of the group quickly raised their glasses and drank the toast, before hastening indoors out of the cold.

'Have you got the rings?' Emma whispered to Leo, and he patted his pocket reassuringly. Franzi joined them, and touched up Emma's face, and then produced a small bouquet of orange chrysanthemums and white asters for her to carry.

'Try to cheer up!' she whispered. 'Everyone is so happy for you, and you should be too. Dear Em, it's the start of a new life. You and Leo will be in charge from now on! Let me see you smile. Come on!'

Emma felt her eyes moisten, but she pulled herself together, and gave her beloved sister a big smile.

'I'll be fine once this is over,' she answered. 'Don't worry. I'm all right. Which door do we take?'

At that moment, one of the five doors in the wide lobby opened, and a wedding party emerged, a very young bride in white, flushed and laughing, and her equally youthful husband, followed by family and friends. Noisily they took possession of the hall, while Emma's much smaller party stood to one side. Moritz cleared his throat loudly – it seemed he was about to make a reprimanding comment, but Franzi stopped him.

'They're just young people. Leave them. Who knows how long they'll be together before he's sent to the front.'

Ten minutes later their names were called, and they filed through the open door. The registrar, an elderly man with doughy cheeks, thin hair sleeked back, and bloodshot eyes, waited until everyone had settled in the semicircle of chairs in front of his desk before welcoming them and starting the ceremony.

After twenty minutes it was all over. Emma Marc had disappeared – she had become Emma Gebhardt.

Immediately she began to feel better. As Leo slipped the ring onto her finger, and they kissed, she felt an unexpected surge of happiness such as she had never experienced before. Franzi was right – a new future was opening up for her, but now it wasn't just her, but *them*, and soon they would be three. She would look after her home and her baby and her husband, helping him in his work by providing a pleasant refuge for him to return to each night, and together they would plan, and undertake holidays, and make decisions, and be there to help and comfort and listen to each other, and sympathise and advise – all the pleasant dealings that make up a successful, trusting partnership between husband and wife. They would hide nothing from each other, and share all their problems, misgivings, joys, successes, failures. They would be as one person.

She smiled to herself as all these thoughts flashed before her inner eye, for she knew it would not be like this. Of course there would be misunderstandings, disagreements, contrasting opinions – but she trusted that they would always be able to reach a consensus and ultimately find solutions to any difficulties together. They loved each other deeply, and felt more at ease in each other's company than anywhere else. That was all that mattered. That was the basis of their partnership.

Showing her happiest, most infectious smile, she allowed herself to be congratulated by her parents, sisters and their partners, her aunts and uncles, and by her new father-in-law. He paid her a lovely compliment:

'My dear Emma, welcome to our tiny family. You are a jewel and an enrichment, and I cannot think of anyone I would rather see at the side of my dear son than you. My blessing on you both. If ever you need help, I will do whatever is in my power. You can always depend on me.'

The whole party moved across the Town Hall Square to the Flensburger Hof, where a long table had been set for a festive lunch. The low-ceilinged room resonated with animated conversation and the clinking of cutlery on plates. Later, Herr von Franken made a short speech in which he stressed the talents and gentle character of his niece, and congratulated Leo on his good taste in choosing such a perfect partner. Soft laughter and appreciative murmurs accompanied the applause. Other toasts followed, by Uncle Hans and even by brother-in-law Benno. With a sigh, Emma saw Uncle Otto rising from his chair.

'Dear wedding party,' he began. 'This is a special day not just for our happy couple, but, in a humble manner, for our whole nation. We are all aware of the importance of marriage and family in the central plans of our Führer, to enable our nation to grow and to pass its beneficial influence on to other less fortunate regions of the world. Emma and Leo, may your marriage be blessed with happiness and fortune in the form of sons and daughters, who will bring joy to you both and to our whole nation. I am here today, in the honoured uniform of our beloved Führer, to pro...'

'Yes!' hissed Elisabeth, so that half the company could hear her. 'Because he can't afford a *cut!*'

Franzi laughed out loud, and others were smiling, so that Uncle Otto, who hadn't heard the remark, was distracted and lost his thread.

'To Emma and Leo,' he finished lamely, and raised his glass.

By the time they returned to the house in Flensburger Strasse, it had stopped drizzling, and so the families gathered in the back garden for photos: the three parents with the newly-weds, the three young couples, the newly-weds on their own. The whole party.

Shivering, they were glad to move into the reception rooms – the big connecting doors had been opened – for coffee and liqueurs. The men lit cigars, and Elisabeth and Franzi cigarettes. Benno turned on the radio and found a station broadcasting dance music. The war in Poland had ended a month ago, after a duration of only five weeks, with the fall of Warsaw and the Polish capitulation. The invasion by Germany's ally Russia on the eastern border of the country had speeded up the campaign. Now Poland was being divided up between its two powerful neighbours. Fortunately, and unexpectedly, France and England had not moved after declaring war. At any rate, it meant that light music was no longer non grata, and it played softly in the background to the hum of voices and laughing.

After a while, the women disappeared into the kitchen to prepare the supper, leaving the men to themselves.

Herr Marc and Herr Gebhardt were trying to find common topics, not an easy undertaking. Paul's hobbies were gardening and hunting, while Herr Gebhardt was really only interested in wine and socialist politics. Ferdinand politely asked Paul where he had shot the magnificent capercaillie in the hall, where it was mounted with wings outspread above the door into the dining room.

'That was on a shoot of a colleague of mine in West Prussia, near Elbing, where we used to live. It was a wonderful morning in winter, deep snow on the ground crunching underfoot, a freezing sun just rising, as we set off with our dogs from the hunting lodge where we'd spent the night. Our guide knew where the capercaillies gathered, and sure enough we saw them in the distance. They're extremely shy, so we had to advance on them on our stomachs, not very comfortable in the snow. The dogs were panting with excitement, but cowered down as we commanded. Centimetre by centimetre we crawled closer to them till we were within range and could get a clear shot, and my first try was a hit.'

Herr Gebhardt's eyes were slightly glazed. West Prussia was flat and had no vineyards. He'd never been there.

'The only thing I know about hunting is what I gleaned from a book by a Russian author, Turgenev, "Reflections of a Hunter", which is mostly about the atrocious conditions under which the country population in Russia was living in the mid-1900s. It's unpopular to say so nowadays, if not dangerous, but the Russian revolution was long overdue. Perhaps you know it? He describes how hard the serfs had to work and how little they got to eat. Admittedly, many of the landlords were also very poor – the whole system needed reforming.'

'Their agricultural methods were completely outmoded,' began Paul, and launched on an account of the farming estate of his uncle Wolff, where he used to spend his holidays. Uncle Wolff was very progressive in his farming ideas and introduced modern machinery and also new types of crop plants which produced higher yields.

And so on. Leo, who was listening to the two older men with half an ear, was amused, and left them to it. He glanced across the room to where Aunt Charlotte and the von Frankens were deep in conversation; he couldn't imagine what they were talking about. He turned in the other direction, where Lise's husband Benno and Moritz had their heads together. Benno had met Moritz once or twice, but had never had a chance to talk to him.

'Lise tells me you were in Spain for a few years with the Condor Legion,' said Benno.

'Yes, I was. I started training as a criminal investigator, but when the chance came to join the Luftwaffe, I grabbed it. It changed my life completely, I must say. Best move I ever took.'

'It certainly sounds very adventurous.'

'Doesn't it just! Flying itself is wonderful. Being up in the air, released from the ground, turning the aircraft this way and that. At times the horizon is below, at times at eye level, and then again above me! Great fun! You need strong nerves. Mind you, it was tough enough in Spain. The heat in the summer! And often no water, no place to wash for days on end. And freezing in winter. No heating.'

'Did you get much combat experience?'

'A fair bit, though I only had one strike. Not much compared to some. I'm a fighter pilot, fly a Messerschmitt 109, which is very nippy, great for aerial combat. My main task in Spain, though, was as liaison officer between the German Luftwaffe and the Spanish air force, such as it was. My Spanish is pretty good, since I used to visit an uncle who lived in Spain quite often when I was a kid. In the end I stayed in Spain all of four years, during the whole civil war, while the run-of-the-mill pilots just got three months' experience and were then exchanged. Mind you, not a bad system. We have a large number of experienced pilots to fall back on, now that it's getting serious here. Or might get, if and when England wakes up and decides to make a move.'

'Can't say it's something I'm looking forward to,' said Benno drily. 'I'm working in a clinic north of Berlin at present, but there's a good chance that the Army will be sending me to some godforsaken place in Poland. For the benefit of the occupying forces, and perhaps of the locals, though I gather they're of secondary importance. At any rate, Lise and I will be cut off from civilization for years.' And he stared morosely into his empty cognac glass.

Moritz launched into a long, amusing story of a bizarre wine-tasting he'd experienced in Spain, together with two hospitable tramps, unshaven in their well-worn collarless shirts, one of whom, it turned out, was the local lord mayor and the richest man in the area, and the other the chief of police.

'The caves in the hillside for storing the wine were many hundreds of years old,' said Moritz, 'and held absolutely enormous barrels of wine. We were told to choose which we wanted to taste. I'd been on a wine-tasting tour in the Rhineland, so I knew what to do: I stole around until I found a small cask hidden in a dark corner. "Ah!", said the owner, "you have the nose! That's the most valuable wine we have here!" And he poured it for us. A red wine which had taken on an orange tint – it was fifty years old and went down like honey. Such generosity! None of us really remembers how we got down the mountainside and home after that.'

Paul and Ferdinand had been listening to him, and a general conversation about great wines of the past, unforgettable drinking experiences, and remarkable characters among the vintners developed, leading to a lively exchange with much laughter.

'... Schriesheimer Kuhberg Cabinet, a Sylvaner, 1934, unsurpassable, a wine of the century,' Herr Gebhardt was proclaiming, 'and what does he do? He adds soda water to it! Americans! Barbarians!!'

Uncle Otto moved over to stand beside Leo.

'When did you join the Party, Herr Gebhardt?' he asked.

Leo glanced at him. 'In 1933,' he answered shortly.

'I've been a member since 1929,' said Otto proudly. 'It was clear to me very early on that our future lay in the hands of this genius. The history of our nation and our race is being rewritten, and I'm proud to be able to contribute my humble bit to the glorious future which lies ahead.'

'Indeed,' commented Leo. 'I must say this Armagnac is exceptionally good, don't you agree?'

Uncle Otto stared at his liqueur glass is if he'd only just realised that it was in his hand.

At that moment Franzi and Emma entered with trays of snacks and pumpernickel sandwiches and sweet-smelling rolls, crisp on the outside, fluffy inside, thickly spread with fine cheeses, sausage meats, gherkins, sliced chicken. Paul went into the unheated veranda where some bottles of white were cooling, and then opened the reds he'd left in the front room. He wondered if Herr Gebhardt would approve of his selection. Benno chose a beer. Plates with forks and napkins were distributed, and soon the clink of cutlery on china was the predominant sound in the dining-room, as the company fell on the food. Emma was suddenly aware that she was really hungry. She'd only picked at her lunch, but now she chose a smoked meat roll decorated with a slice of orange and some capers, and ate it with relish.

Suddenly the lights went off. Exclamations of surprise! The door opened, and Lise came in with a large, iced cake, in the middle of which were three or four sparklers in full glitter. Ooohs and aaahs and applause greeted her, Emma and Leo were called to cut the cake together, and then Paul tapped his spoon on his glass and announced that he was going to make a speech. He rose.

'Herr Gebhardt, my dear family,' he began. 'This is one of the happiest days of my life, and I am delighted to see you all here together. But it is also a sad day, for my beloved Emma is passing out of my ... jurisdiction ...' – smiles from the listeners – 'into the hands of this fine gentleman, whom I am proud to call my new son. My blessing and best wishes be with both of you, my children, for a healthy, and safe, and prosperous future, in mutual harmony and well-being.'

Murmurs of 'Hear hear!' from his listeners.

'It is uncertain when the future will allow us an opportunity such as we have now, where all the family, and only the family, are assembled. I would like to use it to pass on to you some thoughts which have been going through my mind in recent days.'

He paused for a moment, and gave his little dry cough.

'Unfortunately, the present time is one which brings with it many question marks about the future. Every era confronts the people living in it with boundaries, trends, rules, a culture, which affect their own will and activities in one way or another, sometimes more, sometimes less. The life we live is always a compromise with our surroundings. It is up to the individual to find his way in this maze, to live his life as fully as he can in the environment in which he finds himself.'

His listeners were very quiet. Herr Gebhardt had his eyes glued on Paul. Moritz and Leo were staring at their shoes, listening intently. Benno was trying to keep his eyes open. Lise was staring out the window, wondering whether she and Benno would get back home before midnight, it was such a long drive. Franzi and Emma had their eyes on their father's hands, which rested on the table in front of him – they were trembling slightly. Elisabeth was annoyed: how could he start such a serious lecture on this of all days! Uncle Otto was frowning.

'What I want to tell you today is that no individual is alone in the decision he takes when finding his way. He is supported by the law. By natural law. There are many kinds of law, as you know. They change and come and go, but there has always been one natural law. It was first written about by the Greeks, and was firmly outlined a thousand years ago by Thomas Aquinas, so it is a law with a long and proud family tree. It is the law given us by nature, based on our human feelings, our ability to think, and our sense of morality and ethics. We know by instinct what is right and wrong in our daily doings. We might tell a lie, to help ourselves, or to protect someone, but we are *aware* that it is a lie and not correct behaviour.'

The silence in the room was accentuated by the soft throbbing of the dance music on the radio. Moritz reached back and turned it off.

'The ideal law promulgated by any country is that which comes closest to matching natural law. Thousands of books and treatises on this topic have been written by very many clever people, but in the end, every individual should be able to distinguish between what is a good law and what is a bad one. In times when there are laws that are not in harmony with natural law, it can be more difficult for a single person to act in accordance with his natural instincts, for the human law which governs his movements might force him to react otherwise. He lives in a conflict which is not only difficult but can also be dangerous. He is faced with many decisions, and his answers to them can affect not only himself but also his wife, his children, his whole family, his friends and colleagues.

'I have no answer to this dilemma. I can only hope that none of you will be involved in situations where you will be confronted by such deep-reaching choices. But I would like you to be aware of this issue, and to be prepared, when the time comes, to act in a way which will bring you the peace of mind that rewards actions which accord to your own view of how life should be lived.'

The silence in the room was steeped in thoughtfulness.

Lise was shifting her feet restlessly.

'Eras come and go. I want to end on a lighter note, and to offer you a poem. You may not yet know, Leo, that Emma's secret passion is poetry, and her favourite poet is our wonderful Heinrich Heine – non grata now, because his ancestry is unacceptable, but a great poet nonetheless, and a friend of humour and satire. Here's what he has to say about change:

'A damsel young stood on the shore –
She sighed; her eyes were wet,
So moved was she by what she saw:
It was the fiery sun that set.

'Young lady! Be more cheerful!
This trick's an ancient kind:
It sinks away before your eyes –
And comes back from behind.'

There was laughter and a hint of applause, but Paul raised a hand, and continued:
'And another short verse from Heine, this time addressed to my dear Emma:

'I behold in you a flower,
So chaste and pure and fine,
Wistful and tired my heart is,
To know that you were mine.

I want to lay my hands
In blessing on your head,
Praying that God preserve you
Whatever path you tread.'

And he stood back. Now everyone joined in the applause.

Emma rose and went over to him. She put her arms around his neck and sunk her head into his shoulder.

'Dearest papa,' she whispered. 'You haven't lost me. Whatever else I am now and will be, wife, mother, maybe even grandmother some day, I am and always will be your daughter.' And she tenderly kissed his cheek.

Now Leo was at her side. He took his father-in-law's elbow.

'Thank you for those wise and inspiring words, my dear papa. You can rest assured that I will bear them in mind in whatever the future holds for us. And thank you again for entrusting Emma to my care. I am beholden to you and mama for making me so welcome in your family.'

First Lise and Benno, and shortly afterwards Moritz, the von Frankens and the others took their leave. Uncle Otto, who had become very quiet, bade his brother and sister-in-law a cool farewell. Herr Gebhardt, Leo and Emma had ordered a taxi to take them to the flat in Charlottenburg. In the early evening, only Franzi and Aunt Charlotte were in the family home with the parents. Franzi cleared away the dishes for the girl in the morning, and then they sat together for a while, going through the various events of the day. Aunt Lotte retired not long after. Franzi felt her parents might want to be alone for a while, so she went to bed early too.

'Well, Paulus,' Elisabeth began, as they settled on the sofa with a glass of wine, 'that was a fine speech. It'll give poor Leo something to think about. I wonder what he made of it.'

'I can't make him out,' said Paul. 'He's so intelligent and knowledgeable when it comes to music. How can he be so convinced by these politics? I don't even think he's a bad person, or I'd never have agreed to let Emma go so easily. He just seems to be turning a blind eye to what's happening around him – only interested in getting on with his career.'

'He knows now that you've seen through him, and that might help him to – I don't know –, develop better or stronger principles or something.'

'That was my intention,' said Paul quietly, taking a sip of his wine. 'Otherwise he'll be in trouble with Emma.'

'She's very loyal,' Elisabeth said.

'But she'll draw the line where I would,' said Paul firmly, then sighed. 'Let's leave that now, Lissy. My compliments to you and Lise and Franzi for all the work you did today, you can be proud of yourselves. How long do you think it will take us to get used to being in this big house all on our own? It always seemed a bit too small for all five of us and a maid, didn't it?'

'We can spread out more, and at long last we'll have a guest room for my sister or anyone else who wants to stay the night. And who knows, maybe I'll find a live-in maid again. The girls will come by if their husbands are away on duty somewhere. There'll be coming and going, wait and see. We'll take it as it comes.'

They rose and embraced. Elisabeth tidied away the wine glasses, Paul switched off the lights, and they followed Franzi upstairs. The wedding day was over.

1940

16

23 February: Sonntags and Liepmanns

The kitchen was cold after Emma had aired it to remove the smell of cooking. She hastily closed the double windows, and gave one of her short dry coughs. As she reached for the cookery book to check the recipe for the sauce it slipped from her hand and fell face down on the floor.

'Sh...ugar!!' she hissed. 'Slow down, Emma!'

She'd started cooking in the morning, had prepared the broth and the meatballs for Königsberger Klopse. She'd finished the dessert, spoonfuls of egg white whipped to the dry stage and poached in a delicate custard sauce, 'Islands of Snow' her mother called them. It was keeping cool out on the balcony. The starter was done too, Russian Eggs on a bed of chopped spinach together with thin segments of toast spread with a vegetarian sandwich spread, an economical recipe she'd learnt at the cookery course in the Women's Work Union she'd joined last year. Now she only had to finish the cream sauce and simmer the dumplings, and then to keep everything warm while the guests were arriving and settling themselves. She'd managed the timing quite well, she found.

She drew a deep breath to calm herself.

It had been Leo's idea to invite the Sonntags and the Liepmanns to dinner. The Sonntags had the other flat on the same floor as theirs, and they had given Emma and Leo a warm welcome when they went to introduce themselves as their new neighbours. They were a generation older. Frau Sonntag reminded Emma of her own mother, with a full, matronly figure, a soft face and grey hair parted at the side with only a token attempt at curls. Leo was clearly impressed by Herr Sonntag's standing in society: he was a colonel in the army. He was of medium height, a dapper figure with thinning hair and sharp little eyes. The Sonntags, it turned out, had a high opinion of their former neighbour, Herr Liepmann, and since Emma and Leo had already promised to invite him and his wife some day, Leo suggested that they give a little dinner party for the two couples. This was the first dinner she was cooking for strangers.

The table was already set. She went to check it again. The dining-room looked lovely. The furniture with its walnut veneer gave off a deep gleam – the oval table, now extended to seat six, the large sideboard with the pull-out marble tray, the beautiful, tall glass cabinet with its plate glass shelves and curved corner panes. It had been part of her dowry from her generous father. The table was laid with the china that Leo's father had passed on to them, the blue-and-white onion pattern Meissen. The table glittered and glowed, snow-white, blue and silver contrasting with a small bowl of burnt amber chrysanthemums in the centre, creating a warm but festive atmosphere.

In the bathroom Emma checked that everything was clean, and that Elsa had left guest towels as instructed. Bending in to the mirror, she touched up her lipstick and gave her hair a flick. She wore it loose now, the new style – Leo had suggested it. Definitely more modern. She looked at herself again, sideways: she was wearing a loosely cut dress, which, she hoped, hid the slight bulge. It was hardly noticeable.

She returned to the kitchen for the final stage of the cooking. Leo should be arriving any minute – he'd rung, very annoyed, to say that Bischoff had roped him in for a last-minute discussion about some vaudeville group from Bulgaria whose political credentials seemed untrustworthy. He'd just have time to wash and change. The guests would be arriving in forty minutes.

Two hours later, Emma leant back in her chair and began to take a deep breath, but stopped herself just in time. Everyone else was smoking, Leo and Herr Liepmann drawing on cigars, Colonel Sonntag and his wife had cigarettes, and Frau Liepmann an Egyptian cigarillo which looked quite exotic. She was dying for a cigarette herself. The two ladies had helped Emma to clear the table, as if it was the most natural thing in the world for the guests to take things into the untidy kitchen, but they both did it so casually that Emma didn't feel at all embarrassed. They had lavishly praised her cooking, Frau Liepmann wanted the recipe for the vegetarian sandwich spread, and the men had taken second helpings of everything that was available, so that she feared she hadn't made enough. But in the end there were a few dumplings left over – she'd fry them tomorrow for Leo – and some sauce from the meatballs. Luckily she'd found a packet of rye biscuits and a big hunk of Dutch cheese she'd bought for the coming week, and they were chopping away at that in between their cigars and cigarettes. In her mind she scanned the whole evening so far, and was happy.

They were unexpectedly interesting guests. Herr Liepmann had stayed in his two rooms just once since they'd moved in, but she hadn't met his wife. Frau Liepmann was quite a bit younger than her husband, and attractive in a sensible way, with a broad face, blond wavy hair, pale blue eyes and a comfortable figure. She was wearing a light woollen suit in pale blue, a fine emerald brooch pinned to it. She and Herr Liepmann were obviously very fond of each other, and he kept turning to her for confirmation of what he was saying.

The conversation during the meal had meandered lightly around themes such as cooking, the problems caused by rationing, the traffic and public transport, entertainment, the restriction on sporting events. Emma found out that the Liepmanns had no children, while the Sonntags had two sons, one the same age as she was, the other younger. Both had been called up. And they had a daughter, a nurse, who was still living at home.

'Oh,' said Emma, 'we should have invited her too! I haven't met her yet.'

'She's out and about with her friends,' said Frau Sonntag. 'They're exploring shops in Wedding and Kreuzberg where they're hoping to find cheaper dress-making material than here in our area. You can't imagine, Frau Gebhardt, how they reacted when the textile coupons were introduced. Barbara almost went berserk! One hundred points for a whole year! I don't know if you've used any of yours yet. A jumper takes 25 points, a dress 45, and even a pair of socks costs 4 points! That allows about one outfit per annum! So now they're all taking dressmaking courses and hoping to make their own.'

A Normal Couple

'My sister makes most of my clothes, fortunately,' commented Emma. 'I wonder how much is needed for a pair of shoes. I'll be needing new ones for the summer, and shoes aren't mentioned at all on the coupon.'

'I believe that's a separate paper. But it's a problem I won't have to deal with from now on,' said Herr Liepmann, with a wry turn of the lip. 'The latest is that people like me with ancestors from the wrong side of the street won't be allocated any leather or shoes at all. So before you throw out your old used ones, think of us!'

'Speak for yourself,' said his wife, with a typical loud laugh. 'You should see his wardrobe! He has about ten pairs of shoes in it, and most of them he's hardly worn. He just walks around in the same old ones all the time.'

'Because they're comfortable!'

But the other four people around the table had fallen silent, the light conversation had broken apart. Leo picked up the pieces by proclaiming, 'Why are we still sitting at the table? Please, come and sit over here, it's much more comfortable.' And he drew back Frau Sonntag's chair for her and led them all into the adjoining sitting-room. Emma switched on the floor lamp and began to move one of the big armchairs closer into the circle, but Colonel Sonntag gently moved her aside and did this for her.

'You're carrying enough already,' he joked.

Emma was startled, then smiled. Her parents would never have made a remark like that. In their world, pregnancies were never even alluded to in public! She was quite taken by him. His eyes underneath arched eyebrows seemed to be constantly either laughing, or sceptical and mocking – he reminded her of a friendly pixie. If she hadn't known he was a colonel, she would never, ever have guessed it; he was a complete contrast to any of the other military big wigs that were strutting about in Berlin.

They settled on the three-piece suite, also provided by her father as part of the dowry. Its box shape hinted at an art deco design, and the cover was a strawberry-coloured velvet. She loved it. Leo filled up the glasses, handed round cigarettes and cigars, and got the conversation going again by asking Herr Liepmann if he and his wife had settled in well in Klobbicke. It was Frau Liepmann who answered.

'Yes, indeed. But you know, we've had that house for a number of years. In fact, it belongs to my father, quite Aryan, otherwise we'd have had to give it up by now. He lets me use it, it's been our country retreat. Very convenient, because it's not so far from here. But when Herr Hitler in his wisdom confiscated my unAryan husband's Aryan car last year, we found it was impossible to run this flat *and* the house, and we decided that the way things were going we'd be better off out in the country.'

'I thought they'd be staying the night with us,' said Frau Sonntag. 'We have plenty of room now that the boys are gone. Now I hear they've got two rooms here. That's very convenient!'

'Have you heard from your boys recently?'

'Achim, my eldest, is an adjutant to an officer in the artillery. Harald is in Poland, near Warsaw. They're both doing very well, thank God. Have you anyone in service in your family, Frau Gebhardt?'

'My brother-in-law is a fighter pilot in the Richthofen squadron. He's stationed in Normandy at present. It's hard on my sister – they got married only eight days ago.'

'Well, the military is a good training for any career,' said Colonel Sonntag. 'Teaches you discipline and self-control. Also how to lead others and command respect. Even without active service. How about you, Herr Gebhardt, have you been called up yet? Are you in any regiment?'

'No, I haven't been drafted yet. And as I belong to the generation which missed out on military service, I joined the general SS some years ago to get some experience – and to do my bit for the movement! But of course they're not a fighting unit. I've just been to a few training sessions, mainly athletics and gun practice – and then the lectures. They really are very tiresome! All that political indoctrination, so oversimplified, as if we were children learning the alphabet. It's hard to remain serious, or even awake, in the lectures.'

Leo was examining the tip of his cigar while speaking, and so he didn't catch the bland expressions that appeared on the faces of Colonel Sonntag and Herr Liepmann, and the quick glance they exchanged. But Emma, who had caught her breath at Leo's last statement, had immediately focused on her guests for their reaction. She didn't know what to make of it.

'Yes, indeed,' answered Sonntag. 'Surprising, considering the SS tries to recruit its candidates from the top strata of our society. I should imagine most of them would welcome a more sophisticated approach to the issues of our time.'

Frau Liepmann joined in. 'Exactly. What amazes me is how undifferentiated all political discussions are nowadays. A science as complex as politics surely requires many different approaches, with contrary opinions from which a consensus can be reached, one which will satisfy a majority. But such debates never take place now.'

'Well, my dear,' said her husband, 'you're harking back to the bad old days of democracy, when everything was topsy-turvey. The Führer has things under control now, and it's all running more smoothly. Don't you agree, Herr Gebhardt?'

Emma was still holding her breath. The others remained silent, clearly awaiting Leo's opinion. Emma found that she, too, didn't know how he would react.

Leo tapped his cigar over the ashtray while answering.

'Of course! That experiment with democracy was doomed from the start. A nation has to be schooled to a democratic way of governing, has to learn the system gradually, and Germany had never had such a government before, unlike the English, who have been moving that way for hundreds of years. Germany was just not ready for it. Our most successful rulers in the past were those who governed with a strong hand, like Frederick the Great, and Bismarck. After the chaotic post-war years, it was clear that a new start was required, and this could only take place under a strong ruler. I'm sure you will agree that the present government has been very successful in reviving our fatherland and in motivating our people to look forward with optimism.'

The Sonntags and Liepmanns remained uncommitted and silent, but, in fact, Leo hadn't finished.

'Which is not to say that things might not be better in the future. At present there are so many ridiculous rules and maxims and even laws. Take Mendelssohn! His magnificent music for "Midsummer-Night's Dream". Banned because he was Jewish! Instead we have to play a modern composition – absolutely fourth rate! – whenever the play is performed.'

Emma began to relax, and noted that Frau Sonntag was smiling slightly.

Leo continued, 'World-class musicians like Richard Tauber or Bruno Walter are banned from performing, and colleagues in my office have to scour the provincial music halls to find half-way adequate substitutes for those first-class members of orchestras like the Berlin Philharmonic who've had to emigrate. It's all very awkward!' He paused to snuff his cigar, and Frau Sonntag seized the opportunity to put in a word.

'Dear Herr Gebhardt, you are quite right. And isn't all you've said an example for what Frau Liepmann pointed out just now – that there is no room at present for contrary opinions.'

'My dear lady,' Leo pronounced, 'you've hit the nail on the head. The examples I just named are hard to justify. But our state is making a new start, and it seems impossible to implement what this requires unless we all pull in the same direction. Any new start means uprooting unwanted weeds, no matter how pretty they may be. When the garden is in order, then we can allow more diversity again.' And he leant back, at ease, and drew slowly on his cigar.

Emma caught another quick exchange between Herr Liepmann and Colonel Sonntag.

'Well,' began Sonntag, 'I'm not sure what you mean by "unwanted weeds". You surely wouldn't include Mendelssohn and Richard Tauber. And then there are all the smaller weeds that are being forcefully uprooted, like the half-hearted attempt at our good friend Herr Liepmann. Would I be right in thinking, dear Herr Gebhardt, that you would not condone Herr Liepmann being uprooted from his idyllic country refuge and, like so many of his ... *ilk* ..., forced to sell it for a fraction of its real value, purely because of his ancestry?'

'By no means!' Leo pronounced firmly, rising from his chair. 'And especially since I see his glass is empty. This will never do!' He carefully topped up Herr Liepmann's glass, and then continued to see to his other guests, while they watched him in quiet anticipation.

Emma had grown tense again. She could sense that Leo was beginning to feel annoyed. She hesitated, trying to gather her thoughts, and then began to speak.

'Whatever is happening, it seems we cannot greatly influence the trend in our fatherland at the present time, and have to find our way through life as best we can, without harming anyone ourselves, while at the same time caring for our families. My father used to be a state prosecutor and is now a judge ...' she saw Sonntag's eyebrows shoot up in sceptical query, so she quickly added: '... in the divorce courts,' and the eyebrows relaxed. 'And he taught us that even in times when our laws might not seem as ... just ... as they ought to be, we can still try to live by our conscience, to help where possible and to compromise no one. As far as possible, at any rate ...' she finished, and flushed.

Frau Sonntag nodded and the Liepmanns smiled at her kindly. She got up to fetch a dish of nuts and fruit she had prepared.

Leo had regained his composure and took the initiative.

'Herr Sonntag, are you stationed with any particular regiment? Or are your active days safely in the past?'

'Oh, long in the past, dear Gebhardt, though it was an interesting enough experience. But for several years now I've been in the administration; at present I'm involved in personnel and finance matters, a far remove from the excitement and terror of the battlefield. In the last resort, I must say I prefer it.'

A Normal Couple

What he preferred was unclear, and no one probed any further.

Frau Sonntag began to question Leo about his work, and he described the trials and tribulations in the Ministry in an amusing fashion, poking fun at all his superiors, and especially those who knew nothing about music. From there he drifted to his earlier Leipzig days, and he was able to offload several amusing anecdotes about the big names in the music world that he'd had dealings with. They included the radically Aryan Winifried Wagner, Richard Wagner's English daughter-in-law, the so-very-British conductor Sir Malcolm Sargent, the German Jewish conductor (emigrated) Otto Klemperer and many more. Emma was pleased to note that he was interested only in basking in the shade of these names, and his stories displayed no preference or prejudice on account of anyone's origin or religion. Herr Liepmann picked up on this and described how he was accepted in the tiny community of Klobbicke, where the farmers, very down-to-earth, no-nonsense types, judged people only by their characters and the qualities they displayed, not by their allegiance to any particular form of politics or race.

Frau Sonntag asked tentatively whether there were any sources in Klobbicke for extra rations of meat, fat, potatoes and other foodstuffs that Herr Liepmann could, perhaps, organise? To which Frau Liepmann said she'd see what she could do, and then admitted that the farmers were annoyed at not being allowed to sell their produce at market price, and were, actually, always willing and able to sell supplies under the counter. A complete turnaround from their attitude in 1933, when to a man they'd voted for Hitler, because the Nazis had succeeded in raising the market price of pigs for slaughter. But now the tables had been turned.

Their politics was based solely on what they could get for their farm products.

Emma relaxed. To be discussing these subversive topics with people who had been strangers of unknown political allegiance only a few hours earlier was very refreshing. It seemed their view on political issues was more liberal than Leo's, but there was a general consensus that the letter of the law was a pliable object rather than an unbending hammer. She felt she could trust them with any misgivings she might have about how life in Germany was developing, and at the same time they knew just how far they could open themselves to her and above all to Leo.

Leo's stories were very funny, and both Sonntag and Herr Liepmann were quick to respond with witty comments, so that the atmosphere became more and more convivial, and they were all surprised when, in a sudden moment of silence, the grandfather clock (a present from Uncle Fritz) struck midnight.

'Bedtime for the ladies!' announced Sonntag in a military tone, and Leo re-joined with one of his favourite lines: 'What are we going to do with the rest of this afternoon?!' Amid laughter, thanks, promises of return invitations, wishes for a good night, and praise for a wonderful evening, the Sonntags took their leave at the hall door, and the Liepmanns retired to their rooms inside the flat.

Leo closed and locked their front door, then turned to Emma. He drew her in his arms and kissed her on the cheek.

'That was wonderful! What a successful evening! What pleasant people! But I'm feeling a bit peckish. Weren't there some dumplings left over?'

17

15 July: Leo's birthday and Jochen's birth

Leo switched on the desk-lamp in the study and opened the top folder of the pile. He glanced at the first typewritten page and sighed, pulled out his office chair and sat down to work. It was already 10.15 at night, and he was tired after the eventful day, but the controversy about Bohemia had to be resolved, and he could think better here than in the office, where Bischoff tended to poke his nickel spectacles and fleeing chin round the door at the most inconvenient moments with some absurd request. He leafed through the correspondence again.

Elly Ney had contracted for three concerts in Bohemia next summer, and Leo was supposed to finalise the authorisation by the Ministry. This application had brought to a head the dispute within his section about the status of Bohemia with regard to concert exchanges. The cultural office in Prague had requested that all correspondence be conducted through the Foreign Department of the Music Section of the Ministry. An eagle eye in the Ministry, however, had detected the explosive potential of this and attached a memo to the file. Officially, Bohemia, of which Prague was the capital, had been annexed after the German army had occupied it in March of the previous year. Before that, it had been labelled a 'protectorate', but now it was considered part of the Greater German Reich, with limited powers of self-administration. So what was it? Was it a foreign state? An autonomous region governed by the Reich? A state within the Reich, like Bavaria or Saxony? If Leo of the Foreign Department in Section M were to rubber stamp Elly Ney's concerts there, the implication was that the section was recognising the autonomy of Bohemia as a foreign state, as opposed to its integration in the Reich. It was definitely a hot potato.

Leo had no intention of getting his fingers burned. He wrote a note forwarding the whole file to the attention of the Legal Department, clipped it to the cover, and dropped it on the floor beside his chair. He leaned back and stretched his long arms and his back. A sound out in the corridor caught his attention, a gentle slurring of footsteps, a knock on the door of the room. He opened it immediately, and, as he expected, found his father standing there in his dressing gown.

'Are you still at your desk, my boy?' asked Ferdinand. 'I was on my way back from the toilet and saw the light under the door. You shouldn't have to be working so late on your birthday.'

Leo drew his father through the connecting door into the sitting-room and placed him in a comfortable armchair.

'Would you not like a glass of wine or a little brandy before you go back to bed, father?' he asked.

'I wouldn't say no to a brandy,' Ferdinand answered, with the hint of a wink, very untypical

A Normal Couple

for him. Leo drew the bottle out of the drinks cabinet hidden inside the little round side table and poured each of them a generous tot.

'To your health, father,' he said, and indicated a toast.

'To yours, my dear boy, on your special day. Do you always work so late?'

'Yes, unfortunately. Either I have to attend a concert, which often involves entertaining the artists afterwards, or I take files home to study in peace, like this one,' indicating the one on the floor. 'But now ...,' he glanced at his wristwatch, '... I'm staying up until Emma has to give the baby his midnight feed. Then we can go to sleep together for a few hours, till he comes again.'

Ferdinand took a pensive sip of his brandy. His tired eyes strayed around the room.

'I wish your mother could have been here today, to see the way you're living now. How overjoyed she would have been to have had this gentle, gracious daughter-in-law, and a wonderful little grandson. And to have seen you in this flat, with its beautiful furniture, right in the middle of the capital city. Not to mention the important position you fulfil in the Ministry, whatever its value.'

At the mention of his mother, Leo's mouth drooped and he fell into his morose mood; it helped him to ignore the end of his father's sentence.

After a moment, he nipped at his brandy and drew himself up in the armchair.

'This has been the happiest year in my life, there's no doubt about that. Meeting Emma is the best thing that could ever have happened to me. And with the birth of Jochen, everything is perfect. The work is sometimes on the tedious side, but other aspects are extremely pleasant. I meet interesting people, and at the end of this month I travel to Italy again for a few days, which I love.

Even though it means being separated from my Rose and my Bud.'

'Are you not anxious about how this war might develop? Now that Germany has occupied all these West European countries – Denmark, Norway, the Netherlands, Belgium, even most of France! – it's only a matter of time before the Allies increase their aerial shelling and destruction of our cities.'

Allies! Leo noted silently, and he gazed at his father with hooded eyes. He was still listening to foreign stations.

'We gave them a thorough trouncing in France, didn't we?' he countered. 'Over three hundred thousand of them having to scuttle back to England in those hundreds of little boats! Dunkirk was the highlight of our campaigns so far, I think. It doesn't look as if our troops are in danger. Their RAF attacks have been very timid too. No, I'm not anxious, I think our military command knows what it's doing.'

'That first raid on Berlin five weeks ago was only a test, Leo. You can't believe that that's all they're capable of! The raids on our industrial plants in the west, in the Ruhr area, paint a completely different picture. Mark my words, this is only the beginning of what's in store for us!'

Leo didn't want to pursue this train of thought tonight. So far his birthday had been very pleasant and harmonious.

It had started with a surprise: his application for the birth subsidy had come through more quickly than he'd expected, and among a pile of birthday cards in his letter box he'd found a cheque for 500M. That covered 80% of the expense of Jochen's birth, a very welcome extra, especially today. His father had travelled up from Dresden the night before, Emma's parents and Aunt Charlotte had arrived after lunch – Leo had taken

A Normal Couple

the day off – , and together with the nanny and Jochen they had all strolled to the café in the grounds of Charlottenburg Palace. The weather had been perfect, not as hot as on the previous days. Ferdinand and Paul had reminisced about the era before the Great War, when the world was ruled by emperors and kings, and the social ladder was a rigid construction with the aristocracy at the top and the working class at the bottom, where each knew its place and acted accordingly. Everything was clear and predictable and orderly. ('Though the living conditions of the workers were atrocious,' Ferdinand interspersed.) All that had changed – had vanished. The map of Europe had been redrawn by the Treaty of Versailles in 1919, the first heave of the axe, and now it was being redrawn again. The people in power today – it was impossible to tell what class *they* belonged to, there was no name for it.

The two grandfathers agreed amiably that they had grown up in the best of times, and pitied their descendants, who had to cope with this complex, demanding, erratic environment. Leo had caught some of their conversation, and was pleased that they were getting on so well.

Mama and Charlotte had concentrated on the nanny, Lisl, and Jochen. Although Emma had told him that her mother couldn't even darn a sock and had probably never changed more than half a dozen nappies by herself, she was now quizzing the nurse on all aspects of her work with Jochen, and dealing out old-fashioned advice, which Lisl, for all her youth, accepted with due respect and a hidden smile. Charlotte, who had never married – her fiancé had fallen in the Great War – spoke very little, as usual, but was smiling happily with a sparkle in her eye. He and Emma trailed behind the others, her hand tucked under his arm, observing the older folk, quietly relaxing in the aura of content that this outing and the company were providing, and happy to be able to focus on each other.

In the late afternoon, they returned to the flat for a dinner cooked by Emma. She had prepared roulades, stuffed meat rolls, the day before, using all of her and Leo's meat rations for the month. There had been a disaster with the gravy, she'd told him. For the roux, instead of flour she had stirred cornflour into the precious melted butter, so that the stock had turned into a gelatinous clump. In tears, she had wanted to call her mother, despite knowing that she was an amateur herself – she'd always had a woman to cook for her. But Lisl had stepped in, although it was not part of her job, and saved the dish with a smile and a few tricks that she had learnt at home. In the end, the dinner was a great success, and Emma had accepted the praise with only a slightly guilty conscience.

All this had flashed through Leo's mind while listening to his father.

'Well, father,' he began, 'I don't believe the war will last much longer. If Hitler had wanted to invade England, he would have done so by now. France is pacified and largely unharmed, Paris is an open city. It will benefit from being ruled by Germany. Let's close the evening of this lovely day with a toast to the future.' He poured a little more brandy into the glasses and raised his. 'To the future, may it be a peaceful and prosperous one for all of us.'

His father, too, raised his glass with a tight little smile. At that moment there was a wail from the nursery, and Ferdinand stood up.

'Goodnight then, my boy,' he said, and took his son's hand in his. 'Sleep well, and may all your

A Normal Couple

wishes for your and Emma's and your boy's life be fulfilled.'

Leo watched him as he turned and carefully made his slippered way to his room.

Emma was already awake when he poked his head round the door of the bedroom. Lisl brought her Jochen, and while Emma was nursing him, he got ready for bed. They chatted about the day and their parents. Jochen was a lazy feeder, and it was an hour before Emma could fall asleep again.

There was no sleep for Leo. His father's words about the possible development of the war ran through his mind. He had never thought about the future this way before, he'd never had time. Should he be making emergency preparations? Would he be called up again? He recalled the shock he'd felt three months earlier, when he found the official postcard in the letterbox: he was to report to the Recruiting District Headquarters the following Monday at 7.00am. That was only five days later. He'd broken out in a cold sweat, and to make it worse, Emma had appeared just then and noticed his consternation. He'd had to tell her, and she grew pale and swayed, her right arm looking for support. He'd caught her, and they wrapped themselves around each other for support.

In the office half an hour later, he'd informed the Personnel Department, and the following day a long letter was sent to the Recruiting Office listing in detail his many duties and his special, unique qualifications. 'The significance of music propaganda abroad has increased since the outbreak of war; the number of musical exchanges with neutral countries has risen considerably. Every single tour to a foreign country by a German artist, and every engagement by a foreign musician in Germany is processed by Dr Gebhardt. This requires both highly specialised knowledge, and personal contacts to musicians in other countries, a combination of qualities which are impossible to replace, so that Dr Gebhardt's services are indispensable to the department. We therefore request the status of Reserved Occupation for Dr Gebhardt as soon as possible.'

That had done the trick. Weeks later he'd received a document confirming that he was exempt from military service 'against his own personal wishes'(!), and that he should not suffer any disadvantages on this account. So he was safe for the moment. But if the war situation deteriorated, as his father feared, he was sure to be called up again. Today was his thirty-sixth birthday, and the age limit was forty-five. It wasn't that he was really against the war effort. He was in two minds about it; in fact, he preferred not to think about it at all. But he was definitely not of the stuff soldiers are made of. He'd never been interested in sports. At school, all forms of physical activity had lowered his grade average. He liked walking and canoeing, and even skiing, but he'd always abhorred team games, as well as sports and athletics for their own sake. He was hopeless at gun practice, and by no stretch of the imagination could he imagine shooting anyone.

Emma murmured in her sleep, and he turned on his other side. 'Time to think of something more pleasant,' he thought. And what was more pleasant this year than the birth of his son.

He had been so surprised when Emma told him back in September that she was expecting. It would complicate everything, he had complained, but as tears came to Emma's eyes he had immediately repented and enclosed her in his arms. Everything would be fine, it was wonderful news, it would make everything even better. And Emma was reassured. Since then he had taken special care of her and had constantly admonished her to rest and eat well. He had even found a source for real cream, bringing her a small bottle every now and again, and making sure she ate it!

The due date had been around the 4th of June. Emma's twenty-sixth birthday was on 31 May, and they planned to make it a very festive occasion, the first birthday they were celebrating together, and the last birthday they would have on their own. Emma thought they would get up early and have a leisurely breakfast before Leo had to go to the office. He planned to come home as soon as possible, and had made sure not to have any appointments for that evening. Emma wanted to prepare sauerbraten, a beef roast marinated in a spicy broth, then seared and served in a gingerbread sauce with red cabbage and dumplings. It was one of Leo's many favourites. She'd refused his invitation to take her out to dinner. 'I'm far too huge!' she said.

She woke up to a surprise on the morning of her birthday. Leo had got up long before her and set the table for breakfast, with a crispy white tablecloth. The smell of fresh coffee and baker's rolls permeated the room. Not only that, on the sideboard was her birthday cake, complete with candles, beside a huge bunch of red roses in the crystal vase, and a colourful basket full of fruit, chocolate, biscuits and sweets. Next to these lay a pile of birthday presents.

Leo's eyes lit up when he saw the look of delight on her face as she turned to him.

'I've never had such a lovely birthday table! Thank you! How did you think of it?!'

'That's how we always celebrated our birthdays at home,' he replied, embracing her carefully. 'My mother used to set up birthday tables for each of us. Didn't your mother do that? I thought everyone did!'

'Not at all,' she said. 'We got our cake and our presents, and had friends in for a little party in the afternoon or evening, but nothing as personal and loving as this. Thank you, my dearest.' She tried to kiss him but her belly was in the way. From now on, she resolved, that was how all their birthdays would be celebrated.

After breakfast he set off, but he had hardly reached the office when he got a call from Emma to say that her pains were starting. At least, she thought that's what it was, although it was earlier than predicted. Fortunately, he was able to return home at once, and he contacted the midwife. After that, everything happened very quickly. He bundled Emma up and hired a cab to the clinic in Bendler Strasse; the nurses took her from him and very decidedly sent him home, and only four hours later the hospital called to tell him he was the father of a healthy son. Mother and child were well.

He was the father of a son.

A feeling of happiness such as he had never experienced before overcame him.

He was overwhelmed. He not only had the sweetest wife he could have wished for, he was also a father. Two years ago he had been alone in the world, now he was the head of a family, with a wife and a son whom he loved more than anything he had ever loved before in his life. It was miraculous! This was worth living for, this was what gave his life a purpose, a direction. From now on, no difficulty, no hindrance, no setback would ever get him down. He would only have to think of his family to set problems into their proper perspective and to find solutions which would leave his private life as perfect as it was now.

A Normal Couple

He poured himself a small brandy, and then rang his parents-in-law. Franzi took the call. When he told her the news, she gave a little shriek, then produced one of her piercing whistles and yelled: 'Granny, you're wanted on the phone!'

There was no reaction, and Franzi called again: 'Elisabeth! Your grandson wants you!'

Now he could hear an exclamation of delight from Mama, and he was able to repeat the wonderful news to her, and then to Papa, who had joined the little group. The line linking them transported not only their voices, but even more their mutual joy, so that they were all laughing at the same time.

After that, Leo called his father, who expressed his satisfaction in an heir for the family name, and formally sent his congratulations to Leo and Emma. Despite his stiff words, his voice was softer than usual, and he was clearly very pleased and moved. Leo wished he could have been with him to celebrate, and to talk about how happy his mother would have been.

Emma remained in the birth clinic for a few days before returning home, tired and smiling, with her bundle wrapped in a soft white shawl crocheted by Franzi – 'my pregnancy gift!'. They had arranged for a nanny to come and stay with them for the first few weeks. Notices were sent to all their friends and relations, and congratulations and presents began to pour in.

And from now on, Emma and Jochen would be celebrating their birthdays on the same day.

There was only one negative reaction. Aunt Dorothea von Franken sent a stiff little card with her congratulations and best wishes for mother and child. Inside the envelope was a further note:

'I am happy to hear that your son is healthy and fully developed. However, the irregularity of his early date of birth implies a standard of morality which does not measure up to that which must be expected in an heiress to the von Franken estate. Therefore I regret to have to inform you, my dear Frau Gebhardt, that I can no longer consider you for this position. I am sure you appreciate that I have no other choice. With my deepest expressions for a blessed and healthy future for you and your family, I remain, Yours sincerely Dorothea von Franken.'

Leo was smiling as he finally drifted off to sleep.

18

30 July: Lise and Gostynin

The hot weather had kept up for the rest of July. It was hard to tell whether it was more bearable indoors or out. Lise wiped her face with a towel, leaned into the big square mirror on the dressing table and stretched the skin of her cheek with two fingers. She thought she'd seen some tiny red veins when she was in the bathroom. She turned her head from side to side, but her skin was as clear and unblemished as ever. With a sigh of relief she sat back and took a brush to her thick, naturally wavy brown hair. She applied some mascara to her eyelashes, which added lustre to her deep-set, dark blue eyes. A bright red lipstick highlighted her full lips. As a second thought she patted some pink powder on her cheeks. Another careful stare into the mirror, and she felt better. Reiner was asleep, and his next feed wasn't due for another two hours. She wondered if she could leave him alone for a short time and go down into the garden where her mother was pottering about. How lucky Emma was to have a nanny for Jo! She was free to do whatever she wanted whenever she wished.

She peered into Reiner's cradle. He was lying on his back, his arms at neat right angles to either side of his little head, his waxen hair lying in damp tufts. She pressed a soft kiss on his satin cheek, smiled at the red print left by her lips, and tiptoed out of the room.

It was definitely hotter in the garden, even in the shade of the old walnut tree. Her mother was resting in a wicker chair, reading a fat book. She looked up without smiling as her daughter fell into the chair next to her.

'Well, is he asleep?'

'Yes, fast. I left the door and the window open, we can hear him if he wakes. What're you reading?'

'I thought I'd have another go at "War and Peace". It seems the right thing to read these days. Might give us a little more insight into the overall picture.'

'I doubt it. I'd say Moritz could tell us more, and even Benno in Poland has hinted at happenings that don't reach the newspapers. But I must say I'd rather not know about anything like that. Where's Franzi?'

'Gone to the market. Would you like some lemonade? I left some in the ice box.'

'Darling ma, I'd love some!'

After the capitulation of France six weeks earlier, Moritz's squadron was still posted in Normandy, probably in preparation for the invasion of England, said Franzi. Franzi and he had been married for six months now, and she was expecting their baby at the end of December. Because he was constantly being transferred to new postings, they'd decided not to establish their own home for the moment, and she was still living with her parents.

A Normal Couple

The defeat of Poland was already eight months old, and with the annexation of large western segments of the country, Benno had been sent to a surgery in a small Polish town about 500 kilometres to the east of Berlin. Barely integrated in the Greater German Empire, Gostynin had immediately been given a more Germanic name, Waldrode. Lise and Benno had been provided with a large house there, fully furnished, but Lise had preferred to have her baby in Berlin, and was staying on at her parents' place while recovering. Reiner was born at the end of June, just a month after Jo, and was now four weeks old.

The clatter of the garden gate being slammed open told them that Franzi had returned, and Lise went round to meet her. She was pushing her bike up the brick path to the side of the house, and Lise saw that it was heavily laden with bags and sacks.

'My goodness! How could you ride that? What did you get?'

'I didn't ride, I had to push it all the way home. They were selling potatoes without coupons, and I got twelve kilos. They wouldn't give me any more, but maybe we can try again tomorrow. And two huge Savoy cabbages. I know Pa has them in his vegetable beds, but his aren't ready yet, so I got these. Here, help me to carry this in. I'm exhausted!'

'Ma has a cold lemonade, come and get some before we bring all this in,' said Lise.

'Ma? I made it! Oh never mind!' And her skirt flared as she swept into the house and the kitchen for the cool drink.

'Paulus!' They could hear their mother calling their father, who was working somewhere down in the garden. 'The girls are here! Come and join us for a lemonade!' By the time they'd stowed away the vegetables and other shopping and had re-joined Elisabeth, Paul was relaxing beside her under the walnut tree, his broad-brimmed straw hat resting on his knee.

'A shame Emma isn't here with Jo,' said Elisabeth. 'I'll give her a call and ask her to come out tomorrow. I'm sure she'd want to see you before you take off for Waldrode, Lise.'

The next day was just as fine. Emma and Jo arrived in mid-morning, before it got too hot. The two little boys were placed side by side in their prams under the green shady tree, and mothers, aunts and grandmother gathered around them silently, full of wonder, praise and gratitude. Paul was watching them from his wicker chair.

'Well, this is a moment I think we'd all like to have preserved for eternity,' observed Paul. He didn't want to continue: he was wondering how often the future would allow him and his wife to enjoy the company of all three daughters and their children at the same time. They would soon be scattered to different corners of the rapidly expanding Third Reich, and the unpredictability of the present time left little hope for many repeats of such harmonious and peaceful meetings as this.

'Is Leo coming out this evening?' Elisabeth asked Emma.

'No, he left for Italy early this morning. He'll be back on Sunday.' That was five days later.

'Oh! Will you stay here tonight?' Franzi wanted to know.

'I thought about it, but I think, no. I'd have had to bring too many of Jo's things with me. It'll be easier if I go back home this evening.'

'Nonsense!' said Franzi. 'I'm sure Lise can give you anything you need for Jo. Isn't that right, Lise?'

A Normal Couple

'Yes, of course, do stay Emmi. I'll be leaving the day after tomorrow, let's stay together as much as possible,' said Lise in her husky voice, drawing on a cigarette.

'I'll think about it,' answered Emma. She had a problem with spontaneous changes of plans. But in the end she did stay. Franzi and Elisabeth made a huge potato salad, a Silesian recipe from Elisabeth's childhood kitchen, with snippets of onion and apple, and real mayonnaise, and little gherkins, and frankfurters from a glass that they'd stored last year. For dessert they had a fresh fruit salad with berries from the garden: strawberries, raspberries, black- and redcurrants, gooseberries, and a custard sauce made from powdered eggs, which, they agreed, didn't taste too bad. Pa opened a bottle of white wine and poured Elisabeth and Franzi a glass, but Emma said no, on account of her nursing, and Lise, who had wanted to accept, also turned it down, and then Franzi, too, decided it would be better if she kept off alcohol for a while.

'A good long while! Until you stop nursing!' said Lise, with a touch of bitterness.

'What about your smoking, Lise?' asked Emma mildly. 'Don't you think that might be bad for Reiner?'

'Oh goodness, I don't think so. I think it would be worse for him if I was nervous and jittery all the time. The cigarettes help to keep me calm. And I've cut down, you know.'

'What have you heard from Benno?' asked Emma. Lise had not yet been to Gostynin.

'He seems to have landed us in a one-horse town. He says he's being treated like a lord by the locals. When he enters a crowded shop, they all step back and allow him to advance to the counter and be served first. In fact he says they doff their caps when they see Dunja loping in wagging her tail, before he's even rounded the corner.'

'I'm sure they're very grateful to have a doctor there at last, from what you told us the other day. And Benno will be very popular with them, he's got such a fantastic bed-side manner.'

'I think he's only there to serve the German community. From what I gather, the Poles are to be left to their own fate. But knowing my husband, he won't be able to resist helping anyone who needs his help. I just hope it doesn't get him into trouble.'

'But why should he only be there for the Germans?' Elisabeth wanted to know. 'Surely the best way to pacify a conquered country is to treat the population better than they've been treated by their own leaders?'

'Oh well, ma, you know the Poles aren't in the same category as us. They might be all right as workers and servants, but they don't need the same privileges that we've grown up with. They don't feel things as intensely as we do. Benno says the secondary schools and universities are being closed, at least for Polish children, because they'll all be needed to work here in the factories and in agriculture in Germany while our soldiers are away fighting. They won't need any education for that.'

There was silence for a few moments. Emma looked shocked.

'Lise, you can't believe that!' said Franzi. 'There are intelligent and less intelligent people in every country, and the Poles have professional and academic and artistic classes just like we do! You can't deny their children a proper education and proper medical care. And anyway, isn't it the aim of education to better everyone, to provide everyone with a chance to improve themselves and their lot? I know they've been telling us for years that we're the master race and all that, and it's a very attractive notion that I enjoy basking in now and again, I must admit. But do you really believe all that? I don't!'

'I do,' said Lise firmly. 'How many great and famous Poles can you name, offhand? Well?'

Franzi and Emma were stumped for a moment.

'Chopin,' said Emma, 'and ...'

'There you are! They've had the same chances that the German race has, and that's the only name that comes to you.'

'They haven't had the same chances.' This time Paul was putting in his word of wisdom. 'If you look at their history, you'll see that Poland has been conquered and divided and subjugated again and again over the centuries. They do have a rich cultural tradition, which hasn't reached us because of the language problem and because of their relative isolation in the east of Europe. But the main cause is the political weakness imposed on them by their aggressive neighbours.'

He paused, but he was clearly not finished, and no one said anything.

'I hope, Lise, when you settle in Gostynin, you'll open your mind a bit more to the people around you, even if they are simple and primitive. You'll find many warm-hearted neighbours, I can assure you, men and women who will welcome you, and who will deserve any help you can give them. Please don't go there thinking you're a representative of the master race. You're the doctor's wife, and as such you'll have a responsibility and the opportunity to do good, and that is your duty there.' He paused a moment and looked at Lise. She avoided his eye.

'Your life will still be glamorous and there's sure to be a lively German community. Of course there'll still be the normal class distinctions that exist in every society. You'll have servants in your house and a nurse for Reiner, things you couldn't afford here, but never forget *why* you and Benno can suddenly afford a style of living that in the normal run of things you could enjoy here only if Benno was a professor at a university clinic.'

Lise sucked in her lower lip, raised her eyebrows and stared down at her fingernails. She reached for her cigarettes. Her mother cleared her throat, and Lise withdrew her hand. She said nothing.

Emma didn't expect to get much sleep that night. She and Jo were sharing the big back-bedroom with her sister and Reiner. They were able to nurse both babies at more or less the same time, and after putting them back in their cradles, the two young women sat out on the balcony overlooking the back garden. It was still very warm; every now and again a waft of honey from the night-scented stock below the balcony reached them, sown there by Paul in kindly anticipation of an occasion just like this, and the only sound was that of the resident hedgehog snuffling through dry leaves around the woodpile next to the rabbit hutch.

Lise lit a cigarette. Emma would have loved one too, but she was able to resist.

'How will you get to Gostynin?' asked Emma. 'It's a long journey, isn't it?'

'It takes ages. There's a through train from Friedrich Strasse, thank God. It leaves at eight in the morning and Benno said he'd send someone to pick me up at a place called Kutno. About eight hours later, God help me. And only if the train gets through. But of course if there's military being moved it might take much longer. I'm just glad I don't have to change.'

'How are you finding married life, Lise? Are you happy? Is it what you expected?'

A Normal Couple

'Typical Em questions! Yes, in fact I'm very happy. Benno is easy to manage and lets me do whatever I want. He's nearly always good-humoured. The only downside is that he's often tired in the evenings after a long day in the surgery and I can't get him to go out with me as often as I'd like. Well, now with Reiner, that's a thing of the past anyway.'

'Just as well, from what you've been saying about the cultural life of Gostynin.'

'I wish everyone would stop calling it Gostynin. It's part of Germany now and I much prefer the name Waldrode. What about yourself, though, Em. You're so soft. How do you find married life, living with a big husband, running a household, taking care of a baby? Of course you're lucky to have all that staff.'

'What do you mean?!'

'Well, the nurse, the nanny ...'

'I only had her the first six weeks! It was a great luxury, I must admit, and it was so good of Leo to finance it. Since she's gone I realise how much she did for me. I get much less sleep now. Isn't it just amazing how such a small baby can take up so much time! Still, I wouldn't miss it for all the world. I thought my wedding day was the most wonderful day in my life, but when Jochen was born, I saw there was no comparison. It was the happiest experience I've ever had, despite the pain. My God!'

'Yes, same here. It's such a shame that Benno hasn't had more time with Reiner. When he was here just after the birth – you won't believe this – he insisted on learning how to change him, and he did it so gently! I think he'll be a great help to me with the baby. He says he's really looking forward to pushing him in the pram when we go out! Can you imagine!'

Emma laughed. 'No, I can't. Leo would never push the pram, and I can't see him changing nappies either. That's definitely the woman's job. But he's so busy at work, and brings it home with him too, so I'm all right with the way things are. I do love being together with him, we talk all the time and he's always bringing me flowers or cakes, and brings me my morning tea in bed and wants to spoil me all the time. I feel really … I don't know how to describe it … sheltered … in his company. As if I was the only thing that existed in his world. And now Jochen, of course. It's such a … complete … feeling. If this goes on for the next fifty years, I'll be the happiest and luckiest being on earth.'

Lise stubbed out her cigarette. 'Sounds like you've drawn four aces. And you didn't even know each other all that long before you married! Just don't forget to keep both feet on the ground and make sure the practical things in life are taken care of. I've a feeling your Leo is romantic by nature, and he could lose touch with reality if he's not careful.'

'I don't see that at all,' answered Emma. 'He is romantic, no doubt, but he's also very down-to-earth. Don't forget he's from Saxony, and you know the reputation they have – careful with money, live in your own house, be it ever so small, look twice at strangers before welcoming them, all those kinds of things. He's very like that, for all his romanticism.'

'Well, I know that you'll take good care of him and of your family life. You probably augment each other very well. You've a touch of the romantic about you too, you know.'

'I suppose I do.' Emma yawned. She was growing tired of this conversation. 'Let's try to get some sleep, Lise. The babies will be wanting us shortly, and you'll be busy packing tomorrow.'

The sisters went inside, checked on their boys, then both lay down in their clothes and fell asleep at once.

19

28–30 August: The First Air Raids

Emma was awake immediately. She looked at her luminous alarm clock: twenty-five minutes past midnight. At first she thought it was Jo crying, but then remembered that he'd just been fed. No: the steady wailing tone – rising and falling, rising and falling, impersonal and relentless, for two interminable minutes, a frequency which penetrated her whole being. She must have missed the earlier 'aircraft approaching' signal – this was the full alarm: they had ten minutes to reach a shelter.

Leo was up. This time they'd gone to bed fully dressed, as recommended by the authorities. In the first three alarms two weeks earlier, they'd gone to bed as usual. But no raids followed, and this had given them a false reassurance. On the fourth night the full alarm had barely ceased and they were still in the flat when they could make out the rumble of aircraft. But they passed over them to offload their cargo on some other less fortunate part of the city. After that they decided it would be safer to be better prepared.

A Normal Couple

Emma grasped the baby and wrapped him in a blanket, Leo snapped up their two emergency suitcases at the hall door, and they were out of the flat just as the signal wailed itself to silence.

'Cellar or Post Office?' called Emma.

'Post Office.'

As they rushed downstairs they were joined by Frau Sonntag. The other inhabitants of the apartment house must already have left or fled into the cellar.

'We're going to the Post Office, Frau Sonntag,' gasped Emma, changing Jo to her other arm so that she could grasp the handrail. They didn't dare use the lift. 'Is your husband in the Ministry?'

Frau Sonntag just nodded.

Five minutes later they had reached the modern building on Konstanzer Strasse. It had extensive cellars with several exits, which, as was common knowledge, had been built five years earlier for just such a purpose, long before there was even talk of a war. People had joked about it. 'Good for growing mushrooms!'

Emma almost panicked when she saw the crowd, mainly women and children and older people, trying to elbow their way in, but the wide entrance doors admitted them all quickly, and the broad stairs down into the cellars allowed them to scramble into the shelter in less than a minute. The vast area was furnished with rows upon rows of benches and some wooden tables, and streams of people were milling about settling themselves in small groups. Together with Frau Sonntag, they pushed their way as far into the centre as possible, away from the heavy metal doors which would close off the room. Emma and Leo immediately began to unpack their gas masks and the gas tent for Jo and to pull them on. It was still an awkward struggle, despite having practised it several times.

She was familiar by now with the correct sequence for adjusting straps, goggles and mouthpiece. Jo whimpered as Emma pulled the rubber tent over him, and she hoped he'd go back to sleep quickly. How fortunate that his next feed wasn't due for another three hours.

She looked around the huge, low-ceilinged room, which was illuminated by long stretches of neon lamps. It was filling up rapidly, and later she wondered if it hadn't contained far more than the four hundred people for whom it was planned. Almost everybody was wearing their gasmask, and the sea of alien, insect-like heads was grotesque and frightening. People were talking in low, muffled voices, the sheer number of them creating a soft cacophony, like an army approaching from afar.

At the far end of the cavern were extra rooms, she knew. These had beds in them, for people who were ill, or even expecting mothers. There was also a kitchen back there, and the washrooms.

She moved closer to Leo and searched for his firm hand.

'You look terrible!' she said.

'Do I? But this is my favourite piece of clothing!'

'It doesn't suit you! I hope it goes out of fashion soon!'

Emma turned to her neighbour.

'Are you all right, Frau Sonntag?' she asked.

'Yes, my dear, thank you. Oh!'

The murmured conversation of the people in the shelter stopped abruptly as the droning of the approaching aircraft became audible. Despite the huge building above them and the reinforced ceiling and walls of the shelter, the rumbling grew louder and louder, and Emma felt herself beginning to tremble. Now nobody was talking; the only sound came from the excited chattering of some small children and a wailing baby. She moved even closer to Leo, pulling Jo in his tent with her. The roar of the enemy planes seemed to be directly above their heads. The sudden clatter and boom of the anti-aircraft guns from a post somewhere in the vicinity added to the racket. She was anticipating the whining of the first bombs, the crash of the missile hurtling through a roof, the explosion, the thunder of disintegrating buildings above their heads, the screams of terrified women as the first whiffs of gas seeped through the crack under the iron doors, the heat of flames outside .... The planes roared on and on, their sound muted by the shelter around them, and gradually the droning faded away. The nearby guns stuttered and ceased, and after fifteen minutes there was silence. There was deadly silence too in the huge shelter. They waited.

'There go the bombs,' murmured Leo.

'What do you mean?' asked Emma.

'They've dropped their bombs. Can't you hear them?'

'No, I heard nothing. It must be very far away. God help the poor people there, wherever it is.'

Now and then there were bursts of distant anti-aircraft fire, but they could hear no explosions. The danger seemed to have bypassed them. Yet it was almost three hours before the all-clear sounded, people began to pull off their gas masks, the heavy doors were opened, and the first hardy locals emerged cautiously up the stairs to street level. More and more people streamed out of the shelter. When Emma, Leo and Frau Sonntag reached the surface, they were relieved to see that nothing had changed – nothing at all. It was still a warm, late August night, or rather early morning. A slight breeze was moving the leaves at the tops of the lime trees on either side of the road, a black-and-white cat raced across the deserted street and ducked under a garden gate, the waning moon provided just enough light to demonstrate that life in Charlottenburg at 3.20am on this twenty-ninth of August was absolutely and completely normal.

Emma felt almost light-headed as they hurried back to their house. Leo invited Frau Sonntag in for a small brandy to settle their nerves, but she refused, knowing that the young couple needed to get back to sleep as soon as possible. Jochen had slept soundly through all the panic.

In the morning, Emma made sure to listen to the official army news bulletin on the radio. Severe bombing raids with many casualties had taken place in the heavily industrialised Ruhr area in the west of Germany. A school and two hospitals had also been hit, an injustice which the report capitalised on with great indignation. The Berlin bombing came at the end of the report. Most of the bombs had fallen on open ground in the eastern part of the city, but one of the main railway stations had been demolished. Twenty-eight people had been injured, and twelve had been killed. It was the first time that destruction had hit Berlin, and these were its first casualties. Emma was shocked. Surely it was only a matter of time before their area would also be targeted. True, there were no major train stations in their direct vicinity, nor were there any industrial plants. She thought it through and came to the conclusion that, in fact, there was nothing that would justify (if one could even call it that) an attack on Charlottenburg. If both parties to the war continued to play a fair game, selecting to bomb only military infrastructure, then the three Gebhardts (and Frau Sonntag) should be safe.

During the day, she talked to her parents and Franzi on the phone, and they reassured each other that the areas they were living in were safe.

That applied especially to her parents, whose house was on the south-west perimeter of Berlin, almost in the forest which grew around that area of the city. Her father was able to tell her that the station which had been bombed was about eight kilometres from her flat as the crow flies, which would explain why she hadn't heard the bombs.

'Leo must have very keen hearing,' he commented, when she told him that he had heard them exploding.

But how would this go on? How often would the bombers come? Surely not every night? How were people to live under such conditions, how were they to work, to go about their business, to take care of their families – without sleep? Why had the anti-aircraft defence even allowed the British bombers to reach the capital? Hadn't Göring promised that this would never happen?

'I'll change my name to Meier if any enemy aircraft reach Berlin,' he is supposed to have boasted some time back. Now everyone was talking about Herr Meier under their breath.

Sure enough, only two nights later, the alarm sounded again. They had been fast asleep. It was two am. Yet both Emma and Leo had developed a lighter sleep after the past raid, and they had left the bedroom window open, so that this time they heard the first alarm, warning them that an attack might be expected. They had trouble staying awake for a possible second signal. But, once it started, there was no missing it. For two minutes the oscillating tone penetrated every wall, window, eardrum, urging sleepers to rise and run. Fear enveloped them instantly. Yet this time they decided it would do if they sheltered in the cellar of their apartment house, where one room had been converted to serve as an air-raid shelter. Again

Emma looked after Jo, while Leo took their cases, which contained all their important documents, small valuables, some clothes, food and money. He also grabbed the bag with the gasmasks and their steel helmets.

This time they didn't see Frau Sonntag. Emma even ran to her door and rang and knocked, but Leo bellowed at her to leave it and to go downstairs. When they reached the shelter, they found that two other couples from the floors above theirs had sought refuge there too.

The room was more intimate than the big shelter in the Post Office. Each apartment had contributed one or two old armchairs or deckchairs. There was a little table, and a radio on a shelf attached to the wall. Buckets of water lined one side, with a pile of old towels and blankets folded next to them. The walls of the cellar were clean and freshly whitewashed after they had been reinforced the previous year, when detailed directives obliging all homeowners to carry out these 'improvements' had been issued. In the centre of the room, a newly constructed column of steel and cement added support for the ceiling, but it was commonly known that the arched ceilings of the old Berlin cellars were immensely strong. Should it come to the worst and the house collapse on top of them, they offered a good measure of protection. The former wooden door had been replaced by a strong steel panel within a rubber frame, to prevent gas seeping in, and a second exit had been opened to the courtyard at the back of the house. There were no windows to the room, and no ventilation system like in the public shelter, and Emma thought the air would get very stuffy if they had to stay there longer than a couple of hours.

Again Jo slept on while she fitted the gas tent around him. They didn't know these neighbours well, had only greeted them briefly whenever they'd met in the stairwell or in the lift. The middle-aged couple from the smaller apartment on the top floor hadn't bothered to pull on their gas masks, and were joking about 'laughing themselves to death' if gas should enter.

'That's not funny,' snapped Emma, and they both stopped sniggering immediately, and even indicated apologies. She snubbed them when they offered a friendly comment on Jo. She and Leo settled into their deckchairs as well as they could, and began to listen. After a moment their light-hearted neighbours fell silent too. The first floor had just taken their seats in grim silence. All were quiet, tense, and frightened – all except Leo. He moved his deckchair closer to hers, and searched for her hand.

'Try to sleep, dearest,' he said, 'I'll watch out.' He stroked her hand.

Emma almost smiled. Sleep? Now? In a few minutes? And he would watch out? He was sweet.

And then they could hear the aircraft approaching. At first they sounded very far away, but their deep roar drew closer and closer. The sudden outburst of the anti-aircraft guns pounding nearby made Emma jump. The floor under her feet vibrated softly. The droning and rumbling grew ever louder, and when it seemed to be directly above them, Emma heard the whining sound she had been dreading. Louder and louder, closer and closer – and then a thunderous explosion. The floor under her feet trembled, crumbs of plaster fell from the ceiling and the cellar light flickered. Emma cried 'No! No!' and threw herself over the basket with Jo. Already Leo was beside her, throwing his arm over her.

'It's all right, Em, it's all right, it wasn't for us, we're all safe.'

Crying, she clung to him, and he pulled her close with his long arms wrapped around her. The other people in the cellar had also changed position – the joking husband was crouching on the floor with his arms shielding his head, his wife was clinging to the pillar in the centre of the room, and the other couple were cowering in a corner with their faces to the wall. Hardly had they all drawn breath when a further explosion followed, not so close, but this in turn was succeeded by an even louder bombardment which seemed to have struck their house. Everything vibrated. The noise was unbearable, the cracking, bursting, shattering. The cellar door shivered, and Emma thought she could smell smoke.

Leo firmly pushed Emma away from him and told her to sit on the floor. He took one of the blankets, folded it and placed it for her to sit on. Then he took three of the towels and steeped them in the water in the buckets, wrung them out and handed one to each of the women in the room.

'Wrap this around your head,' he told them.

Everybody was sitting on the floor by this time. Emma had taken Jo out of his basket and was holding him on her lap. He had woken and was yelling. She tried to calm him, but with the noise and the panic in the air, it was hopeless. She decided to ignore the strangers around her, and unbuttoned her blouse and her nursing bra, opened Jo's tent so that his head emerged, and laid him at her breast. Fortunately, when he realised what was on offer, he quietened down, producing only a yell of protest at intervals.

The thunder of the bombing, the explosions, the lifting of the floor and the grit showering from the ceiling, together with the shattering bursts of the anti-aircraft guns continued unabated for a further ten minutes. Then it all gradually subsided. Then suddenly ceased. They could hear crackling noises in the outside world, and Leo made out the wailing of a fire-brigade or an ambulance. But the bombers had gone.

They stayed where they were until they heard the all-clear. The joking man cautiously turned the lever which had sealed the door of their shelter. Emma anticipated that a load of rubble would tumble into the room, but it opened easily. The stairway outside was covered in dust, but otherwise clear. They climbed up into the lobby of their building. There was nothing special to be seen. Leo opened the door to the street and stepped outside. Everything appeared unchanged. He walked to the corner and looked around into Dusseldorfer Strasse. Two houses down, on the far side of the street, flames were shooting from the top floors of a building, and the fire-brigade was already in action. All the windows of this house and the house opposite, on their side, were shattered. He could see no further damage. Where had the other detonations taken place?

He returned to their house and helped Emma upstairs, then went back down to the cellar to fetch the cases. Their flat was intact, except for a large, ornate, rather hideous vase a colleague of Leo's had given them as a wedding present. They had placed it on top of the glass cabinet, but now it was lying on the floor, shattered. The vibrations from the detonations must have caused it to shift.

'That's the silver lining on the edge of the cloud,' observed Leo, as he shoved the shards aside with his foot.

Emma was still shivering and crying, so Leo made her a cup of hot cocoa with a shot of rum in it. Then he made her undress and tucked her into her bed.

'Try to sleep now, my love,' he said, and placed a kiss on her forehead. 'We'll talk about all this in the morning,' he promised. 'It's not going to happen again.'

20

30 August: After the Air Raid

Emma dreamt that she, Leo and Jochen were sitting on a beach. It was sunny and warm and very quiet, the water of the lake or the sea was lapping gently on the shore, but she felt uneasy. Some people were approaching her and she thought at first they wanted her to go away, but instead a kind woman produced a beautiful Dresden china coffee pot, poured her a cup of real coffee and handed it to her. 'For your nerves,' she said, and Emma had to laugh. She dug her nose into the cup before tasting it to enjoy the wonderful, intensive smell that she had missed for so long now.

Her eyes opened slightly. It was morning – the morning after that terrible night. Her dream vanished, and the memory of the terror she had felt brought tears of self-pity to her eyes. She buried her face in the pillow for a moment. Raising her head, she peered over at Leo's bed and saw it was empty, the cover drawn far back to allow it to air. At the same time she became aware of the wonderful scent of coffee, real coffee, just like in her dream – and it was real! She sat up. She could hear a movement outside in the passage, the door opened, and Leo appeared, bearing a tray.

'Breakfast in bed for tired mothers,' he announced. 'Special orders straight from the Führer!'

He waited until she had smoothed her bedcover, placed the tray on her lap and kissed her gently on her mouth.

'Good morning, my sweet, have you slept well? Have your breakfast and then we'll make our plans for the day. I've rung the office to say I'm not coming in. The phone rang for a long time before anyone answered – I think I'm not the only one taking the day off after such a night.'

'We have to ring my parents and your father to let them know we're all right! They'll be worried!'

'All done,' said Leo, drawing back the curtains and allowing morning sunlight to flow into the room.

Emma smiled at him gratefully, and then admired the breakfast tray. On a pretty paper napkin, Leo had used the good china for a cup of real coffee and two halves of a crisp roll, one spread with cheese and the other with strawberry jam. The tray also held a miniature cut-glass vase with a white rose in it, freshly picked from the climber he had planted on the balcony. It all looked so pretty and delicious, and so normal! Her anxieties evaporated and she felt only gratitude for his love and care.

'Have you been up long? What time is it? Is Jo awake?'

'It's nearly nine o'clock. Jo is just beginning to whimper; I'd say you have another five minutes.'

'Have you been outside? What does it look like?'

'The house around the corner was hit, but they managed to get the fire under control. The top floors are badly damaged. The poor people. They've started bringing their furniture out onto the street before more collapses. All the windows in the house opposite were shattered. It backs onto our house, at the side of the yard. That must have been the noise we heard when it sounded as if our house was struck. We've been very lucky. It's amazing. The streets have been swept already, there's rubble only in front of the house that was damaged.'

'But we heard all those explosions and detonations! Where did the bombs fall?'

This question was answered later. After breakfast, they quickly got themselves ready to go away for the day. They decided to prepare a picnic and take the train out to Grunewald, the extensive forest between Charlottenburg and Zehlendorf. They would find a clearing where they could be alone, to absorb the cleansing pine scent of the forest, the songs of the birds, the peacefulness of eternal nature that knew no war. Their way to the station brought them through the local park, Bayerischer Platz, and they were shocked to see two huge craters in the lawn in its centre. Earth had been splattered over a wide area, the lime trees were ripped apart, stark and maimed, and pieces of iron piping and underground cables were projecting in agonised chaos from the sides of the craters, already full of black water. Two apartment houses on the edge of the park had also been hit, one of them destroyed completely. In the row of tall, ornate late 19th century buildings, a smoking gap and tall pile of rubble marked the site which only twenty-four hours earlier had held the homes of families like theirs. Heavy machines were pulling carefully at pieces of jagged, broken walls and girders. Figures clambering over the ruins and trying to lift stones told them that people were missing, perhaps dead, or trapped in the air-raid shelter in the cellar. It was terrible. It was the first time either of them had seen such a sight, and they were deeply moved.

Forty minutes later they were in the forest. Other people had had the same idea, and it took them a while to find a grassy spot off the beaten track. Leo spread out the blanket he had brought for them to sit on, and Emma placed Jo on it. She and Leo lay down too, arm in arm, but it wasn't terribly comfortable, and after a while they each found their own positions. In no time, Leo was asleep, snoring gently. Emma held Jo in the crook of her arm, closed her eyes, and made herself think pleasant thoughts: happy memories of similar outings with her parents when they were children, or the holiday plans she and Leo had made for next winter, maybe skiing in the Bavarian Forests. This brought her to Franzi's wedding last January: her sister all in white and a large crowd of guests in a freezing church, and afterwards Franzi running through the snow in her white slippers, laughing, holding hands with handsome Moritz in full dress uniform. Lise had been furious at the fuss – Franzi had even organised young Peter Marc, a cousin, to scatter rose petals on the white path to the horse-drawn coach. Goodness knows where she'd found all that.

Emma smiled to herself.

Leo woke refreshed an hour later, and saw that his wife and Jo were asleep. He rose quietly and moved back into the thick of the forest. With his hunting knife, he began to cut lush branches from the bushes and undergrowth, and to collect handfuls of the soft moss which grew in the shade of the tree trunks. Back at their resting place, he constructed a soft seat for Emma next to a mossy rock, and began to unpack their little picnic. Emma was awake and watching him.

'Let's just stay here, Leo,' she said. 'We'll sleep under the trees, you'll make us beds of moss, and traps to catch rabbits and squirrels for us to roast, and I'll collect blackberries and pine nuts, and we'll be safe from the bombs and all the other terrible things out there. Don't you think that's a good idea?'

'That's what we'll do,' agreed Leo, looking so patrician as he poured her a glass of lemonade. 'But come and eat first. I'm a bit hungry.'

He spread the blanket over the leafy seat he'd made, and Emma and Jo sank down on it.

'It's very comfortable! Dear love, how you take care of me! I feel safe and have no worries when you're near me. Promise you'll never leave me!'

'Why should I promise not to do something that would kill me if I did! No, my Em, you and I will always stay together. If ever a marriage was made in heaven, it's ours.'

And he took a big bite out of his sandwich. 'This is delicious!' he said, and Emma laughed again. When Leo was hungry, even artificial sausage tasted good.

When they got home in the early evening, they called on the Sonntags to see how they had got through the night. Both of them were home, but Barbara was out. Frau Sonntag said they'd come over in half an hour to compare notes on the events of the past night.

Leo busied himself in the kitchen while Emma was looking after Jo. He produced a bottle of white wine and made some little cubes of sandwiches with alternate layers of brown bread and pumpernickel, garnished with parsley from the balcony. He had switched on the radio while he was working to listen to the official Armed Forces report. The speaker said that sections of the residential inner city had been targeted, but the attack was so uncoordinated and the air defence so effective that the bombs fell on open spaces and hardly any damage was done. There had been no casualties, the voice said.

Emma was putting Jo to bed when her guests arrived. Before she joined them, Frau Sonntag asked Leo how Emma was managing, and Leo reassured her: she'd been nervous in the cellar, but had got over it. Frau Sonntag made no comment, merely nodded, and looked thoughtful.

She and her husband had spent the air raid in the public shelter. They compared the advantages of one over the other for a while, and related curious incidents they had observed.

'Where's Herr Meier now?' a stalwart local dame had proclaimed. 'I'd like to help him celebrate his new name!'

Leo mentioned the report he'd just heard, and while he didn't agree that no damage had been done – he'd seen the damage round the corner with his own eyes – he was glad that no one had been killed.

'I'm afraid you have to take those reports with a grain of salt, my friend,' said Sonntag. 'The statistics are sometimes delayed. Did you see the house that was destroyed on Bayerischer Platz? The tenants were all sheltering down in the cellar, about ten of them, and their exits were blocked by the falling masonry. Part of the cellar roof collapsed, and smoke from the burning house penetrated the room. They were all asphyxiated.'

Leo was shocked again. He just had time to say: 'Emma mustn't hear that!' when she came to join them. After warmly greeting her guests she sank into one of the armchairs, and Leo silently handed her a glass of wine. He placed the platter with the snacks on the little round drinks cabinet, and the men smoked while helping themselves to the refreshments.

The two couples had sat together several times since the dinner party in January, and were getting more comfortable with each other. Colonel Sonntag, despite his position and despite Leo's membership in the party and the SS, allowed himself witty or flippant remarks about the government and their plans, without mentioning any specific names, and Leo would smile or even laugh at his comments. Leo, too, made the occasional derogatory remark about his superiors, and about the rigid official position on so-called Germanic music and musicians. He was often openly dismayed at the senseless restrictions on what works could be performed or what artists invited, but avoided any direct criticism of politicians.

Leo said, 'Colonel Sonntag was just advising us to go to the public shelter instead of our cellar in future.'

'All this might be easier to bear if we knew how long it was going to last,' sighed Emma. 'The British must be beaten soon. They're suffering so much bombardment from our planes. My brother-in-law is involved in the aerial battles over the south of England, and the amount of bombing that is going on there sounds terrible. They can't hold out much longer.'

'I'm afraid, my dear,' said Colonel Sonntag gently, 'that you'll have to prepare yourself for a long campaign.'

'What do you mean?' asked Emma. 'Until Christmas?'

'Longer, I fear, much longer. The British are only just beginning to get their show together.'

'But they were routed so easily in France, and their attacks on Berlin ... well, last night was awful, but compared to what we're doing to them, I think it was probably harmless.'

'Yes, but as I say, they're only just beginning. Don't forget that they have a whole empire behind them. They're far from beaten, and they're very determined to conquer us from the air. Their air force is growing rapidly, and they have a couple of very good new fighter planes. Their morale is high. You might think they have their backs to the wall, but that would give them even more will-power to continue.'

'But isn't the invasion of England imminent?' asked Emma. 'It's been in the air for weeks. And people say that with our air strikes and our ground forces, London can be taken in four weeks, and then the rest of the country will collapse, just like France.'

'That is more than unlikely to happen. The logistics involved in invading England are enormous. Their defences along the coast are very, very strong, and moving an army across the channel to England would require more naval power than is at our disposal at present. No, our government realises that now and has changed its policy. They're focussing on completely different invasion plans at the moment. In fact, the Brits can relax – if only they knew it.'

'How do you know all that?' Emma didn't like to ask if he had been listening to foreign radio stations. The penalty for doing so was now up to eight years' imprisonment.

Colonel and Frau Sonntag looked at her and Leo for a moment. Then Herr Sonntag said:

'You may not be aware of it: I told you I was working for the administration, but I think I never told you where. I'm in the Military Intelligence, which allows me insights which are not suitable for the tender ears of the general public, if you know what I mean. In confidence, of course,' he added in his usual casual manner.

Emma held her breath. Her first thought was to try to recall anything she or Leo might have said which was unsuitable for the ears of someone who might want to interpret it as defeatism, which was also punishable. Leo's mind was occupied with the same idea, but then he realised that Colonel Sonntag had put himself at much greater risk with his revelation to someone like himself. Sonntag was not in the party, and he had criticised it and the ways things were moving in Germany more than once. He relaxed, took a deep breath, and filled up the glasses. Emma refused, asking for some water instead.

'Well,' said Leo, 'that puts us all on a clear footing. Thank you for your confidence. We both have illustrious bosses, in that case. Mine being Goebbels, and yours Admiral Canaris, I take it.'

'Indeed,' smiled Sonntag. 'You might say I'm his second in command, just to make that clear before you hear it from someone else.'

'Oh, no risk of that. I don't move in those kind of circles,' answered Leo. 'And of course I'm very far removed from my own top boss. In fact, I still haven't had the pleasure of being introduced to him – or he to me, for that matter.' He drew on his virginia.

'So to return to your worry about the future, Frau Gebhardt,' continued Sonntag, 'my advice to you would be to look around for a place outside Berlin, somewhere out in the country, a nice harmless little town or village with no industry or railway junctions nearby, where you and your baby can sleep the night through without having to stumble down into cellars or out to public shelters. Think about it.'

Emma's heart plummeted. Only hours earlier, she and Leo had sworn each other never to be separated, and now here was someone who knew what he was talking about advising her to do just that. It was unbelievable! Never! She could never leave Leo on his own here in the capital. There must be a different solution.

Frau Sonntag noticed that Emma was fighting to hold back her tears. So much for her iron nerves! Her suspicions were confirmed: Herr Gebhardt's estimation of his wife's mental state after the experience of the past night was far too optimistic. The poor girl was clearly close to breaking point.

'Now, Hans,' she addressed her husband, 'I think it's time we let these young people get to bed. Who knows what the next night will bring? Frau Gebhardt, my dear, you know I'm usually at home. Please don't hesitate to drop in on me any time you want to chat or talk about anything. Good night, and sleep well, both of you.'

The two men exchanged some friendly comments, and Sonntag clapped Leo on the shoulder in an intimate greeting as he stepped out into the hall.

Frau Sonntag looped her arm under her husband's elbow as they strolled round the corner to their flat.

'Well, Hans,' she whispered, 'was that wise?'

'If he has anything on me, I have plenty on him. No, I think he's happy to use the present system to rise in the world, but he's not an ideologue. My instinct tells me he's all right, and you know my instinct has never let me down. He won't endanger our work.'

Frau Sonntag smiled and waited as her husband unlocked their front door.

21

27 December: The New Year's Party

Even from the highest rung of the step-ladder, Moritz had to stretch to reach the candles at the top of the Christmas tree. Leo held the side rails in case Moritz overbalanced. When the highest candles were lit, he took one step down, lighting more on his way until he reached the floor.

'Twenty-eight candles!' he said admiringly. 'Not bad for such a small room.'

Emma wondered why he called it a small room. In her eyes her parents' sitting room was really quite large. They all fitted in comfortably, Paul and Elisabeth, Franzi and Moritz, Leo and Jo, Aunt Charlotte, and herself. But then she recalled that one of Moritz's grandfathers had been a millionaire at some stage, before the Crash, and she assumed he was thinking back to some opulent Christmasses of his childhood days in some enormous palace, compared to which this room would, indeed, be a poor second. She smiled to herself, then moved aside as he folded the ladder, gave her a wink, and brought it out to the cupboard in the hall.

Paul turned off the top light, and the room was illuminated only by the candles. As always, the beauty of the tree brought a lump to Emma's throat. It reached almost to the ceiling of the high room, and the branches were spread out by the weight of the fat red apples hanging from their tips. The whole tree was glittering with icicles made of tinsel laid strand by strand on its branches. Golden chains were looped gracefully from the end of one branch to the next, encircling the tree, while green, silver, red and purple glass globes hung in its interior, from where they mirrored the flickering candles. The garden smell of the apples mingled with the honey smell of the bees-wax candles, filling the air with a festive scent unique to this time of the year.

Cinnamon, lemon and cloves added their seasonal touch to the air. Aunt Charlotte and Emma had poured out glasses of hot punch, and now they handed these round. Only Franzi refused. Her baby was due any day now, and she was feeling uncomfortable. Emma slipped out to the kitchen to make her a herbal tea, and when she brought it, Franzi gave her a grateful smile and a kiss on her cheek in thanks.

'Let's drink a toast to absent friends,' announced Paul, and they raised their glasses and murmured the words. Lise, Benno and Reiner were spending Christmas in Waldrode, and Leo's father, who had been invited to join them for the New Year, had refused, saying that, under the present circumstances, the capital city was the last place he wanted to be right now. If his son couldn't make the time to come down and see him, his aged and only parent, then he would celebrate on his own. It wouldn't be the first time. Leo had felt bad about it, but his own family had precedence now, and this was the first New Year's that the three of them would be spending together. He would see his father early in January.

Everybody had their eyes on the tree, lost in their own thoughts. No one felt like disturbing the gentle mood that enveloped them all. Emma relished the feeling of harmony which prevailed; it was rare to experience moments such as this, even with the people she loved most. Jo was lying on a rug on the floor, staring at the tree, gurgling to himself and contentedly blowing bubbles. She sat on the floor at Leo's knee and reached for his free hand, and he pressed hers and kissed it softly.

'How much leave have you got, Moritz?' asked Elisabeth.

'Just two days. I have to be back at the base on Sunday evening. Gosh, Fra, can't you do something to make that young lump get a move on? Jump off a chair or something? I want to be here when she comes!'

'He'll come when he sees fit!' retorted Fra with a sceptical moue, and everyone smiled.

'Have you come to terms about names yet?' Aunt Charlotte wanted to know. They had all witnessed the dramatic discussions on this important issue.

'Fra is still insisting on an alphabetical order, and it has to be something august and ... imposing. Augusta, Agrippina, Alexandria – Aida!'

'That's just a silly superstition in the Richthofen squadron, that all their pilots produce girls! It's going to be a boy! Alexander, Arminius, Achilles, Adolphus ...'

'God forbid, not Adolphus,' said Moritz.

'How far down the alphabet do you intend to go in the next few years?' asked Leo, laughing.

'Well, I love the names Jocasta, and Jonathan, but that would mean ...' She paused, screwing up her eyes in concentration.

'Ten! Ten children! You're mad!' said Moritz. 'Cleopatra or Constantine will be as far as it goes! And not one letter more! Anyway, I'd much prefer normal names like Hans or Franz or Eva. But they're not grand enough for madame. Where did she pick up those ideas? You and Ma aren't like that at all, Pa.'

Everyone was laughing now, and Emma scrambled to her feet to top up the glasses and to hand round a platter of Christmas biscuits. They had already eaten. Some days earlier, Paul had been out with a friend with whom he shared a shoot, and had come home with two hares and a pheasant. Elisabeth had managed to find some speck – a layer of pork fat from just under the skin, pickled and smoked – with which she and Franzi had larded the dry meat, and she had produced succulent roasts which had earned her heartfelt thanks and compliments, especially from her two sons-in-law.

'Don't worry, my boy!' said Elisabeth. 'Once the baby is here she'll come to her senses. She won't have any time for her funny ideas.'

'Will you be returning to the attacks on Britain?' Emma wanted to know.

'I suppose so. Our last sorties were against Liverpool, but as you know – well, you've been there – Britain has a large number of manufacturing cities, and they're all legitimate targets in a war.'

'Yes, maybe. But so many civilian buildings have been hit too, so many homes destroyed, so many ancient and beautiful buildings. Coventry Cathedral! How can that happen if everything is planned so carefully?'

'It can't be helped, Em,' said Moritz, with an untypical frown. 'It's all part of what makes a war. Our palace in Charlottenburg was damaged too, don't forget. It's give and take. The sooner the other side realises that it hasn't got a chance and decides to capitulate, the better for all of us.'

'But who says it's the English side that doesn't have a chance? Perhaps their fortunes will turn and we'll be the ones to have to surrender!' Emma gave a dry cough. She was recalling what Herr Sonntag had said in August, after that first air raid.

'There's absolutely no sign of that. The size of our country is working in our favour. We can reach London and the other cities in one or two hours from France, but for them to reach Berlin they have to fly four hours over enemy territory – each way. They have very few planes with that range. They have to fly under cover of darkness, and once the nights start getting shorter and the days longer, it'll be too dangerous for them to fly all the way to Berlin. Mark my words! We, on the other hand, can continue to hammer them, almost from our own armchairs, so to speak!'

'Well, I just hope it ends as soon as possible.'

'It will. Remember a year ago? My squadron was assigned to the air defence of Berlin. And then our defence command realised that our anti-aircraft guns were doing a great job dealing with the British fighter bombers and their covering planes. So we fighter pilots were posted to Normandy and the attack on Britain. OK, we didn't defeat them from the air as fast as we'd hoped, but there's no doubt we've weakened them. The ultimate proof of that is Dunkirk.'

Emma was fighting with a heavy bout of coughing. She signalled her apology and removed herself to the kitchen for a glass of water. When she returned to the sitting room, Paul was speaking.

'It has certainly been an extraordinary year. It has brought Elisabeth and me great joy, with our daughters married and with two, and soon three, grandchildren. This is more happiness than we could ever have anticipated in so short a time. But these air raids are a terrible thing, especially for people living near the city centre, like Emma and Leo. Almost forty air raids since the end of August, forty nights without proper sleep, rising in fear, leaving one's warm bed and stumbling out into the cold, to sit for hours together with strangers in an inhospitable cellar, not knowing if one's house is still standing at the end of it.'

'It's bearable for me when Leo is there to share it,' said Emma. 'But he's away so often. That time at the end of October, from the 21st, I think it was, to the 27th – they came every night, and I was on my own with Jochen, Leo was at a conference in the Rhineland. He wrote me lovely letters, how peaceful it was, going for walks in the forests, enjoying the cold winter weather and the food. And I spent the nights struggling down to the shelter in our house with the baby and our bags. Frau Sonntag was away at the time, I had no one to help. It was so very, very frightening.'

She wrung her hands in her lap and paused to try to regain control.

'Oh, I know I shouldn't be bringing it all up again. There's no point. But four and a half hours! It lasted four and a half hours on the 25th!'

'That's right,' said Paul sombrely, 'that was the time they dropped bombs on Zehlendorf as well. We didn't realise until the next day that our suburb was hit. It was on the other side of the village centre. But it was in our local area. Frightening.'

Leo was looking very dismal, and Emma, noticing this, said: 'Don't look so sad, Leo dear, you couldn't help it. It's just the way it is. It's what makes war, Moritz would say. But when will it end? There's no indication! On the contrary – we all remember just before Christmas, the 20th and 21st – only a week ago. Leo was in Brussels. It began on the Friday night from ten until one, and then we thought it was over. I even got undressed and went to bed.'

Franzi took up the tale. 'And then at a quarter to five in the morning, it started again, with bombs dropping around Alexanderplatz, right in the centre. The all-clear came two hours later, but hardly had we taken off our gas masks and started upstairs when the sirens went off again, and the planes returned until half past seven.'

'Frau Sonntag and Barbara were able to help me that time, and we went to the public shelter. But Jo woke up and I wasn't able to calm him, and the bombs were falling so close to us! Or so I believed. It was so awful. He was yelling and the bombs were thundering around us and exploding and everything was shaking and shuddering and people screaming.'

'And the damage done in Charlottenburg was considerable.' Aunt Charlotte had joined the narrative. 'All those beautiful houses destroyed. And in the city centre the cathedral was hit, and the Armoury and the Antiquities Museum. It's a miracle that only six people were killed.'

'It's no way to live!' exclaimed Emma.

When the raids had continued at the end of August, all through September and into October, Leo had persuaded her to leave Berlin for a couple of days. He arranged for her to visit distant cousins on her mother's side in Breslau, an ancient town in Silesia, far away from Berlin. Memories of her stay there surfaced now.

A Normal Couple

'Those few days I had in Breslau in October, how peaceful they were! So normal! I'd almost forgotten what it was like to be able to sleep without having to stay dressed and keep half an ear open for the sirens. The sirens! How I hate them! Am I the only person to start shaking with fear as soon as I hear them?'

'By no means!' came two or three voices.

Moritz had been keeping quiet, but was listening carefully. For one thing, he was the only one who hadn't experienced hiding in air raid shelters to the same degree as the Marcs and, even more so, the Gebhardts had. And for another, he was aware that the horrors his friends and family were describing was exactly what the population of the cities that he and his comrades were attacking was going through. He himself wasn't a bomber pilot, he flew a Messerschmidt air fighter. His job was to protect the bombers on their way to and from their targets. But he knew he was just as responsible for the results as the airmen who released the bombs from their hatch. He tried never to think about it.

He moved in his armchair. But it was war. He didn't make the rules. They were targeting industrial and military complexes. If occasionally a bomb went astray and hit a civilian target, it was regrettable, but it was not intended. It happened, just like a tornado, or a ship sinking in a storm.

In the meantime, the candles on the tree had burned down and were extinguished one by one, and Paul had switched on the overhead light and two standing lamps.

'A nightcap before we retire?' he asked, waving a bottle of brandy. But everyone was too tired. It had been arranged that they would all sleep in the house in Zehlendorf. Franzi and Moritz would have Franzi and Lise's old room. Emma and Jo would be in her room. Aunt Charlotte was sleeping in what used to be the maid's room. And Leo was going to make do with the big sofa downstairs.

Emma started a long stretch of coughing as she was preparing for bed, and Franzi caught her on the landing.

'Did your application for the spa come through?' she wanted to know.

'Yes, it did.' And Emma's anguish from the past conversation fell away and she smiled happily at her sister. 'I'm going to Reichenhall Spa at the beginning of February. And Leo is hoping to get holidays at the same time, so we can be together.'

'That's wonderful, my Em. Now try to sleep. Surely the Brits want to celebrate New Year with their families too and won't disturb us tonight. Sleep well, dearest.'

'And I hope you and Moritz can sleep well, and that your baby will come soon and quickly.'

Franzi's pains started during the night. Moritz drove her calmly to the local hospital, where arrangements for the birth had been made. He wasn't allowed to stay, but six hours later he received a call announcing the arrival of his son and heir, Alexander Paul Wilhelm.

Grandfather Paul opened the bottle of real champagne he had been saving for the event. Three grandsons! All within one year! He felt an inner glow. Elisabeth was beside herself with pride. And Emma, when she heard the news, burst into tears. With this new baby, all the tension and horror of the past months was washed away, and she was able to revel in the happiness of her sister and her brother-in-law.

'Alexander!' Moritz proclaimed. 'What a mouthful! Well, I'm glad he's got at least one normal name. I'm going to campaign for calling him Paul.'

And Leo had already decided that, from now on, he would rechristen his younger sister-in-law 'Aida'. It suited her down to the ground.

1941

22

1 January–7 March: In the Spa

Emma loved bedrooms that had a balcony. She pulled on a thick cardigan and draped a rug over her head and shoulders before stepping outside, drawing the glass door closed behind her. It was completely black outside. Her breath shimmered in the air; she inhaled slowly. A sweet smell of wood-smoke softened the smell of the piercing cold. Gradually her eyes began to make out details in the night. From the slope where her pension was located, the shallow snow-filled valley flowed away into darkness. It was protected left and right by a wall of hills, velvet silhouettes in the light of the half-moon which hung suspended in centre stage like a lantern. Outcrops of rock and forests formed darker shadows against the silent snow. Specks of light here and there pinpointed homes of isolated families, and at the end of the valley a spray of sparks like a scattering of jewels marked the little town. She looked up. Stars, myriads of them, littered the sky from horizon to horizon, an infinite unorganised glitter against the deep black void. She searched for and found Orion with his dog, and her favourite, Cassiopeia, the sprawling W. It was absolutely silent, and she allowed herself to be enfolded and lost in the immensity and purity of the scene before her, an impartial world without any constraints or demands on her.

She pulled the rug tighter, aware that what she was doing was not what her doctors would have ordered. But her soul needed care and aesthetic nourishment as much as the rest of her, and this would aid her cure.

She had been in the spa for almost a week. The therapies that had been prescribed were gentle and, she hoped, helpful, but there was no doubt in her mind that the main benefit was the peace and quiet of the nights. She was able to sleep as long as she liked, and without any interruption. Much as she missed them, neither Jo nor Leo could disturb her sleep, but above all there were no sirens, no alarms, not even the fear of them, which had been present even when they didn't come. She could go to bed in a normal nightdress, not fully clothed. It took her three days to be able to sleep without half an ear open for the first alarm. The constant presence of the cellar, the neighbours in the middle of the night, the baby in its gas-tent, the droning of the planes, the explosions and shuddering of the walls and floor – it was only now that she realised how deeply all this had penetrated her consciousness, had got under her skin, into her bones, making her start at the least unexpected sound.

Chronic bronchitis was the diagnosis she had received, but by then her application for the cure had already been granted. Her coughing at night had been an additional strain during the few hours of rest they were allowed. Leo had recommended the little clean-air spa in the mountains not far

A Normal Couple

from Salzburg. His mother had stayed there several times; he had visited her, and was enthusiastic about the clinic and the surroundings. In fact, he had been able to arrange twelve days holidays for himself during the five weeks that she would be spending there.

A door opened below at the side of the boarding house, and the voices and laughter of people leaving brought her back to the present. She turned and slipped into her room. It was not very large, but comfortably furnished with picturesque rustic furniture: a soft bed, half of a pair of twin marriage beds, with a colourful headboard and a heavy feathered quilt, a wardrobe painted with country scenes, an oak table with curved legs and a drawer, and an upholstered chair. A wall mirror in a blue wooden frame over a small shelf served as her dressing table. She was pleased that she had a table lamp, which she could use for reading in bed. Best of all, the house was centrally heated, and the warmth of the room was like a welcoming robe as she closed and barred the balcony door.

Sitting down at the table, she opened the drawer and took out the letters she'd received from Leo since she'd left home. On her journey here she'd spent several days in Innsbruck with friends of his from his student days, and his first letter to her, written on the day she'd departed, was full of requests for items that were now hard or impossible to come by in Berlin. Black or grey socks, darning wool, any face and body creams she could find, toothpaste (but only if it was the old kind, the new ersatz paste ruined one's tooth enamel). Warm underwear for herself. Shaving soap, and his March allocation of normal soap. Some lovely, scented soap for his sweet wife. A pair of braces for his trousers. Enclosed in the letter were 60 Marks and his clothing coupons. She'd spent a whole day walking around the centre of Innsbruck, to the chemist he'd named, and the haberdashery where he used to shop, and had succeeded in finding all the items he needed for himself.

In his next letter he'd sent her another 20 Marks, and hoped she'd find some pretty things for herself. And could she buy some twine, and if she had any money left, perhaps one or two night-shirts for himself, his were all worn.

She had found these articles too, and now everything was stowed away in the bottom of her wardrobe, awaiting his arrival. She had a dim feeling of pride at having been able to meet all his requests so precisely.

For herself she had found a chic, warm, beret-like hat in Innsbruck, in a dark green felt with a little feather at the side. Hats were coupon-free, and it was noticeable that while fashions hadn't changed much in the past year, an amazing variety and creativity in ladies' headgear had blossomed on the streets and in the cafés.

She in turn had written to him, asking him to forward her February allowance of butter, bread, sandwich spread, dried sausage, ersatz coffee and some eggs, as her coupons were not valid in Innsbruck, and it would take a few days for new ones to be issued. And sure enough, a small parcel arrived the day before she was leaving, with all of the raw eggs still intact! So she'd been able to recompense her hosts, who had shared their rations with her. She hated being in anyone's debt.

Leo wrote that he'd been invited out to his parents-in-law's house for dinner a few times, where Mama had served him delicious food, and her father had spoiled him with a new Mosel wine. And he'd enjoyed one really spectacular evening, an invitation – she had been invited too, *such* a pity

A Normal Couple

that she wasn't there – by the ambassador of Manchukuo, who lived in a dream of a house in Grunewald, with grounds running down to a lake. They'd had afternoon tea with real tea and coffee, and for supper, crayfish. Just the ambassador, the Japanese conductor Ekikai Ethu, Dr Bischoff and himself. It had been charming.

He missed his Rose and the Bud immensely, but whenever he saw the small Bud at her parents' place, he had the impression that Jo recognised him, for he immediately wet himself and had a big smile on his face.

There was a smile on Emma's face too, as she stacked the letters and stowed them away. Tomorrow she would write to Leo, the last letter he would receive before setting out to join her here. She was still coughing at night, but on the whole already felt better, and was looking forward to going hiking and skiing with him in the beautiful winter scenery around the village.

A week later, Leo was checking the contents of his old canvas knapsack before setting out for the boarding house. There was an extra scarf for Emma, an extra pair of gloves, a flask of tea with milk and sugar, and four rolls spread with real butter and cheese, as well as half a smoked sausage. His lodgings consisted of a room in a farmhouse not too far from Emma's place, where his breakfast was served by the pretty, shy teenage daughter of the house. The sausage and the two extra rolls were the result of a diplomatic conversation with the young lady that morning. Moved by his gentle charm and his sad description of the frail state of his dear young wife, she had slipped back into the kitchen while her mother was out in the cowshed, and brought him the additional food for their picnic.

He laced up his boots, shouldered the knapsack, then the two pairs of skis, picked up the ski sticks and headed out. The sun was shining; its reflection on the snow was blinding, and he stopped to dig out his snow goggles before proceeding. Another beautiful day! He'd been here for four days now, and the very cold weather had been reliable and fine all the time. In the mornings, while Emma was taking her therapies, he was out and about at an early hour, climbing the surrounding hills, and once he'd skied back down. In the afternoons, he'd joined Emma and they'd undertaken shorter walks together.

Today, Saturday, there were no treatments, and they'd planned to walk up to a knoll on the slope of the nearest mountain, Wappachkopf, and then ski down from there. He had arranged to pick up the skins and two pairs of skis and boots from the forester nearby. Would Emma be up to it? It meant walking uphill for about three kilometres, to an altitude 450 metres above their village. Emma was sure she could do it, and if it turned out to be too much for her, they could turn back at any point.

She was waiting for him in the hall of the house, and as always his heart gave an extra beat when he saw her. She always looked so refined, a real lady! It was such a shame that she had been unable to book a double room for them – he had hoped they would be staying closer together, so that he could interrupt his bachelor existence at least now and again. She was wearing dark green skiing pants which fell loosely to her ankles, where they were gathered in her woollen socks. The matching jacket was closed with a sensible zip and had red applications on the shoulders, and a high collar which could be buttoned. A red bonnet, scarf and gloves rounded off the smart outfit. Her face was already glowing, and beamed as she advanced to meet him. She laced up the ski boots and they set off right away.

After ten minutes, Emma unwound her scarf and stowed it in her own little knapsack.

'Phew, it's warm!' she said. 'Aren't we lucky!'

At the edge of the forest the road changed to a logging trail. They continued for another thirty minutes until the snow got too deep. Leo, who had been carrying the skis on his shoulder, set them down and took the seal skins out of his rucksack. Emma, who had never before walked up a ski slope – there had always been at least a drag lift when her family went skiing – was unsure how to fasten them to her skis, and Leo helped her.

'The fur on the outside, and the hair pointing behind you. That acts as a break so you won't slip back when walking uphill, but you can glide forwards if the road takes a dip.'

She slipped her right foot into the binding and placed the cable in the notch around the heel of her boot before firmly snapping down the fastener in front. When both skis were attached, she attempted a few steps and found she could, indeed, move uphill without sliding back down again. She leaned over to Leo and raised her face to his for a kiss. Some minutes later, grasping their ski sticks, they set off.

The going was slow, and it was colder in the forest, but the walk was so exerting that she soon had to unzip the top of her jacket. It was wonderful! The air was dry and cool, the pine trees gave off a resinous smell which she drew into her damaged lungs as deeply as she could. The only sound was that of an occasional rustling of snow as it scattered from the tops of the tall trees, where the sun had softened it. On and on they climbed, not talking; she had no breath for that. Whenever there was a break in the forest, they could see the village below them, already apart, another life, remote. There was just Leo and her. If only Jo were with them! Then everything would be perfect.

After three hours they had reached the knoll of Wappachkopf. It was free of trees, and the view across the valley and down to Reichenhall was stupendous. Across the valley, range upon range of craggy, snow-covered mountains graduated into the anonymous distance. The sun was burning down on them, and although there was a breeze, Emma took off her jacket. They removed their skis, and Leo found a sheltered niche where they could sit comfortably for their picnic.

'My dearest Emma, if you are only one tenth as happy as I am right now, I'm sorry for you, it must hurt so much!'

Emma laughed.

'Oh stop! You're just hungry! Let's see what you've managed to scrounge! They wouldn't give me anything extra in the boarding house, even though I said I wouldn't be there for lunch. Mean!' She was starving herself, and they both enjoyed their meal.

'It tastes better than lobster or steak or smoked salmon ....,' said Emma, and Leo nodded. He pulled out his pipe and the tobacco pouch, filled the bowl and lit it. The scent gradually mingled with the clean air, a sweet odour of caramel.

'When the war is over, we'll come here every year for a winter holiday with the children,' said Leo. 'I'll teach them to ski, and the baby will be on a toboggan which I'll attach to my belt. I've seen other men do that.'

'How many children were you thinking of?' asked Emma.

'Three,' answered Leo promptly. 'Like in your family. Jo must definitely not be an only child. I hated not having any brothers or sisters to play with. Four would be all right too.'

'Whoa!' laughed Emma. 'Three would be enough for me. Nicely spaced. And where would we be living then?'

'What would you think of Munich? The last time I was there, Clemens Krauss dropped some hints about bringing me down to the National Theatre. How would you like that?'

'I wouldn't like that at all! You know I don't have a high opinion of Bavarians. They're loud and opinionated and much too full of themselves. And it would be much too far away from my parents. No, Leo, not Munich or Bavaria, please!'

'Well, we'll see what happens. The work at the Ministry is interesting, but there's also a lot of infighting, and I'm away so often. At present it's still enjoyable, but I can see a time coming when I'd rather be at home each evening with my Rose and all my little Buds.' And he hugged her closer to him.

'At any rate,' began Emma with a sigh, 'it'd be heavenly to be living a normal life again, like it was before all this started. If only there was a way of knowing when it's going to end. That would make it all more bearable.'

'It can't last much longer. The air raids on Berlin have stopped. Great Britain is getting such a hammering, they'll have to give up soon. Then Hitler will have achieved what he set out to do, and things will quieten down.'

'I don't know about England being ruled by Germany. I can't imagine it, somehow. The British are so ... self-contained, so insular, as if the rest of the world existed just for their convenience, whenever they might need it. And in the meantime they just go on living their own culture and take it for granted that it's superior to everybody else's.

Don't forget, England hasn't been conquered by a foreign power since 1066, whereas I think there's no country on the mainland which hasn't been overrun by one or more of its neighbours in all that time. That kind of experience leaves its mark on a nation!'

'Clever Em! What deep thoughts run through that little head! You're such a clever little thing! You'll be the ideal mother for our three children, able to answer all their questions and explain the world and its ins and outs and teach them what's right and how to behave.'

Emma smiled. 'It'll be a while before I get to that stage. At the moment I'm still trying to get used to looking after one infant with a very limited though loud vocabulary. It's a full-time job. I can't think that far ahead, to a time when I have three children old enough for political discussions. What will the world be like then?! We'll wait until the whole contingent has arrived, and then we can continue this conversation.'

They both laughed.

There was a pause. Leo drew on his pipe and they admired the scenery and enjoyed the thin warmth of the winter sun.

'What are those birds?' asked Emma. A rabble of small, crow-like birds with bright yellow beaks and red legs were hopping and flying around near them, producing short sharp whistles. They came quite close, perhaps hoping for some food.

'They're Alpine choughs. They live high up in the mountains. They belong to the crow family, though their sound is so different.'

'They're pretty. Oh!' One of the choughs had performed an acrobatic loop in flight.

'The word "contingent" reminds me of my days in Innsbruck,' began Leo. 'I joined a student militia there. Things were getting restless out in the streets, and we wanted to make sure law and order was maintained. We used to have kinds of military exercises, we even had a sort of uniform, but the best part was the training on skis during the winter, patrolling the trails and passes up in the mountains. It was wonderful. Such a fine group of young men, all proud of their nation and its values, very patriotic. They knew whose side they were on!'

'Did you have any encounters with the ... opposition?'

'Not really. Just once. We knew of a cell of Bolshies in a village in one of the side valleys, and we went up there to check on them one time. They were just coming out of a house, must have been having a meeting. Well, they weren't prepared for us, and we gave them a thorough trouncing. We never heard any more about them. But mostly we just did our training once a week and then went to the local pub, where we sang and made a nuisance of ourselves until they threw us out. Nothing dramatic ever happened. It was just wonderful camaraderie, a change for me after my lonely childhood.'

He knocked the bowl of his pipe against a rock to empty it, then stowed it in his pouch and began to gather their belongings together. Emma had remained silent.

'Time for the exciting part of the day!' he announced.

After removing the skins from the skis, they strapped them on. Leo shifted his knapsack on his back so that it lay comfortably. Emma zipped up her jacket and pulled on her scarf and bonnet. She was tucking her hair firmly under her hat when Leo, without another word, took off, gliding down the track with an elegant Telemark curve. When she looked up, Emma was amazed to see him disappearing down the hill. Her dismay turned into anger. She picked up her sticks, stamped the skis once or twice to warm her feet, and followed him. She was an able skier, but she'd have preferred Leo to be behind her, in case she fell and needed help. The trail was quite smooth, in fact, and she had little difficulty in keeping up with him. She was able to proceed at a gentle pace, just fast enough to feel the thrill of the cold afternoon breeze on her face. It had been several years since she had skied, and, despite her confused annoyance, her heart swelled at the enjoyment of the movement, the swish and squeak of the firm snow under her skis as she made a turn, the slight shifting of her weight and the adjustment of her legs to stay balanced on the boards while changing direction, all the while speeding – now it seemed like speeding – downhill. She finally suppressed her anger at his unannounced departure; she had decided not to spoil their day by mentioning it.

After twenty minutes they had reached the end of the forest trail that had taken them three hours to ascend, and slid on down the snowy village street to her hostel. Dusk was falling as they left their skiing gear in the ski-shed, and they tiptoed in their stockinged feet up to her room. Without speaking, they quickly undressed and huddled into her bed to warm themselves. And then Leo's bachelor interlude received a temporary remission.

The following day, they decided to attend the Catholic mass in the little village chapel. Emma's landlady had pointedly asked if they intended going, and on discussing it, they found that they both wanted to give thanks to whatever celestial powers had allowed them such happiness together. And to experience more of the village atmosphere.

The church lay beyond Leo's lodgings, so that Emma arranged to meet him there. As she came into the little hallway, she could hear him shouting upstairs. She quickly ran upstairs. Cowering in his doorway was the girl who did the cleaning and inside was Leo, holding up his shirt, which had dark stains on the front.

'You stupid girl! Is that how you learnt to work? What kind of idiot taught you?! It's ruined! That was a good shirt, and where will I get a new one now? For God's sake!'

'Leo!' called Emma. 'What's wrong? What's happened?'

'This stupid girl washed my shirt without checking the pockets! There was an ink pencil in one of them! My best shirt! It's ruined!'

Emma was stunned. She had never experienced Leo like this. At the same time she felt angry. She was still sore at his sudden departure the day before, and the sight of the girl, red-faced, with tears pouring down her full country cheeks, roused her. It wasn't even his best shirt.

'Well, Leo, you know, I really think you could have checked your pockets yourself before you got someone else to wash your shirt for you. It was your shirt and your pencil. Surely it's not too much to ask if you make sure your things are ready to be laundered before you send them off. Come here, my dear,' and she put her arm around the shoulders of the young girl. 'Go back downstairs, we'll settle this.' And quickly opening her handbag and pulling a 5M note out of her purse she pressed it into her hand. Then she entered the room and closed the door.

'You didn't give her money, did you?!' asked Leo.

'Yes, I did!' Emma took a deep breath. She was trying to catch up on her own display of courage. 'She's just a poor little girl with no experience, and you've no right to be shouting at her like that. Just because she's a servant – she can't even defend herself! You men! You're all spoilt, with us women doing everything for you. It's time that things evened out a bit between the genders!'

'Emma, everyone has their place in the world. Mine is to work and earn money for you to spend...'

'I worked too, and I enjoyed it, and I wouldn't mind doing it again! And men can cook or wash clothes just as well as women. It's not part of a natural law that tasks are divided up that way.'

'It's the way our culture is organised, and I think it works very well!' Leo turned his back to her and started rummaging in the wardrobe for another shirt.

'Well, our culture is being turned head over heels at present, so maybe it's a good time to reform this part of it too! It's very unfair! And to shout at that poor girl like that! Do you call that culture?!'

But Leo had his head buried in the wardrobe. She observed him for a moment, then looked at her wristwatch.

'I'll wait for you downstairs,' she said. 'We'll be late.'

And she left, closing the door loudly behind her.

23

23–24 February: A Day at the Office

The faint February sun spread a glitter of sparks on the thick snow in the allotment gardens near the tracks, as the train from Munich approached the outskirts of Berlin. Leo carefully stretched his long legs under the seat in front of him, and settled into a more comfortable position. It was a modern carriage, with upholstered seats, and he had been able to sleep most of the time, but after ten hours he needed to move and walk about to get his circulation going. He'd be home in an hour. He was dying for a solid meal and a bath. The bath meant filling all the big saucepans with hot water and heating them on the cooker. Just as well that they'd decided on the bigger model with four jets. There'd be one left over for him to heat some food. He hadn't really eaten since midday yesterday, when he and Emma had gone back to the farmhouse-pub in the village. They'd had several meals there, and when he was leaving he'd been able to buy two pounds of home-churned butter and a large slab of smoked bacon. The farmer's wife, who had taken a shine to him, wrapped it up for him, and then added half of one of the six huge crusty loaves that she had just hauled out of the community baking oven. So while the water was heating, he'd open a jar of stuffed cabbage rolls donated by his mother-in-law and heat them, and then fry a slice of the bacon, and have that together with a thick slab of the pungent bread spread with real butter. His mouth watered as he sorted all this out, and he again shifted in his seat to try to ease his shoulders.

    He stared out at the small industrial complexes, the untidy backs of tenement houses, local stations crowded with travellers, the odd gutted building or factory, parks with bare trees mingled with snow-laden evergreens. But his mind was still back in the village. It had been a wonderful holiday. How welcome the uninterrupted nights had been, the reliable peacefulness, the fresh, cool air, the sunlight glistening on the glaring snow, so clean and pure. Even the locals, seemingly dour at first, with an impossible dialect, revealed a gruff friendliness as he came to know them. Best of all was being there together with Emma. She seemed newly made, relaxed and happy, like she was when he'd first met her. It was a shame they hadn't been able to get a double room, but the cosy closeness of her bed had had its own charm, and the landlady, he suspected, had turned a blind eye, so that they had been able to spend quite a few nights together. Of course, there'd been that silly incident with the girl. Emma had looked wonderful – he'd never seen her angry before. It had frightened him at first, but she just needed to let off steam, and he had used his usual strategy in such a case, which was to ignore it. They'd come together again quite normally a day or so later, and the rest of the holiday had been as perfect as the first few days.

A Normal Couple

As the train drew into Anhalter Bahnhof, passengers began to scramble out of their seats, and Leo retrieved his knapsack from the luggage rack, taking care not to jostle the six bottles of Enzian schnapps he had wrapped up in his socks and his extra pullover. He always liked to bring little presents for close friends or colleagues when he'd been away, and the strong, delicately flavoured spirits distilled from the Alpine gentian was perfect. There was nothing like it to be found in Berlin right now. When the train had stopped, he climbed down onto the platform and found the luggage car for his suitcase. As he made his way to the tram, he was whistling a snatch from 'Aida'.

Five hours later he was out at his in-laws' place in Zehlendorf. The first thing he saw, after Elisabeth had opened the door, was his 9-month-old son crawling towards him, a wide smile of triumph vying with a look of stern concentration on his face. He swooped him up and gave him a hug and a big kiss, and then held him at arms' length. Jo had definitely put on weight: he now had three chins, and had grown five sharp little teeth. He beamed at his father and tried to grab his nose, but after a few seconds he began to wriggle, and Leo set him down to crawl again. Jo wiggled off round the corner to the kitchen.

In the meantime, Paul had appeared, also smiling widely, and behind him were Moritz and Fra. What a pleasant surprise! They drew Leo into the drawing room, where plates with remnants of cake and glasses of wine and cognac on the side tables showed that they had been celebrating Moritz's birthday. Leo hadn't forgotten it, and presented him with a half-bottle of gentian. For his father-in-law he had a large bottle, and for Elisabeth a soft white shawl embroidered with

Alpine flowers. Fra got a small enamel brooch depicting an edelweiss.

'You seem to have had good skiing weather,' commented Moritz, and made circles of his thumbs and index fingers in front of his eyes. Leo smiled. Shaving after his bath, he'd noticed that his face was quite sunburned, with abrupt white areas around his eyes and at the top of his forehead, where his skiing cap ended.

'It was indescribable,' he said.

He gave them all the news about Emma, the village and her cure. 'The best part was being able to sleep through the nights. There haven't been any more attacks, have there?'

'No,' answered Moritz, 'not since …. Not for some weeks, actually.'

They all thought hard, and then Paul said, 'I think the last raids were those just before Christmas. Since then there haven't been any. Nearly eight weeks. I wonder what that means.'

All eyes turned to Moritz.

'I think it's just too far for them to fly from Britain. And the cold weather is dangerous too; ice can form on the wings. My guess is that they won't start again until it gets warmer. But then, of course, they'll lose the advantage of being able to fly the whole stretch here and back under cover of darkness. Our air defence will get them.'

Leo remembered that Colonel Sonntag had said the same.

'So we can hope that the worst of it is over,' he smiled, forgetting the rest of Sonntag's assessment.

'Maybe,' said Moritz, setting down his glass. 'Only maybe.'

The positive effects of his holiday began to crumble away as soon as he entered the office next morning. He'd hoped to slip straight into his own room, picking up his mail from his secretary on the way, but before he'd even turned into his corridor he bumped into young Eckart.

'Ah, Herr Gebhardt, welcome back. Have you had a good time? Been able to relax?' And before Leo could reply, he dropped his voice. 'You've been sorely missed. Klaus is on the warpath against you, says he can't find his way round your files. But I believe Bischoff has sent him off with a flea in his ear. Oh, and Dr Strauss rang several times looking for you. Your secretary will tell you. Good to have you back!' And he hurried on.

Leo changed his mind about going into his office and headed for Bischoff's door instead.

'Ah, Gebhardt! Back at last! I must say you look very well, typical skiing suntan!' and he laughed heartily as he joined his index fingers and thumbs in the goggles symbol. Leo smiled. They shook hands, and Leo presented him with a (small) bottle of gentian, which Bischoff accepted with sincere thanks and the comment that it was impossible to get in Berlin.

Dr Bischoff asked how Emma was doing, and Leo told him that she had sent her regards. Bischoff smiled gently.

'So what's new?' asked Leo. 'Is there an earthquake anywhere?'

'Well, I don't want to swamp you after you've so obviously had a restful holiday, but yes, it's one crisis after another. The Bulgarian tour you organised is jeopardised since our troops marched in. I suppose it's not surprising that they're reluctant to applaud a German orchestra at the moment. Though the Wehrmacht report said they welcomed the army with open arms. I don't know. I suppose they always say that. Let's hope it'll blow over. But all those cancellations need to be organised, the hotels, soloists and so on!'

'My secretary will deal with that,' said Leo in a friendly tone.

'Then there's an awkward matter, I don't know how we're going to get out of this one. Meister Konoye wants to conduct Beethoven's Ninth here in Berlin next winter. I can't see the German public going for a Japanese conductor for this work. What do you think?'

'I can't decide that right away. I'll make a note of it and get back to you. Who was the application addressed to?'

Bischoff turned to his desk. It was covered with a sprawl of papers, which he shuffled around, picking up and discarding a couple of pages.

'Ask my secretary, she'll be able to tell you. And then there's Professor Molina from Milan. Apparently Furtwängler has promised him a tour of Germany this autumn, but we have no capacity for a series of full orchestral concerts. He's been on the phone about it, I think your secretary took the calls. Oh yes, and Dr Strauss called about five times asking for you. Something to do with the Japanese Festival Music last year. I thought all that was wrapped up.'

'I think I'd better get in touch with both our secretaries, and see what's in my In-box before we talk any further, Dr Bischoff. But I'm sure we can find solutions to all these queries. I'll look into them right away.'

And he escaped to the relative calm of his own room and sat down at his desk. He'd left it with just a large blotting pad, a marble pen and ink set, and a set of reference dictionaries on it – now it was covered in papers: correspondence, sheet music, new sets of regulations in small print, hand-written memos, as well as random paper files.

He sighed, and called his secretary on the phone. She came immediately.

Fräulein Schubert was a complete contrast to Emma. When she was first presented to him, he was immediately convinced that Bischoff had been induced to accept her in the hope that her appearance would guarantee a longer career in the ministry than Emma's. She was almost as tall as he was, and as thin as a laundry pole. In fact, she seemed to consist mainly of corners. Her long narrow face, closely set pale eyes and thin mouth were framed by wispy hair of an undefinable colour shaped into limp curls. She was usually clothed in a grey suit or dress, with strong, sensible shoes. When she moved, her arms and legs seemed to go different ways, reminding him of a crab. Her redeeming feature was her voice, which was a pitch lower than normal and had a pleasant timbre, so that he sometimes wondered if she took singing lessons. That was an area he hadn't wanted to explore so far.

For all that, she was excellent at her job, very efficient and level-headed, well able to deal with Dr Bischoff and people like Klaus. So he was all the more surprised at the state of his desk.

'Welcome back, Dr Gebhardt,' she said. 'I hope your wife is enjoying the cure and that it's helping her?'

'Thank you, she's doing quite well. We had a very restful holiday.' And he presented her with a little box. She opened it right away – it contained a brooch, an enamel painting of an edelweiss, identical to Franzi's.

'That's very pretty, thank you so much for thinking of me. You shouldn't have!'

'Well, you seem to have had a lot on your hands while I was away.'

'It certainly wasn't boring,' she smiled tautly. 'I see Herr Klaus has been in over the weekend. I swear I left your desk completely tidied on Friday afternoon, but this has happened before. Herr Klaus works very hard, I must say, even at the weekends.'

'Can you sort it for me? You'll be able to see what goes where much faster than I. Then I can settle down to work.'

'Of course. There's one thing though, Dr Gebhardt. Dr Strauss called twice. He says he hasn't yet received the tea and the statue, and he'd like you to look into it. I hope I have that message right, I've no idea what he meant.'

Leo laughed. 'It was part of his fee for the Japanese Festival Music he composed last year, commissioned to celebrate the 2600th anniversary of the Japanese Empire. Besides his fee he asked for ten pounds of tea and a statue of a buddha. I'll call him now and try to calm him down, and then we'll have to find out where they are. Can you put me through to his house in Garmisch before you start on my desk?'

Richard Strauss, now in his 77th year, was Germany's leading composer and world famous for his operas. He had been appointed head of the Music Department when it was formed back in '33, but differences of opinion between him and the politicians on cultural matters had soon induced him to resign. He lived in Bavaria, from where he made sure to keep on the right side of the administration while staying as far away from them as possible. This was not only for his own peace of mind, but also to protect his Jewish daughter-in-law, Alice, and her family.

A Normal Couple

Leo had organised the liaison between the Japanese agents and Dr Strauss last year, and had visited him in his house several times. On his second visit, he'd been presented with a haunch of venison that Strauss's son had shot, a welcome addition to his and Emma's meat rations.

The call came through in ten minutes and was taken by Strauss's wife. Leo chatted with her for a few minutes.

'How is Dr Strauss?' he asked. 'Is he planning any more concerts?'

'Oh, I don't know what he's about at the moment. At least he sits at his desk and his piano and works every morning, and he still gets his Skat games in the afternoons. But we're worried about Alice, and especially her mother. She's still in Theresienstadt Concentration Camp, and they won't even let us visit her. One hears terrible things about the conditions there. The poor old lady. What harm did she ever do anyone? Our grandsons' ID cards have been confiscated, and other children spit on them on their way to school. Where will all this end? Do you not know anyone, Herr Doctor, who has a say in those circles and can do something for her?'

'If the maestro himself couldn't move the authorities, I'm afraid there's nothing I can do, dear lady. I'm so sorry,' replied Leo gently. 'The main thing now is to look after yourselves, I mean ... not to draw attention to yourselves. But you know all that. These are difficult times and they seem to be getting more so.'

'Yes, indeed. But I don't want to keep you any longer. I'll get my husband.'

The conversation with Dr Strauss was even shorter. Leo promised to try to find out why the two consignments from Japan were taking so long, and they both hoped that the ship transporting them hadn't been torpedoed.

Fräulein Schubert had opened and sorted his mail, and he began to go through it when he got another call. It was the office in Prague. An official there wanted to know if there would be any political objection to the Czech violinist Jan Kubelik appearing in Liege in Belgium. Leo said he'd call back, and passed the query on to his assistant Klaus, asking him to report back. The reply came two hours later: the Czech violinist Jan Kubelik had died nine months earlier. Should the office in Prague mean his son, Raffael Kubelik, the conductor, there were, indeed, strong objections to his appearing there. It was well known that he refused to conduct works by Wagner, Hitler's favourite composer, and he declined to give the German salute.

'My God,' groaned Leo. 'How can you run international music exchanges with officials who don't even know if the person they're talking about is alive or dead?! What backwater have they come from?! What a waste of everyone's time!'

His attention was drawn to a letter from the Finnish Embassy addressed to Dr Leo von Gebhardt and ending 'With sincere expressions of respectful esteem'. The Finnish composer Yrjö Kilpinen wished to attend the Mozart Festival in Vienna at the end of the year, and hoped that some of his compositions – he was second only to Sibelius – might be performed there. Leo scribbled a memo in the margin of the letter: 'K. should apply to fringe events organisers, be polite!' He'd met Kilpinen some years earlier. He was a staunch supporter of the Führer and what he stood for, and though he was a wonderful composer, as a person Leo found him fawning and unpleasant.

The cancellation of the Bulgarian tour was urgent. He wrote a memo for young Eckart, their legal expert, asking him to deal with the contract end of matters, and another to Klaus, requesting him to cancel all the travel arrangements. He smiled as he noted this. Klaus would be furious at being landed with such a menial task. But someone had to do it. He'd probably pass it on to one of the secretaries.

Konoye conducting Beethoven's Ninth, the Choral Symphony, in Berlin, was a trickier matter. Personally, he saw no reason for turning it down. Konoye was a brilliant musician, and had been described as the 'Furtwängler of Japan', a comparison with Berlin's world-famous conductor of the Berlin Philharmonic. It could be an exciting project. But at the same time, he suspected that some of the leading knuckleheads at the top of the administration would object. They were people who held German music to be superior to that of all other nations, revering it regardless of its quality. He had talked to a top official from the newspaper department recently who confused the opera-composer Richard Strauss with Johann Strauss, the composer of pleasant light dance music like 'The Blue Danube'. Nonetheless, they would consider it irreverent for a Japanese person, someone who was visibly non-Aryan, to be conducting this monumental German work, one of the few they actually enjoyed listening to and could understand. He decided to put in a query to the programming section for a time slot and appropriate venue, and then see what results that might produce.

So the day passed. He dictated a request to the Head of the Passport Office in the Police Headquarters, authorising a passport for the opera soprano Rosalind von Schirach. Her brother was the Reich Governor of Vienna. He approved an application for travel subsidies by a North German choir for a concert in Pressburg in Slovakia. The contracts for four soloists for the Ninth Symphony in Prague in three months' time appeared on his desk – four weeks after the date of the signing! Where had they been all this time? Why hadn't they been sent to the singers? Who had messed this up?

And so on.

At four thirty he decided to call it a day. He would just have time to get back home, grab a bite to eat, and change. At six pm he was due to attend a piano recital in the Singakademie, part of the German-Yugoslav Music Exchange Programme. Nearly all the pieces were familiar, and he hoped he wouldn't fall asleep. As he packed his briefcase, his thoughts wandered back to the evening he'd had in that august auditorium with Emma, their first evening out together. How he wished she were here in Berlin with him. Together with Jo. Just the three of them. A peaceful evening at home.

His job looked very glamorous on paper. But behind the scenes, what he was doing was not much different from a sweeping brush clearing away some glamorous rubbish thrown in its path.

24

18 May: Some tensions in the family

'Fra, what do you think of this new fashion for the summer, those funny puff shorts under an open skirt. Aren't they a bit – you know …?'

'Why? Do you need something for the beach?'

'Well, yes, I could do with something that I could just walk about in and then quickly change into for sunbathing. Do you think they'd suit me?'

'Of course! I think they look pretty and summery, and you'd find them useful even inside the house if it got very hot. Do you have any material?'

Emma didn't. And she had given Leo most of her clothing coupons because he needed a new outfit for all of the receptions and concerts he had to attend.

'I told you not to give them all away, no matter how urgently he needed them!' scolded Elisabeth. 'It was clear as daylight that you'd be needing them yourself at some stage. How could you be so stupid!'

Emma flushed.

'He needed them more than I did!' she began.

Franzi broke in.

'Stop it, Ma! That's not fair! We're all in a tight spot when it comes to using our rations, and of course we try to help each other. Don't talk to Emma like that! What about that summer dress with the pattern of garlands that you bought two years ago. Didn't you say it doesn't fit you any more?'

'That's right, since rationing started. I've hardly worn it.' She hauled herself out of the outstretched garden chair and stomped up the steps into the veranda. Emma was foolish. She'd never learn, no matter how often she snapped at her.

After a long and cold spring, the weather had been fine for several days, and Emma had brought Jo out to Zehlendorf to see his grandparents. It was a Sunday. Leo, who had been in Italy for the week, was expected back shortly, and would come straight out to meet them here on his arrival in Berlin. They were expecting him for lunch.

Elisabeth reappeared with a cotton dress on a hanger. It had sleeves which ended just above the elbow, a fitted bodice, and a long loose skirt which reached almost to her ankles. Franzi regarded it with an expert eye.

'I could make a little jacket top with the bodice and the bottom of the skirt,' she said. 'But we'd need more material for the shorts. What do you think?'

'Could you not make a narrower skirt, and then have enough material for both?' asked Emma. 'The shorts needn't be terribly puffy.'

Fra laughed.

'I'm two sizes smaller than Ma as it is,' pleaded Emma.

'All right, all right!' smiled Franzi. 'Come inside and I'll take your measurements.'

Elisabeth kept an eye on the babies while the girls were in the house. Jo was trying to walk, hauling himself up on anything his little hands could grasp. Axel was starting to sit up on his own. Her heart swelled as she watched them, and a faint memory rose before her. The scent of recently cut grass, the gracious warmth of the early sun, the peacefulness of the Sunday morning – all this opened the window to a long-forgotten vision from the early days of her own motherhood. She and her sister Lotte were staying in Moehlten, at the estate of her maternal grandfather. Emma was four, and Lise just two, and while the children were crawling and playing in the long, dusty grass, she and Lotte, in voluminous cotton lawn blouses and ankle-length summer skirts, were watching the farmhands cutting the hay on a slope beyond the end of the extensive garden, a long row of them swinging their swishing scythes in unison across the endless meadow. It was just this picture she recalled, like a photograph. What was special about it? Had she been particularly happy? Had something unexpected happened? She didn't know. Why just this one image? Moehlten had always been a place apart, a safe constant in her unhappy childhood. Her own mother had died young, just like her grandmother, and her grandfather had married again, a school-friend of his daughter's. Elisabeth's step-grandmother was the same age as her dead mother had been. She was warm-hearted and enterprising, quite different than the new wife her father took. Her hobby was photography, and with her heavy mahogany-mounted lenses on awkward long tripods, she followed them and the babies around and produced the most charming photos that Elisabeth had ever seen, quite different from the formal poses of the photographer's studio that she was used to. Pictures of Emma as a baby studying her toes, as a toddler swinging a spade in the sand pit, as a four-year-old sitting in a wicker chair, her hands hugging her crossed legs, a pensive expression on her sweet little face – the expression she still had now, when she thought she was alone. How she loved them all! A happiness overcame her like a God-given shower. At that moment she would have done anything for them!

She shook her head. She knew that she was often sharp with the children, even unjust, her own and her grandchildren, small as they were. She knew she mustn't spoil them – the modern books on bringing up children had taught her that. But she felt now that her own childhood, with a stepmother who had been cold and overly strict, a father always away working, then dying before his time, had left her bereft of a pattern she could easily fall back on when responding to her own offspring.

She leant over to help Jo, whose arm had got stuck between the legs of the chair, and gently helped him to stand. He beamed at her and then pushed her away.

Paul came round the corner from the front of the house, a large bunch of fresh dandelion leaves in his hand.

'If I'd known we'd be keeping rabbits I wouldn't have done away with all those dandelions underneath the lilac trees last year,' he said ruefully. He smiled when he saw Jo. 'What a big boy! Standing already! Clever lad!'

Jo squealed in pleasure and waved his fat little arm, then turned abruptly and plonked down on his bottom. He immediately rolled over and tried to stand again.

Leo arrived two hours later, tired, and very hungry after the over-night train journey from Florence.

Before they ate, he distributed the gifts he'd brought for everyone: a litre bottle of olive oil for his mother-in-law, a bottle of grappa for Paul, a pair of ivory earrings for Franzi, and an ivory comb with a prettily carved shaft for Emma.

'You shouldn't have,' said Franzi. 'I'm sure you were much too busy to have time for shopping. They're lovely, thank you!' And she smacked a kiss on his cheek.

Elisabeth had managed to produce a large batch of rissoles, though they consisted more of bread than meat, but they were well seasoned, and together with a large helping of mashed potato and lots of kohl rabi in a light sauce, he was soon feeling fit again.

The conversation turned to the sensation of the moment: Rudolf Hess's mad flight the previous Sunday in a Messerschmidt 110 to Scotland, where he abandoned his plane and parachuted on the Duke of Hamilton's estate. Hess was, after all, no less than the Führer's deputy. According to the news, he had believed he could convince British politicians it was in their best interest to end the war and leave Germany a free hand.

'He's clearly crazy,' said Leo. Bischoff, who had been part of the delegation in Italy, had passed on the official explanation issued by the government, together with instructions to the media to downplay the whole escapade. Nonetheless, people were fascinated and amused, and in line with the Berliners' talent for turning anything unusual into a joke, a few good stories were doing the rounds.

'Have you heard this one?' asked Franzi. 'An announcement by the BBC: No further German cabinet ministers are expected to land by parachute this Sunday evening.'

'And the German High Command communiqué has announced that Göring and Goebbels are still firmly in German hands.' That came from Elisabeth.

'Where did you hear that one, Mama?' asked Emma smiling.

'At the butcher's yesterday. They were all talking about it. I wish I could remember more …. Oh yes! The 1000-year Reich has shrunk to 100 years. Why? One zero has dropped out!'

They all laughed at that one.

Franzi had heard lots of talk and quips in the clinic.

'Churchill asks Hess: "So you're the madman?" "No," says Hess, "only his deputy."'

'Well now,' said Paul, smiling, 'that's a risky one. You'd better be careful where you pass that one on, Fra. Certainly not to Uncle Otto!'

'Don't worry, Pa. But it's really surprising how openly people are talking about all of this, and making these comments. It's as if a veil of repression had been lifted. Very refreshing!'

'It's amazing they haven't clamped down on it,' said Emma.

'What was it like in Italy, Leo?' asked Elisabeth. 'How did the people react down there?'

'Oh, they all thought he was mad too. But there were no anti-government comments like you seem to have heard. Anything in that line took place very much behind closed doors, and only in absolutely secure company.'

'Talking about secure company,' Franzi said, leaning forward eagerly, 'do you know what a nurse on my floor told me? Her sister works in the Foreign Office, and she said the conditions there are absolutely chaotic. Everyone just goes around doing whatever they like. And documents marked Top Secret make the rounds in open envelopes. Anyone who wants to takes a peek at them, and then discusses the content over the phone. Can you believe that?!'

'I well can,' said Leo firmly, 'if it's anything like the madhouse I work in. They're great at putting on an efficient and strong face in public, but behind the scenes the left hand often doesn't know what the right hand is up to.'

'Did your friend have any information about the content of these secret documents?' asked Emma slyly.

Paul raised his eyebrows, but said nothing. Franzi was bursting to pass on the news she'd picked up from her friend, who had it from her sister.

'There's something going on at the Russian front. Troops are being withdrawn from the west, Normandy and so on, and sent to the east. All along the border to Russia. The girls didn't know why, but there were lists of numbers of regiments and divisions and so on, and where they were coming from and where they were going to. Says my colleague.'

Nobody said anything.

Leo spoke first. 'Why should troops be deployed to the Russian frontier? That doesn't make any sense. Russia and Germany signed a non-aggression pact before the war even broke out. Russia has been fighting on our side. They helped us in Poland and are helping to secure the eastern territories. Why should they attack us? They wouldn't have a chance! I don't believe what you heard, Fra. I'm sure it's just a rumour. All our efforts are concentrated on conquering England. That's why Hess took that mad step.'

'Maybe he took it because he knew that our troops were going to be taken away from Normandy, and he was hoping that England would capitulate before it became obvious that our army and air force were giving up on England, because they were pinned down somewhere else. Or something like that,' said Emma.

The others, all except Leo, stared at her. Each one of them considered whether what she'd said made sense or not.

'You could be right. Though maybe it's not a question of Russia attacking us,' said Paul thoughtfully, 'but the other way round.'

'What do you mean?' asked Emma.

'That we might attack Russia.'

A silence of consternation broke over them. Then all began speaking at once.

Leo: 'Excuse me, Papa, but that is complete nonsense!'

Franzi: 'That would be the absolutely ultimate madness!'

Elisabeth: 'Why on earth would we want to attack Russia?'

Emma: 'Dear God, I hope not!'

Paul raised both hands in a 'Hold on!' gesture.

'I think we should forget this conversation as soon and as thoroughly as possible. It is based on hearsay, on a possible rumour and pure speculation, and that is a poor foundation for a serious and profitable discussion. And the topic is much too dangerous to mention to anyone else. *Anyone*! And I mean it, so pay attention!'

Emma and Franzi started clearing the table, and, with the clattering of the dishes, no one talked. They brought in the dessert, bottled pears with a custard sauce.

'How was Italy, Leo?' asked Paul mildly.

'Very successful. Cooperation with the orchestras in Bologna and Florence is developing. With a bit of luck, Emmi, we can both travel to Florence for a festival of German Romantic Music sometime next year. I'm just dying to show it to you. The streets lined in bougainvillea and oleander, and wonderful little cafés on every corner. The old palaces and the little courtyards, so charming, and world-famous works of art at every turn!'

Emma smiled as she scraped her dessert bowl clean. Who knew what next year would bring? But it was pleasant to forget the present, even for half a minute, and dream of a more pleasant future.

Emma, Leo and Jo took their leave in the late afternoon. As they were sitting in the underground, Leo said, 'I met the most charming group of Spaniards at the conference in Rome. We spent a whole afternoon together walking in Monte Albani outside Rome, very interesting, cultivated people. One of them is a count!'

Emma leant over to check on Jo, who was asleep on the seat beside her. She waited for Leo to continue. He drew on his cigarette and expelled the smoke slowly.

'They'll be coming to Berlin at the end of the month, and I told them so much about you that they absolutely insisted on meeting you. So I've invited them for dinner at the end of the month. You'll love them!'

'That's nice,' answered Emma. 'How many did you say there were?'

'Just five, a lady and four gentlemen. Really pleasant, normal people. We'll have an enjoyable evening.'

'Yes, indeed,' said Emma. 'We'd better start saving our coupons, or will you be getting an allowance from the Ministry?'

'I'll look into that on Monday, shouldn't be any problem, as their visit is official.'

'That's nice,' said Emma again. 'We can look forward to it,' and, though she had to force herself, she smiled at Leo, loyally. She and Jo would be celebrating their birthdays at the end of the month, too. She wanted to invite her parents and Fra and Aunt Charlotte. She wondered how she'd manage.

25

19 June–18 July: Holidays at the Baltic Sea

Leo and Emma arrived in Prerow looking forward to lying on the beach in the sunshine. Indeed, the evening of their arrival was promising, warm and bright. But next morning they woke to grey and drizzle, which gradually developed into uncompromising rain. They decided to make the best of it, and went back to bed after breakfast. Jo was still tired from the train journey. He lay on his back in the cot in their room, one arm over his eyes, the thumb of the other firmly in his mouth. Leo made some suggestive sounds and movements, to which Emma responded, and they had a comfortable, relaxed session before both dropping off to sleep again.

A loud wail from Jo woke them. It was almost past lunch time and still raining. Leo suggested he go out and see if he could get some fish-rolls and a bottle of wine, and they would have a picnic in their room. Emma would like to have snuggled back under the bedclothes, but she got dressed and turned her attention to Jo. She took him up and smelt him, was tempted to feed him first and then change him later, but decided against it. He didn't like being changed, so she found a rusk in her food bag and gave it to him. It kept him busy till she was finished. Then she ran downstairs to her landlady's kitchen to heat the milk she knew was there waiting for her. Frau Hass was used to having small children stay, and had a fixed and smooth procedure for providing suitable food for babies and toddlers.

When she tried to settled Jo in his cot with the bottle, he protested loudly. She tried to ignore him while she finished unpacking and tidying away their things. Suddenly she heard him shouting: 'Mama! Mama!' in the midst of his crying. She dropped what she was carrying and picked him up, laughing, then walked around the room with him.

'Say it again, Jo! Mama! Say Mama!'

They had a large room, with an old-fashioned bedroom suite with twin beds, and a small round table and two chairs in one corner. In another corner was a bathroom sink and a mirror with some shelves for toiletries. Perfect. The floorboards creaked when one walked on them, but a worn, once valuable Persian carpet covered most of it. It was a corner room, with a window to the garden on one side and a balcony looking onto the street on the other. She stood at the glass door with Jo on her arm, looking out at the rain. To the left and right were lattice fences overgrown with wisteria, and the front wall was topped with heaps of petunias spilling over and out to the front, providing absolute privacy. A little basketwork table and two wicker chairs held the promise of cosy sunshine hours to come.

She put Jo down on the carpet and kept an eye on him while she found the tea towels she had packed for just such an occasion and spread them on the table. She removed the toothbrushes from the tumblers and rinsed them. Two fresh face cloths would serve as napkins. From their last holiday in Austria she had learnt the usefulness of bringing their own knives and forks, and these she laid carefully on the tea towels. The table was set for lunch.

Leo returned with four pickled herrings and some rolls, and a bottle of white Mosel wine.

'Not really right for herrings,' he said, 'but it was the only white they had.'

'It'll be fine!' said Emma. She was looking forward to their unusual meal – it was all so carefree and effortless! 'And guess what Jo just did!'

Their holiday in the Baltic Sea resort of Prerow had been planned some time ago. It was a small village located on the peninsula of Darss, west of Danzig, and the whole area consisted of sand dunes. Emma had spent a restful holiday there some years previously. The landscape reminded her of her beloved Kahlberg, hundreds of kilometres eastwards along the same coast, where she and her parents and sisters used to spend their summer holidays years ago. It was all new for Leo, and she was looking forward to showing it to him as soon as the weather permitted.

After their meal, Leo cleared everything away while Emma played with Jo, and then they all three went downstairs to the communal sitting room of their lodgings. The house was a villa run by a lady whose seafaring husband had passed away some years previously, and she had converted it into a boarding house. Though the bathrooms were old-fashioned and the wallpaper faded, it was spacious and comfortable. The sitting room was furnished with groups of armchairs and sofas, allowing several parties to sit quietly by themselves.

Now it was occupied by a young lady and an elderly gentleman; they were not together. The man rose as Emma entered the room, and introduced himself. He was portly and going bald, with a cheerful expression around a snub nose. The party button was pinned to his lapel.

'Schumann, from Bremen,' and he gave a little bow as he held out his hand.

Emma and Leo introduced themselves, and then turned to the young lady. She stood up to greet them, and they were surprised at how short she was.

'Emma Klinke,' she said, 'from Potsdam. Pleased to meet you.'

'Emma Gebhardt,' said Emma, and they both laughed. 'This is my husband, Dr Gebhardt, and this here,' and she held up Jo, 'is Jochen. He's a year old. I hope he won't disturb you, or else I'll take him back up.'

But Fräulein Klinke and Herr Schumann had no objections, and the Gebhardts chose a small sofa and armchair in a far corner. Jo was playing with a plush toy lamb, and Emma settled him on a blanket and cushions in a corner of the sofa. She took her book out of her handbag and snuggled into the other corner of the sofa. Leo had bought a paper and shook it open with a clatter. Jo blew bubbles for a while, then began to whimper. Emma took him on her lap, where he played with his left foot until his eyelids drooped and he fell asleep. It was still raining.

At 3.30 the door opened, and the maid came in with a trolley laden with cups and saucers, and a cake. Frau Hass followed with a big pot of ersatz coffee. Everyone smiled, and gathered round the table in the centre. In the end they all sat down at the table.

'How long have you been here?' Emma asked Frl. Klinke, admiring her handsome face and thick brown hair.

'I came last Saturday, and I have another week. The weather was lovely at first, and I'm sure it'll get better again. How long will you be staying?'

'My husband is here for a week, but I'll be staying longer, maybe four weeks. My mother will be coming to join me when he leaves.'

Leo had been given a pay rise, and he had decided the sea air would benefit her lungs and that she should stay on. He could afford it now.

'How nice!' said Herr Schumann. 'I arrived yesterday too, and will be here for just a week.'

It turned out that Herr Schumann was retired. He had been in charge of a department of the famous coffee importers Dahlmayr, and had 'closed shop' as he called it, a year previously.

'There's not much going on in the coffee business right now,' he said dryly. 'So I was glad to be able to leave.'

'Well, I'm kept busier than ever,' said Frl. Klinke. 'I'm a secretary, and my employer is the UFA!'

'Oh!' said Emma admiringly, but Herr Schumann said, 'Ufa?'

'The film company in Babelsberg, in Potsdam. "The Cabinet of Dr Mabuse", "The Blue Angel", "Metropolis" – you know!' said Emma.

'Ah, of course. Well, I never go to the cinema, I must admit. But I've heard of those films, of course.'

Emma was dying to ask if Frl. Klinke had met any of the big stars – Heinz Rühmann, Lilian Harvey, Marlene Dietrich, Gustav Gründgens – but she assumed everybody asked her that, so she held back.

It seemed no one dared to ask Leo where he worked, so Emma said: 'My husband works in the Propaganda Ministry, in the Department of Music. He looks after concert arrangements abroad. I used to work there as a secretary,' with a smile at Frl. Klinke. She really had a beautiful face, with strong features and large, clear brown eyes.

Herr Schumann found this interesting. It turned out that he was a great Wagner fan, and the two men were soon dissecting the various interpretations of the operas that they had seen.

'But "Rheingold" is the best by far, wouldn't you agree, Doctor?'

'Oh yes, there's no doubt about that!'

Frl. Klinke asked Emma what she was reading.

'"The Good Earth", by Pearl S. Buck. Do you know it?'

'Indeed I do, I loved it, and I've read all her other books too.' And the two young women spent an enjoyable ten minutes talking about Miss Buck's love stories, which were all set in China, and the exotic life and conditions she described in such a lively way. A squawk from Jo ended their conversation. Emma said she would take Jo up on her own, but Leo insisted on accompanying her.

'What pleasant people, Leo, aren't they?' said Emma, when they had reached their own room.

'Very nice! Though I wouldn't mind having seven days in a row when I *don't* have to give my opinions on music.'

'I heard you say you preferred "Rheingold" of all the Ring operas. I thought you didn't have a favourite?"'

'I don't, but I wasn't going to get into a deep discussion about the merits of all the Wagner operas. It would never have ended. After all, I'm on holiday! I need a break!'

'Quite right,' smiled Emma, and she pulled his face down to hers and gave him a kiss. 'They're nice people, but we want to be on our own for now. We'll have to watch out that they don't latch onto us. What's this? Don't move!' And she pulled a hair from the side of his head. 'Going grey already? You must relax this week, old man! We could go back to bed, if you like!'

The next morning was fair. Emma and Leo assembled their beach equipment and set off. They had the big pram for Jo. Sandy trails led slowly uphill from the houses through a band of scattered pine forest. Although the sandy trails were still dampened down from the rain, the wheels of the pram kept getting stuck on the flat roots of the trees. It was hard work, and they paused for a moment in a clearing. Emma breathed deeply, filling her lungs with the healthy, resinous-laden air. The forest ended where the sand dunes fell down to the shore. They paused again, admiring what lay spread out before them. The white beach was very wide, curving along a shallow bay which stretched and narrowed to distant points on either side. The sea lay in varying shades of blue and pale green near the shore, and deep blue at the sharply drawn horizon, where it met an almost white sky which, in turn, showed in deep blue overhead. Short busy waves splashed and broke and withdrew with the comforting sound of eternity.

They made their way down to the beach, which was not nearly as crowded as they had feared, but it was very windy, whipping up the fine sand. They rented a beach basket chair, and Leo immediately set about constructing their fortress. It took him an hour to dig the depression of about five metres in diameter, with the basket chair and the pram in the middle; with the sand removed from the centre he built up a wall all around, so that they were sheltered from the wind and from the eyes of most other bathers. This would be their home on the beach for as long as they were staying.

Leo went for a swim right away, after his heavy work.

'Wonderful,' he enthused when he returned, 'though pretty rough, and not very warm yet. But you must try it, Em, it'll do you good, toughen you up for the coming winter.'

'Hold on, not so fast, I'm still recovering from the last one!' laughed Emma.

'Not at all! You look as if you've been bedded on silk and fed on strawberries and cream!' said Leo. 'I could eat you up!'

Emma laughed. Her face looked as fresh and open as a flower bed in spring, thought Leo. She was wearing the beach suit Franzi had made for her, a short-sleeved, loose-fitting blouse and a flowing skirt, which ended just above her knees. She slipped this off now to reveal a pair of pleated shorts with a neat turnup. They emphasised her slim figure. All three parts were of the same material, reworked from Elisabeth's summer dress; Fra had produced an eye-catcher. Leo glowed with pleasure as he watched her. He hissed. She wagged her finger at him reprovingly, and he leant over and kissed her, intensively.

The morning passed in leisure. They walked to the water's edge with Jo, and let him dabble his feet in the shallows. It was his first time at the seaside. He squealed in delight when the waves broke, and stamped and splashed, and would have sat down if they hadn't held onto his arms.

'You'll be giving him swimming lessons soon,' said Emma.

In the afternoon, the sky began to cloud over, and they went back to the boarding house. They lay down for a while, and then went down for their evening meal. By now it was raining again. Before retiring for the night, they listened to the news on the radio in the sitting room. There had been no further air raids on Berlin. In fact, there had been very few raids there this year, compared to the year before, though the same could not be said of the heavily industrialised Rhineland. Victories were announced in North Africa, in Yugoslavia and Greece. Crete had been taken by the German Wehrmacht. Everything was working in favour of Germany.

Emma and Leo had had a restful day, and felt relaxed and very happy as they snuggled into each other for the night.

'Have you heard the news, Herr Gebhardt?!' Their landlady's face was sweating and her cheeks were bright red. She placed the coffee pot on their table and wiped her hands on her flowered apron.

'Good morning, Frau Hass,' said Leo calmly, peering out the window at the weather. Yesterday's rain had stopped, and the sky was a promising blue with white clouds racing out to sea.

'Good morning, excuse me, I'm all over the place! Have you heard?'

'Heard what, dear lady?' asked Leo, tucking his white table napkin into the collar of his shirt.

'It's Russia! They've attacked Russia. We ... The army has advanced on Russia, they crossed the border along the entire eastern front! During the night. We're at war with Russia!'

The two other guests had entered the room. They stopped when they heard her.

'That cannot be!' This from Fräulein Klinke. 'We signed a non-aggression pact with Russia before the war, and ...'

'And Foreign Minister Molotov was here on a state visit just before Christmas! The streets were lined with people cheering for him! Why should we attack Russia?' exclaimed Herr Schumann.

'There must have been some provocation,' said Leo. 'The Bolsheviks might have been planning to attack us, despite the pact. There must have been some reason for it. There was no inkling of this happening ....'

Emma caught his eye, and he stopped. They both recalled the conversation they'd had earlier that month, when Franzi had passed on the rumours that were coursing through the Foreign Department. And a colleague of Leo's had told him, in a quiet moment, that his son's regiment was being transferred from Italy to the east, and he didn't know what to make of it. This had been brewing for some time, it seemed, and if he had enquired more seriously, he could possibly have found out more. But it seemed so preposterous. The repercussions were enormous! The whole strategy of the war, its development, its aims and its end – had all this changed? For a moment he was thunderstruck.

'Those Bolsheviks can't be trusted,' Herr Schumann was saying. 'It might not be a bad idea at all to get rid of them. Murdering their royal family like that. And Stalin allowing his own people to starve just to push through his primitive ideas of collective farms. Dispossessing landowners who had farmed their estates for generations!'

'Indeed!' said Leo. 'And they want to spread their creed around the rest of Europe too. Who knows if they mightn't have tried to turn Poland or Bulgaria communist too! They need to be shown how far they can go, and who better to teach them that than our Führer!'

'It's an excellent policy,' said Herr Schumann brightly. 'This alliance with us must have been a mere cover for their real plans. World domination! They have to be stopped. Our Führer has landed another wonderful coup!'

'Well ... but...,' began Frl. Klinke in a clear voice, 'they're an independent country, aren't they, and they haven't attacked or harmed us so far. What international law of warfare gives us the right to attack them?'

The men stared at her.

'I really don't know!' she said. 'I'm just asking. As far as I know a war is justified only if there is a serious reason. Our leadership is always emphasising that we act according to international law. So what is the position here? Do either of you gentlemen know?'

'It's too early to answer those questions now,' said Leo, with a frown. 'The next few days will bring more background information, so that we can understand the whole picture. We can rely on the Supreme Command to know what they are doing. If they've decided to attack Russia, then it must have been unavoidable. And the German army is so well set up, its equipment so up-to-date, our soldiers so motivated – the Bolshies have nothing to set against us, they're unprepared, their equipment outdated, their troops semi-barbaric for all I know. It should be another blitz for the German army, just like in Belgium and Holland and France last year. A couple of weeks, and the whole thing will be over. We'll have taken Moscow, and that will be that.'

Frl. Klinke looked at him from keen eyes, her face expressionless.

'All those soldiers, young lads, whether on our side or theirs.... All those young lives, lost, wasted....'

'Not wasted, dear lady,' said Herr Schumann. 'On our side, it's for a good cause. And the Russians, like all Slavs, well, they haven't reached our level of development, it's different for them. They don't feel such a loss the same way as we do.'

Frl. Klinke sat down at her table, and poured herself some coffee.

'They are all some mother's sons, and I can't imagine a Slav mother is less devastated by the death of her child than a German one.' She spooned sugar into her coffee.

An awkward silence fell.

Leo took another roll, cut it open, and spread plum jam on it.

'What do you think, Emma, should we try the beach again this morning? Perhaps Jo is ready for his first swimming lesson? What do you think, Jo?'

Jo was sitting at the table on a high chair, and Emma had been soaking pieces of bread in milk and feeding him. She had been so busy making sure he didn't mess up the table, his chair, his clothes, the carpet, that she had been unable to contribute to the conversation – for which she was grateful. In the process she had hardly eaten anything herself, but now she just wanted to get away.

The piercing June sunshine had dried the sand by the time they reached their fortress on the beach, and the wind had died down. They made themselves comfortable. Leo went for a swim while Emma and Jo paddled in the shallows, jumping together over the little waves. Jo laughed loudly, throwing his head back and enjoying every minute of this new adventure. Later, she put him down on his blanket, where he practised rolling over and crawling. She and Leo took turns hauling him back when he went too far.

Emma's head was still racing from the morning's news.

'This new war – it'll be fighting on two fronts now. How can the country afford that? It's crazy!'

'Well, there's not much fighting on the western front any more. France and Belgium and Denmark and so on are all firmly in our hands, and like Paul said earlier this month – was it Paul? – anyway, it looks as if we've given up on taking England.'

'That's what Fra suggested too. Herr Sonntag hinted at something similar, didn't he? Can you remember exactly what he said? And I imagine there's all kinds of resources in Russia that we could use – the Ukraine is the breadbasket of Europe, and there's oil there somewhere too, isn't there?'

Leo lit a cigarette. 'In Azerbaijan. But that's pretty far to the east. Still, I'd say it'll all be over in a couple of weeks. They have nothing, those people.'

'That's what they said about England too, when we started bombing their cities. Five weeks it was supposed to last, and no longer, and look at where we are now! Russia is so huge. If this campaign goes on into the winter, well, you know what happened to Napoleon, and I don't see it being any different now.'

Emma had read the full version of 'War and Peace'.

'Look, Emma, I can't imagine our High Command would send such a huge army into Russia without being prepared for all possible developments. It goes without saying that our soldiers will be properly equipped even if the campaign does last longer. You can't possibly doubt their ability to plan such a project down to the last woollen mitten and fur-lined snow hat. Or can you? Now really!'

Emma was silenced. She very much could doubt that such extensive and expensive preparations had been implemented, especially since the news reports never ceased to emphasise that victory would be theirs in only a few weeks.

Leo must have read her mind.

'We'll just have to wait and see, I suppose. And listen to the Armed Forces Reports.'

Emma took Leo's hand in hers, and they sat in silence for a while. It was a Sunday, and families with children had come to the beach for the day. Near them, a group of boys was playing chasing around the sand fortresses, yelling and kicking up sand, pushing and knocking each other over in good humoured exuberance. A group of teenage girls went by, chattering and laughing loudly, their eyes wandering towards the boys in search of possible admirers.

'It's almost like the old days in Kahlberg,' smiled Emma, 'except that the beach there was always much fuller.'

'Frau Hass was telling me that the number of visitors has plummeted. I suppose it's to be expected. You can see there are no young men here, just grandparents and mothers. Mainly.'

They glanced quickly at a family group sitting near them, a white-haired couple, a younger woman, and a young man with a bandage over his left eye and the empty sleeve of his right arm pinned to the shoulder of his shirt.

'At least he's still alive,' said Emma quietly. 'An arm for a life. His active days are finished.'

Leo put his arm around her shoulders and drew her closer. She closed her eyes.

'Leo, there's something I've been meaning to talk to you about. I know the bombing has almost stopped. But if it should start again, when the nights get longer, I don't want to be in Berlin. I've been thinking and thinking about what Herr Sonntag advised, about finding somewhere out in the country. You're away so often, it's all so difficult on my own, and I'm sure you too would feel easier in your mind if you knew Jo and I were somewhere safe. What do you think?'

'You know I never like to be in the flat on my own, all alone without my Rose and my Bud near me. I don't think the bombing will ever be like it was again. And don't you think you could organise things better? Leave the bags down in the shelter in the cellar and then you'll only need to bring down Jo and our papers and a bag of fresh food.'

Leo shaded his eyes from the sun with his hand, and stared intently out to sea at a small sailing boat.

'Oh Leo,' said Emma. 'You know it's not as easy as that. It's not just getting downstairs, it's the whole experience, the noise and stress and fear ...'

'Well, if it makes you feel better, there's no harm in looking around at where you could go. You can always come here, I suppose, though it might get a bit expensive if you stayed longer.'

'No, I was thinking of staying with family or friends. With Lise and Benno in Waldrode, for example. Or maybe with Marie in Elbing.'

'That's awfully far away,' said Leo morosely.

'Well, it's just a thought. I'll talk to my parents about it, they might have an idea. My uncles live out in the country too, some of them. There are probably lots of places that aren't as far away as Marie and Lise. I just wanted to have your approval for the idea before I undertook anything.'

'Of course, my sweet. Make your arrangements, by all means. It's just that I don't think it'll be necessary.'

'All the better,' said Emma. 'But I like to be prepared.'

The rest of Leo's week passed quickly and uneventfully. The weather remained fine, and they spent all their time on the beach. Emma had finished Pearl Buck and was reading a small volume by Stefan Zweig, 'Decisive Moments in History', which she had missed when it first appeared many years previously. This was Elisabeth's copy. She'd made a jacket of brown paper for it so that no one could see the title. Zweig was banned – his books had been burned in Berlin in 1933.

Leo had brought a novel by Agatha Christie, 'Peril at End House'. But he could never sit still for long. The wall of their fortress needed constant attention, he believed, and he would wander off into the forest to collect fallen branches with which to strengthen it. He made sure the floor of their refuge was even, and then fetched clumps of pine twigs with their long needles to construct an attractive green fence on top of his wall. In between he slept, and swam, and played with Jo.

The official news provided by the Armed Forces reported speedy advances with little or no resistance from the Bolsheviks. On the 25th it announced that the threat of a massive Russian invasion of the Reich had been warded off by the advance into Russia, where the Wehrmacht arrived just in time to prevent the enemy forces from forming. The Wehrmacht was actively supported by the air force right from the start.

'I wonder how that will affect Moritz,' said Leo. 'Poor Aida!'

Frau Hass drew out the footstool from under her armchair and settled herself comfortably, a tiny glass of sherry from her precious store in the back

A Normal Couple

cellar on the side table next to her. She sighed. It was 2pm, and this was her holy hour – it was an iron rule in the house that nobody was allowed to disturb her until after 3.00. She set her alarm for 2.55, sipped her drink, and closed her eyes.

Her work tired her more and more every day. The difficulty of procuring enough food for all her guests, the bureaucracy involved in collecting and passing on the ration coupons, finding enough meat or meatlike foodstuffs to satisfy her guests, even things like locating that awful soap for the laundry, or always making sure the windows were blacked out. Her guests were usually understanding, but there was the odd one who expected pre-war standards, and it was always unpleasant to have to lay out her position and to bring them round to her point of view without being rude or overly adamant.

Like Frau Marc, the mother of that lovely young Frau Gebhardt. She'd been here for a fortnight now, arrived the day after charming Herr Gebhardt departed. He was some big shot in one of the ministries, she had gathered, but really quite down-to-earth and easy to deal with. Though he'd put on airs when he found the parcel his father had sent him had been left waiting for him in the sun. As it turned out, it contained butter and eggs. That had been unpleasant. The postman, Erich, couldn't know what was in the parcel, and it was good of him to leave it at the door, so Herr Gebhardt wouldn't have to walk all the way to the post office at the other end of the village to pick it up. Yet Herr Gebhardt gave Erich a nasty talking to the next day. On the other hand, the day before he left, he brought her a beautiful bunch of wildflowers, most tastefully arranged and bound, and he gave Magda 5M as a tip. That was nice of him.

But the mother was something else. She noticed that Frau Gebhardt – Emma – was nervous on the morning her mother was coming. She arrived with a huge suitcase, and insisted on a man being found to carry it upstairs for her, though Frau Hass knew they could have managed it between them. Luckily Arno was working in the garden. She hardly thanked him. Frau Hass heard her voice upstairs all afternoon, with just a low comment from Emma now and again. And during the evening meal – Frau Hass had produced a tasty soup with little croutons floating in it – Frau Marc had commented loudly that she had expected something more substantial than these bits of dry bread floating in coloured water. She'd handed in her coupons and wanted her money's worth – probably the landlady was using the coupons to feed her own family. At this Emma had reacted sharply, poor thing, and her mother had been silenced. But the older lady clearly had a mighty appetite, and possibly she left the table still feeling hungry. Frau Hass had noticed that the summer dresses she wore hung loosely on her.

She sighed again.

Luckily they spent most of their time on the beach. Young Frau Gebhardt could never have managed that pram, with the baby and all her things for the day, on the strand by herself. Frau Hass had long intended to get Arno to make her one or two little wagons, with wide wheels and a long handle, that one person could pull through the sand even when it was fully loaded. She should have taken care of it before the war. Now it was almost impossible to get the materials. She must check her late husband's workshop. She might find enough nails and screws, and maybe even some planks, that Arno could use. But where to get the wheels?

There'd been a real row upstairs three days after Frau Marc arrived. Frau Hass couldn't hear what it was about, but when she checked that the room had been cleaned properly, she noticed a small change, and imagined that that might have been the cause. Frau Gebhardt – though probably it had been Herr Gebhardt – had made three little washing lines, by tying parallel lines of string across one corner of the balcony, from railing to railing. They must have brought the string with them, and even some clothes pegs. Frau Gebhardt obviously had a system whereby she washed small items up in their room every evening, and hung them outside to dry. With the fine weather, this worked well, and she had come down only twice a week with all the nappies, to have them boiled on the stove in the laundry room. But now, these lines were gone, and she had been bringing washing down every second day, saying she would pay for the extra work. It was clear that the mother had objected to the arrangement that had worked so well up till then. And she was constantly asking for extra food. The bloom that had grown on Emma's face during her first week with her husband was faded, just like the happy sparkle in her eyes. Frau Hass felt sorry for her.

At least the house was full again. Frl. Klinke and Herr Schumann had left, and a family of five had arrived, so that all three of her rooms were let again. It consisted of an elderly pair, the grandparents, their daughter, and her two children, a boy and a girl aged about eight and ten. Like the Gebhardts, they were from Berlin, and from what she could gather, they too lived in the inner city and had experienced the bombing last year. The father was safe in Norway, and they were staying for three weeks, which was nice for them and for her. The grandfather took the children for long rambles, so that the women could relax. They spent most of their time on their balcony.

She wondered how long she would manage to run the boarding house. While her husband was still alive, she'd enjoyed a comfortable lifestyle. He'd been a captain on one of the ferries to Sweden and Denmark. He loved his work, was often away longer than Frau Hass would have expected, but she never questioned him. When he was home, he was always good-tempered and loving. He'd had a rich sense of humour, and their hours together were filled with laughter and fun. Then, on his last holiday here, he suddenly got a heart attack, and died before help arrived. It had been a terrible shock, but with the aid of her sons-in-law, she'd set up the boarding house, and she enjoyed her new lifestyle and the variety it provided, now that the children were gone and she was alone. She and Wilhelm had had three, all girls (thank goodness!), married now and living in Hamburg and Rostock. In the winters, when things were quiet here, she visited Erna in Rostock regularly and could see her little grandchildren. Erna, dear child, would spoil her on her visits, and after rationing began she, in turn, had been able to supply her with extra butter and bacon. Her neighbour, Frau Bauer, gave it to her, in exchange for putting up some friends of hers free of charge every now and again.

That brought her back to Herr Gebhardt. Before he left, he'd dropped a hint about her supplying Emma with a pound of the wonderful local butter when she departed for Berlin? She'd replied in a vague way. He was clearly disappointed and even annoyed. All her guests were always asking her for extras on the side. They thought that because she was living out in the country, it was easy to get hold of these luxuries. But anything she could find was either used up in the boarding house, or else she sent it to her daughters in the cities. They needed it just as much as these strangers.

She dropped off. When the alarm rang shortly afterwards, she felt refreshed. She thought of Frau Gebhardt and the butter again. She'd wait and see. Perhaps she could wedge off some for her. It all depended.

26

18–21 July: Home from Prerow and Herr Liepmann makes a proposal

Emma would never have managed the return journey from Prerow on her own. She had Jo in the big pram, a bag, a rucksack, and a heavy suitcase. Elisabeth also had a bag and a suitcase. But between them, one minding Jo while the other brought the big luggage to the luggage van, they dealt with it.

Every seat in their compartment was taken. The other passengers were pleasant, and one lady entertained Jo for about ten minutes, playing peeky-boo by hiding her eyes behind her handbag. He was fascinated, and Emma and Elisabeth used the interlude to draw breath.

Franzi was at the station to meet them.

In Prerow the weather had continued fine and the temperatures had risen to record levels. They all had deep suntans. Emma and Elisabeth had settled into a ceasefire routine for the remainder of their stay. Elisabeth had tried hard not to cross or annoy Emma, and Emma had decided not to be so critical of her mother. That is not to say she wasn't constantly scared of what her mother might say in public. Elisabeth was as outspoken as she was unabashed in her views on Hitler and the regime. She had received news that the son of one of her best friends had fallen in Russia, and she was unable – and unwilling – to curb her indignation.

'Poor Elsa! Her darling Heinrich. Such a fine young man, so gentle. I knew him since he was a baby. And that ratpack sent him off to be slaughtered, just like that, while their own sons, nephews and in-laws are wrapped up in tissue paper and left doing "indispensable" work in some cosy office in town, beside an underground station which will take them back safely to their luxury flat close to a government bunker. How long will people stand for it!' Spoken in her normal speaking voice, if not even a little louder, during breakfast, in the presence of Frau Hass, Magda the maid, and the entire Trumpeter family.

Emma hissed at her to lower her voice. Elisabeth added, 'I'm only saying what everyone knows!' and truculently spooned honey on her bread. Emma needn't have worried. Frau Hass was neutral in her political opinions. All she was concerned about was that her business shouldn't get a bad name, either one way or another. All the adult Trumpeters were smiling, without meeting anyone's eye. Magda was deep in thought about what her Fritz might have meant last night when he said she'd have to reach a decision soon. The children were squabbling about the last bit of cheese.

Similar situations followed, even down at the beach, where it was worse, because she didn't know what kind of political animal might be listening. She developed a tactic whereby, as soon as she realised where her mother's tongue was going, she would interrupt and say the first thing that came into her head.

'That's a lovely bathing suit that young woman is wearing, look, over there, the blue one.'

'Frau Hass was looking tired this morning. I'm sure it isn't easy for her to run such a big place on her own.'

'Tell me again what Fra wrote to you in her last letter.'

Fra, in fact, had reported that Moritz had been moved from Brittany to Denmark. It meant they still couldn't live together, and she missed him terribly. When would she have a household of her own? But at least he wasn't being sent to Russia. Her colleague with the contact to the Foreign Office had passed on details that were not even hinted at in the official announcements. It seemed the advance wasn't going as smoothly as the Supreme Command had anticipated. Although the Wehrmacht had taken almost 330,000 prisoners at the battle of Minsk, (though in fact the majority of these were the civilian population), they had been unprepared for the power of the Russian heavy tanks that opposed them. The 'primitive Slav subhuman' proved to be an inventive, dauntless and highly motivated fighting machine, one, moreover, that had the advantage of being familiar with the territory. The German troops were surprised and impressed. They had been equipped with two months' supplies. Now it was rumoured that that wasn't nearly enough. Emma recalled her conversation with Leo about this eventuality and smiled to herself, despite the gravity of the situation.

Denmark was definitely a safer base for operations.

Emma also passed on the news she received from Leo. He had spent a week at conferences in

Karlsbad and Bad Elster, on the Czech border, where he had had a wonderful time. The food had been more than reasonable, and the surroundings! An upper-class spa, everything in tip-top condition, the baths a dream. He had gone swimming every day. If only she could be there with him!

And on the 18th, the day of her return, he had to leave Berlin again for five days. He was attending the Wagner Festival in Bayreuth; normally he looked forward to this, but the idea of his Rose and their Bud returning to an empty apartment didn't appeal to him at all. They would make up for it when he returned! At least she could enjoy their balcony. Their maid, Rosemarie, had done a good job watering everything. The roses and gladiolas he'd planted were in full flower, as were the sweet peas, absolutely beautiful, except that they had no scent! That crook of a gardener had sold him the wrong seeds! What a shame Frau Hass hadn't come up with the butter! The tomatoes on the kitchen table were from Kempinski, delicious! He sent a thousand million kisses.

Emma was delighted to be at home again. It was much easier to look after Jo here, and she had Rosemarie to help her. Franzi and her mother dropped her off at her flat, and she arranged to go out and see them all the following day. There had been no more air raids. She could relax, free from having to fit in with anyone's demands. She missed Leo, but she didn't mind spending some time alone. And indeed, the balcony was a dream.

And Leo had left a beautiful surprise for her, a small amber casket for her necklaces. Amber nuggets were washed up on the shore of the Baltic every spring, and all the shops had amber jewellery and other artefacts on sale. But she hadn't noticed him buying this pretty little box. She was very touched.

She arrived at her parents' house just before lunch the next day. Elisabeth and Fra had made a salad with lots of vegetables from the garden, and a dessert of late red- and blackcurrants and raspberries, sweetened with honey that Elisabeth had bought coupon-free in Prerow.

After lunch, Elisabeth went to her room for a lie-down. Emma asked Fra about Moritz's work in Denmark.

'He's been assigned to some office, planning. I imagine it has to do with Russia. I suppose they can reach targets to the north more quickly from there. I don't really know. Anyway, he insists I really needn't worry about him right now. And I'm relieved, of course. Oh – he does get some flying in. He mentioned something about private flights for his boss, Göring, bringing crates to a small airport not far from Carinhall.'

'Where's that?'

'Carinhall? Göring's palace in the forests north of Berlin. His private hunting grounds. I thought everyone knew about it!'

'New to me,' said Emma. 'But all that's great news. Is there any chance you can join him in Denmark? I'd say life there would be more pleasant than in Berlin right now!'

'No, no sign of that at present. But we've looked at the possibility of me staying in a hotel on the German side of the border, so that we can meet more often. And! – he's got a month's leave in August, and then we're going to Spain together! He wants to show me everything! Ma has said she'll take Axel, I'm just weaning him. I thought first I'd bring him along too, but it's not a good idea. It'll be so hot there, and their hygiene might not be up to scratch, contaminated water and so on. He'll be

A Normal Couple

safer here, and Moritz and I have a lot of catching up to do! It's a chance I can't let pass.'

'I'm delighted for both of you! Don't worry about Axel. Jo and I will spend time out here as often as possible. He'll be well looked after. I do envy you! Will you be going down south to Grenada and those other Moorish towns? I've always wanted to see them!'

'I hope so, but I don't know yet what he's planned. It'll be a change just to get away from a country that's actively at war. He only told me a week ago, so it's all new for me too.'

The afternoon passed quietly and harmoniously. Emma felt safe and happy. Yet she was aware that she was no longer part of this world. Her married life had formed her new. She belonged in her own surroundings, her own home, together with her husband and her child. The sudden realisation of this surprised her, and pleased her at the same time. She was on the right path, her life was on course. Suddenly she missed Leo very much. She looked forward to writing to him when she got home in the evening. She wouldn't tell him what she had just discovered about herself, but she was sure her new-found happiness would find an outlet in the words she chose to let him know how much she loved him.

Two nights later. Emma had trouble falling asleep. Jo was teething and was cantankerous, and she was unsure of how to deal with him. She'd got a baby syrup from the chemist, and had given him a teaspoonful at midnight. After that they both fell asleep.

Only two hours later the sirens started their ominous wailing. She woke up heavily, then mechanically followed the safety procedure. She had packed their necessities in a rucksack, so that she would have her hands free to carry Jo. She bundled him up in his blanket and set off down to their own cellar. Sonntags were away, she knew – he was in the office, she was visiting family in the east. Some other inhabitants of the house were also away, so that she was joined in the cellar only by Stegmanns from the top floor, and Frau Koske, who lived under her. She settled in Leo's deckchair. It was cool down here and she pulled the blanket they kept there around her. The iron door had hardly been closed when they could make out the rumbling of the aircraft overhead. It got louder and louder, and suddenly the anti-aircraft guns from the nearby defence post opened fire, much louder than the noise of the planes. Sporadic, muffled, yet frightening gunfire penetrated the cellar – but there was no response from the enemy bombers. They just flew on.

'Some other poor souls further on are for it,' observed Frau Koske

The sound of the guns grew thinner; the planes were out of reach. Silence.

Emma slept for a while. At 3.15 the all-clear sounded, and they stumbled upstairs, glad of another few hours' sleep before the daily routine of jobs and chores called. It was getting bright outside, the dawn chorus was in full volume. The heavy scent of the lime trees emphasised the promise of another hot summer day. Emma didn't care. All she wanted was to get back to bed.

At the baker's, some hours later, Frau Althaus scrutinised Emma's ration coupon.

'Is anything wrong with it?' asked Emma, irritated.

'I have to make sure...'

'What?'

'Don't you know? They dropped bundles of forged rationing coupons everywhere.'

'Who?'

'Last night, early this morning. Those planes. The Tommies.'

'They dropped ration coupons?!'

'Yes!'

Emma had to laugh.

'And have you been given any of them yet, Frau Althaus?'

'Not yet, but I have to watch out!'

'No one would dare to pick them up, let alone use them.' There were strict prohibitions, with dire punishments for picking up any leaflets dropped by the enemy.

'You can't be careful enough!'

Emma smiled and shook her head as she left the shop.

That evening, Emma was sitting listening to a concert on the radio while darning stockings. Jo was asleep in the nursery. Emma had left the doors open so that she could hear him if he got uneasy. His tooth had emerged, but his little cheek was red and sore. She was giving him the syrup every few hours.

Her doorbell rang. She looked at the clock on the bookshelf. 8.30. Who could it be at this hour? Was it one of the late-night visitors for the Sonntags, mistaking her door for theirs? She put aside her needlework and opened the door without removing the safety chain. Herr Liepmann, her landlord, was leaning against the wall opposite her door.

'Good evening, Frau Gebhardt, I saw a light on in your sitting room, so I didn't want to let myself in.' He had a key to the flat so that he could use his two rooms when they were away. But if he thought they were in, he always rang the bell.

Emma closed the door, removed the chain, and opened it again.

'Come in, Herr Liepmann! I'm sorry ... My husband isn't here ... '

Herr Liepmann gave himself a shove to stand upright, and then moved towards the door. He stumbled, then steadied himself, grasping the doorpost. Emma realised that he was drunk. She eyed him cautiously as he swayed into her hallway.

'Forgive me for being so late.' He spoke slowly and overly loudly. 'I was celebrating with some friends. Such a wonderful occasion!'

'Come in and sit down,' said Emma, slightly reassured. 'I'll make you some coffee. Have you had something to eat?'

Herr Liepmann waved his hand vaguely and sat down in Leo's armchair.

'Such a triumph, such a triumph,' he said. 'Such a *triumph*!'

'You must tell me all about it,' smiled Emma. 'Just excuse me a moment.'

She walked down the hall to the kitchen, and leant against the counter to think. How did you treat someone who was intoxicated? He probably needed liquid. And something to soak up the alcohol. She put on the kettle and prepared the coffee pot. Then she cut two big slices of bread and smeared margarine on them. She had two slices of real cheese left from Prerow. With a sigh, she decided to sacrifice one of them. For the other piece of bread she used ersatz sandwich spread and one of the precious tomatoes. She placed everything on a tray and brought it into the living room.

Herr Liepmann was sitting with his eyes half-closed, but when she entered he stood up politely, then sat down again quickly.

'Dear lady,' he said. 'You are so kind. It's just ... I didn't expect it! It all worked out perfectly! All those bicycles! One thousand two hundred and five bicycles. They want to win the war with them.'

'That's wonderful,' said Emma. She had no idea what he was talking about. She poured the coffee – it was ersatz – , added milk and sugar, and pulled over a little side table for him.

When he had finished everything, she brought him a glass of water.

'I must apologise for bursting in like this, Frau Gebhardt,' Herr Liepmann began. 'I had a busy – business meeting here in Berlin today. There was a certain trans- transaction which would be very profitable for me. The t- chances were fifty-fifty, and to be honest, I wasn't very *con*fident. Especially in my position. But, you know, the other party was even *more* nervous than I was. They were *dead* keen to buy what I was offering. In fact they were *so* keen,' and Herr Liepmann's voice almost broke, 'that I risked raising the price, and would you believe it, they took the bait! I – I had such a battle not to shtow – show my surprise! We settled everything, sealed and signed. And all above board! Everything legal – except for my position, of course. But the other party knew about that.' He drew a deep breath, raising his eyebrows as high as they would go. 'He was very fair, I must say that, a really good fellow. My wife and I are set up now for the next two years. *Such* a wonderful coup! My dear lady, you are so kind! Where is your good husband?'

'He's in Bayreuth, he'll be back on Tuesday. How long will you be staying?'

'Oh, I'm returning to Klobbicke tomorrow. I must tell my wife. She'll be worried if I stay away too long, thinking all kinds of black thoughts about what might have happened to me.'

'How is she?'

'Very well, thank you. She sends her regards. This was wonderful, just what I needed. It was ...

My dear, would you think me very impolite if I retired now? I really am awfully tired.'

'Of course, Herr Liepmann. Can I get you anything? Do you have towels there? I don't even know if your bed is made up?'

'It should be, and we have towels, thank you. I'll leave you now. Are you in tomorrow morning?'

'Yes. Just come in here whenever you wake up. I hope you can sleep well. And congratulations on your wonderful success. I'm so pleased for you and your wife.'

Much more in control of himself than he had been on his arrival, Herr Liepmann walked carefully to the door and along the corridor to his rooms.

Emma was dying to know what kind of deal he had pulled off. From previous little meetings with him, she and Leo had gathered that he was an accomplished businessman, but they had never found out what line of business he was in. Leo surmised that he bought up property or goods of some kind cheaply and sold them to the right clients at a huge profit. Neither of them were versed enough in business matters to be able to imagine what kinds of objects might be involved. And in truth they didn't want to know.

Next morning, Herr Liepmann appeared at 8 o'clock. She was just setting the table for breakfast. He had shadows under his eyes, and his voice, when he greeted her, was dry and cracked. His hand shook a little. He was less talkative than the night before, and so Emma busied herself with Jo, who was very suspicious of the stranger and glowered at him, until he took Jo on his knee and jiggled him up and down. Jo loved it, laughing, waving his arms and demanding repeats, till Herr Liepmann set him firmly down, gave him a toy to play with, and then ignored him. Jo, to Emma's

A Normal Couple

surprise, accepted this rejection as the natural order of things and played quietly with his toy.

Herr Liepmann commented on Emma's tan, and she told him about Prerow. She emphasised how safe she had felt there.

'I've decided I'm not spending any more bombing nights in Berlin if I can help it,' she said. 'If things get really bad again, Jo and I'll move to my sister's place in Poland or to my schoolfriend in West Prussia.'

'My dear, you needn't go so far away. Come and stay with my wife and me. If someone can bring you by car, it takes only an hour. Longer with public transport, but it can be done. We live in a tiny ... it's not even a village, just a collection of houses. We've seen planes passing over, mostly on their way back from Berlin, but we haven't had a sleepless night in the past two years. At least not from air raids. And we have plenty of room. We could put you and your little boy up easily, and even fit in your husband when he came to visit. My wife and I would be delighted to have you there.'

Emma didn't know what to say. She bent over and removed a crust from Jo's hand that he had picked up from the carpet and was now pushing into his mouth. Such kindness, from someone who had to watch out for his own well-being all the time! She felt a flush of warmth.

'Thank you so much, dear Herr Liepmann,' she began, and he interrupted her.

'No, my dear, it is the least we can do. We have to help each other in these times. You would be wonderful company for my wife. She gets rather bored out there, with only the pine trees and the wild geese to talk to.'

Emma smiled.

27

18–26 August: Indoctrination Course

Leo found it strange to be sitting at a desk in a schoolroom, waiting to write an essay for a test. After his final written exam at university, a dozen years ago, he had felt an overwhelming relief that all this pressure was over, forever. Yet here he was again. He looked around at the other candidates. They were about thirty in all, most of them younger than he, probably all thinking the same rueful thought. It wasn't even a proper schoolroom – it was the library of a former monastery in which he now found himself.

He and the others, all members of the SS, had been sent here for a ten-day refresher course on the movement's ideals and aims. There had been a preparatory evening course in Berlin six weeks ago, attended by over eighty people, and he wondered where the rest of this group were.

He had arrived the previous evening after a five-hour train journey. His luggage contained his black parade and his service uniforms, both worn with the uncomfortable long leather boots – quite unsuitable for this hot August weather.

Fortunately the thick stone walls of the old building provided a cool interior, and his room, a former monk's cell, faced east, so that the temperature was bearable and guaranteed a good night's sleep. He shared the room with a man who introduced himself as Dr Lothar Weltz, from the Ministry of Finance. He was slim and lively, with a quick wit, and a heavy smoker, who didn't bother to conceal from Leo that he wasn't prepared to obey all the rules to the last letter. This suited Leo fine, and he knew they would get on well.

'Comrades, you have ninety minutes time,' said the instructor, as he wrote the theme of the essay on the blackboard: 'The Eastern Policy of King Henry I'. Well, that was no problem. The papers had been full of it in the past few years. Henry I, early tenth century king of East Franconia, founder of the Ottonian dynasty and ultimately, some writers believed, of the First Reich. He was known as Henry the Fowler because he was said to have been setting up his hunting nets when emissaries appeared to offer him the crown. He was a character in Wagner's opera 'Lohengrin'. Leo was quite familiar with his story.

Again he looked around at his fellow examinees. None of them looked flustered. A grey-haired man three desks away was examining his fingernails. The balding young candidate on his other side was resting his chin on his folded hands and had his eyes closed. A couple of others had started writing at high speed. As a former music critic and music correspondent for the Leipzig paper, he himself was well used to writing texts to a deadline. He knew how to plan a text, how to express himself, how to make an impression. He started writing.

Of course it was clear why they had been given this particular theme. Henry's predecessors had been threatened for decades by the Magyars, the

Hungarians, who invaded the Franks' eastern territories again and again, and it was he who finally succeeded in routing them, expanding his lands to the east, and laying the foundation for the German Empire. Or so it was believed and propagated by the National Socialists. It was even said that Himmler, the chief of the SS, believed he was the reincarnation of Henry the Fowler. Some years ago he had held a midnight torchlight ceremony at Henry's grave in the abbey in Quedlinburg, the king's final resting place, on the 1000th anniversary of his death. It had received a big spread in all the national newspapers and magazines. Today, with the invasion of Russia, history was repeating itself, and a new and equally glorious age was dawning for Germany.

Leo knew what the examiner wanted to read, and he set about producing it. After an hour he had written twelve pages and handed in his paper.

At lunch in the old refectory, conversations sprang up and the participants got to know each other. The grey-haired man with the manicured fingernails was a professor of history at Kiel University; a rotund man with full lips and red rimmed eyes was an economist in the Ministry of Labour, and there was even someone from the Foreign Office. Leo understood now why they were so few: of the group of eighty at the preparatory course, the organisers had selected the academics as an elite group for this one. Why, he couldn't imagine. Not that they could be identified as such by sight – the ages ranged from late twenties to mid-forties, he estimated. They presented a normal cross-section of the population, tall, short, slim and athletic, or arm-chair types with a paunch. There was a fair sprinkling of Hitler moustaches and the forelock over half the forehead; the Nazi salute was the standard greeting; heels being clicked together and military feet stamped was part of the general background noise. Still, in a confined environment like this, it was much more pleasant to be among people of one's own culture and upbringing. None of them left their elbow on the table while eating, or spoke with their mouth full. Not that the food warranted such polite manners – cabbage soup – but at least one's visual aesthetic sense wasn't offended. In fact, he had an interesting conversation with a Dr Levin about Wagner's treatment of Henry the Fowler. Dr Levin had well founded ideas on why the composer had changed some of the historical facts. Leo was impressed – yet how could an SS officer sport such a Jewish surname? If it had been his, he'd have changed it.

Athletics were scheduled for the afternoon – a thousand metres and long jumps. In the evening there was a lecture and discussion on the history and ideals of the SS. The general consensus was that the SS rested on a solid foundation and had an important historic task to fulfil. Its members were particularly loyal to the Führer, trained to fulfil his commands and wishes even before he had uttered them.

Leo wondered if what he had overheard earlier, as he was awaiting his turn at the long jump, had also been carried out as an act of loyalty to the Führer: a young officer was telling his neighbour about a letter he'd received from his brother, who was fighting in the Ukraine. He reported that he had witnessed mass executions of Jews and other civilians – old people, women, children – in the villages that had been taken by the German army. The executions had been carried out by members of the SS and a police execution squad specially formed for this task. Leo heard no more, for his jump was due; he managed a miserly 2.7 metres.

Now, during the evening lecture, he came to the conclusion that these excesses were an exception, an aberration. This kind of treatment was not part of the normal duty of an SS man.

At ten pm he collapsed onto his straw mattress and fell asleep right away.

The following day brought another test, this one on military theory. He knew next to nothing about it, but decided to apply his common sense, and was pleased with himself when his paper was collected. Lunch consisted of a vegetable stew. In the afternoon they had shooting practice, using Browning pistols. He failed miserably. As he later wrote to Emma: 'My hand was shaking so much I couldn't hold the gun steady.' In fact his hand hadn't been shaking, but something stopped him from making an effort to aim precisely. He was shouted at by the instructor, an old World War veteran with a leg missing, and he submitted to the rebuke with admirable regret. However, this was the one area where his ambition to succeed was zero.

The lecture this evening was on the Jews. The instructor posed the question: were the Jews a race, a nation or a religious group? There was some discussion on this before the lecturer launched into his topic. Leo began to get bored and switched to dual concentration: listening and taking enough notes to be able to answer a future test, at the same time wondering what Emma was doing. The radio had reported a bombing raid on Berlin two days previously – a lone Russian plane, not much danger there. A serious raid had taken place a week previously, the heaviest so far, when over 80 tons of bombs fell in the eastern sections of the capital, with many casualties. He hoped she was all right. Right now she was probably sitting in the living room, listening to a concert on the radio. Jo

A Normal Couple

would be asleep. Or perhaps she was out on the balcony with her darning or a book. He wished he could be there together with her. The balcony had come along splendidly, the pompom dahlias he'd set were magnificent, sprightly red baubles that made him smile. Next year he must try that new breed of dahlia .... The talk was now arriving at the predictable verdict that the Jews were a race, an inferior one, and could therefore never become German Aryans. And presumably it would conclude with the national ideal of racial hygiene and the creation of an Aryan core area free of Jews. The lecturer was a good sort – he'd been in charge of the preparatory course in Berlin – but Leo noticed his eye was resting on him, and with a concentrated frown he leaned over his paper and scribbled a few more notes.

Three days later, a new challenge was presented. They were divided into groups of five, and in each group they took it in turns to act as commander. A target was set, and the leader had to command his group so as to achieve this. When it was Leo's turn, his target read: 'Defend your stand against an attacking group'. Their stand was in a corner of what used to be the cloister. It lay slightly higher than the rest of the square. Nearby was a clump of wild lilac bushes, forming a good shelter. Drawing himself up and assuming a loud and snappy tone, he marched his group smartly to their post, positioned two men behind the clump of lilac, and withdrew into the gallery with the other two. Using Macduff's ploy in Birnam Wood, the three of them kept moving about quickly behind the pillars of the outside wall, taking shelter only when the 'enemy' started firing their blanks as they approached. The trick worked – the attacking force had passed the lilac bush without noticing the soldiers hiding there, and were caught in the ambush. They surrendered easily, with mock indignation. Leo was relieved that 'his' men had actually carried out his amateurish commands without arguing. Praise came from the commanding instructor, with some hints on what could have been done better. Nonetheless, he knew that this little game by no means proved that he was qualified to lead a group of soldiers in a genuine battle scenario.

For lunch there was cabbage soup, and a severe athletics test took place in the afternoon. The group was reminded that all SS members were expected to participate in sports on a regular basis and to achieve the SS athletics diploma. This was one of the criteria which set them apart from the common members of the Wehrmacht. He felt he excelled himself in the long jump – three metres thirty; the shotput, normally his strong point, went awry; in the 3000m race he came in third in his group of six. But he totalled only 18 points – the target was 50. Next morning the results for the whole group were posted on the notice board: he was number twenty of the twenty-nine. Only three candidates had reached fifty points or more.

'Not too bad,' he thought. 'Middle of the road. Too weak to be used for special tasks, not bad enough to be subjected to severe criticism.' He wondered what the average number of points attained had been. It was clear that the talents of this group of eggheads lay in other regions.

That evening's lecture was on Jewry's subversive moves towards global domination. It was a more academic lecture than the previous ones, quoting precise examples and sources to support the thesis. The main source was 'The Protocols of the Elders of Zion', an old text which revealed the detailed plan for this dire undertaking. Leo knew of this book. It had been widely read about ten years ago, even though some historians claimed it was a fake. But the examples used by the lecturer rang bells. 'As you will have experienced yourselves' was a phrase which was used more than once, and heads nodded in agreement. Leo recalled fellow trainees at the bank, back in the '20s, stalwart German boys, who'd later been unable to find a position. On the other hand, there were his former Jewish friends and colleagues. Several had been extremely witty, and one of them, Karl Sanders, had also been a wonderful cook, who opened his own restaurant. The best operatic singer at the theatre in Görlitz, where he had trained the choir nearly twenty years ago, had been Jewish. As had his doctor in Leipzig, a wise and kindly old gentleman, with a bright family of blond, blue-eyed teenagers that were always coming and going whenever he attended the surgery in the doctor's house. And all his colleagues at the paper … ! But he supposed that these were exceptions, just the tip of the iceberg as numbers go, and not representative. What did he know about the mass of working-class Jews, or the Jewish shtetls in Poland? Those people were barely civilised! On the other hand, global domination could hardly be achieved by labourers and peasants without the leadership of educated and trained people like his friends and ex-colleagues. Yet none of these, as far as he could judge, had ever shown the slightest interest in global domination. When not working, their attention was occupied with quite different – normal – matters. Sanders had been worried about his mortgage, the doctor in Leipzig was more interested in his butterfly collection than his patients. His own colleagues had all safely emigrated, as far as he knew; at any rate, he'd lost touch with them. But not for a moment did Leo doubt that somewhere there were groups of Jews who were plotting to take control of the international economy and to gain control of the leading nations of the world. This ran counter to natural selection, as he had learnt on lectures on Darwinianism. He knew that the Aryan race had evolved through adaptation, which had endowed it with qualities and strength that gave it the right of domination, based on the theory of the survival of the fittest.

   Well, anyway, Hitler was doing his bit to put a stop to any rivals for world domination, that was certain. Just as well, maybe.

   After the first few days, the men were less tired in the evenings, and sat around in the garden or in the former chapter house, which served as a casino. They were all part-time members of the General SS, which meant that they were in full-time employment elsewhere. A handful of them had already received their call-up papers, with a date in the middle future. Leo noted that some of the younger ones were eager to engage actively in the war, to teach the Bolshies a thorough lesson they wouldn't forget. Several of them had been involved in operations in Poland that had required a degree of ruthlessness he could not envisage for himself. Inevitably he recalled the conversation he had overheard some days earlier. He paid lip-service to their opinions, but tried to avoid their company. The older men were generally more reserved in their expressions of national commitment. Like himself, they had lived through the Great War, had lost fathers, uncles, even brothers in the trenches, had starved in the turnip winters, and were not eager for a possible repeat.

   The following days brought military training – scrambling over wooden walls, crawling through rolls of barbed wire and muddy ditches, and the like – written and oral tests, and lectures which highlighted the status and nefarious history and aims of the Jews, as well as on the ideals of the SS movement. The highlight of the sports events would take place on Sunday, the required 25-kilometre cross-country march with a fully loaded backpack, to be completed within a maximum of 4 hours. He looked forward to it – cross-country walking had been a passion of his ever since his years at Innsbruck University, with the Alps on his doorstep.

They woke at 6am to the sound of water shooting out of a flooded gutter. It was pouring rain, the landscape outside their little windows hidden in a haze of mist, and there was no sign of improvement. Groaning, they dressed, loaded their packs, and helped each other to drape their heavy raincapes over themselves and their luggage. Three officers accompanied them.

It was soon obvious that several of the men were not used to this kind of activity at all, and the muddy tracks, the runnels of water shooting downhill towards them as they struggled up through forests and between pastures, the increasing weight of their soggy clothing slowed them all down considerably. The officers were soon shouting at them as if they were raw recruits – which in a way they were – and made no allowances. In particular they picked on three of the men who were unable to keep pace with the rest, berating them, and poking or even striking them with their batons. A scheduled stop was cancelled to make up for lost time, and Leo realised that the officers were also under pressure to produce good results from their group for the monthly SS statistics. The merciless rain continued unabated, alternating only with aggressive thundery downpours.

'It's more like swimming than marching,' quipped Dr Weltz. 'And I thought swimming was scheduled for this afternoon! At least we won't need a shower tonight.'

The group began to stretch out, the faster ones keeping to the pace dictated by their officer, and aiming their own abusive comments at the stragglers, who were holding them back. More and more of the men slowed down. Leo, who could have kept going for several hours, paced himself to stay in the middle of the spread-out hikers. An unspoken solidarity with the weakest in the group was developing, and the officers accompanying this part of the troop were helpless in the face of the mass of men squelching through the mud at their own speed, regardless of shouts and threats.

Five hours later, shortly before reaching the monastery, the leading troops were halted to wait for the rest, which made the former even more angry. They were reassembled and marched back into the courtyard in a closed formation. The leading officer delivered an angry lecture about the group's disastrous performance, and announced an extra round of press-ups for later in the evening. Then they were dismissed.

A disgraceful scene developed in the showers. Several of the most ardent marchers were commenting loudly about those whose 'laziness' had brought them the coming penalty. This culminated in them ganging up on their victims and attacking them both verbally and physically. Luckily, others intervened, and the incident ended there. From then on, there was a clear divide in the group. The tone was now set by the younger, more radical SS adherents, while the more moderate majority were intent on getting through the last few days without drawing undue attention to themselves.

On their last evening, Leo sat in the cloister garden with Professor Behrenberg, the history man from Kiel, and his roommate, Dr Weltz. Leo was enjoying a long thin cigar, a virginia, and Dr Weltz was on his fifteenth cigarette. Their conversation drifted to the world domination lecture they had heard several days earlier.

'The evidence of the "Protocols of the Elders of Zion" is very convincing, I must say,' commented Leo. 'I recall how difficult it was for an uncle of mine to find a position in a lawyer's office. It was a closed shop – the employees were all Jews. In the end he was taken on only because they had so many cases to deal with after the Great Crash. But he always felt a bit like a fish out of water there.'

'That book, the Protocols, is an absolute forgery,' said Professor Behrenberg calmly. 'A British journalist proved this conclusively in a series of articles in the London "Times" in 1921. Numerous passages were plagiarised from, among others, a political satire called "Dialogue in Hell Between Machiavelli and Montesquieu", written in 1864 by a French author, Maurice Joly. It has a long history of falsification, all of which has been researched and revealed. It proves absolutely nothing about a Jewish desire for world domination.'

'Except that it's been quoted by reliable experts!' said Leo suavely. 'And the theses it presents have all been verified by recent history!'

'Even experts can't be trusted nowadays, my dear Doctor,' said Behrenberg. 'And just because a theory seems to be proven by contemporary events doesn't mean it's true. It depends on how you interpret the events. If you explain them using the theory you believe in as a basis, then you seem to have proved the theory too. But perhaps the events can be looked at from a completely different angle, and then your theory is left hanging. You can't prove a theory with another theory.'

Leo hesitated. The issue was a central theme of Third Reich propaganda; it justified the Nurnberg Laws and all other measures against Jewry in Germany. He needed more time to absorb this new information. Was it true? Professor Behrenberg had spoken so calmly and precisely. He was aware that he had never immersed himself in the details of Nazi ideology and preaching – he'd never had time. But he was familiar with the most notable tenets, and integrating this piece of information in his world view was proving difficult. It would need more thinking about. Perhaps there were other sources, more reliable and more convincing, to bolster the state agenda with regard to antisemitism. Such a crucial political policy could never, ever have grown and reached its present significance if based on a mirage. It belonged to the foundation of his own adherence to party policies.

Dr Waltz had started on the campaign in Russia, and was wondering if it would be completed before the Russian winter set in. Tolstoy's 'War and Peace' had demonstrated in dramatic scenes what the German army might expect if the invasion was not successful before then.

'A wonderful book,' said Professor Behrenberg with feeling, 'so warm-hearted, yet so precise in his observations. And the battle scenes are rendered in so many dimensions, astounding how he kept it all under control. Just phenomenal! Such an interesting and disciplined writer. A pity the Nobel Prize didn't exist in his time. And yet, you know, he has the simplest grave one could imagine, just a small green mound in a loose stand of birch trees, unmarked. He chose the site himself. An unbelievable experience. You know, he said he didn't need a bombastic tomb. He said these overstated tombs were visited by people just to see the artwork. But if a personality was revered for what he had achieved in his lifetime, people would visit even an unmarked grave. And they do.'

'You've been to Russia, then?' asked Dr Weltz.

'Yes. I was writing a book about the aftermath of Napoleon's campaign, and that took me to Moscow. That was in 1928. So much poverty! Terrible. Even worse than it was here at that time. But Moscow was, or is, a wonderful city. Such distinguished buildings, such cultivated people, even today, after the Revolution.' He looked aside, away from his two listeners. 'I wonder what it's like now.' Exactly a month earlier, the German Luftwaffe had dropped bombs on Moscow.

'Have either of you gentlemen been given your marching papers yet?' asked Leo.

They both shook their heads.

'I often wonder how they'll use us. Quite honestly, I'd be quite hopeless in a battle situation. Shooting is not my thing, I cannot muster any enthusiasm about fighting or living in trenches or fighting mosquitos or lice or whatever. I'd probably be one of the first to get shot,' he ended glumly.

Dr Weltz smiled. 'What you've just described so graphically would apply to seventy-five percent of the armed forces, I believe. If not in the first few days, then certainly after the first week. You'll have to come up with something more convincing if you want to avoid being sent to the front.'

'What they will probably do with us,' began Professor Behrenberg, 'is either place us in an office somewhere behind the lines, where intelligence and the ability to plan strategies is required ....'

'Such as?' asked Leo.

'Well, logistics, for example in the national rail system, planning supplies for the front, coordinating troop movements and transport, dealing with mail to the front – there are hundreds of possibilities.'

'You said "either",' said Dr Weltz. 'What's the "or"?'

'I don't know if you're aware, it's not generally known. Dr Himmler has established a war reporter company exclusively for the SS. It corresponds to the war reporter units that Dr Goebbels drew up for the army some years ago. They recruit mainly journalists and writers or photographers. I should imagine that any of us with experience in that line will be ideal for them. With ever more regiments being sent to Russia, they'll be needing more and more reporters. Of course it's not as safe as a desk job, but still better than being cannon fodder at the front.'

They were silent for a moment. The sun had set and the gloaming was casting long shadows over the bright flowers in the garden. Dr Weltz pulled on his cigarette, and slowly blew pale grey smoke rings into the darkening sky. In the distance a train whistled.

'If you gentlemen have any good friends in positions where strings can be pulled, now would be the time to contact them,' said Professor Behrenberg quietly.

28

October: Franzi travels to Vienna, Emma and Leo to Klobbicke

After settling Axel in a corner of the compartment, Franzi let down the window as far as it would go and leant out. On the platform seeing her off to her new home in Vienna were her parents, her sister and her nephew. Elisabeth was well wrapped up in her second-best fur coat and a thick scarf, and Pa was protected in his greatcoat and homburg. Fra could see that Emma was red-eyed and trying not to cry.

'Now don't leave the window open too long, child, there'll be a draught and the baby will catch cold,' scolded Elisabeth.

Fra ignored her. 'Cheer up, Em,' she said. 'I'll write as soon as I land and then every week. And I hope you and Jo will come and visit us as soon as possible. Though it might be better to wait till the weather gets a bit warmer.'

'You'll be so busy for the next few weeks,' said Emma bravely. 'And you and Moritz deserve to be left alone for a while, after waiting so long for your own home together.'

The train gave a whistle, and a cloud of smoke drifted towards them.

'Good-bye, my loves,' called Franzi, 'good-bye, and don't forget me!' And to everyone's surprise, she started to cry herself. In the end they were all in tears.

They waved and waved, Emma lifting Jo's chubby fist and shaking it, and Franzi stretched out of the window more and more until the train had rounded the bend and she had passed from their view.

'Well,' said Paul, 'who would have thought that our Fra would end up in Vienna! She'll take to it like a duck to water, and she'll be fluent in the accent in no time at all. We won't understand her.'

'I hope Moritz won't be as busy as Leo has been lately. At any rate, he probably won't have to travel so much. Poor Fra, waiting nearly two years before she can set up her own household as a married woman. I hope she'll make nice friends.'

'She's sure too, and she'll have all the young men buzzing around her like she always had. Viennese men don't have any compunctions about whether an attractive young woman is married or not. She'll have the time of her life.'

After their holiday together in Spain, Moritz had been appointed commander of the Aviation School at Vienna Airport to the southeast of the city. It meant that at long last he and Franzi could begin to lead a normal family life. Franzi had hardly been able to sleep all night when she heard the news. Moritz had found a large flat ('Almost as large as yours, love,' she told Emma coyly, and Emma guessed that it was even bigger). September had been taken up with planning and trying to find utensils and bedding, packing and unpacking, meeting friends for the last time, making lists and losing them – all moments of busy happiness and anticipation.

'You'll get all those things much more easily down there,' Paul told her. 'There won't be the same shortage as there is here. And of course you won't have to worry about air raids.'

'I know,' answered Fra. 'I've told Emma to come down and stay with me if and when things start to get awkward again up here.' She turned to her mother. 'Why did you and Pa never take us to see Vienna on our family holidays? I've read so much about it – the huge palaces and the opera and the theatre, the public buildings, just en*orm*ous. There seems to be nothing like it here.'

'Well, there might be, when we have peace and Hitler can go ahead with his gargantuan plans for rebuilding the capital,' said Elisabeth in a derogatory tone. 'Vienna's showy architecture developed because it was the capital of one of the greatest empires the world has ever known – before it was dismantled. That role will be taken over by Berlin, if things go the way our megalomaniac leader envisages in his sleepless vegetarian nights. Except that Vienna evolved over centuries, and wasn't produced overnight, like a product of our Aladdin's lantern.'

'You're talking nonsense,' said Paul mildly, though with a slight edge to his voice.

'Yes, of course,' snapped Elisabeth. 'And the Third Reich will be the Thousand-Year-Reich, while the Holy Roman Empire only lasted ... how long did it last, Paul?'

But Paul had drifted into his den and closed the door.

The following Sunday, Leo had no commitments. He had considered going to the SS barracks in Zehlendorf, where he was now registered, to do his monthly round of weekend duty. As a member of the movement, he was supposed to attend a two-hour meeting once a week, and to do duty for four to six hours one Sunday a month. But he had rarely been able to fulfil this schedule. He was away so much, or whenever he was in Berlin his evenings were taken up with official concerts or hosting visiting musicians from abroad. Not to mention reserving time for his beloved Emma and Jo. He'd received some sharp memos from the command post, but had forwarded them to the Personnel Department in the Ministry, and they had dealt with it for him. Still, considering what might yet happen, he felt it wiser to keep on good terms with the local authorities who could have a say in his future.

The advice that Professor Behrenberg had given him had not fallen on deaf ears. On his return journey from the training in the monastery, he mentally went through his many friends and acquaintances, searching for someone who would be able to help him to enter the War Reporter Regiment. It meant joining the newly formed Waffen SS, but this was a technicality, for the non-combatant General SS, the organisation he had joined several years before, was gradually being dissolved, its members transferred to the Wehrmacht, or guard duty in the camps, or to other organisations where their special skills and dedication were required. The War Reporter unit would be right up his street. He would be working more or less autonomously, responsible only to a headquarters located far from his field of operations, and he would not have to fight. Or, he hoped, be involved in any of the atrocities associated with his organisation.

The only person he could think of who might be able to pull the strings recommended by Professor

Behrenberg was Emma's cousin Walter. He was a lawyer. Leo had met him some months earlier at a gathering of Elisabeth's branch of the family to celebrate the seventy-fifth birthday of her step-grandmother, who had moved from the Moehlten estate to a small town near Berlin. Emma's gift for her great-grandmother was a beautiful volume of art photographs, since this had always been the old lady's hobby. Walter and Leo had got on well – they both had the same pragmatic attitude to the issues of the times and the solutions that were being applied to them.

Walter was also in the SS, in the Equestrian Company, and Leo knew that the members of this group were well networked in the upper echelons of the SS organisation. He had written to him in September, and Walter had replied right away, saying he would see what he could find out. He firmly believed that the War Reporter Regiment was the only one that Leo would be considered for, so that he shouldn't worry.

Leo knew Emma would be disappointed if he didn't spend the Sunday with her and Jo, but he also knew that it would probably be his last chance in the coming two months to put in a showing at the barracks. They discussed it the evening before.

'What will you be doing the following weekend?' Emma wanted to know.

'Working, probably. The planning for the Mozart Festival Week in Vienna at the end of November is gathering pace, and I can see a flood of work and difficult colleagues heading towards me. But I don't think I've any appointments. Why? Is there something my little Rose wants me to do?' And he reached for her and drew her towards him.

She snuggled into his arms and rested her head on his shoulder.

'You remember Colonel Sonntag advised me to look around for places where I could find refuge outside of Berlin. And I told you that Herr Liepmann invited me to stay with him and his wife in Klobbicke. Before you disappear to Munich and Vienna again, I'd like to pay them a visit, and I'd like to do it together with you. Do you think we could manage that next Sunday?'

'Oh dear. Yes, well, of course, I think I can manage it. How long do you think we'll be gone?'

'I've made some enquiries. It'll take us about three hours to get there. The bus for the last leg of the trip doesn't run very often. So it looks like we'll be gone most of the day, my sweet. It would take a load off my mind if we could do it. I could write to them straight away.'

'All right. I'm very curious to see how they live. He's a funny character. He seems very clever at avoiding awkward situations and always landing on his feet. How he manages it with his ancestry is beyond me. And his wife is charming. We'll make an excursion of it and have a lovely day.' As a reward for his acquiescence he garnered a long and intensive kiss.

Autumn had set in early this year, and by mid-October the weather had turned very blustery and wet, with some night frosts. They wrapped themselves up well. The parents had taken Jo for the day. Although it was early on Sunday morning, the platforms at Stettin Terminus were surging with people of all classes and ages heading out to relatives or friends in the country. Ladies in heavy coats with showy bonnets were using their umbrellas to clear a way to the first- and second-class compartments. Working-class women wrapped in plaids and wearing men's boots, thin, pale housewives with several children in tow,

A Normal Couple

youngsters in Hitler Youth uniforms, old men in worn coats and baggy trousers were struggling for places in third and fourth class. Mingled in the crowd were military and policemen. Most of the people were carrying empty shopping bags and rucksacks, hoping to come home laden with the foodstuffs that were in such short supply in the capital. Leo pushed his way through the throng purposefully, Emma sticking to his heels. It was an old train – each compartment had its own carriage door, with a narrow wooden board running along on the outside for the conductor to move from one compartment to the next during the journey.

They reached a second-class section at the same time as an elderly couple. The man was small, with soft cheeks and sunken eyes; the satin collar of his coat was shiny from wear and the ends of the sleeves had been darned. His wife, her face still pretty and lady-like, held onto a ruffled cashmere shawl wrapped around her head; her gloves were well worn. On the left side of their coats were the startling yellow stars that had been prescribed for Jews just three weeks previously. Leo was bending towards them to help them in when a policemen appeared at his elbow.

'You're not helping them into the train, are you, my friend?' he asked. His tone was not unfriendly.

'Why, yes, that was my intention,' answered Leo.

'Now, Grandma and Grandpa, you know you can't take the train on the weekends. You'll have to postpone your trip for during the week. Get in, Sir, and I'll help your good wife.' And he pushed the old couple aside firmly and turned to Emma.

She was too shocked to react, but once in the compartment she turned to Leo.

'They're not allowed to use the train at the weekend? Why on earth not? Can't you do anything?'

Other travellers had climbed up and the compartment was now full.

'Jews!' said a man sitting next to them sharply. No one else showed any reaction.

Through the window Emma could see the policeman talking to the old couple, bending down so that they could hear him. A second policeman joined them, frowning, and the first man straightened and pushed the old couple towards the exit. The door of their compartment was slammed shut. A long whistle came from the guard on the platform, the train gave a jerk and started slowly huffing its way out of the station.

'Since when has this rule ... law ... been in operation?' asked Emma.

No one answered.

A thin man with round glasses and dry mousy hair sitting in the opposite corner spoke.

'Since Thursday. Word hasn't got round to all of them yet, it seems. They want to limit the number of people travelling at the weekends, so that ... well, like now, you know ....' He glanced at the bags and rucksacks in the luggage rack.

'Although it's not as if they couldn't do with some extra food too.' This came from the middle-aged woman sitting opposite Emma. A plump young teenager sat next to her, her mittened fists scrunched in her lap. She was staring at the floor.

The man who had spoken first broke in. He had a fleshy, red face with a small nose over wide lips. A long scar on his left cheek identified him as a former member of a nationalistic students' union whose initiation rites included duelling.

'They kept us short of everything during the economic crisis, and look at what they've done in Russia, dispossessing all the farmers. It's time they found out what it's like to be at the receiving end.'

A Normal Couple

'That's nonsense. Excuse me, Sir, but there's no other word for it. Nonsense!' The loud voice, like that of an officer, came from an elderly man with a full moustache and a beard, dressed in plus-fours. 'You can't for a moment believe that that old couple is responsible for what the communists are doing to the farmers in Russia?! That's ridiculous!'

'We can't make any exceptions!' snapped the first speaker. 'The whole race is a problem, and that's how we have to deal with it. Of course there are always innocents in such an action, but there are millions of them, and we can't examine and investigate every single one of them. They have to be shown how far they can go, all of them, and then we can take it from there.'

The officer-type in the corner turned to answer him.

'No person in their right mind would agree that millions of people should be discriminated just because a few of them have too much power. And that isn't even proven! It's just a vague theory, a notion!'

'It's the policy of our Führer and our government! And who are you to question that?! It's a whole race that are infiltrating our society and corrupting it from the inside! There is no place for them in our world – they need to be dealt with, all of them!'

'Still, they are human individuals, like you and me,' began Emma, but she was interrupted.

'That's exactly what they are not! They're an inferior race, and we don't want them contaminating our Nordic blood. We have a mission to fulfil, an enormous task, which our ...'

'Our enormous mission today is to see if we can find some extra potatoes or carrots or a bit of bacon for our housewives at home,' interrupted a young soldier, a conciliatory smile on his badly scarred face. One arm was in a plaster cast and sling. 'Whatever mission our wise leaders are working on, all I'm interested in today is filling my belly before I fall into bed tonight.' And he smiled at the young woman at his side.

She laughed back at him, shaking her brown curls and settling her coat more tightly around the bulge in her middle. She turned to the other passengers.

'Have you heard this one?' she asked. 'Why should we be so grateful to Hitler, Goebbels and Göring?'

Silence, and a few apprehensive smiles.

'Hitler thinks for us, Goebbels speaks for us, and Göring gobbles for us!'

Some chuckles. Göring was indeed more massive every time he appeared in public.

The teenager sitting opposite Emma raised her head.

'Hitler, Goebbels and Göring are sheltering in a bunker. It gets hit by a bomb. Who will be saved?'

They stared at her in surprise.

'Germany!'

This time there was a burst of laughter, though not from scarface who had spoken first. Other jokes followed. It was the first time that Emma had experienced such openness among strangers. Her fingers searched for Leo's warm dry hand, and he grasped hers firmly in his.

The woman opposite her leant forward. Her broad, weathered face, the eyes slightly too far apart giving her a look of surprise, appealed to Emma.

'I have a small grocery shop in Dahlem,' she began quietly. 'You know how the system goes. Ration cards for everyone, but far less for them than for us. And they're only allowed to shop between three and four in the afternoon, and then there's often nothing left by the time they come in. My father had the shop before me, some of them have been customers of ours for years, and their parents before them. It's heart-breaking not to be able to give them anything when that happens. Though I do try to make up for it at other times ...' and she looked out of the window into the distance.

'That yellow star,' said Emma. 'Up till now you didn't know who was Jewish and who wasn't. But now ...! It's so humiliating. Those poor people.'

'It's an absolute disgrace,' said the woman bitterly.

The last passenger in the compartment, a plump young woman with pretty Madonna-like features, wearing a thin, wine-red coat, looked up. She had a runny nose and sniffed constantly. Emma was wondering how she came to be in the second-class compartment.

'Joking aside,' she said in a husky voice, 'I'd be glad if we was rid of the lot of them. We'd be much better off! They've caused us so much trouble and robbed us of our due. Living in luxury while us simple people struggle to get by. Their posh houses and big cars – and I don't believe they're starving like the rest of us. Away with them, that's what I say!'

Her listeners stared at her, with expressions ranging from curious to aghast. The scarred cheek was the first to speak.

'My dear young lady, whom, precisely, do you mean by "they"?'

'Well them, of course, them Jews, what are causing all the trouble. Why? What did you think?' A taut pause, some suppressed smiles. 'Them yellow stars are a great idea. Now they can't hide any more! Now we can deal with them.'

Most of the passengers produced bland expressions, with the odd raised eyebrow. Her questioner sat back, pleased.

'Absolutely! Precisely! It's the first step towards complete segregation. We've drawn a clear line, and everyone knows where they are. It's better for them too, they don't need to hide any more. Two nations, two sets of rules!'

The vegetable woman made a sound close to 'Pshaw!'. Emma fell back in her seat. She wished the journey was over. She glanced up at Leo. He had closed his eyes, but his typical tobacco-and-shaving-lotion scent was much stronger than usual. She felt a twinge of disappointment that he hadn't joined in the altercation.

The train drew into the first station, where the vegetable lady as well as the soldier and his girl descended, giving Emma and Leo a smile and a friendly 'Good day!'. Other people took their places, but there was no more exchanges beyond a polite 'Hallo!' or 'Good-bye!' and an occasional 'Heil Hitler!'

An hour later, Leo and Emma reached their destination. The bus for the next stage of their trip was already waiting, and in twenty minutes they had reached Klobbicke. It was a typical Brandenburg village, a long street with an S-bend in the middle winding around the squat brick church and the manor house. Large farmhouses lined the road on either side, attractive low brick buildings with farmyards at the side and a wide grass verge in front.

Herr Liepmann had told them his house was near the end of the village, about five minutes' walk from the church where the bus had dropped them. Alone at last, Emma took up the question that had been bothering her.

'Leo, why didn't you say anything during that discussion in the train? That awful man! He said such terrible things about the Jews. Why didn't you put him in his place?'

'You know very well that that would have been impossible.'

'But the man in the corner contradicted him! Why didn't you support him?'

'He was obviously an old soldier, an officer, he could afford to risk an opinion like that. It goes entirely against our official stand. The government has a policy with regard to non-Aryans, and it expects full backing and loyalty from the population.'

'But do you really think that this policy is right? They've lost their citizenship, their doctors and lawyers have lost their licences, they're being driven from their homes ... I keep thinking of what my father said at our wedding party, about following natural law, about listening to one's own instinct. And my instinct tells me that this policy is not right, that it is unjust. What do you think?' She didn't want to start an argument, so she tucked her hand under his arm and gave it a squeeze.

'I think there are reasons behind all this that we don't know or don't understand. I trust our leadership; I believe that what they're doing is what is best for our nation and our future and the future of our children.'

'But Leo, I don't want my children to profit from the suffering of other people. Everything was fine after Hitler became chancellor, his policies obviously helped the broad mass of the population. If he had continued like that, everyone would have been happy, including the Jews.'

'Agreed, it is hard on individuals, but we have to keep the whole picture in mind. And protesting against official policy can be dangerous, you know that. It would be nothing less than stupidity, endangering oneself. And besides, protest wouldn't change anything at all. No, it's much better just to keep a low profile and stick to one's job and let others look after the politics.'

Emma was about to say that nothing would ever get better if nobody was prepared to speak out against the government, but they had reached what was clearly the Liepmanns' house ('the small one without hens or a dung heap in the front yard'). She straightened her hat and pulled at her gloves, and she and Leo proceeded to the front door.

29

27 November: Mozart Festival Week

Leo couldn't believe his eyes. He read the telegram again.

The Mozart Festival Week in Vienna was opening on 28 November. That was the following day. It had been an annual event since 1920, and the plan was that this year's should be the most prestigious so far, a triumphant manifestation of the artistry, power and organisational skills of the Third Reich. Aryan culture must be supreme even without the participation of famous non-Aryan composers and artists. It was the 150th anniversary of Mozart's death. This, combined with the international popularity of his music, provided ideal propaganda material aimed not only at countries allied to or integrated in Germany, but also at the envious, excluded opposition. The Music Department in Berlin had been working on it all year, and the last few weeks had seen tension and tempers building up as threatening deadlines loomed and more and more last-minute omissions were surfacing from the organisational mire.

The main events of the week included six operas, eighteen concerts, twenty-one lectures and countless fringe events. Leo was busy on all fronts – of which there were dozens. For weeks he had negotiated with radio stations in other countries, arranging broadcasting rights for the festival productions. The Viennese Brass Consort had not yet(!) received its contract and was therefore unable to arrange rehearsal dates with Professor Elly Ney. Please redress immediately!! He organised a grant for an impoverished composer colleague (and acquaintance) who had been invited but was unable to finance his journey. Dozens of representatives of the foreign press were expected: who was organising them?! He learned that the magnificent ceremonial hall of the Viennese National Library, the scheduled venue for a Mozart exhibition and an international congress, had no central heating! In late November! Could they not at least organise electric heaters?! Otherwise the congress would have to be cancelled!

But his main task had seen him drawing up lists of foreign musical luminaries and music organisations that were expecting an invitation. They amounted to many hundreds of names from more than fifteen countries, including Japan. Those impossible names, spelt differently each time! He saw to it that invitations were dispatched; when the bookings for tickets arrived, he made sure that wishes were met as far as possible, seats reserved as requested, reservations and names confirmed, and the confirmations sent back to the correct addresses. His head drummed with the strain of it all at the end of every day.

Then, only one month ago, the Reich Governor of Vienna, Baldur von Schirach, had announced that he could guarantee the safe transport of only 450 guests, no more. So the whole list of invitees had to be reworked, people uninvited, tickets returned, apologies forwarded. A nightmare!

Next, it dawned on someone that the Music Department employees who would be hosting the foreign invitees would also need tickets – that was just ten days ago. Panic! While the demands for tickets for all concerts kept coming in.

And now this telegram:

following twenty-two musicians from poland, bohemia, austria, belgium request tickets for all events. positive response required for propaganda reasons. immediate reaction requested.

Said the head office.

He couldn't believe it. It was Thursday night. The opening ceremony was less than twenty-four hours off.

He had been on his feet all day, talked to dozens of people, made innumerable phone calls, dictated umpteen memos, pleaded, placated, argued, persuaded, praised, bullied, flattered – had he been himself for even one minute? Certainly, he hadn't had time to eat properly – a waiter had brought him a cheese sandwich and a glass of beer some hours ago.

It was almost midnight, and he was in his hotel room at the Grand Hotel Vienna, looking forward to a bath and a few hours of sleep. And now this.

It was fortunate that the ticket office was in operation all night. Wearily, he reached for the phone and asked to be put through.

An hour later, he was lying in the bath. On a locker beside him was a sparkling glass of beer, a cold salad and a sandwich. As always, at the end of the day when he was travelling, his thoughts drifted to Emma. He'd written to her two days ago, a cheerful letter, making fun of Bischoff, who was causing chaos as usual, and downplaying the mayhem he was working his way through. He wouldn't be able to write to her in the next few days, he told her. Once the foreigners arrived, he'd have even less time.

They'd had an argument a week earlier, the day he was leaving. Emma was feeling under the weather, and she was fed up with him being away so much. He'd been to Munich and Vienna in early September, in Richard Strauss's house in Garmisch, Bavaria, in mid-October, in Munich and Vienna again from the end of October until well into November, and now these twelve days for the festival, which ended on 5 December. But on top of all that, she'd made a list of all the evenings he'd been away at concerts, hosting foreign musicians – in fact, he'd spent only nine evenings at home during November. Nine! Thirty days hath September, April June and November. She'd been alone at home for twenty-one evenings! Three weeks out of four! Of course, she said, she realised all this was part of his work. But she wanted him to see to it that he had a different work schedule when the festival was over. She wanted a normal family life. It was all difficult enough without his being away all the time. And anyway, he was killing himself, she said.

He wondered what she would think of the offer he'd received.

He sighed, opened the hot water tap, and reached for the soap. It was pre-war and smelt so good! He was lucky to have got this room, though he'd had to fight for that too. That idiot of a receptionist had sent him up to a tiny room on the fourth floor, with only a washstand and the bathroom on the landing half a flight down. He'd gone straight back down and made a huge scene, shouting and thumping on the counter. That had put the man in his place. And lo and behold, there was another room available! You had to know how to deal with these people! It was one of the few useful things he'd learnt from his father.

With a surge of foamy warm water he hauled himself upright, shook his hand dry, and took a big bite of the sandwich.

What was his father doing right now, he wondered. Asleep, he hoped. He knew the old man was still listening to foreign stations. The old fool! Didn't he realise that the death penalty had been passed for this breach of the law? And that the first executions had already taken place?! And the way he expressed himself in his letters! As if there was no such thing as censorship! Any one of them would be enough to have him shunted off to a camp. Why did he insist on thinking himself immune to all these perils? But there was no talking to him, he refused to listen to anyone.

As if he didn't have enough worries of his own – his work, Emma's demands, justified though they were, and this new offer!

And now the letter he'd received today. Or rather yesterday. Forwarded to him from Berlin. His call-up papers.

He'd been assigned to the SS War Reporter Regiment. A small mercy. And he wasn't due until April of 1943, almost a year and a half off. It seemed his prayers had been answered. He dreaded having to tell Emma, but it could have been much worse. The war might be over by then, and perhaps he wouldn't be drafted at all. There was plenty of time.

He finished the sandwich and all the trimmings, and took a slow draught of the beer. Delicious. He'd enjoyed the short telephone call to Moritz this afternoon – a few moments of sanity in the midst of all the madness. He was sorry he didn't have time to see him and Franzi, it would have done him good. Which reminded him: he'd promised to get them tickets for Cosi fan Tutte at the weekend. He'd do that first thing in the morning. Emma and he had talked about inviting all the family to their flat for New Year's this year, and they would see each other then. Something pleasant to look forward to. And perhaps his father would come too.

He sighed again, and slowly climbed out of the bath.

Eight days later, after another very short night – the closing ceremony had lasted until 3am – he was standing in the doorway of the dining-room. Despite the early hour, all the tables seemed to be occupied. Everyone was keen to get back home. The high room was resounding with the clatter of cutlery on china plates, the chatter of countless conversations, and, as usual, a small string quartet was playing Mozart on the little podium in the far corner. Waitresses in black dresses with frilly white aprons were working the tables efficiently, carrying baskets of fresh rolls and platters of sliced cheeses and cold meats to the tables. The delicious smell of real coffee filled the air. The Minister had spared no effort or expense to ensure that his august and influential guests would return to their own countries with a glowing image of life in Greater Germany.

Across the room he saw his Japanese colleague Ritsuki Ogu sitting alone at a table for two. Leo had met and worked with him the previous year in connection with the Japanese Festival Music that Strauss had composed, and he had invited Ogu to his and Emma's home for dinner one evening. He was a cultivated man, very musical, with a great sense of humour. And his German was excellent. They enjoyed each other's company and had developed a certain degree of intimacy. He made his way over, weaving through the tables, briefly returning friendly greetings from some of the guests who knew him.

'Good morning, Herr Ogu, may I join you?'

'Well, good morning, Herr Gebhardt, yes, please sit down!' And Ogu rose from his chair as Leo took the chair opposite him. A waitress appeared at once and he placed his order.

'Well, Dr Gebhardt, I'm sure you're glad all this is over. I must say it was a very impressive event. Are you satisfied with how everything worked out?'

'On the whole, yes. Of course there were a lot of snags, that's to be expected in these big festivals, but I didn't notice any complications or disturbances in public. Or did you hear of any?'

'No, I didn't. All my compatriots were full of praise for the organisation. My ambassador will be passing on his congratulations to the Minister in the next few days. And the music was, on the whole, of a very high standard.'

'We were fortunate in having all our top musicians taking part. Though ... did you see "Don Giovanni"?'

'Yes. I thought that was rather uneven. Donna Anna was weak. I was surprised.'

'I thought so too. Don't spread the word, but the little word "quality" is rated higher in Berlin than in Vienna. Too much Austrian schmaltz around, I think.'

Ogu smiled. 'And Maestro Strauss wasn't quite in control of his choirs in "Idomeneo", am I right? He got a wonderful reception, which of course he deserved, but I think he's past it as far as conducting is concerned.'

'I'm afraid you're right. Though to be fair, he wasn't at all keen on doing that concert. My guess is that from now on he'll be able to stay at home in Garmisch and play cards with his friends, which is what he likes best.'

'Well, he's deserved that,' said Ogu again. 'His achievements for the world of music are considerable and of lasting effect, and need no further proof of his genius.'

'I'm glad we met here, Herr Ogu,' said Leo. 'There's something I wanted to tell you before we send it in writing. You recall that Professor Konoye inquired about conducting the Ninth Symphony in Berlin earlier this year.'

'In February, to be exact,' said Ogu dryly.

'Well, yes. I did get in touch with the music publishers Peters about the score for him. I hope he received it?'

'I must assume so, I don't know for sure.'

'However, in September the Concert Board informed me that there were no halls available for a concert of that size during the winter. I insisted that they look further. I thought it unlikely that all concert halls would be booked for the whole season. So I put some pressure on them.'

Ogu's left eyebrow rose slightly.

'A few days ago, I received a very firm refusal. They see themselves in no position to schedule this performance in the present concert season. It's extremely regrettable, for I know it would be a magnificent occasion, and a wonderful example of our international cooperation in the field of music. I'm not leaving it there, Herr Ogu, believe me, but Professor Konoye should be informed that nothing may come of his project. Unfortunately.'

Leo drained his cup, avoiding Ogu's eye.

What he could not afford to tell Ogu was that the letter from the Concert Board had stated in very clear and unmistakable terms that there were very severe reservations about having Beethoven's very German Ninth Symphony, with its glorious Ode to Joy by the national poet Schiller, performed under a Japanese conductor. It was inconceivable that a German public would accept such a clash of cultures.

Ogu stood up. 'Thank you for telling me, Dr Gebhardt. It is, indeed, regrettable, and not wholly understandable, considering our request was lodged so early. I'll be expecting the Department's letter, and will take up the matter then. Are you returning to Berlin today?'

'No, I have an appointment with Dr Strauss in Garmisch this evening and will stay the night there.'

'Well, my best regards to the maestro, and also to your charming wife when you get home. May I ask you to present her with this little token of my esteem?' He bent over to his briefcase and extracted a small packet. 'It's a little tea. She might appreciate it. I look forward to seeing her and you, dear Doctor, in more relaxed circumstances.'

Leo thanked him sincerely, they shook hands, and Ogu slowly left the room, stopping at one or two other tables for short conversations on the way.

Leo, too, was approached by three or four of the foreign guests he had taken care of in the time leading up to the festival. They were full of praise and appreciation for his help, and thanked him sincerely and heartily for his commitment and attention to detail. He replied courteously in his usual friendly manner. It was past ten when he finally left the breakfast room. He had missed his train for the eight-hour journey to Garmisch. He was aware that he felt relieved about this. He didn't think that Strauss wanted anything of great importance – a telephone call might solve the problem. He went to the telephone counter in the huge lobby. Twenty minutes later the call went through and he had the great composer on the line.

He explained that he would not be able to come to see him in his home after all.

'No matter, dear Gebhardt,' said Strauss. (Indeed! thought Leo. An eight-hour-train and bus journey for no matter?) 'Has there been any news of my Buddha statue and the ten pounds of tea? You recall that was part of my fee for the Festival Music.'

'Yes, I do remember, Professor. I put in a reminder with the Japanese Embassy some time ago, but they had no information to give me. I'll enquire again.'

'I only hope the ship hasn't been torpedoed. My wife is just dying for the tea, we're down to nettles and mint. But there's another matter I wanted to talk to you about. It's a neighbour of mine. His stepson is the opera singer Wilhelm Hiller. He was called up when the war broke out and is now a lorry driver in France. All protests by his theatre manager have been ignored. He's not a young man any more, born in '01, and he has a family. His whole future career can be ruined! Please do me the favour, dear Doctor, and approach the president of the Theatre Department in the Ministry, with my special regards, and ask him to undertake the required steps to get this man classified "indispensable" and out of the military. I would be most grateful if you and he pursued this problem with the utmost energy.'

'Of course, Professor, I'll see what I can do. As soon as I have any news – or even if I don't have any – I'll get back to you about it.'

With a few more general remarks about the Festival, and regards to each other's wives, Leo was able to end the conversation. Regardless of how deserving the rescue of Opera Singer Hiller might be, it did not, in his opinion, justify the arduous journey to Strauss's home in a side valley of the

Alps. How lucky he'd been to have missed the train!

Next he went to the travel desk in the hotel and got tickets for the next train back to Berlin. With a bit of luck, he could be home in time for breakfast with his darling Emma and Jo. Much earlier than he'd thought. This notion caused him so much pleasure that his weariness began to drop off, and he returned to his room to pack.

Very early the following morning, Leo carefully inserted his key into the lock of their hall door and turned it softly. Em would still be asleep. He dropped his bags gently and peeped into the nursery. As he had expected, it was empty – Em would have taken Jo to sleep with her in her bed. He went into the kitchen and closed the door.

Ten minutes later he opened the bedroom door with his elbow and edged in with a pretty breakfast tray. He set it down on the dressing table, and chinked a spoon against the teacup.

'Your eye-opener!' he said, but her eyes were already open and smiling.

'My sweet! You're home earlier than you said! That's wonderful!'

He took her in his arms and kissed her on her mouth, and embraced her till she gasped for breath. Then he bent over Jo, who was still asleep with his thumb firmly anchored in his little mouth.

'Look what I have for you!' said Leo, placing the cup of tea on her bedside table.

She sniffed the aroma.

'Real tea! You miracle worker! How did you manage that?'

'Ogu gave it to me, specially for you. I knew he'd taken a shine to you when he was here.'

'Oh!' was all Emma could say. She sipped the tea and gave a luxurious sigh. 'Wonderful!'

'I got some rolls on the way home. Perhaps we can have breakfast, and then, if you don't mind, I'd like to lie down for a while. I got hardly any sleep on the train. And this afternoon I'll tell you all my news.'

'And I'll tell you mine,' laughed Emma. 'But don't worry, that won't take long!'

Over a cup of ersatz coffee in the afternoon, Leo told Emma some of the more amusing incidents from the festival.

'I also have something important to discuss with you,' he went on. 'You know I've been writing articles for Clemens Krauss on the side.'

'"On the side" is good,' said Emma. 'You write them in the middle of the night after a full day's work plus a concert in the evening. Has he offered you a job again?'

Clemens Krauss was the highly regarded intendant of the Munich National Theatre, one of the country's leading musicians. Leo had mentioned earlier in the year that Krauss was interested in getting him to join the theatre in Munich.

'It seems he likes what I've done. Anyway, he's asked me to start working for him in Munich in January. He needs a right-hand man to organise his day-to-day affairs and to represent him at rehearsals. It would be an enormous boost to my career. If I have my foot in the door in Munich, lots of other doors will open – I'll be on my way to the top.'

Emma was silent. He watched her, his heavy eyelids drooping. He recalled their earlier conversation about this. He knew what she was thinking.

'That's a wonderful compliment to you, and recognition of all your work and your abilities.

Dear Leo, I think if you were a single man, this is a chance you'd jump at. But if you work for Krauss, you'll be away from home even more often than you are here. Jo and I will see even less of you than now. You'd be at the theatre every evening and every weekend, and writing papers for that man in your free time. Where would that leave our family life?'

'I thought you'd say that, my Rose. And in my conversations with him I put out feelers about the hours that would be involved. The office work could be done during the day, and the rehearsals are in the afternoons. The orchestra has concerts in the evening, they wouldn't have rehearsals then. I'd make absolutely sure that my schedule would be organised so that I'd have regular hours, more or less.'

'You don't believe that yourself, my sweet. You've worked long enough in the theatre and with concert people to know that they have the most irregular hours of any profession, except maybe firemen. And there's something else I don't like. The Bavarians. I can't stand them. We've talked about this before. Munich and Bavaria are wonderful for a holiday, the people are friendly and welcoming. But only because you're a guest and you're leaving your money in their shop or their inn or spa. All friendly up front, and cold and calculating as soon as they feel they don't have the advantage. I could never live in Bavaria. I'm sorry, but that's how it is.'

A sudden thought came to her. She recalled how he had rented their apartment without consulting her.

'You haven't committed yourself, have you?' she asked, anxious and ready to be vexed.

'No, no! He's left it up to me to take the first step. In fact I told him it would be impossible, I couldn't just leave the Ministry, and certainly not at such short notice. I thought I'd let him dangle a bit. No, I'm quite free.'

He tried not to show his disappointment and frustration. He himself loved Bavaria. He enjoyed the warmth of the people, their homeliness, their local patriotism, their eagerness to enjoy themselves in public – so different from the dour Berliners. And the Alps just on the doorstep, so much more challenging and spectacular than the mildly undulating scenery around Berlin. The hiking, the skiing! He decided he'd drop the subject for the moment, but a degree of pessimism about his chances of convincing Emma to take this move with him had set in.

'Never mind, my Rose. I don't need to decide anything now. We can go on as we have been. And I will try to cut down my hours away from home. Klaus or Witschoss can take over more concerts or hosting, at least now and again. You'll see, it'll get better. The hours I spend with my Rose and my Bud are the best of all. There's nothing I love doing better. And now we have the whole weekend before us. Let's go out for a breath of fresh air, and then settle down for a cosy evening beside the radio or the gramophone, what do you think?'

Emma smiled at him gratefully. She'd make him something special for tea. It would help him to forget his disappointment. That always worked. But wild horses wouldn't drag her to Munich.

Yet that night, as they lay in his bed together, he kissed her on her forehead and said, 'You will think about Krauss's offer again, won't you?'

It was hours before she was able to fall asleep.

30

15–20 December: Franzi and Moritz

Franzi switched off the radio. The news – she'd had enough of it! Since the attack on the Americans in Pearl Harbour – where was that anyway? – and Germany's declaration of war on the U.S. and vice versa, just a few days ago, the outlook was getting blacker and blacker. How fortunate that Vienna had never been subjected to an air raid. In that respect, at least, life here was a great improvement on Berlin. Though even Berlin had suffered very few attacks since October, unlike the Rhineland – it must be hell living there, those poor people.

She fiddled absent-mindedly with the Christmas decorations she'd spread out on the dining-room table. Most of them were little wooden figures of people and animals, brightly painted. She'd bought them at stalls at the edge of the local market from wrinkled old men whose Viennese dialect she could barely understand. They'd made them themselves, and they cost almost nothing. She picked up a little goose-girl, a fretwork silhouette of a girl in a long blue smock, with a yellow kerchief round her head and clogs on her feet, leaning forward and holding a gosling in her hands. It was so pretty, and so lovingly made, and it had cost 75 pfennigs. Nothing! In one of the junkshops along the banks of the Danube she'd been lucky enough to find a dusty box with delicate glass globes in red, gold and silver. New ones were unobtainable nowadays. The selection of tinsel chains and the packet of real tinsel for the twigs of her tree were a present from her mother. And she could make some paper stars herself – they used to make them at home when she was small. Which wasn't that long ago. She even had a dozen candle holders, and had found real wax candles in a shop which supplied the clergy and the church.

At any rate, she had enough decorations to make a pretty tree, the first one in her own home. Her first Christmas together with just her husband and her baby. They'd both saved their meat coupons, and with a bit of luck she'd get a fowl of some kind, or a bit of beef, for a rich dinner on Christmas day. Rationing wasn't as hard here in Vienna as it had been in Berlin. Quite often it was possible to get something under the counter. She might even get a hare, or a duck. She looked at her watch. Six o'clock. Moritz should be landing in Dresden around now.

A clatter of something falling over in the hall and a loud wail had her running out to see what Axel was up to. He'd managed to throw over the umbrella stand, and frightened himself doing so. She scooped him up and cuddled him, and brought him back into the living room. It really was terribly quiet here. She switched on the radio again and turned the tuner until she found some dance music. Holding Axel like a dancing partner, she waltzed around the room with him, swinging around and bowing up and down. He squealed in delight, and when she stopped for breath, he jerked himself back and forth, demanding 'More!' So off she started again. She'd turned the music up so loud that she almost missed the phone ringing in the hall. She ran out with Axel still in her arm.

It was Moritz, to say he'd arrived safely.

'That's wonderful, dearest. Have you been to your hotel yet?'

'Yes, that's where I'm calling from. Look, write down the number. It's Hotel Berthold, the number is Dresden 4351. I'm in room 15. How are you? Is everything all right?'

'I'm so bored! Which means everything is all right. Dying for you to get back. What time does the trial start tomorrow?'

'Nine a.m. It'll probably just be taking personal details. If I'm lucky and I'm on tomorrow, I could get back a day sooner. But I'll ring tomorrow evening and let you know. Will you be home, Madam? Or have you a swain escorting you out?'

'Ha ha! The only going out I'm allowed is to the shops or the market with Axel.'

When he heard his name, Axel started wriggling on her arm.

'I need to stop, Axel is impatient. We'll talk again tomorrow evening! Be good!'

'I'm the image of chastity! But what about you, with no one to keep you under control! Just watch out!'

They laughed, and Fra was about to replace the receiver when Axel made a grab for it. She held it to his ear for him, and he spluttered into the shell. Before letting the receiver go, she held it to her ear, in case Moritz was still on the line. But all she heard was a crackling, then a click, and then the dialling tone, so she replaced it on its cradle.

Her live-in maid, Katja, was in the kitchen preparing the evening meal. Her eyes were red again. Franzi felt a twinge of impatience. She knew it was not easy for the young girl – she was fifteen – to be so far away from her home and her relations. She came from some hovel in a village somewhere in Bohemia, could speak hardly any German, and was constantly homesick. As a housemaid she was very good – she'd been the eldest girl in a family of nine, and had been trained by her grandmother. Franzi revised her idea of her home being a 'hovel'; that wasn't fair. She herself had been to some of those villages, and the houses, usually whitewashed single-storey farmhouses, were often beautifully decorated with colourful stencilled designs on the outside walls, amid gardens tumbling with flowers.

But she was homesick herself, and the last thing she wanted was sharing her flat – which wasn't as large as Emma had supposed – with someone who was moping all the time. She, too, missed her parents, and Emma and Jo, and her friends in Berlin. The Viennese suburb where she now lived, Loav, was quite far outside the lively city centre. There was a local library, a small cinema, and a dance hall – so much for the cultural offerings. She missed the operas, concerts and recitals of Berlin, and the shows in the huge Admirals Palast, which seated an audience of twenty-two hundred. True, Moritz had fairly regular hours and was home most evenings, and with Katja there to baby-sit Axel, they were able to get out once or twice a week, to a film, or to go dancing. But it was during the daytime that she felt alone. She hadn't yet met anyone she could really talk to, or drop in on for a chat, or invite to join her when she took Axel for a walk in his pram. Moritz had introduced her to some of his colleagues' wives, usually young women her own age, but they were either extremely taken up with their own importance and social standing (based solely on their husband's importance and social standing), or else boring and interested only in make-up and film stars.

'Now, Katja,' said Franzi kindly. 'Please feed Axel. Make his bottle and his mash. I will make us some soup and sandwiches. All right?'

Katja looked at her, then nodded. She loved looking after Axel; Franzi knew it would help her to get over her momentary sadness. Katja lifted the little boy into his high chair and gave him a spoon. He squealed and spluttered his own language loudly, banging the spoon on the metal tray. It was surprising how comforting the racket was – anything was better than constant silence. Snatches of a popular love song drifted in from the radio in the living room, and Fra caught them up and started singing along, rolling her eyes, waving her wooden spoon around and executing little dance steps in time to the beat. Katja laughed, and even Axel stopped in amazement, then flung his spoon on the floor and started slapping the tray with both hands. From then on the mood improved. When their meal was ready, Katja brought Franzi's into the dining room, while she had hers in the kitchen. It became quieter in the flat. Katja changed Axel and brought him to bed, then retired to her little room. Franzi took out her knitting – a pullover for Axel – and settled beside the radio to listen to a talk about a journey to Greenland. At nine thirty she, too, went to bed.

Moritz called at seven o'clock the following evening.

'Just a short call, Fra, so it doesn't get too expensive! I've nothing much to report. They took my particulars today, but the main questioning will happen tomorrow.'

'Was the big man there?'

'No, he won't appear, just his lawyers. Look, I must stop now. More tomorrow! Be faithful, my dutiful wife!'

'Your wish is my command, my lord and master!'

The following evening's call came at six p.m. She'd been looking forward to it all day. Moritz hadn't told her much about the trial he was being called to as a witness. It wasn't a normal trial, it was at the Military Tribunal. It had something to do with corruption or bribery or something of that kind, and it involved a highly placed personality. From the way Moritz expressed himself, it sounded as if his own boss, the Commander in Chief of the Luftwaffe, Marshal Göring, might be involved, though he never stated this directly. It was quite plausible. Göring was renowned as a passionate art collector, and helped himself liberally to any works that caught his fancy in the fine art museums of countries that had fallen into the hands of the Reich in recent years. Not to mention his benefitting from private collections that had been 'dissolved' because their owners had 'disappeared'. Franzi recalled that Moritz had been on 'extra' missions for Göring himself while he was stationed in Denmark, but she had never given these any further thought.

Moritz sounded tired.

'All right, Fra, I'm through today. I can come home tomorrow.'

'How did it go? Were you able to help?'

'Look, it's too … complex to discuss right now. I mean, it's a dicey matter. I'll tell you all about it when I get back.'

'Did you have any problems? You sound a bit down.'

'No no! I'm fine. It went very well. I just don't want to talk about it now. I might be needed again some time tomorrow, so I'm taking the 22.33 from Dresden to Vienna tomorrow night. It's a through train, and I should arrive shortly before 2 pm on Friday.'

'Oh, so you're not flying back?'

'No, there's no plane available.'

'That's fine, my best one. I hope the train gets through without any delays, and I'll have a nice meal and a hot bath waiting for you here.'

'Just what I'll need, dearest. I won't call again. Give Muppet a big kiss and see you on Friday.'

'Sleep well, lover, safe journey!'

Next afternoon, Franzi got out her new 1942 diary to check her appointments. Not that there were many. In fact, the only entries were for festivals and family celebrations. Christmas in a week's time, Axel's first birthday at the end of December, followed by New Year's – Emma and Leo had invited them to Charlottenburg, but it was such a long, arduous journey in the winter, especially with a small child, so that she was undecided. She'd discuss it with Moritz when he got back. Then their second wedding anniversary on 17 January, her twenty-third birthday four days later, and Moritz's twenty-ninth in February. What would all those 'happy' events be like? How could you have a party to celebrate if you didn't know anyone?

On the other hand, Moritz was a wonderful socialiser. He got on well with everyone, was funny and charming, made friends easily, everyone liked him. She would let him invite whoever he wanted – the main thing was to have a crowd of people around who were eager to have a good time. She thought back to their engagement party – twenty people at her parents' house! What fun they'd had!

The hall clock – a present from Moritz's mother – struck four. She looked out the window at the fields at the back of her house. It was almost dark outside, yet there was still that special, calm brightness. Everything was white, had been for weeks. She hadn't seen so much snow since the time when they'd been living in West Prussia, in Elbing. She and Moritz had done a little skiing at the weekends, but she'd been busy settling in and they hadn't yet had time to explore the slopes in the vicinity. That was something to look forward to! She should try to get Moritz some new ski-boots for his birthday. His Christmas present was new ski-pants and a jacket to match, bought with the option of changing them if they didn't fit his muscular six-foot frame.

Axel would be waking from his midday nap soon. She wondered what Katja was doing. To give her her due, she usually found something to occupy herself, whether washing or ironing, or polishing silver. She was really a good girl.

The doorbell rang. It happened so rarely that a joyous rush of blood rose to her head. She got up to press the opening mechanism, but Katja was there before her. She left the door on the chain until she could see who it was. Franzi advanced to the door.

'Thanks, Katja, I'll get it.'

A man in a Luftwaffe uniform was coming up the stairs to their first-floor apartment, his cap already in his hand. She recognised the slim figure and slightly balding head, a colleague of Moritz's. Habig was his name, she recalled.

'Good afternoon, Frau Birkenfeld,' he said, 'Captain Walter Habig, you may remember me.'

'Of course,' said Fra, removing the chain and opening the door wide. 'Do come in. My husband isn't here though. He won't be back till tomorrow.'

'That's why I'm here, Frau Birkenfeld. Can we sit down for a moment?'

Franzi instantly felt cold. She led the way into the sitting room, indicated an armchair and sat down heavily herself.

Habig glanced around at the Christmas decorations, and Axel's soft toys scattered on the carpet.

'Frau Birkenfeld, I'm afraid I have some very bad news for you. I received a phone call from Dresden a short while ago. I'm sorry to have to tell you that Captain Birkenfeld had an accident on his return flight to Vienna. His plane crash-landed in a place called Ilgau, that's about half-way between Dresden and Vienna, in Moravia. It must have happened during the night. He was found by some farm labourers this morning.'

Fra felt as if she was sleep-walking. As if she was outside her own body. Her hands were freezing.

'That can't be, Captain Habig. My husband is returning by train tonight. He gets in at 2 tomorrow. He said he ...'

The expression on Captain Habig's face made her stop.

'I'm so sorry to have to bring you this news. But I'm afraid there's no doubt about it. The commander of the airport in Dresden rang me personally. He died instantly. His body has been retrieved and is being brought back to Dresden. I'm afraid he's no longer alive, my dear.'

Franzi stared at him. She didn't know what to say. She couldn't understand what he was saying, it made no sense. What was wrong? Five minutes ago, everything was utterly normal. Plans for Christmas, birthdays, anniversaries ... Now there was only chaos. A void, black. What had happened? She couldn't think. She couldn't breathe.

'What did you just say?' she whispered.

'His plane was found in a field. It was lying upside down. He was inside it, alone. We don't yet know the exact cause of his death. He must have been trying to land – maybe he'd lost his way in the dark, or had engine trouble. All that is being investigated, but it'll take a few days. My dear lady, I'm so terribly sorry. Can I get you something? Would you like some brandy? To help you recover?'

'Yes, yes, please. Here, in the drinks cabinet …' She waved her hand vaguely.

Captain Habig filled a glass half full of brandy and handed it to her. She took a gulp as if it were a potion to set things right. Then she stared at Habig again with stark eyes.

'You say he set off from Dresden last night to fly back here? But he rang me yesterday evening and told me very clearly that he would be taking the 22.33 overnight train to Vienna tonight. The direct train. He wouldn't even need to change. He should be packing his bags now. He may have visited my sister's father-in-law in Dresden this afternoon … Why should he have changed his mind? It's not like him.'

'I can't answer your questions yet. Believe me, this is a great shock to me and to all my colleagues and the students at the academy. In the short time I was working with him I grew to like him very much, and to appreciate his handling of our students as well as his flying abilities. He was ideal in this position.' He drew his hand over his head, his eyes and mouth drooping. 'It's possible that he had a chance to fly this plane back to Loav and wanted to surprise you by arriving earlier than announced. I gather you and he have only just been able to set up your household together ...'

Franzi gave a loud wail. She bent over and hid her face in her hands, sobbing and wailing loudly. Looking for relief from her pain by expelling it from her body. By force. She groaned and cried 'No! No!' Habig went over to her and lifted her and put his arms around her, pressing her head against his shoulder. She grasped his arms as if to hold herself upright. Katja had come into the room, frightened, and Habig nodded at her. She came over and put her hand on Franzi's. Franzi shook her hand free and said, 'He's dead, Katja, he's dead, say it's not true, it can't be true.'

Habig handed her the glass of brandy and she took another gulp. Now she was sitting in the armchair, her head still buried in her hands, shaking backwards and forwards, moaning.

'Can I get anyone to come and be with you?' asked Habig gently. 'Is there anyone I can ring for you?'

'I don't know anyone here yet,' said Fra. 'I'll be all right in a moment. I just need a moment.' She took a deep breath, and lifted her head. Katja handed her a big handkerchief. This act of kindness started the tears again, but she was calmer. Habig and Katja waited.

'Has his mother been informed?' asked Franzi.

'No, I don't think so, I imagine not.'

'You said he flew back last night?'

'So I was told.'

'But he thought he might be needed in the tribunal today. He wouldn't have left early.'

'I'm afraid I know nothing about that, dear lady. I'm so terribly sorry ...'

'I must ring my parents. No, my sister. In Berlin.' The tears started again.

'I'm sorry, I have to ask you something practical. I hope you don't mind. I was requested to ask you where the funeral should take place, here or in Berlin or somewhere else?'

'In Berlin. We have no one here. My son and I will travel to Berlin right away. I think that would be best. I can get help there. Perhaps you can help me to book a train as soon as possible, a sleeper for myself and the child.'

'Yes, of course. I'd be only too pleased to help in any way I can.' He rose. 'Here is my telephone number,' placing a note on the table. 'Ring me at any time, day or night. And as soon as I have your tickets I'll let you know. This has been the hardest day in my career, believe me, dear Frau Birkenfeld. And remember, even if you don't have any close friends here, very many people in Loav will be thinking of you and your dear husband right now and sharing your grief. Finish the brandy and lie down. I'll call again later.'

'Thank you, Captain Habig, you've been very kind and sympathetic. Thank you.'

Habig nodded to Katja, and left the apartment quietly.

Later, Captain Habig's wife Maria called at the flat. She was one of the giddy ones, but in this emergency she was warm-hearted and practical. She helped Franzi to pack a suitcase for Berlin. She rang her husband for Franzi, to inform him that Moritz's brother Walter would need to be informed. He was a flak soldier stationed in Russia at present, at Orel, south of Moscow. When Franzi made the difficult call to Moritz's mother, Maria sat quietly at her side. Frau Birkenfeld was collected and said little. Of her four children, Moritz was the second she had lost. A daughter had died of pneumonia some years previously.

Maria and Katja made supper while Franzi tried to take care of Axel. Tears came again and again as she fed and changed the child, thinking of his coming birthday and of how he would have to grow up without a father. Not even a year old! His father hadn't even been able to celebrate one single birthday with his son! With his black hair and blue eyes he would be the image of Moritz. And she a widow at twenty-two! Emma had been terribly upset on the phone, she'd hardly been able to talk. She'd offered to come down to Vienna right away. But Franzi couldn't wait to leave, to get away from this place and return to her family home, where she would feel safe and be surrounded by the people who – now – loved her most in the world.

Later Captain Habig called to say he'd booked tickets for the 14.25 tomorrow. It got into Anhalter Station at 8.31 on the 20th. He'd booked a sleeper, as requested. Second class, was that all right? He'd send a car to bring them to the station at one thirty tomorrow. Maria said she'd be happy to accompany Fra and Axel and help with the luggage.

Franzi worried about Katja. She didn't think she'd ever come back. She asked Maria if she could look for another position for the young girl. She was very good in the household and excellent with children. Maria said she'd look around, and Katja could stay with her until she was settled somewhere else. Franzi explained this to Katja, who, when she'd understood what Franzi was telling her, thanked her profusely in Czech and tried to kiss her hand.

Maria found some pills in the bathroom which would calm Franzi down, and persuaded her to take two of them before going to bed. She waited until Fra was asleep before she left the flat.

The funeral took place on the 23rd, a day before Christmas Eve. She had received a phone call from the Air Ministry insisting that it take place immediately. The Woodland Cemetery in Dahlem was a stage-set in black and white, the ground covered in snow, the naked skeletons of the trees dark and damp against the slate-grey sky. Fortunately the ground wasn't frozen. Franzi, a wisp of her usual self, was wrapped in a black coat of her mother's. She clung to Emma's arm on one side, and leant against Moritz's brother Walter on the other. Walter had learnt of Moritz's death from his commander.

'Ah, Birkenfeld, get yourself ready to depart for Berlin immediately. Your brother's funeral.'

Death was part of their life. There was no space for emotions.

He drove to the nearest military airport, where he was lucky enough to meet a pilot who had known Moritz in Spain. This man was on his way to the Führer's bunker in East Prussia, and he took Walter with him as a passenger. From there he organised a flight to Berlin for him, so that he was able to arrive on time. Moritz's parents were there too, pale faced and grim. Franzi hardly knew them, the father was strange. Lise had made the long journey from her new home in Poland without Benno, who had been refused leave. Some of Franzi's friends from her work as a physiotherapist in the Charité Hospital were there, as well as Erika Lenz, her old friend, who had introduced her to Moritz only three years ago. Paul, Elisabeth, and Aunt Charlotte kept close to the girls, silent, frightened and very downcast. Leo looked grim.

The coffin was already standing in the chapel of the Woodland Cemetery in Dahlem when they entered. A guard of honour, six young lieutenants flown up specially from Loav, stood guard around it. Their commanding officer stood at the side.

Franzi froze when she saw where her husband was now. She had not seen the body, she had received no further information about what had happened. All enquiries by her father had been blocked by excuses and polite evasions. She turned to look at Walter, and saw that he, too, was stunned. The coffin was much too small to contain a powerfully built man of over six feet. What was going on?

The pastor arrived and started the ceremony, delivered the sermon and held a eulogy; there was music, hymns were tentatively sung, and, after the last Amen and blessing, the six young men lifted the coffin onto their shoulders and carried it out of the chapel.

Franzi searched for Walter's hand. He squeezed it briefly, then he pushed her gently towards Emma, and fell behind as the funeral party followed the bearers out into the graveyard and to the grave. They stood in silence as the pastor spoke another prayer. A final tortured hymn was rendered. So far, she had been able to control her pain, but as the coffin was lowered jerkily into the dank hole in the ground, her tears took over again, wracking her whole body.

The undertakers had arranged for a reception in a café near the cemetery. Moritz's parents did not attend. They had offered their sympathies again at the graveside, the mother, Clara, warm and sorrowful, the father, Wilhelm, detached, stern and watchful. They drove off in a horse-drawn cab. Some former colleagues of her husband's were here now, and her own family, and Walter. He reminded her so much of Moritz, dark like him, though with sharper features, and not so tall. He drew her aside as soon as he saw a chance. What had he found out? Could he help her?

'Fra, I have to leave this evening. I have to return to my regiment. But I want to talk to you first. What do you know about what happened to Moritz?'

She looked at him with troubled eyes. She spoke in a whisper.

'Only that his plane crash-landed half-way between Dresden and Vienna, apparently on the night of the 18th. I couldn't understand it, because he'd rung me specially earlier that evening to say he'd be returning by train the following night and arriving on the 20th, last Friday. My father has tried to find out more, but he's got nowhere.'

'Exactly. I couldn't believe my eyes when I saw that coffin. It was much too small for a man of Moritz's build! As we were leaving the chapel I asked the officer in charge to open it, but he refused. He said he'd had strict orders to keep the coffin closed, no one was to open it. I also asked him if he had any other information about what had happened. Like everyone else, he said Moritz had crashed on the return flight from Dresden and suffered a fractured skull. I asked him what plane Moritz had been flying, and he said a Focker Wulf Harrier, and he'd been alone. And that settled it for me.'

'What do you mean, Walter?'

'I don't know exactly, Fra. But something is very much not in order. The flying orders for a Harrier prescribe a crew of three, the pilot, co-pilot and a rear gunner. No one would be allowed to take off if these rules weren't adhered to. He'd never have been allowed to start on his own. And he'd never have done so either – he was much too careful and experienced a pilot to risk such an adventure.'

'Walter, I've just remembered something. I took no notice at the time. But after one of his telephone calls, I didn't replace the receiver for a few seconds – Axel wanted to play with it – and then I heard static and a click, and only then the normal dial tone. Do you think all this has something to do with the evidence he gave at this military tribunal in Dresden?'

'I don't know, love, but one thing is certain: all these discrepancies don't add up to a round number. I'm going to keep my ears open.'

'I can't believe it, Walter. It can't be true! Moritz dying is terrible enough, but the possibility that he was killed on purpose … . It's unbearable! And you need to be careful too, Walter. You can't risk anything happening to you. Your mother wouldn't survive it.'

Walter didn't comment. He knew his mother was tough.

'You're right. Enough strange things have happened. Our Aunt Marie and Uncle Robert – our father's siblings – did Moritz tell you about them?'

'No. He mentioned them once or twice. They live in Frankfurt, don't they? I think he visited them a couple of times. Why?'

'They were arrested and have disappeared. Moritz was convinced they've been murdered.'

Franzi was more and more amazed.

'But why? Arrested for what? Who would have done that? They were old, weren't they? Like your father?'

Walter stared at her. She could see he was thinking.

'Look, Fra, did Moritz ever give you a document of some kind and tell you to keep it very carefully in case you ever had any … queries … about us … your marriage to him … our family?'

Now it was Fra's turn to stare.

'Well yes, in fact, he did. In a sealed envelope, I don't know what's in it.'

'Just hold onto it very carefully. You might need it some day. In the meantime, keep a low profile on Moritz's death. All we know is that he died when his place crashed, and that's what you should tell people if anyone asks. That's the official version, stick to it and you'll be on the safe side.'

'But what does all this mean?'

'Never mind. Best keep that envelope sealed, but take good care of it, for the boy's sake too.'

Franzi couldn't believe her ears. Her head was full of questions, but she controlled herself.

'I have to go,' said Walter, looking round. 'I'll just get something to eat, if I may, and take my leave from your family. You're a brave girl, Moritz was so proud of you. Before I met you he told me he'd met the most beautiful, intelligent, practical, artistic, humorous, athletic – and half a dozen other positive attributes I can't recall – girl in the world. You're going through a tragic period right now, but you'll come out on top, I'm certain. It's the way you're made. Do keep in touch with me, write to me, will you? I'd like that. And I want to know how my nephew is progressing.'

'Dear Walter,' and Franzi embraced him warmly. 'You're the one who needs to take care of himself, in that bad, dangerous Russia. Don't take any unnecessary risks. I will write to you, I promise.'

They kissed cheeks, and Walter drifted off. Fra remained where she was, motionless. What had Walter not told her? She saw the other people in the room as if through a glass wall. As if she were in a glass box, seeing, hearing them, watching them move, live, yet she was remote from them. Words had taken on new content; the old meanings were warped. Shapes were blurred, sounds distorted. Was she the only one in a glass box? Weren't the others too? What was real?

She took a deep breath and consciously pulled herself together. Her father came over to her and took her hand.

'Are you all right, my Fra? My dearest?'

'Yes, Pa. But I need a cigarette. I'll just pop outside.'

She stood in the porch and pulled on the cigarette, then realised she hadn't lit it. What was there about Moritz's family she didn't know? Surely not what Walter had hinted at – his aunt and uncle 'disappeared' or even 'murdered'! That didn't happen to normal people. It was all too much. Too much.

She shook her head and decided that, like her heroine Scarlett O'Hara in the novel, she wouldn't think about it right now. Later. But unlike Scarlett, she knew she would face up to reality when the time came. She wasn't afraid of solving problems. She could do it. That's how she was made.

31

24 December–1 January: The New Year's Party

'January 1, 1942: May the rest of this year continue as joyfully as it began.'

Viktor Sell signed his name boldly under the sentence he'd written in the Gebhardts' visitors' book. His wife Gertrude added her name, and young Charlotte Pommer, and two others followed amid laughter and the clatter of plates being stacked, with the odd piece of cutlery landing on the floor.

'Please! Leave the dishes, we'll do that tomorrow – later today,' called Emma, her face flushed and her eyes slightly puffed. It was 3.15 am.

Horst Amery wrote a line of music and a text which was greeted with a roar of approval by Leo. Everybody crowded over to see what he'd written: under the opening bars of the Ode to Joy were the barely decipherable words 'A joyous year and a joyous party, My thanks are really ever so hearty.'

Groans of mock disapproval mixed with calls of 'It's time you went home, old boy!' and similar remarks were interrupted by Leo, who was opening another bottle of sparkling wine and refilling glasses. His guests sank back in their armchairs, and Marin Swarowsky spoke for all of them when he said: 'Definitely the very last one, Doctor!'

Gertrude Sell raised her glass: 'A last toast to our hosts – thank you for a wonderful evening, an unforgettable end to a remarkable year, and may we all be together again in happiness and in health one year from now.'

The 'Hear hear!' which followed was more subdued and sincere than the joking that had gone on before, and everyone was thoughtful for a moment. Then Charlotte Pommer shoved herself up from the low sofa.

'I have a paper to finish for the clinic tomorrow, I mean today! Bedtime for busy med students!' And she headed out to the hall, stretching out to support herself on the back of a chair as she swayed on the way. All the others followed suit, the hall was a muddle of coats and hats and arms, scarfs and muffs and people looking for their overshoes which had been left outside in the stairwell. Noisy cheerful thanks and farewells were called, and Emma hoped the Sonntags were also up and celebrating and not being woken once again by the late departures issuing from the Gebhardts' place – a ritual which seemed to occur every few months.

Scarcely had the door closed on Hans Swarowsky when Emma, who had kept up her happy façade to the last, collapsed on the edge of the sofa. She sat hunched up for a moment, her hand over her eyes, then reached for a biscuit. Leo moved about the room, collecting glasses and carrying them carefully into the kitchen. When he returned to the drawing room, he saw that Emma hadn't moved.

'Go to bed, my Rose,' he said. 'I'll take care of everything.'

'Like you always do!' hissed Emma, avoiding his eye.

Leo said nothing. With a doleful expression he moved about, picking up bowls with the remains of food, collecting crumpled damask napkins strewn about the table, and moving chairs out of the way. Then he sat down next to Emma, but she got up at once.

'I'm going to bed,' she said. 'We'll talk about all this later on.' And she left the room.

Leo remained alone, slumped on the sofa, his long hands hanging between his knees. He groaned loudly, then got up and continued to clear the remains of the party. When the lights had been dimmed, he opened the blacked-out windows to air the room while he was in the bathroom. He looked in on Jo, too. He had been sleeping badly lately, but now he was asleep, his thumb in his mouth, his cheek red and swollen where a new tooth was being born.

Leo stood beside the cot for a while. What should he do to placate Emma? He pulled Jo's cover up and smoothed it. She was overreacting, of course. She was too sensitive. He'd have to assert himself. After all, he was the head of the household. He was the breadwinner; her job was to run the house and to keep things going smoothly. But he didn't want to hurt her. He would get up early and do all the dishes before she woke. And then he would bring her her breakfast in bed, and they would spend the day together quietly, which is what she enjoyed most. Perhaps they would take the tram out to Zehlendorf, if that was what she wanted. He would get round her.

Emma lay in bed, but was far from asleep. Her mind was racing. Although the party had been a success, it seemed to her that the events of the past two weeks had culminated in this evening, in a situation where she had lost all control. There had been signs and symptoms in the past, she realised, but only now was she aware of what they implied.

She had been deeply hit by Franzi's losses – the loss of both her husband and the family life she'd waited for so long. So soon before Christmas, the festive days which revolved around home and the family! She and Leo had planned to spend Christmas in their own flat, leaving her parents alone for the first time in many decades. That was what they wanted, they maintained. Now Franzi and Axel had moved in again. Then Leo got a phone call from his father's neighbour: the old gentleman was feeling unwell, it might be best if he came to see him. Leo was reluctant to go, but Emma felt relieved, and persuaded him to take the train on the morning of Christmas Eve, so that he could keep his father company over the holiday. And she and Jo could spend the festive season – which no one really wanted to celebrate any more – with her parents and her sorrowing sister and her little nephew.

They got through the festivities somehow. There was only a small Christmas tree, and though Emma brought what she could from her own larder, the food did not measure up to the usual standard, despite extra rations being issued for the festive season. The weather was gloomy, with snow showers and cold night frosts, which left the roads and pavements icy in the mornings. At least the central heating was working.

When Leo returned three days after Christmas, Emma was out in Zehlendorf, and he phoned her there. His father was feeling better, he said, it was just a cold and loneliness. And he had a surprise for her: he had bumped into his old colleague Sell in Dresden. Sell was now working for a newspaper in Berlin, but he had been visiting his parents – coincidence! – and on the spur of the moment Leo had invited him and his charming wife for a new year's party in their flat. And he'd rounded up four more friends, two of whom she already knew. They'd have a jolly party and that would help to drive away the gloom of the past weeks and the unfriendly weather. And, he added quickly, they'd all bring their ration cards so that she could buy whatever she needed to make it all a success. What did she think?

She was beside herself. A party?! she exclaimed. Just two weeks after her brother-in-law, her dear sister's husband, had been killed? It was the last thing she wanted! How did he expect her to concentrate on organising food for eight people at such short notice, in this awful weather, when all she wanted was to be near her sister and her parents and to comfort and help them? How could he be so thoughtless? Why hadn't he consulted her before inviting anyone? Did he think she could just jump and run whenever it suited him? Didn't she have a say in what was planned? Whenever she wanted him to do something for her, didn't she always ask him first? It would never occur to her to make plans involving him without consulting him beforehand.

'Well,' he mumbled, 'it *is* part of your job, isn't it?'

Emma caught her breath. The telephone was in the hall, and one of her parents or Franzi could pass by at any moment.

A Normal Couple

'I'll come home now,' she said, 'and we can talk about it then. I can't talk here.' And she banged down the phone. She had never done that before.

She had never been so angry. What did he think of her? Was she his servant? She knew he loved her, deeply, but it seemed that at the same time he believed he could dispose of her – or at least of her time and work – as he wished. There had been earlier incidents: the five Spaniards he'd invited without asking her, renting the flat before she'd even seen it. It made her feel she was on hold, to fulfil his whims *and* then praise him for organising 'surprises', which he expected her to enjoy. He'd been lucky with the flat, but the five Spaniards at the end of May had ruined her and Jo's birthday party. And, it occurred to her, how could she be sure that he wouldn't accept Krauss's job offer in Munich without telling her after all? This latest coup was too much. He'd have to disinvite his guests. She'd insist on it. She had to draw a line.

But by the time she got home, he had gone out. He'd left a note for her: there was a crisis in the ministry – a Finnish concert pianist needed hosting – that required his immediate attention. She made a meal for both of them, but had eaten hers and was in bed before he returned. When he came into the bedroom, she pretended to be asleep. In the end, though, she heard the grandfather clock in the hall chiming four times before she dropped off.

The following day was a Monday, and he'd left for work before she woke. In the evening she broached the problem as they were having their evening meal. But her initial anger had waned, she felt drained and unable for a conclusive discussion.

'Leo, I feel in no mood or capacity to deal with a party at this time. I want you to ring those people

Olga Peters

and tell them something has come up and the party is off.'

To her surprise he banged his fist on the table and shouted at her.

'I've invited them and I'm not going to take back the invitation now! We have two days and it must be possible to organise a buffet meal in that time!'

She had been totally unprepared for this reaction.

'But Leo,' she said, trying to keep her voice calm, though she felt like crying, 'think! How can you expect me to be part of a cheerful party when my heart is breaking for my sister? I have the image of Moritz before my eyes all the time, that handsome young man, and his little boy, who will never know his father! It's only just happened, just a few days ago! I can't bring myself to organise a party! Please! It's too much to ask!'

Leo had calmed down. 'You're overreacting,' he said coolly, spreading vegetable paste on his bread. 'Of course you can do it. And wait and see, you'll enjoy it, it'll do you good.'

'I doubt that very much. It goes against everything I feel.'

'Well, I can't disinvite them now, it's much too late.'

'Surely you can. If you explain our situation – my situation ….'

'There's nothing to explain,' he said. 'We're having a party on New Year's Eve and that's that.' He was folding his napkin as he spoke. He slipped it into its ring, then rose and left the room for his study, closing the door behind him.

For the next two days, Emma felt as if she was functioning outside her own body. She would stand with a plate in her hand wondering what she wanted it for. Leo had never spoken to her like that before. She had seen this side of him last winter, when he attacked the girl who had ruined his shirt. But she had never dreamt that he would behave like that towards her, and had no idea how to react. Did he have a right to behave this way? Had she done something wrong? It was the first time they'd had such a serious quarrel. Was it a marriage crisis? Could the damage ever be healed?

She bought the most essential things she could find for the party, cooked the meals, organised the flat with the help of her maid. Jo was teething and very cantankerous, his left cheek burning where a tooth was breaking through. She was very gentle with him, and he responded to her caresses and soft words. She loved him more than ever. Leo helped her when he was at home, with a serious expression on his face, and she was polite to him, even smiling occasionally, but feeling a pit of emptiness inside.

Now, in her own bed, she sat up to wait for him, her arms wrapped around her drawn up legs, her chin on her knees. She looked pale, with shadows under her eyes.

Tired as she was, it was now clear to her that the marriage she had envisaged for both of them, the marriage she believed she had been living for the past two years, was a chimera. It was not a partnership based on equality, not a functioning unity. Leo was not the modern partner she had taken him for. He was kind, considerate, warm-hearted, empathetic, he trusted and respected her – but he did not regard her as an equal. She had overlooked the signs last winter in the spa. Perhaps he had been a bachelor for too long. He was in full control of his life, of which she was a part; there was harmony between them as long as her wishes corresponded to his. But where her desires differed, only his counted. And not because they were better or more valuable, but simply because he was the man. He was the head of the family. He was following in his domineering father's footsteps.

But she would not take on the role of his submissive mother. Leo might be harking back to the old, paternalistic tradition, but she had been brought up differently. She had other expectations of her life and her future.

It was a new, though unwelcome, challenge.

He came in eventually, already in his pyjamas, and stood beside her bed, looking down at her.

'My Rose,' he began, 'what can I do to make you happy again? It was a wonderful party, everybody went home in high spirits, thanks to your efforts. And I promise you I won't invite people again without asking you first.'

'It's not just that, Leo,' said Emma, looking up at him sadly. 'I think I've learnt something about us, about you and me, or maybe about all married couples, that I hadn't realised before. It's something I don't like, and I have to decide if I need to get used to it, or if I'm going to try and change it. But I'm too tired to go into it now. Go to bed, Leo, and get some sleep. Jo will be up soon, and God knows the night is short enough already.'

He bent down and kissed her on her cheek, and her mouth tipped the side of his nose.

'Happy New Year,' she said.

The story of Emma and Leo continues in Parts 2 and 3 of this series.

You can contact the author at:

olgapeterswriter@gmail.com

Acknowledgements

This book owes its creation to the invaluable guidance and belief of Frank Fahy and Dr Ursula Naumann. Frank, a seasoned publisher, and Ursula, an accomplished professional writer, have been pillars of inspiration. It was their astute recognition of my storytelling aptitude and their persistent encouragement that fuelled the genesis of this work.

The Write-On Group, nestled in Galway, Ireland, deserves sincere appreciation for their unwavering support, insightful feedback, and constructive critiques on individual chapters. Their collective wisdom and encouragement have significantly shaped the narrative's evolution.

Special gratitude extends to Hans Bauer and Renee Freeling, two nonagenarians whose first-hand experiences provided crucial insights into the historical backdrop of wartime conditions. Their contribution enriched the authenticity and depth of the narrative.

Heartfelt thanks are owed to a circle of friends who dedicated their time to reading drafts and offering meticulous critiques. Mary Rose Tobin, Connor O'Donnell, Penelope Nicholson, Brian Rosen, Nora Ziprian, Rachel Nicholson, Heike Ochs and Dylan Clancy provided invaluable feedback, each insight contributing to the refinement and enhancement of this work.

Lastly, a profound and special acknowledgment to Frank Fahy, whose time, expertise, and unwavering enthusiasm in overseeing the publication of my inaugural novel have been indispensable. His guidance has been instrumental in bringing this project to fruition.

Sources & Bibliography

Sources: Private letters, diaries, family reports, oral accounts, photos; and The German Federal Archives, Berlin.

Bielenberg, Christabel. *The Past is Myself: The experiences of an Englishwoman in wartime Germany.* Chatto & Windus, London, 1968.

Bode, Sabine. *Nachkriegskinder.* Klett-Cotta, Stuttgart, 2011.

Friedrich, Jörg. *Der Brand: Deutschland im Bombenkrieg 1940-1945.* List Verlag, Berlin, 2004.

Giebel, Wieland (Hg.). *Bomben auf Berlin: Zeitzeugen berichten vom Luftkrieg.* Berlin Story Verlag, Berlin, 2012.

Girbig, Werner. *Im Anflug auf die Reichshauptstadt: Die Dokumentation der Bombenangriffe auf Berlin.* Motorbuch Verlag, Stuttgart, 2001.

Große Geschichte des Dritten Reichs und des Zweiten Weltkriegs. 7 Bände. Naturalis Verlag, München/Köln, 1989.

Hein, Bastian. *Elite für Volk und Führer? Die Allgemeine SS und ihre Mitglieder 1925-1945.* Oldenburg Verlag, München, 2012.

Hein, Bastian. *Die SS: Geschichte und Verbrechen.* C.H.Beck, 2015.

Kästner, Erich. *Das blaue Buch: Geheimes Kriegstagebuch 1941-1945.* Hrsg. Sven Hanuschek. 2021.

Klemperer, Victor. *Ich will Zeugnis ablegen bis zum letzten: Tagebücher 1933 – 1945* (2 Bde). Aufbau-Verlag, Berlin, 1995.

Vassiltchikov, Marie. *Berlin Diaries 1940 – 1945.* Vintage Books, New York, 1988.

The Author

Olga Peters was born in Germany towards the end of the war and her family later settled in Ireland. She attended Trinity College Dublin, where she studied History and obtained her teaching diploma. In the early seventies, she returned to Germany. After retiring from her career as an English teacher at a technical college, she relocated to the small country town of Brandenburg. There, she pursued her interests in ornithology, gardening, and playing the piano.

During this time, she also honed her writing skills. Her writing experience encompasses a multitude of long narrative letters, translations of German city guides into English for a Leipzig publisher, and a self-published book about her family home in Dublin. Inspired by two experienced writers and by members of the zoom Write-On Group in Galway, Olga directed her focus towards a long-cherished project: the events portrayed in this book.

'We are all apprentices in a craft where no one ever becomes a master.'

Ernest Hemingway, *The Wild*

Printed in Great Britain
by Amazon